KAINE
PUBLISHING

Warning: This book may become subject to retrospective book-burning legislation. To comply with Kaine Directive CSBO-812864, the **Mandatory Combustibility Information** of this novel has been calculated as follows:

Energy Content: 19,180 Btu
Combustibility: Medium
Flash Point: 451°F

Something Rotten

ALSO BY JASPER FFORDE

The Eyre Affair

Lost in a Good Book

The Well of Lost Plots

*I tried to imagine the whole room full of Shakespeare clones
clattering away at their typewriters....*

THURSDAY NEXT
IN

Something Rotten

A NOVEL

Jasper Fforde

VIKING

VIKING
Published by the Penguin Group
Penguin Group (USA) Inc., 375 Hudson Street,
New York, New York 10014, U.S.A.
Penguin Books Ltd, 80 Strand, London WC2R 0RL, England
Penguin Books Australia Ltd, 250 Camberwell Road, Camberwell,
Victoria 3124, Australia
Penguin Books Canada Ltd, 10 Alcorn Avenue,
Toronto, Ontario, Canada M4V 3B2
Penguin Books India (P) Ltd, 11 Community Centre, Panchsheel Park,
New Delhi–110 017, India
Penguin Group (NZ), Cnr Airborne and Rosedale Roads, Albany,
Auckland 1310, New Zealand
Penguin Books (South Africa) (Pty) Ltd, 24 Sturdee Avenue,
Rosebank, Johannesburg 2196, South Africa

Penguin Books Ltd, Registered Offices: 80 Strand, London WC2R 0RL, England

First published in 2004 by Viking Penguin, a member of Penguin Group (USA) Inc.

3 5 7 9 10 8 6 4 2

Frontispiece and text illustrations by Maggy and Stewart Roberts

Frederick Warne & Co. is the owner of all rights, copyrights, and trademarks
in the Beatrix Potter character names and illustrations.

Publisher's Note: This is a work of fiction. Names, characters, places, and
incidents either are the product of the author's imagination or are used fictitiously,
and any resemblance to actual persons, living or dead, business establishments,
events, or locales is entirely coincidental.

LIBRARY OF CONGRESS CATALOGING-IN-PUBLICATION DATA
Fforde, Jasper.
Thursday Next in Something rotten : a novel / Jasper Fforde.
p. cm.
ISBN 0-670-03359-6
1. Next, Thursday (Fictitious character)—Fiction. 2. Characters and characteristics
in literature—Fiction. 3. Women detectives—Great Britain—Fiction.
I. Title: Something rotten. II. Title.
PR6106.F67T484 2004
823'.914—dc22   2004049497

Printed in the United States of America
Set in Berkeley Medium   Designed by Francesca Belanger

For Maddy, Rosie,
Jordan and Alexander

With all my love

April 2004

Contents

Author's Note

This book has been bundled with **Special Features,** including
The Making of documentary, deleted scenes from all four books,
outtakes and much more.

To access all these free bonus features,
log on to www.jasperfforde.com/specialtn4.html
and enter the code word as directed.

Dramatis Personae

Thursday Next: Ex-operative from Swindon's Literary Detective office of SpecOps-27 and currently head of Jurisfiction, the policing agency that operates within fiction to safeguard the stability of the written word.

Friday Next: Thursday's son, age two.

Granny Next: Resident of Goliath Twilight Homes, Swindon. Age 110 and cannot die until she has read the ten most boring classics.

Wednesday Next: Thursday's mother. Resides in Swindon.

Landen Parke-Laine: Thursday's husband, who hasn't existed since he was eradicated in 1947 by the Goliath Corporation, eager to blackmail Miss Next.

Mycroft Next: Inventor uncle of Thursday and last heard of living in peaceful retirement within the backstory of the Sherlock Holmes series. Designer of Prose Portal and Sarcasm Early-Warning Device, amongst many other things. Husband to **Polly**.

Colonel Next: A time-traveling knight errant, he was eradicated by the ChronoGuard, a sort of temporal policing agency. Despite this, he is still about and meets Thursday from time to time.

Cat formerly known as Cheshire: The ex–Wonderland über-librarian at the Great Library and Jurisfiction agent.

Pickwick: A pet dodo of very little brain.

Bowden Cable: Colleague of Thursday's at the Swindon Literary Detectives.

Victor Analogy: Head of Swindon Literary Detectives.

Braxton Hicks: Overall commander of the Swindon Special Operations Network.

Daphne Farquitt: Romance writer whose talent is inversely proportional to her sales.

The Goliath Corporation: Vast, unscrupulous multinational corporation keen on spiritual and global domination.

Commander Trafford Bradshaw: Popular hero in 1920s ripping adventure stories for boys, now out of print, and notable Jurisfiction agent.

Melanie Bradshaw (Mrs.): A gorilla, married to Commander Bradshaw.

Mrs. Tiggy-winkle, Emperor Zhark, the Red Queen, Falstaff, Vernham Deane: All Jurisfiction operatives, highly trained.

Yorrick Kaine: Whig politician and publishing media tycoon. Also right-wing Chancellor of England, soon to be made dictator. Fictional, and sworn enemy of Thursday Next.

President George Formby: Octogenarian President of England and deeply opposed to Yorrick Kaine and all that he stands for.

Wales: A Socialist Republic.

Lady Emma Hamilton: Consort of Admiral Horatio Lord Nelson and lush. Upset when her husband inexplicably died at the beginning of the Battle of Trafalgar. Lives in Mrs. Next's spare room.

Hamlet: A Danish prince with a propensity for prevarication.

SpecOps: Short for Special Operations, the governmental departments that deal with anything too rigorous for the ordinary police to handle. Everything from time travel to good taste.

Bartholomew Stiggins: Commonly known as "Stig." Neanderthal reengineered from extinction, he heads SpecOps-13 (Swindon), the policing agency responsible for reengineered species such as mammoths, dodos, saber-toothed tigers and chimeras.

Chimera: Any unlicensed "nonevolved life-form" created by a hobby genetic sequencer. Illegal and destroyed without mercy.

St. Zvlkx: A thirteenth-century saint whose revealments have an uncanny knack of coming true.

SuperHoop: The World Croquet League finals. Usually violent, always controversial.

Lola Vavoom: An actress who does not feature in this novel but has to appear in the Dramatis Personae due to a contractual obligation.

Minotaur: Half-man, half-bull son of Pasiphaë, the Queen of Crete. Escaped from custody and consequently a PageRunner. Whereabouts unknown.

Something Rotten

1.

A Cretan Minotaur in Nebraska

Jurisfiction is the name given to the policing agency *inside* books. Working with the intelligence-gathering capabilities of Text Grand Central, the many Prose Resource Operatives at Jurisfiction work tirelessly to maintain the continuity of the narrative within the pages of all the books ever written. Performing this sometimes thankless task, Jurisfiction agents live mostly on their wits as they attempt to reconcile the author's original wishes and readers' expectations against a strict and largely pointless set of bureaucratic guidelines laid down by the Council of Genres. I headed Jurisfiction for over two years and was always astounded by the variety of the work: one day I might be attempting to coax the impossibly shy Darcy from the toilets, and the next I would be thwarting the Martians' latest attempt to invade *Barnaby Rudge*. It was challenging and full of bizarre twists. But when the peculiar and downright weird becomes commonplace, you begin to yearn for the banal.

Thursday Next, *The Jurisfiction Chronicles*

The Minotaur had been causing trouble far in excess of his literary importance—first by escaping from the fantasy-genre prison book *Sword of the Zenobians,* then by leading us on a merry chase across most of fiction and thwarting all attempts to recapture him. The mythological half-man, half-bull son of Queen Pasiphaë of Crete had been sighted within *Riders of the Purple Sage* only a month after his escape. We were still keen on taking him alive at this point, so we had darted him with a small dose of slapstick. Theoretically, we needed only to track outbreaks of custard-pie-in-the-face routines and walking-into-lamppost gags within fiction to lead us to the cannibalistic man-beast. It was an experimental idea and, sadly, also a dismal failure. Aside from Lafeu's celebrated mention of custard in *All's Well That Ends Well* and the ludicrous four-wheeled-chaise sequence in *Pickwick Papers,* little was noticed. The slapstick either hadn't been strong enough or had been diluted by the BookWorld's natural disinclination to visual jokes.

In any event we were still searching for him two years later in the western genre, amongst the cattle drives that the Minotaur found most relaxing. And it was for this reason that Commander Bradshaw and I arrived at the top of page 73 of an obscure pulp from the thirties entitled *Death at Double-X Ranch.*

"What do you think, old girl?" asked Bradshaw, whose pith helmet and safari suit were ideally suited to the hot Nebraskan summer. He was shorter than I by almost a head but led age-wise by four decades; his sun-dried skin and snowy white mustache were a legacy of his many years in colonial African fiction: He had been the lead character in the twenty-three "Commander Bradshaw" novels, last published in 1932 and last read in 1963. Many characters in fiction define themselves by their popularity, but not Commander Bradshaw. Having spent an adventurous and entirely fictional life defending British East Africa against a host of unlikely foes and killing almost every animal it was possible to kill, he now enjoyed his retirement and was much in demand at Jurisfiction, where his fearlessness under fire and knowledge of the BookWorld made him one of the agency's greatest assets.

He was pointing at a weathered board that told us the small township not more than half a mile ahead hailed by the optimistic name of Providence and had a population of 2,387.

I shielded my eyes against the sun and looked around. A carpet of sage stretched all the way to the mountains, less than five miles distant. The vegetation had a repetitive pattern that belied its fictional roots. The chaotic nature of the real world that gave us soft, undulating hills and random patterns of forest and hedges was replaced within fiction by a landscape that relied on ordered repetitions of the author's initial description. In the make-believe world where I had made my home, a forest has only eight different trees, a beach five different pebbles, a sky twelve different clouds. A hedgerow repeats itself every eight feet, a mountain range every sixth peak. It hadn't bothered me that much to begin with, but after two years living inside fiction, I had begun to yearn for a world where every tree and rock and hill and cloud has its own unique shape and identity. And the sunsets. I missed them most of all. Even the best-described ones couldn't hold a candle to a real one. I yearned to witness once again the delicate hues of the sky as the sun dipped below the horizon. From red to orange, to pink, to blue, to navy, to black.

Bradshaw looked across at me and raised an eyebrow quizzically. As the Bellman—the head of Jurisfiction—I shouldn't really be out on assignment at all, but I was never much of a desk jockey, and capturing the Minotaur was important. He had killed one of our own, and that made it unfinished business.

During the past week, we had searched unsuccessfully through six Civil War epics, three frontier stories, twenty-eight high-quality westerns and ninety-seven dubiously penned novellas before finding ourselves within *Death at Double-X Ranch,* right on the outer rim of what might be described as acceptably written prose. We had drawn a blank in every single book. No Minotaur, nor even the merest whiff of one, and believe me, they can whiff.

"A possibility?" asked Bradshaw, pointing at the PROVIDENCE sign.

"We'll give it a try," I replied, slipping on a pair of dark glasses and consulting my list of potential Minotaur hiding places. "If we draw a blank, we'll stop for lunch before heading off into *The Oklahoma Kid.*"

Bradshaw nodded and opened the breech of the hunting rifle he was carrying and slipped in a cartridge. It was a conventional weapon, but loaded with unconventional ammunition. Our position as the policing agency within fiction gave us licensed access to abstract technology. One blast from the eraserhead in Bradshaw's rifle and the Minotaur would be reduced to the building blocks of his fictional existence: text and a bluish mist—all that is left when the bonds that link text to meaning are severed. Charges of cruelty failed to have any meaning when at the last Beast Census there were over a million almost identical Minotaurs, all safely within the hundreds of books, graphic novels and urns that featured him. Ours was different—an escapee. A PageRunner.

As we walked closer, the sounds of a busy Nebraskan frontier town reached our ears. A new building was being erected, and the hammering of nails into lumber punctuated the clop of horses' hooves, the clink of harnesses and the rumble of cartwheels on compacted earth. The metallic ring of the blacksmith's hammer mixed with the distant tones of a choir from the clapboard church, and all about was the general conversational hubbub of busy townsfolk. We reached the corner by Eckley's Livery Stables and peered cautiously down the main street.

Providence as we now saw it was happily enjoying the uninter-rupted backstory, patiently awaiting the protagonist's arrival in two pages' time. Blundering into the main narrative thread and finding ourselves *included* within the story was not something we cared to do, and since the Minotaur avoided the primary story line for fear of discovery, we were likely to stumble across him only in places like this. But if for any reason the story *did* come anywhere near, I would be warned—I had a Narrative Proximity Device in my pocket that would sound an alarm if the thread came too close. We could hide ourselves until it passed by.

A horse trotted past as we stepped up onto the creaky decking that ran along in front of the saloon. I stopped Bradshaw when we got to the swinging doors as the town drunk was thrown out into the road. The bartender walked out after him, wiping his hands on a linen cloth.

"And don't come back till you can pay your way!" he yelled, glancing at us both suspiciously.

I showed the barkeeper my Jurisfiction badge as Bradshaw kept a vigilant lookout. The whole western genre had far too many gunslingers for its own good; there had been some confusion over the numbers required on the order form when the genre was inaugurated. Working in westerns could sometimes entail up to twenty-nine gunfights an hour.

"Jurisfiction," I told him. "This is Bradshaw, I'm Next. We're looking for the Minotaur."

The barkeeper stared at me coldly. "Think you's in the wrong genre, pod'ner," he said.

All characters or Generics within a book are graded A to D, one through ten. A-grades are the Gatsbys and Jane Eyres, D-grades the grunts who make up street scenes and crowded rooms. The barkeeper had lines, so he was probably a C-2. Smart enough to get answers from but not smart enough to have much character latitude.

"He might be using the alias Norman Johnson," I went on, showing him a photo. "Tall, body of a man, head of a bull, likes to eat people?"

"Can't help you," he said, shaking his head slowly as he peered at the photo.

"How about any outbreaks of slapstick?" asked Bradshaw. "Boxing glove popping out of a box, sixteen-ton weights dropping on people, that sort of thing?"

"Ain't seen no weights droppin' on nobody," laughed the barkeeper, "but I hear tell the sheriff got hit in the face with a frying pan last Toosday."

Bradshaw and I exchanged glances.

"Where do we find the sheriff?" I asked.

We followed the barkeeper's directions and walked along the wooden decking past a barbershop and two grizzled prospectors who were talking animatedly in authentic frontier gibberish. I stopped Bradshaw when we got to an alleyway. There was a gunfight in progress. Or at least, there *would* have been a gunfight had not some dispute arisen over the times allocated for their respective showdowns. Both sets of gunmen—two dressed in light-colored clothes, two in dark—with low-slung gun belts decorated with rows of shiny cartridges—were arguing over their gunfight time slots as two identical ladyfolk looked on anxiously. The town's mayor intervened and told them that if there were any more arguments, they would *both* lose their slot times and would have to come back tomorrow, so they reluctantly agreed to toss a coin. The winners of the toss scampered into the main street as everyone dutifully ran for cover. They squared up to one another, hands hovering over their Colt .45s at twenty paces. There was a flurry of action, two loud detonations, and then the gunman in black hit the dirt while the victor looked on grimly, his opponent's shot having dramatically only removed his hat. His lady rushed up to hug him as he reholstered his revolver with a flourish.

"What a load of tripe," muttered Bradshaw. "The real West wasn't like this!"

Death at Double-X Ranch was set in 1875 and written in 1908. Close enough to be historically accurate, you would have thought, but no. Most westerns tended to show a glamorized version of the Old West that hadn't really existed. In the *real* West, a gunfight was a rarity, hitting someone with a short-barreled Colt .45 at anything other than point-blank range a virtual impossibility. The 1870s gunpowder generated a huge amount of smoke; two shots in a crowded bar and you would be coughing—and almost blind.

"That's not the point," I replied as the dead gunslinger was dragged away. "Legend is always far more readable, and don't forget we're in pulp at present—poor prose always outnumbers good prose, and it would be too much to hope that our bullish friend would be hiding out in Zane Grey or Owen Wister."

We continued on past the Majestic Hotel as a stagecoach rumbled by in a cloud of dust, the driver cracking his long whip above the horses' heads.

"Over there," said Bradshaw, pointing at a building opposite that differentiated itself from the rest of the clapboard town by being made of brick. It had SHERIFF painted above the door, and we walked quickly across the road, our nonwestern garb somewhat out of place amongst the long dresses, bonnets and breeches, jackets, dusters, vests, gun belts and bootlace ties. Only permanently billeted Jurisfiction officers troubled to dress up, and many of the agents actively policing the westerns are characters from the books they patrol—so they don't need to dress up anyway.

We knocked and entered. It was dark inside after the bright exterior, and we blinked for few moments as we accustomed ourselves to the gloom. On the wall to our right was a notice board liberally covered with wanted posters—pertaining not only to Nebraska but also to the BookWorld in general; a yellowed example offered three hundred dollars for information leading to the whereabouts of Big Martin. Below this was a chipped enameled coffeepot sitting atop a cast-iron stove, and next to the wall to the left were a gun cabinet and a tabby cat sprawled upon a large bureau. The far wall was the barred frontage to the cells, one of which held a drunk fast asleep and snoring loudly on a bunk bed. In the middle of the room was a large desk that was stacked high with paperwork—circulars from the Nebraska State Legislature, a few Council of Genres Narrative Law amendments, a Campanology Society newsletter and a Sears, Roebuck catalog open to the "fancy goods" section. Also on the desk were a pair of worn leather boots, and inside these were a pair of feet, attached in turn to the sheriff. His clothes were predominantly black and could have done with a good wash. A tin star was pinned to his vest, and all we could see of his face were the ends of a large gray mustache that poked out from beneath his downturned Stetson. He, too, was fast asleep, and balanced precariously on the rear two legs of a chair that creaked as he snored.

"Sheriff?"

No answer.

"SHERIFF!"

He awoke with a start, began to get up, overbalanced and tipped over backwards. He crashed heavily on the floor and knocked against the bureau, which just happened to have a jug of water resting upon it. The jug overbalanced as well, and its contents drenched the sheriff, who roared with shock. The noise upset the cat, who awoke with a cry and leapt up the curtains, which collapsed with a crash on the cast-iron stove, spilling the coffee and setting fire to the tinder-dry linen drapes. I ran to put it out and knocked against the desk, dislodging the lawman's loaded revolver, which fell to the floor, discharging a single shot, which cut the cord of a stuffed moose's head, which fell upon Bradshaw. So there were the three of us: me trying to put out the fire, the sheriff covered in water and Bradshaw walking into furniture as he tried to get the moose's head off him. It was *precisely* what we were looking for: an outbreak of unconstrained and wholly inappropriate slapstick.

"Sheriff, I'm so sorry about this," I muttered apologetically, having doused the fire, demoosed Bradshaw and helped a very damp lawman to his feet. He was over six foot tall, and had a weather-beaten face and deep blue eyes. I produced my badge. "Thursday Next, head of Jurisfiction. This is my partner, Commander Bradshaw." The sheriff relaxed and even managed a thin smile.

"Thought you was more of them Baxters," he said, brushing himself down and drying his hair with a "Cathouses of Dawson City" tea cloth. "I'll be mighty glad you're not. Jurisfiction, hey? Ain't seen none of youse around these parts for longer then I care to remember—quit it, Howell."

The drunk, Howell, had awoken and was demanding a tipple "to set him straight."

"We're looking for the Minotaur," I explained, showing the sheriff the photograph.

He rubbed his stubble thoughtfully and shook his head. "Don't recall ever seeing this critter, missy Next."

"We have reason to believe he passed through your office not long ago—he's been marked with slapstick."

"Ah!" said the sheriff. "I was a-wonderin' 'bout all that. Me and Howell here have been trippin' and a-stumblin' for a while now—ain't we, Howell?"

"You're darn tootin'," said the drunk.

"He could be in disguise and operating under an alias," I ventured. "Does the name Norman Johnson mean anything to you?"

"Can't say it does, missy. We have twenty-six Johnsons here, but all are C-7s—not 'portant 'nuff to have fust names."

I sketched a Stetson onto the photograph of the Minotaur, then a duster, vest and gun belt.

"Oh!" said the sheriff with a sudden look of recognition. "*That* Mr. Johnson."

"You know where he is?"

"Sure do. Had him in jail only last week on charges of eatin' a cattle rustler."

"What happened?"

"Paid his bail and wuz released. Ain't nothing in the Nebraska statutes that says you can't eat rustlers. One moment."

There had been a shot outside, followed by several yells from startled townsfolk. The sheriff checked his Colt, opened the door and walked out. Alone on the street and facing him was a young man with an earnest expression, hand quivering around his gun, the elegantly tooled holster of which I noticed had been tied down—a sure sign of yet another potential gunfight.

"Go home, Abe!" called out the sheriff. "Today's not a good day for dyin'."

"You killed my pappy," said the youth, "and my pappy's pappy. And *his* pappy's pappy. And my brothers Jethro, Hank, Hoss, Red, Peregrine, Marsh, Junior, Dizzy, Luke, Peregrine, George an' all the others. I'm callin' you out, lawman."

"You said Peregrine twice."

"He wuz special."

"Abel Baxter," whispered the sheriff out of the corner of his mouth, "one of them Baxter boys. They turn up regular as clockwork, and I kill 'em same ways as regular."

"How many have you killed?" I whispered back.

"Last count, 'bout sixty. Go home, Abe, I won't tell yer again!"

The youth caught sight of Bradshaw and me and said, "New deputies, Sheriff? Yer gonna need 'em!"

And it was then we saw that Abel Baxter wasn't alone. Stepping out from the stables opposite were four disreputable-looking characters. I frowned. They seemed somehow out of place in *Death at Double-X Ranch*. For a start, none of them wore black, nor did they have tooled leather double gun belts with nickel-plated revolvers. Their spurs didn't clink as they walked, and their holsters were plain and worn high on the hip—the weapon these men had chosen was a Winchester rifle. I noticed with a shudder that one of the men had a button missing on his frayed vest and the sole on the toe of his boot had come adrift. Flies buzzed around the men's unwashed and grimy faces, and sweat had stained their hats halfway to the crown. These weren't C-2 generic gunfighters from pulp, but well described A-9s from a novel of high descriptive quality—and if they could shoot as well as they had been realized by the author, we were in trouble.

The sheriff sensed it, too.

"Where yo' friends from, Abe?"

One of the men hooked his Winchester into the crook of his arm and answered in a low southern drawl, "Mr. Johnson sent us."

And they opened fire. No waiting, no drama, no narrative pace. Bradshaw and I had already begun to move—squaring up in front of a gunman with a rifle might seem terribly macho, but for survival purposes it was a nonstarter. Sadly, the sheriff didn't realize this until it was too late. If he had survived until page 164 as he was meant to, he would have taken a slug, rolled twice in the dust after a two-page buildup and lived long enough to say a pithy final good-bye to his sweetheart, who cradled him in his bloodless dying moments. Not to be. Realistic violent death was to make an unwelcome entry into *Death at Double-X Ranch*. The heavy lead shot entered the sheriff's chest and came out the other side, leaving an exit wound the size of a saucer. He collapsed inelegantly onto his face and lay perfectly still, one arm sprawled outwards in a manner unattainable in life and the other hooked beneath him. He didn't collapse flat either. He ended up bent over on his knees with his backside in the air.

The gunmen stopped firing as soon as there was no target—but Bradshaw, his hunting instincts alerted, had already drawn a bead

... *the gunman disintegrated midstride into a brief chysanthemum of text that scattered across the main street....*

on the sherriff's killer and fired. There was an almighty detonation, a brief flash and a large cloud of smoke. The eraserhead hit home, and the gunman disintegrated midstride into a brief chysanthe-mum of text that scattered across the main street, the meaning of the words billowing out into a blue haze that hung near the ground for a moment or two before evaporating.

"What are you doing?" I asked, annoyed at his impetuosity.

"Him or us, Thursday," replied Bradshaw grimly, pulling the lever down on his Martini-Henry to reload, "him or us."

"Did you see how much text he was composed of?" I replied angrily. "He was almost a paragraph long. Only *featured* characters get that kind of description—somewhere there's going to be a book one character short!"

"But," replied Bradshaw in an aggrieved tone, "I didn't know that before I shot him, now did I?"

I shook my head. Perhaps Bradshaw hadn't noticed the missing button, the sweat stains and the battered shoes, but *I* had. Erasure of a featured part meant more paperwork than I really wanted to deal with. From Form F36/34 (Discharge of an Eraserhead) and Form B9/32 (Replacement of Featured Part) to Form P13/36 (Nar-rative Damage Assessment), I could be bogged down for two whole days. I had thought bureaucracy was bad in the real world, but here in the paper world, it was everything.

"So what do we do?" asked Bradshaw. "Ask politely for them to surrender?"

"I'm thinking," I replied, pulling out my footnoterphone and pressing the button marked CAT. In fiction the commonest form of communication was by footnote, but way out here . . .

"Blast!" I muttered again. "No signal."

"Nearest repeater station is in *The Virginian*," observed Brad-shaw as he replaced the spent cartridge and closed the breech be-fore peering outside, "and we can't bookjump direct from pulp to classic."

He was right. We had been crossing from book to book for al-most six days, and although we could escape in an emergency, such a course of action would give the Minotaur more than enough time to escape. Things weren't good, but they weren't bad either—yet.

"Hey!" I yelled from the sheriff's office. "We want to talk!"

"Is that a fact?" came a clear voice from outside. "Mr. Johnson says he's all done talkin'—'less you be in mind to offer amnesty."

"We can talk about that!" I replied.

There was a beeping noise from my pocket.

"Blast," I mumbled again, consulting the Narrative Proximity Device. "Bradshaw, we've got a story thread inbound from the East, two hundred and fifty yards and closing. Page 74, line 6."

Bradshaw quickly opened his copy of *Death at Double-X Ranch* and ran a finger along the line *"McNeil rode into the town of Providence, Nebraska, with fifty cents in his pocket and murder on his mind. . . ."*

I cautiously peered out the window. Sure enough, a cowboy on a bay horse was riding slowly into town. Strictly speaking, it didn't matter if we changed the story a little, as the novella had been read only sixteen times in the past ten years, but the code by which we worked was fairly unequivocal. "Keep the story as the author intended!" was a phrase bashed into me early on during my training. I had broken it once and would pay the consequences—I didn't want to do it again.

"I need to speak to Mr. Johnson," I yelled, keeping an eye on McNeil, who was still some way distant.

"No one speaks to Mr. Johnson 'less Mr. Johnson says so," replied the voice, "but if you'll be offerin' an amnesty, he'll take it and promise not to eat no more people."

"Was that a double negative?" whispered Bradshaw with disdain. "I do *so* hate them."

"No deal unless I meet Mr. Johnson first!" I yelled back.

"Then there's no deal!" came the reply.

I looked out again and saw three more gunmen appear. The Minotaur had clearly made a lot of friends during his stay in the western genre.

"We need backup," I murmured.

Bradshaw clearly thought the same. He opened his TravelBook and pulled out something that looked a little like a flare gun. This was a TextMarker, which could be used to signal to other Jurisfiction agents. The TravelBook was dimensionally ambivalent; the device was actually *larger* than the book that contained it.

"Jurisfiction knows we're in western pulp; they just don't know *where*. I'll send them a signal."

He dialed in the sort of TextMarker he was going to place, using a knob on the back of the gun, then moved to the door, aimed the marker into the air and fired. There was a dull thud, and the projectile soared into the sky. It exploded noiselessly high above us, and for an instant I could see the text of the page in a light gray against the blue of the sky. The words were back to front, of course, and as I looked at Bradshaw's copy of *Death at Double-X Ranch*, I noticed that the written word "ProVIDence" had been partially capitalized. Help would soon arrive—a show of force would deal with the gunmen. The problem was, would the Minotaur make a run for it or fight it out to the end?

"Purty fireworks don't scare us, missy," said the voice again. "You comin' out, or do we-uns have to come in and get yer?"

I looked across at Bradshaw, who was smiling. "What?"

"This is all quite a caper, don't you think?" said the Commander, chuckling like a schoolboy who had just been caught stealing apples. "Much more fun than hunting elephant, wrestling lions to the ground and returning tribal knickknacks stolen by unscrupulous foreigners."

"I used to think so," I said under my breath. Two years of assignments like these had been enjoyable and challenging, but not without their moments of terror, uncertainty and panic—and I had a two-year-old son who needed more attention than I could give him. The pressure of running Jurisfiction had been building for a long time now, and I needed a break in the real world—a long one. I had felt it about six months before, just after the adventure that came to be known as the Great Samuel Pepys Fiasco, but had shrugged it off. Now the feeling was back—and stronger.

A low, deep rumble began somewhere overhead. The windows rattled in their frames, and dust fell from the rafters. A crack opened up in the plaster, and a cup vibrated off the table to break on the floor. One of the windows shattered, and a shadow fell across the street. The deep rumble grew in volume, drowned out the Narrative Proximity Device that was wailing plaintively, then became so loud it didn't seem like a sound at all—just a vibration that shook the sheriff's office so strongly my sight blurred. Then, as the clock fell from the wall and smashed into pieces, I realized what was going on.

"Oh . . . *no!*" I howled with annoyance as the noise waned to a dull roar. "Talk about using a sledgehammer to crack a nut!"

"Emperor Zhark?" queried Bradshaw.

"Who else would dare pilot a Zharkian battle cruiser into western pulp?"

We looked outside as the vast spaceship passed overhead, its vectored thrusters swiveling downwards with a hot rush of concentrated power that blew up a gale of dust and debris and set the livery stables on fire. The huge bulk of the battle cruiser hovered for a moment as the landing gear unfolded, then made a delicate touchdown—right on top of McNeil and his horse, who were squashed to the thickness of a ha'penny.

My shoulders sagged as I watched my paperwork increase exponentially. The townsfolk ran around in panic and horses bolted as the A-7 gunmen fired pointlessly at the ship's armored hull. Within a few moments, the interstellar battle cruiser had disgorged a small army of foot soldiers carrying the very latest Zharkian weaponry. I groaned. It was not unusual for the Emperor to go overboard at moments like this. Undisputed villain of the eight Emperor Zhark books, the most feared tyrannical god-emperor of the known galaxy just didn't seem to comprehend the meaning of restraint.

In a few minutes, it was all over. The A-7s had either been killed or escaped to their own books, and the Zharkian Marine Corps had been dispatched to find the Minotaur. I could have saved them the trouble. He would be long gone. The A-7s and McNeil would have to be sourced and replaced, the whole book rejigged to remove the twenty-sixth-century battle cruiser that had arrived uninvited into 1875 Nebraska. It was a flagrant breach of the Anti-Cross-Genre Code that we attempted to uphold within fiction. I wouldn't have minded so much if this was an isolated incident, but Zhark did this too often to be ignored. I could hardly control myself as the Emperor descended from his starship with an odd entourage of aliens and Mrs. Tiggy-winkle, who also worked for Jurisfiction.

"What the hell do you think you're playing at?!?"

"Oh!" said the Emperor, taken aback at my annoyance. "I thought you'd be pleased to see us!"

"The situation was bad, but not *irredeemable*," I told him, sweeping my arm in the direction of the town. "Now look what you've done!"

He looked around. The confused townsfolk had started to emerge from the remains of the buildings. Nothing so odd as this had happened in a western since an alien brainsucker had escaped from SF and been caught inside *Wild Horse Mesa*.

"You do this to me every time! Have you no conception of stealth and subtlety?"

"Not really," said the Emperor, looking at his hands nervously. "Sorry."

His alien entourage, not wanting to hang around in case they *also* got an earful, walked, slimed or hovered back into Zhark's ship.

"You sent a TextMarker—"

"So what if we did? Can't you enter a book without destroying everything in sight?"

"Steady on, Thursday," said Bradshaw, laying a calming hand on my arm. "We did ask for assistance, and if old Zharky here was the closest, you can't blame him for wanting to help. After all, when you consider that he usually lays waste to entire galaxies, torching just the town of ProVIDence and not the whole of Nebraska was actually quite an achievement . . ." His voice trailed off before he added, ". . . for him."

"AHHH!" I yelled in frustration, holding my head. "Sometimes I think I'm—"

I stopped. I lost my temper now and again, but rarely with my colleagues, and when that happens, things are getting bad. When I started this job, it was great fun, as it still was to Bradshaw. But just lately the enjoyment had waned. It was no good. I'd had enough. I needed to go *home.*

"Thursday?" asked Mrs. Tiggy-winkle, concerned by my sudden silence. "Are you okay?"

She came too close and spined me with one of her quills. I yelped and rubbed my arm while she jumped back and hid a blush. Six-foot-high hedgehogs have their own brand of etiquette.

"I'm fine," I replied, dusting myself down. "It's just that things have a way of . . . well, *spiraling* out of control."

"What do you mean?"

"What do I mean? *What do I mean?* Well, this morning I was tracking a mythological beast using a trail of custard-pie incidents across the Old West, and this afternoon a battle cruiser from the twenty-sixth century lands in ProVIDence, Nebraska. Doesn't that sound sort of crazy?"

"This is fiction," replied Zhark in all innocence. "Odd things are *meant* to happen."

"Not to me," I said with finality. "I want to see some sort of semblance of . . . of *reality* in my life."

"Reality?" echoed Mrs. Tiggy-winkle. "You mean a place where hedgehogs don't talk or do washing?"

"But who'll run Jurisfiction?" demanded the Emperor. "You were the best we ever had!"

I shook my head, threw up my hands and walked to where the ground was peppered with the A-7 gunman's text. I picked up a *D* and turned it over in my hands.

"Please reconsider," said Commander Bradshaw, who had followed me. "I think you'll find, old girl, that reality is much overrated."

"Not overrated *enough*, Bradshaw," I replied with a shrug. "Sometimes the top job isn't the easiest one."

"Uneasy lies the head that wears the crown," murmured Bradshaw, who probably understood me better than most. He and his wife were the best friends I had in the BookWorld; Mrs. Bradshaw and my son were almost inseparable.

"I knew you wouldn't stay for good," continued Bradshaw, lowering his voice so the others didn't hear. "When will you go?"

I shrugged. "Soon as I can. Tomorrow."

I looked around at the destruction that Zhark had wrought upon *Death at Double-X Ranch*. There would be a lot of clearing up, a mountain of paperwork—and there might be the possibility of disciplinary action if the Council of Genres got wind of what had happened.

"I suppose I should complete the paperwork on this debacle first," I said slowly. "Let's say three days."

"You promised to stand in for Joan of Arc while she attended a martyrs' refresher course," added Mrs. Tiggy-winkle, who had tiptoed closer.

I'd forgotten about that. "A week, then. I'll be off in a week."

We all stood in silence, I pondering my return to Swindon and all of them considering the consequences of my departure—except Emperor Zhark, who was probably thinking about invading the planet Thraal, for fun.

"Your mind is made up?" asked Bradshaw. I nodded slowly. There were other reasons for me to return to the real world, more pressing than Zhark's gung ho lunacy. I had a husband who didn't exist and a son who couldn't spend his life cocooned inside books. I had retreated into the old Thursday, the one who preferred the black-and-white certainties of policing fiction to the ambiguous midtone grays of emotion.

"Yes, my mind's made up," I said, smiling. I looked at Bradshaw, the Emperor and Mrs. Tiggy-winkle. For all their faults, I'd enjoyed working with them. It hadn't been *all* bad. Whilst at Jurisfiction I had seen and done things I wouldn't have believed. I'd watched grammasites in flight over the pleasure domes of Xanadu, felt the strangeness of listeners glittering on the dark stair. I had cantered bareback on unicorns through the leafy forests of Zenobia and played chess with Ozymandias, the King of Kings. I had flown with Biggles on the Western Front, locked cutlasses with Long John Silver and explored the path not taken to walk upon England's mountains green. But despite all these moments of wonder and delight, my heart belonged back home in Swindon and to a man named Landen Parke-Laine. He was my husband, the father of my son; he didn't exist, and I loved him.

2.

No Place Like Home

Swindon, Wessex, England, was the place I was born and where I lived until I left to join the Literary Detectives in London. I returned ten years later and married my former boyfriend, Landen Parke-Laine. He was subsequently murdered at the age of two by the Goliath Corporation, who had decided to blackmail me. It worked, I helped them—but I didn't get my husband back. Oddly, I kept his son, my son, Friday—it was one of those quirky, paradoxical time-travel things that my father understands but I don't. Two years further on, Landen was still dead, and unless I did something about it soon, he might remain that way forever.

Thursday Next, *Thursday Next: A Life in SpecOps*

It was a bright and clear morning in mid-July two weeks later that I found myself on the corner of Broome Manor Lane in Swindon, on the opposite side of the road to my mother's house with a toddler in a stroller, two dodos, the Prince of Denmark, an apprehensive heart and hair cut way too short. The Council of Genres hadn't taken the news of my resignation very well. In fact, they'd refused to accept it at all and given me instead unlimited leave, in the somewhat deluded hope that I might return if actualizing my husband "didn't work out." They also suggested I might like to deal with escaped fictionaut Yorrick Kaine, someone with whom I had crossed swords twice in the past.

Hamlet had been a late addition to my plans. Increasingly concerned over reports that he was being misrepresented as something of a "ditherer" in the Outland, he had requested leave to see for himself. This was unusual in that fictional characters are rarely troubled by public perception, but Hamlet would worry about having nothing to worry about if he had nothing to worry about, and since he was the indisputable star of the Shakespeare canon and had lost the Most Troubled Romantic Lead to Heathcliff once again at this year's BookWorld awards, the Council of Genres thought they should do something to appease him. Besides, Jurisfiction had been trying to persuade him to police Elizabethan drama since Sir John Falstaff had retired on grounds of "good health," and a trip to the Outland, it was thought, might persuade him.

" 'Tis very strange!" he murmured, staring at the sun, trees, houses and traffic in turn. "It would take a rhapsody of wild and whirling words to do justice of all that I witness!"

"You're going to have to speak English out here."

"All this," explained Hamlet, waving his hands at the fairly innocuous Swindon street, "would take millions of words to describe correctly!"

"You're right. It would. That's the magic of the book imagino-transference technology," I told him. "A few dozen words conjure up an entire picture. But in all honesty the reader does most of the work."

"The reader? What's it got to do with him?"

"Well, each interpretation of an event, setting or character is unique to each of those who read it because they clothe the author's description with the memory of their own experiences. Every character they read is actually a complex amalgam of people that they've met, read or seen before—far more real than it can ever be just from the text on the page. Because every reader's experiences are different, each book is unique for each reader."

"So," replied the Dane, thinking hard, "what you're saying is that the more complex and apparently contradictory the character, the greater the possible interpretations?"

"Yes. In fact, I'd argue that every time a book is read by the same person it is different again—because the reader's experiences have changed, or he is in a different frame of mind."

"Well, that explains why no one can figure me out. After four hundred years nobody's quite decided what, *exactly*, my inner motivations are." He paused for a moment and sighed mournfully. "Including me. You'd have thought I was religious, wouldn't you, with all that not wanting to kill Uncle Claudius when at prayer and suchlike?"

"Of course."

"I thought so, too. So why do I use the atheistic line: *there is nothing either good or bad, but thinking makes it so?* What's that all about?"

"You mean you don't know?"

"Listen, I'm as confused as anyone."

I stared at Hamlet and he shrugged. I had been hoping to get some answers out of him regarding the inconsistencies within his play, but now I wasn't so sure.

"Perhaps," I said thoughtfully, "that's why we like it. To each our own Hamlet."

"Well," snorted the Dane unhappily, "it's a mystery to me. Do you think therapy would help?"

"I'm not sure. Listen, we're almost home. Remember: to anyone but family you're—who are you?"

"Cousin Eddie."

"Good. Come on."

Mum's house was a detached property of good proportions in the south of the town, but of no great charm other than that which my long association had bred upon it. I had spent the first eighteen years of my life growing up here, and everything about the old house was familiar. From the tree I had fallen out of and cracked a collarbone to the garden path where I had learned to ride my bicycle. I hadn't really noticed it before, but empathy for the familiar grows stronger with age. The old house felt warmer to me now than it ever had before.

I took a deep breath, picked up my suitcase and trundled the stroller across the road. My pet dodo, Pickwick, followed with her unruly son, Alan, padding grumpily after her.

I rang Mum's doorbell, and after about a minute, a slightly overweight vicar with short brown hair and spectacles answered the door.

"Is that Doofus . . . ?" he said when he saw me, suddenly breaking into a broad grin. "By the GSD, it *is* Doofus!"

"Hi, Joffy. Long time no see."

Joffy was my brother. He was a minister in the Global Standard Deity religion, and although we had had differences in the past, they were long forgotten. I was pleased to see him, and he I.

"Whoa!" he said. "What's that?"

"That's Friday," I explained. "Your nephew."

"Wow!" replied Joffy, undoing Friday's harness and lifting him out. "Does his hair always stick up like that?"

"Probably leftovers from breakfast."

Friday stared at Joffy for a moment, took his fingers out of his mouth, rubbed them on his face, put them in again and offered Joffy his polar bear, Poley.

"Kind of cute, isn't he?" said Joffy, jiggling Friday up and down and letting him tug at his nose. "But a bit . . . well, *sticky.* Does he talk?"

"Not a lot. Thinks a great deal, though."

"Like Mycroft. What happened to your head?"

"You mean my haircut?"

"So that's what it was!" murmured Joffy. "I thought you'd had your ears lowered or something. Bit . . . er . . . bit *extreme,* isn't it?"

"I had to stand in for Joan of Arc. It's always tricky to find a replacement."

"I can see why," exclaimed Joffy, still staring incredulously at my pudding-bowl haircut. "Why don't you just have the whole lot off and start again?"

"This is Hamlet," I said, introducing the Prince before he began to feel awkward, "but he's here incognito so I'm telling everyone he's my cousin Eddie."

"Joffy," said Joffy, "brother of Thursday."

"Hamlet," said Hamlet, "Prince of Denmark."

"Danish?" said Joffy with a start. "I shouldn't spread that around if I were you."

"Why?"

"Darling!" said my mother, appearing behind Joffy. "You're back! Goodness! Your hair!"

"It's a Joan of Arc thing," explained Joffy, "very fashionable right now. Martyrs are big on the catwalk, y'know—remember the Edith Cavell/Tolpuddle look in last month's *FeMole*?"

"He's talking rubbish again, isn't he?"

"Yes," said Joffy and I in unison.

"Hello, Mum," I said, giving her a hug. "Remember your grandson?"

She picked him up and remarked how much he had grown. It was unlikely in the extreme that he had *shrunk*, but I smiled dutifully nonetheless. I tried to visit the real world as often as I could but hadn't been able to manage it for at least six months. When she had nearly fainted by hyperventilating with ooohs and aaaahs and Friday had stopped looking at her dubiously, she invited us indoors.

"You stay out here," I said to Pickwick, "and don't let Alan misbehave himself."

It was too late. Alan, small size notwithstanding, had already terrorized Mordecai and the other dodos into submission. They all shivered in fright beneath the hydrangeas.

"Are you staying for long?" inquired my mother. "Your room is just how you left it."

This meant just how I left it when I was nineteen, but I thought it rude to say so. I explained that I'd like to stay at least until I got an apartment sorted out, introduced Hamlet and asked if he could stay for a few days, too.

"Of course! Lady Hamilton's in the spare room and that nice Mr. Bismarck is in the attic, so he can have the box room."

My mother grasped Hamlet's hand and shook it heartily. "How are you, Mr. Hamlet? Where did you say you were the prince of again?"

"Denmark."

"Ah! No visitors after seven P.M. and breakfast stops at nine A.M. prompt. I do expect guests to make their own beds and if you need washing done you can put it in the wicker basket on the landing. Pleased to meet you. I'm Mrs. Next, Thursday's mother."

"I have a mother," replied Hamlet gloomily as he bowed politely and kissed my mother's hand. "She shares my uncle's bed."

"They should buy another one, in that case," she replied, practical as ever. "They do a very good deal at IKEA, I'm told. Don't use it myself because I don't like all that self-assembly—I mean, what's the point of paying for something you have to build yourself? But it's popular with men for *exactly* that same reason. Do you like Battenberg?"

"Wittenberg?"

"No, no. *Battenberg.*"

"On the river Eder?" asked Hamlet, confused over my mother's conversational leap from self-assembly furniture to cake.

"No, silly, on a doily—covered with marzipan."

Hamlet leaned closer to me. "I think your mother may be insane—and I should know."

"You'll get the hang of what she's talking about," I said, giving him a reassuring pat on the arm.

We walked through the hall to the living room, where, after managing to extract Friday's fingers from Mum's beads, we managed to sit down.

"So tell me all your news!" she exclaimed as my eyes flicked around the room, trying to take in all the many potential hazards for a two-year-old.

"Where do you want me to begin?" I asked, removing the vase of flowers from the top of the TV before Friday had a chance to pull them over on himself. "I had a flurry of things to do before I left.

Two days ago I was in Camelot trying to sort out some marital strife, and the day before—sweetheart, don't touch that—I was negotiating a pay dispute with the Union of Orcs."

"Goodness!" replied my mother. "You must be simply *dying* for a cup of tea."

"Please. The BookWorld might be the cat's pajamas for characterization and explosive narrative, but you can't get a decent cup of tea for all the bourbon in Hemingway."

"I'll do it!" said Joffy. "C'mon, Hamlet, tell me about yourself. Got a girlfriend?"

"Yes—but she's bonkers."

"In a good way or a bad way?"

Hamlet shrugged. "Neither—just bonkers. But her brother—hell's teeth! Talk about sprung-loaded . . . !"

Their conversation faded as they disappeared into the kitchen.

"Don't forget the Battenberg," my mother called after them.

I opened my suitcase and took out a few rattly toys Mrs. Bradshaw had given me. Melanie had looked after Friday a lot, as she and Commander Bradshaw had no children of their own, what with Melanie's being a mountain gorilla, so she had doted on Friday. It had its upsides: he always ate his greens and loved fruit, but I had my suspicions that they climbed on the furniture when I wasn't about, and once I found Friday trying to peel a banana with his feet.

"How's life treating you?" I asked.

"Better for seeing you. It's quite lonely with Mycroft and Polly away at the Fourteenth Annual Mad Scientists' Conference. If it wasn't for Joffy and his partner Miles popping round every day, Bismarck and Emma, Mrs. Beatty next door, Eradications Anonymous, my auto-body work class and that frightful Mrs. Daniels, I'd be completely alone. Should Friday be in that cupboard?"

I turned, jumped up and grabbed Friday by the straps of his dungarees and gently took the two crystal wineglasses from his inquisitive grasp. I showed him his toys and sat him down in the middle of the room. He stayed put for about three seconds before tottering off in the direction of DH-82, Mum's bone-idle Thylacine, who was asleep on a nearby chair.

DH-82 yelped as Friday tugged playfully at his whiskers. The Thylacine then got up, yawned and went to find his supper dish. Friday followed. And I followed Friday.

"—in the ear?" said Joffy as I walked into the kitchen. "Does that work?"

"Apparently," replied the Prince. "We found him stone dead in the orchard."

I scooped up Friday, who was about to tuck in to DH-82's food, and took him back to the living room.

"Sorry," I explained. "He's into everything at the moment. Tell me about Swindon. Much changed?"

"Not really. The Christmas lights have improved tremendously, there's a Skyrail line straight through the Brunel Centre, and Swindon now has twenty-six different supermarkets."

"Can the residents eat that much?"

"We're giving it our best shot."

Joffy walked back in with Hamlet and placed a tray of tea things in front of us.

"That small dodo of yours is a terror. Tried to peck me when I wasn't looking."

"You probably startled him. How's Dad?"

Joffy, to whom this was a touchy subject, decided not to join us but play with Friday instead.

"C'mon, young lad," he said, "let's get drunk and shoot some pool."

"Your father has been wanting to get hold of you for a while," said my mother as soon as Joffy and Friday had gone. "As you probably guessed, he's been having trouble with Nelson again. He often comes home simply *reeking* of cordite, and I'm *really* not keen on him hanging around with that Emma Hamilton woman."

My father was a sort of time-traveling knight errant. He used to be a member of SO-12, the agency charged with policing the time lines: the ChronoGuard. He resigned due to differences over the way the historical time line was managed and went rogue. The ChronoGuard decided that he was too dangerous and eradicated him by a well-timed knock at the door during the night of his conception; my aunt April was born instead.

"So Nelson died at the Battle of Trafalgar?" I asked, recalling Dad's previous problems in the time line.

"Yes," she replied, "but I'm not sure he was meant to. That's why your father *says* he has to work so closely with Emma."

Emma, of course, was Lady Emma Hamilton, Nelson's consort. It was she who had alerted my father to Nelson's eradication. One moment she had been married to Lord Nelson for more than ten years, the next she was a bankrupt lush living in Calais. Must have been quite a shock. My mother leaned closer.

"Between the two of us, I'm beginning to think Emma's a bit of a tram— Emma! How nice of you to join us!"

At the doorway was a tall, red-faced woman wearing a brocade dress that had seen better days. Despite the rigors of a lengthy and damaging acquaintance with the bottle, there were the remains of great beauty and charm about her. She must have been dazzling in her youth.

"Hello, Lady Hamilton," I said, getting up to shake her hand. "How's the husband?"

"Still dead."

"Mine, too."

"Bummer."

"Ah!" I exclaimed, wondering quite where Lady Hamilton had picked up the word, although on reflection she probably knew a few worse. "This is Hamlet."

"Emma Hamilton," she cooed, casting an eye in the direction of the unquestionably handsome Dane and giving him her hand. "Lady."

"Hamlet," he replied, kissing her proffered hand. "Prince."

Her eyelashes fluttered momentarily. "A Prince? Of anywhere I'd know?"

"Denmark, as it happens."

"My . . . *late* boyfriend bombarded Copenhagen quite mercilessly in 1801. He said the Danes put up a good fight."

"We Danes like a tussle, Lady Hamilton," replied the Prince with a great deal of charm, "although I'm not from Copenhagen myself. A little town up the coast—Elsinore. We have a castle there. Not very large. Barely sixty rooms and a garrison of under two hundred. A bit bleak in the winter."

"Haunted?"

"One that I know of. What did your *late* boyfriend do when he wasn't bombarding Danes?"

"Oh, nothing much," she said offhandedly. "Fighting the French and the Spanish, leaving body parts around Europe—it was quite de rigueur at the time."

There was a pause as they stared at one another. Emma started to fan herself.

"Goodness!" she murmured. "All this talk of body parts has made me quite hot!"

"Right!" said my mother, jumping to her feet. "That's it! I'm not having this sort of smutty innuendo in my house!"

Hamlet and Emma looked startled at her outburst, but I managed to pull her aside and whisper, "Mother! Don't be so judgmental—after all, they're both single. And Hamlet's interest in Emma might take *her* interest off someone else."

"Someone . . . else?"

You could almost hear the cogs going around in her head. After a long pause, she took a deep breath, turned back to them and smiled broadly.

"My dears, why don't you have a walk in the garden? There is a gentle cooling breeze and the *niche d'amour* in the rose garden is very attractive this time of year."

"A good time for a drink, perhaps?" asked Emma hopefully.

"Perhaps," replied my mother, who was obviously trying to keep Lady Hamilton away from the bottle.

Emma didn't reply. She just offered her arm to Hamlet, who took it graciously and was going to steer her out of the open doors to the patio when Emma stopped him with a murmur of "not the *French* windows" and took him out by way of the kitchen.

"As I was saying," said my mother as she sat down, "Emma's a lovely girl. Cake?"

"Please."

"Here," she said, handing me the knife, "help yourself."

"Tell me," I began as I cut the Battenberg carefully, "did Landen come back?"

"That's your eradicated husband, isn't it?" she replied kindly. "No, I'm afraid he didn't." She smiled encouragingly. "You should come to one of my Eradications Anonymous evenings—we're meeting tomorrow night."

In common with my mother, I had a husband whose reality had been scrubbed from the here and now. Unlike my mother, whose husband still returned every so often from the timestream, I had a husband, Landen, who existed only in my dreams and recollections. No one else had any memories or knowledge of him at all. Mum knew about Landen because I'd told her. To anyone else, Landen's parents included, I was suffering some bizarre delusion. But Friday's father *was* Landen, despite his nonexistence, in the same way that my brothers and I had been born, despite my father's not existing. Time travel is like that. Full of unexplainable paradoxes.

"I'll get him back," I mumbled.

"Who?"

"Landen."

Joffy reappeared from the garden with Friday, who, in common with most toddlers, didn't see why adults couldn't give airplane rides all day. I gave him a slice of Battenberg, which he dropped in his eagerness to devour. The usually torpid DH-82 opened an eye, darted in, ate the cake and was asleep again in under three seconds.

"Lorem ipsum dolor sit amet!" Friday cried indignantly.

"Yes, it was impressive, wasn't it?" I agreed. "Bet you never saw Pickwick move that fast—even for a marshmallow."

"Nostrud laboris nisi et commodo *consequat*," replied Friday with great indignation. "Excepteur sint cupidatat non proident!"

"Serves you right," I told him. "Here, have a cucumber sandwich."

"What did my grandson say?" asked my mother, staring at Friday, who was trying to eat the sandwich all in one go and making a nauseating spectacle of himself.

"Oh, that's just him jabbering away in Lorem Ipsum. He speaks nothing else."

"Lorem—what?"

"Lorem Ipsum. It's dummy text used by the printing and type-setting industry to demonstrate layout. I don't know where he picked it up. Comes from living inside books, I should imagine."

"I see," said my mother, not seeing at all.

"How are the cousins?" I asked.

"Wilbur and Orville both run Mycrotech these days," answered Joffy as he passed me a cup of tea. "They made a few mistakes while Uncle Mycroft was away, but I think he's got them on a short leash now."

Wilbur and Orville were were my aunt and uncle's two sons. Despite having two of the most brilliant parents around, they were almost solid mahogany from the neck up.

"Pass the sugar, would you? A few mistakes?"

"Quite a lot, actually. Remember Mycroft's memory-erasure machine?"

"Yes and no."

"Well, they opened a chain of High Street erasure centers called Mem-U-Gon. You could go in and have unpleasant memories removed."

"Lucrative, I should imagine."

"*Extremely* lucrative—right up to the moment they made their first mistake. Which was, considering those two, not an *if* but a *when*."

"Dare I ask what happened?"

"I think that it was the equivalent of setting a vacuum cleaner to 'blow' by accident. A certain Mrs. Worthing went into the Swindon branch of Mem-U-Gon to remove every single recollection of her failed first marriage."

"And . . . ?"

"Well, she was accidentally *uploaded* with the unwanted memories of seventy-two one-night stands, numerous drunken arguments, fifteen wasted lives and almost a thousand episodes of *Name That Fruit!* She was going to sue but settled instead for the name and address of one of the men whose exploits is now lodged in her memory. As far as I know, they married."

"I like a story with a happy ending," put in my mother.

"In any event," continued Joffy, "Mycroft forbade them from using it again and gave them the Chameleocar to market. It should be in the showrooms quite soon—if Goliath hasn't pinched the idea first."

"Ah!" I muttered, taking another bite of cake. "And how is my least favorite multinational?"

Joffy rolled his eyes. "Up to no good as usual. They're attempting to switch to a faith-based corporate-management system."

"Becoming a . . . religion?"

"Announced only last month on the suggestion of their own corporate precog, Sister Bettina of Stroud. They aim to switch the corporate hierarchy to a multideity plan with their own gods, demigods, priests, places of worship and official prayer book. In the *new* Goliath, employees will not be paid with anything as unspiritual as money, but *faith*—in the form of coupons that can be exchanged for goods and services at any Goliath-owned store. Anyone holding Goliath shares will have these exchanged on favorable terms with these 'foupons' and everyone gets to worship the Goliath upper echelons."

"And what do the 'devotees' get in return?"

"Well, a warm sense of belonging, protection from the world's evils and a reward in the afterlife—oh, and I think there's a T-shirt in it somewhere, too."

"That sounds very Goliath-like."

"Doesn't it just?" Joffy smiled. "Worshipping in the hallowed halls of consumerland. The more you spend, the closer to their 'god' you become."

"Hideous!" I exclaimed. "Is there any *good* news?"

"Of course! The Swindon Mallets are going to beat the Reading Whackers to win the SuperHoop this year."

"You've *got* to be kidding!"

"Not at all. Swindon winning the 1988 SuperHoop is the subject of the incomplete Seventh Revealment of St. Zvlkx. It goes like this: 'There will be a home win on the playing fields of Swindonne in nineteen hundred and eighty eight, and in consequence of . . .' The rest is missing, but it's pretty unequivocal."

St. Zvlkx was Swindon's very own saint, and no child educated here could fail to know about him, including me. His Revealments had been the subject of much conjecture over the years, for good reason—they were uncannily accurate. Even so, I was skeptical—especially if it meant the Swindon Mallets' winning the SuperHoop. The city's team, despite a surprise appearance at the SuperHoop finals a few years back and the undeniable talents of team captain Roger Kapok, was probably the worst side in the country.

"That's a bit of a long shot, isn't it? I mean, St. Zvlkx vanished in, what—1292?"

But Joffy and my mother didn't think it very funny.

"Yes," said Joffy, "but we can ask him to confirm it."

"You can? How?"

"According to his Revealment the Sixth, he's due for spontaneous resurrection at ten past nine the day after tomorrow."

"But that's remarkable!"

"Remarkable but *not* unprecedented," replied Joffy. "Thirteenth-century seers have been popping up all over the place. Eighteen in the last six months. Zvlkx will be of interest to the faithful and us at the Brotherhood, but the TV networks probably won't cover it. The ratings of Brother Velobius' second coming last week didn't even come close to beating *Bonzo the Wonder Hound* reruns on the other channel."

I thought about this for a moment in silence.

"That's enough about Swindon," said my mother, who had a nose for gossip—especially mine. "What's been happening to you?"

"How long have you got? What I've been getting up to would fill several books."

"Then . . . let's start with why you're back."

So I explained about the pressures of being the head of Jurisfiction, and just how annoying books could be sometimes, and Friday, and Landen, and Yorrick Kaine's fictional roots. On hearing this, Joffy jumped.

"Kaine is . . . fictional?"

I nodded. "Why the interest? Last time I was here, he was a washed-up ex-member of the Whig Party."

"He's not now. Which book is he from?"

I shrugged. "I wish I knew. Why? What's going on?"

Joffy and Mum exchanged nervous glances. When my mother gets interested in politics, it means things are really bad.

"Something is rotten in the state of England," murmured my mother.

"And that something is the English *Chancellor* Yorrick Kaine," added Joffy, "but don't take our word for it. He's appearing on Toad-NewsNetwork's *Evade the Question Time* here in Swindon at eight tonight. We'll go and see him for ourselves."

I told them more about Jurisfiction, and Joffy, in return, cheerfully reported that attendance at the Global Standard Deity church was up since he had accepted sponsorship from the Toast Marketing Board, a company that seemed to have doubled in size and influence since I was here last. They had spread their net beyond hot bread and now included jams, croissants and pastries in their portfolio of holdings. My mother, not to be outdone, told me she'd received a little bit of sponsorship money herself from Mr. Rudyard's

Cakes, although she privately admitted that the Battenberg she served up was actually her own. She then told me in great detail about her aged friends' medical operations, which I can't say I was overjoyed to hear about, and as she drew breath in between Mrs. Stripling's appendectomy and Mr. Walsh's "plumbing" problems, a tall and imposing figure walked into the room. He was dressed in a fine morning coat of eighteenth-century vintage, wore an impressive mustache that would have put Commander Bradshaw's to shame and had an imperiousness and sense of purpose that reminded me of Emperor Zhark. "Thursday," announced my mother in a breathless tone, "this is the Prussian Chancellor, Herr Otto Bismarck—your father and I are trying to sort out the Schleswig-Holstein question of 1863–64; he's gone to fetch Bismarck's opposite number from Denmark so they can talk. Otto— I mean, Herr Bismarck, this is my daughter, Thursday."

Bismarck clicked his heels and kissed my hand in an icily polite manner.

"Fraulein Next, the pleasure is all mine," he intoned in a heavy German accent.

My mother's curious and usually long-dead houseguests should have surprised me, but they didn't. Not anymore. Not since Alexander the Great turned up when I was nine. Nice enough fellow—but shocking table manners.

"So, how are you enjoying 1988, Herr Bismarck?"

"I am especially taken with the concept of dry cleaning," replied the Prussian, "and I see big things ahead for the gasoline engine." He turned back to my mother: "But I am most eager to speak to the Danish prime minister. Where might he be?"

"I think we're having a teensy-weensy bit of trouble locating him," replied my mother, waving the cake knife. "Would you care for a slice of Battenberg instead?"

"Ah!" replied Bismarck, his demeanor softening. He stepped delicately over DH-82 to sit next to my mother. "The finest Battenberg I have ever tasted!"

"Oh, Herr B," said my flustered mother. "You do flatter me so!"

She made shooing motions at us out of vision of Bismarck and, obedient children that we were, we withdrew from the living room.

"Well!" said Joffy as we shut the door. "How about that? Mum's after a bit of Teutonic slap and tickle!"

I raised an eyebrow and stared at him.

"I hardly think so, Joff. Dad doesn't turn up that often and intelligent male company can be hard to find."

Joffy chuckled.

"Just good friends, eh? Okay. Here's the deal: I'll bet you a tenner Mum and the Iron Chancellor are doing the wild thing by this time next week."

"Done."

We shook hands and with Emma, Hamlet, Bismarck and my mother thus engaged, I asked Joffy to look after Friday so I could slip out of the house to get some air.

I turned left and wandered up Marlborough Road, looking about at the changes that two years' absence had wrought. I had walked this way to school for almost eight years, and every wall and tree and house was as familiar to me as an old friend. A new hotel had gone up on Piper's Way, and a few shops in the Old Town had either changed hands or been updated. It all felt very familiar, and I wondered whether the feeling of wanting to belong somewhere would stay with me or fade, like my fondness for *Caversham Heights,* the book in which I had made my home these past few years.

I walked down Bath Road, took a right and found myself in the street where Landen and I had lived before he was eradicated. I had returned home one afternoon to find his mother and father in residence. Since they hadn't known who I was and considered—not unreasonably—that I was dangerously insane, I decided to play it safe today and just walk past slowly on the other side of the street.

Nothing looked very different. A tub of withered *Tickia orologica* was still on the porch next to an old pogo stick, and the curtains in the windows were certainly his mother's. I walked on, then retraced my steps and returned, my resolve to get him back mixed with a certain fatalism that perhaps ultimately I wouldn't and the thought that I should prepare myself. After all, he *had* died when he was two years old, and I had no memories of how it had been, but only of how things *might* have turned out had he lived.

I shrugged my shoulders and chastised myself upon the morbidity of my own thoughts, then walked towards the Goliath Twilight Homes, where my gran was staying these days.

Granny Next was in her room watching a nature documentary called *Walking with Ducks* when I was shown in by the nurse. Gran was wearing a blue gingham nightie, had wispy gray hair and looked all of her 110 years. She had got it into her head that she couldn't shuffle off this mortal coil until she had read the ten most boring books, but since "boring" was about as impossible to quantify as "not boring," it was difficult to know how to help.

"Shhh!" she muttered as soon as I walked in. "This program's *fascinating!*" She was staring at the TV screen earnestly. "Just think," she went on, "by analyzing the bones of the extinct duck *Anas platyrhynchos,* they can actually figure out how it walked."

I stared at the small screen where an odd animated bird waddled strangely in a backwards direction as the narrator explained just how they had managed to deduce such a thing.

"How could they know that just by looking at a few old bones?" I asked doubtfully, having learned my lesson long ago that an "expert" was usually anything but.

"Scoff not, young Thursday," replied Gran. "A panel of expert avian paleontologists have even deduced that a duck's call might have sounded something like this: 'Quock, quock.' "

" 'Quock'? Hardly seems likely."

"Perhaps you're right," she replied, switching off the TV and tossing the remote aside. "What do experts know?"

Like me, Gran was able to jump inside fiction. I wasn't sure how either of us did it, but I was very glad that she could—it was she who helped me not to forget my husband, something at one time I was in a clear and real danger of doing thanks to Aornis, the mnemonomorph, of course. But Gran had left me about a year ago, announcing that I could fend for myself and she wouldn't waste any more time laboring for me hand and foot, which was a bit of cheek really, as I generally looked after *her*. But no matter. She was my gran, and I loved her a great deal.

"Goodness!" I said, looking at her soft and wrinkled skin, which put me oddly in mind of a baby echidna I had once seen in *National Geographic*.

"What?" she asked sharply.

"Nothing."

"Nothing? You were thinking of how old I was looking, weren't you?"

It was hard to deny it. Every time I saw her, I felt she couldn't look any older, but the next time, with startling regularity, she did.

"When did you get back?"

"This morning."

"And how are you finding things?"

I brought her up to date with current events. She made "tut-tutting" noises when I told her about Hamlet and Lady Hamilton, then even louder "tut-tut" noises when I mentioned my mother and Bismarck.

"Risky business, that."

"Mum and Bismarck?"

"Emma and Hamlet."

"He's fictional and she's historical—what could be wrong about that?"

"I was thinking," she said slowly, raising an eyebrow, "about what would happen if Ophelia found out."

I hadn't thought of that, and she was right. Hamlet could be difficult, but Ophelia was impossible.

"I always thought the reason Sir John Falstaff retired from policing Elizabethan drama was to get away from Ophelia's sometimes unreasonable demands," I mused, "such as having petting animals and a goodly supply of mineral water and fresh sushi on hand at Elsinore whenever she was working. Do you think I should insist Hamlet return to *Hamlet*?"

"Perhaps not right away," said Gran, coughing into her hanky. "Let him see what the real world is like. Might do him good to realize it needn't take five acts to make up one's mind."

She started coughing again, so I called the nurse, who told me I should probably leave her. I kissed her good-bye and walked out of the rest home deep in thought, trying to work up a strategy for the next few days. I dreaded to think what my overdraft was like, and if I was to catch Kaine I'd be better off inside SpecOps than outside. There were no two ways about it: I needed my old job back. I'd attempt that tomorrow and take it from there. Kaine certainly needed dealing with, and I'd play it by ear at the TV studios tonight. I'd probably have to find a speech therapist for Friday to try to wean him off the Lorem Ipsum, and then, of course, there was Landen. How do I even begin to get someone returned to the here-and-now after they were deleted from the there-and-then by a chronupt official from the supposedly incorruptible ChronoGuard.

I was jolted from my thoughts as I approached Mum's house. There appeared to be someone partially hidden from view in the alleyway opposite. I nipped into the nearest front garden, ran between the houses, across two back gardens and then stood on a dustbin to peak cautiously over a high wall. I was right. There *was* someone watching my mother's house. He was dressed too warmly for summer and was half hidden in the buddleia. My foot slipped on the dustbin, and I made a noise. The lurker looked around, saw me and took flight. I jumped over the wall and gave chase. It was easier than I thought. He wasn't terribly fit, and I caught up with him as he tried rather pathetically to climb a wall. Pulling the man down, I upset his small duffel bag, and out poured an array of battered notebooks, a camera, a small pair of binoculars and several copies of the *SpecOps-27 Gazette,* much annotated in red pen.

"Ow, ow, ow, get off!" he said. "You're hurting!"

I twisted his arm, and he dropped to his knees. I was just patting his pockets for a weapon when another man, dressed not unlike the first, came charging out from behind an abandoned car, holding aloft a tree branch. I spun, dodged the blow, and as the second man's momentum carried him on, I pushed him hard with my foot, and he slammed headfirst into a wall and collapsed unconscious.

The first man was unarmed, so I made sure his unconscious friend was also unarmed—and wasn't going to choke on his blood or teeth or something.

"I know you're not SpecOps," I observed, "because you're both way too crap. Goliath?"

The first man got slowly to his feet and was looking curiously at me, rubbing his arm where I had twisted it. He was a big man, but not an unkindly-looking one. He had short dark hair and a large mole on his chin. I had broken his spectacles; he didn't look Goliath, but I had been wrong before.

"I'm very pleased to meet you, Miss Next. I've been waiting for you for a long long time."

"I've been away."

"Since January 1986. I've waited nearly two and a half years to see you."

"And why would you do a thing like that?"

"Because," said the man, producing an identity badge from his pocket and handing it over, "I am your officially sanctioned *stalker.*"

I looked at the badge. It was true enough; he was allocated to me. All 100 percent legit, and I didn't have a say in it. The whole stalker thing was licensed by SpecOps-33, the Entertainments Facilitation Department, who had drawn up specific rules with the Amalgamated Union of Stalkers as to who is allowed to stalk whom. It helps to regulate a historically dark business and also grades stalkers according to skill and perseverance. My stalker was an impressive Grade-1, the sort who are permitted to stalk the really big celebrities. And that made me suspicious.

"A Grade-1?" I queried. "Should I be flattered? I don't suppose I'm anything above a Grade-8."

"Not nearly that high," agreed my stalker. "More like a Grade-12. But I've got a hunch you're going to get bigger. I latched on to Lola Vavoom in the sixties when she was just a bit part in *The Streets of Wootton Bassett* and stalked her for nineteen years, man and boy. I only gave her up to move on to Buck Stallion. When she heard, she sent me a glass tankard with THANK YOU FOR A GREAT STALK, LOLA etched onto it. Have you ever met her?"

"Once, Mr. . . . ." I looked at the pass before handing it back. "De Floss. Interesting name. Any relation to Candice?"

"The author? In my dreams," replied the stalker, rolling his eyes. "But since I'd like us to be friends, do please call me Millon."

"Millon it is, then."

And we shook hands. The man on the ground moaned and sat up, rubbing his head.

"Who's your friend?"

"He's not my friend," said Millon, "he's my stalker. And a pain in the arse he is, too."

"Wait—you're a stalker and you have a stalker?"

"Of course!" laughed Millon. "Ever since I published my autobiography, *A Stalk on the Wild Side,* I've become a bit of a celebrity myself. I even have a sponsorship deal with Compass Rose™ duffel coats. It is *my* celebrity status that enables Adam here to stalk *me.* Come to think of it, he's a Grade-3 stalker, so it's possible he's got a stalker of his own—haven't you heard the poem?"

Before I could stop him, he started to recite:

> "*. . . And so the tabloids do but say,*
> *that stalkers on other stalkers prey,*
> *and these have smaller stalkers to stalk 'em*
> *and so proceed, ad infinitum. . . .*"

"No, I hadn't heard that one," I mused as the second stalker placed a handkerchief to his bleeding lip.

"Miss Next, this is Adam Gnusense. Adam, Miss Next."

He waved weakly at me, looked at the bloodied handkerchief and sighed mournfully. I felt rather remorseful all of a sudden.

"Sorry to hit you, Mr. Gnusense, " I said apologetically. "I didn't know what either of you were up to."

"Occupational hazard, Miss Next."

"Hey, Adam," said Millon, suddenly sounding enthusiastic, "do you have your own stalker yet?"

"Somewhere," said Gnusense looking around, "a Grade-34 loser. The sad bastard was rummaging through my bins last night. Passé or what!"

"Kids—tsk," said Millon. "It might have been de rigueur in the sixties, but the modern stalker is much more subtle. Long vigils, copious notes, timed entry and exits, telephoto lenses."

"We live in sad times," agreed Adam, shaking his head sadly. "Must be off. I said I'd keep a close eye on Adrian Lush for a friend."

He stood up and shambled slowly away down the alley, stumbling on discarded beer cans.

"Not a great talker is old Adam," said Millon in a whisper, "but sticks to his target like a limpet. You wouldn't catch him rummaging through dustbins—unless he was giving a master class for a few of the young pups, of course. Tell me, Miss Next, but where have you been for the past two and a half years? It's been a bit dull here—after the first eighteen months of you not showing up, I'd reduced my stalking to only three nights a week."

"You'd never believe me."

"You'd be surprised what I can believe. Aside from stalking I've just finished my new book, *A Short History of the Special Operations Network*. I'm also editor of *Conspiracy Theorist* magazine. In between pieces on the very tangible link between Goliath and Yorrick Kaine and the existence of a mysterious beast known only as Guinzilla, we've run several articles devoted entirely to you and that *Jane Eyre* thing. We'd love to do a piece on your uncle Mycroft's work, too. Even though we know almost nothing, the conspiracy network is alive with healthy half-truths, lies and supposition. Did he really build an LCD cloaking device for cars?"

"Sort of."

"And translating carbon paper?"

"He called it rossetionery."

"And what about the Ovinator? *Conspiracy Theorist* devotes several pages of unsubstantiated rumors to this one invention alone."

"I don't know. Some sort of machine for cooking eggs, perhaps? Is there anything you *don't* know about my family?"

"Not a lot. I'm thinking of writing a biography about you. How about *Thursday Next: A Biography*?"

"The title? Way too imaginative."

"So I have your permission?"

"No, but if you can put a dossier together on Yorrick Kaine, I'll tell you all about Aornis Hades."

"Acheron's little sister? It's a deal! Are you sure I can't write your biography? I've already made a start."

"Positive. If you find anything, knock on my door."

"I can't. There's a blanket restraining order on all members of the Amalgamated Union of Stalkers. We're not allowed within a hundred yards of your place of residence."

I sighed. "All right, just wave when I come out."

De Floss readily agreed to that plan, and I left him rearranging his notebook, binoculars and camera and starting to make copious notes on his first encounter with me. I couldn't get rid of the poor deluded fool, but a stalker just might—*might*—be an ally.

3.

Evade the Question Time

Perfidious Danes "Historically Our Enemy,"
Claims Insane Historian

"Quite frankly, I was yim-pim-pim appalled," said England's leading mad history scholar yesterday. "The eighth-century Danish attack on our flibble-flobble sceptered isle is a story of invasion, subjugation, plunder and exploitation that would remain bleep-bleep-baaaaa unequaled until we tried it ourselves many years later." The confused and barely coherent historian's work has been authenticated by another equally feeble-minded academic who told us yesterday, "The Danish invasion began in 786 when the Danes set up a kingdom in East Anglia. They didn't even use their own names either. They preferred to do their brutal work cowardly hiding beneath the pseudonyms of Angles, Bruts and Flynns." Further research has shown that the Danes stayed for over four hundred years and were driven home only by the crusading help of our new close friends the French.

> Article in *The New Oppressor*,
> the official mouthpiece of the Whig Party

How did Kaine rise so quickly to power?" I asked incredulously as Joffy and I queued patiently outside Swindon's ToadNews-Network studios that evening. "When I was here last, Kaine and the Whig Party were all but washed up after the *Cardenio* debacle."

Joffy looked grim and nodded towards a large crowd of uniformed Kaine followers who were waiting in silence for their glorious leader.

"Things haven't been good back here, Thurs. Kaine regained his seat after Samuel Pring was assassinated. The Whigs formed an alliance with the Liberals and elected Kaine as their leader. He has some sort of magnetism, and the numbers that attend his rallies increase all the time. His 'British unification' stance has had much support—mostly with stupid people who can't be bothered to think for themselves."

"War with Wales?"

"He hasn't said as such, but a leopard doesn't change its spots. He won by a landslide after the previous government collapsed over the 'cash for llamas' scandal. As soon as he was in power he proclaimed himself chancellor. His Unreform Act last year restricted the vote to people with property."

"How did he get parliament to agree to *that?*" I muttered, aghast at the thought of it.

"We're not sure," said Joffy sadly. "Sometimes parliament does the funniest things. But he's not happy just being chancellor. He's arguing that committees and accountants only slow things down, and if people *really* want trains to run on time and shopping trolleys to run straight, it could be done only by one man wielding unquestionable executive power—a dictator."

"So what's stopping him?"

"The President," replied Joffy quietly. "Formby has told Kaine that if Kaine pushes for a dictatorial election, he will stand against him, and Yorrick knows full well that Formby would win—he's as popular now as he ever was."

I thought for a moment. "How old is President Formby?"

"That's the problem. He was eighty-four last May."

We fell silent for a moment and shuffled with the queue up to the stage door, had our identities checked by two ugly men from SO-6 and were then ushered in. We took our seats at the back and waited patiently for the show to begin. It seemed hard to believe that Kaine had managed to inveigle his way to the top of English politics, but, I reflected, anything can happen to a fictional character—a trait that Yorrick had obviously exploited to the full.

"See that nasty-looking man on the edge of the stage?" asked Joffy.

"Yes," I replied, following Joffy's finger to a stocky man with short hair and no visible neck.

"Colonel Fawsten Gayle, Kaine's head of security. Not a man to trifle with. It's rumored he was expelled from school for nailing his head to a park bench on a bet."

Standing next to Gayle was a cadaverous man with pinched features and small round spectacles. He was holding a battered red briefcase and was dressed in a rumpled sports jacket and corduroy trousers.

"Who's that?"

"Ernst Stricknene. Kaine's personal adviser."

I stared at them both for a while and noticed that, despite being barely two feet from each other, they didn't exchange a single word or look. Things in the Kaine camp were far from settled. If I could get close, I'd just grab Yorrick and jump him straight to one of Jurisfiction's many prison books, and that would be that. It looked as though I had got back home just in time.

I consulted the complimentary copy of *The New Oppressor* I had found on my seat.

"Why is Kaine blaming the nation's woes on the Danish?" I asked.

"Because economically we're in a serious mess after losing to Russia in the Crimean War. They didn't just get Tunbridge Wells as war reparations but a huge chunk of cash, too. The country is near bankruptcy, Kaine wants to stay in power, so—"

"Misdirection."

"Bingo. He blames someone else."

"But the *Danish?*"

"Shows how desperate he is, doesn't it? As a nation we've been blaming the Welsh and the French for far too long and with the Russians out of the frame he's come up with Denmark as public enemy number one. He's using the Viking raids of 800 A.D. and the Danish rule of England in the eleventh century as an excuse to whip up some misinformed xenophobia."

"Ludicrous!"

"Agreed. The papers have been full of anti-Danish propaganda this past month. All Bang & Olufsen entertainment systems have been withdrawn due to 'safety' concerns, and Lego has been banned pending 'choking hazard' investigations. The list of outlawed Danish writers is becoming longer by the second. Kierkegaard's works have already been declared illegal under the Undesirable Danish Literature Act and will be burnt. Hans Christian Andersen will be next, we're told—and after that maybe even Karen Blixen."

"They can pull my copy of *Out of Africa* from my cold, dead fingers."

"Mine, too. You'd better make sure Hamlet doesn't tell anyone where he's from. Shhh. I think something's happening."

Something *was* happening. The floor manager had walked out onto the set and was explaining to us exactly what we should do. After a protracted series of technical checks, the host of the show walked on, to applause from the audience. This was Tudor Webastow of *The Owl*, who had made a career out of being *just* inquisitive enough to be considered a realistic political foil for the press but not *so* inquisitive that he would be found in the Thames wearing concrete overshoes.

He sat down at the center of a table with two empty chairs either side of him and sorted his notes. Unusually for *Evade the Question Time,* the show had two speakers instead of four, but tonight was special: Yorrick Kaine would be facing his political opposition, Mr. Redmond van de Poste, of the Commonsense Party. Mr. Webastow cleared his throat and began.

"Good evening and welcome to *Evade the Question Time,* the nation's premier topical talk show. Tonight, as every night, a panel of distinguished public figures generally evade answering the audience's questions and instead toe the party line."

There was applause at this, and Webastow continued: "The show tonight comes from Swindon in Wessex. Sometimes called the third capital of England or 'Venice on the M4,' the Swindon of today is a financial and manufacturing powerhouse, its citizens a cross-section of professionals and artists who are politically indicative of the country as a whole. I'd also like to mention at this point that *Evade the Question Time* is brought to you by Neat-Fit® Exhaust Systems, the tailpipe of choice."

He paused for a moment and shuffled his papers.

"We are honored to have with us tonight two very different speakers from opposite ends of the political spectrum. First I would like to introduce a man who was politically dead two years ago but has managed to pull himself up to the second-highest political office in the nation, with a devoted following of many millions, not all of whom are deranged. Ladies and gentlemen, Chancellor Yorrick Kaine!"

There was mixed applause when he walked onto the stage, and he grinned and nodded for the benefit of the crowd. I leaned forward in my seat. He didn't appear to have aged at all in the two years since I had last seen him, which is what I would expect from a fictioneer. Still looking in his late twenties, with black hair swept neatly to the side, he might have been a male model from a knitting pattern. I knew he wasn't. I'd checked.

"Thank you very much," said Kaine, sitting at the table and clasping his hands in front of him. "May I say that I always regard Swindon as a home away from home."

There was a brief twitter of delight from the front of the audience, mostly little old ladies who looked upon him as the son they never had.

Mr. Webastow went on, "And opposing him we are also honored to welcome Mr. Redmond van de Poste of the opposition Commonsense Party."

There was notably less applause as van de Poste walked in. He was older than Kaine by almost thirty years, looked tired and gaunt, wore round horn-rimmed spectacles and had a high-domed forehead that shone when it caught the light. He looked about furtively before sitting down stiffly. I guessed the reason. He was wearing a heavy flak vest beneath his suit—and with good reason.

The last three Commonsense leaders had all met with mysterious deaths. The previous incumbent had been Mrs. Fay Bentoss, who had died after being hit by a car. Not so unusual, you might think—except she had been in her front room when it happened.

"Thank you, gentlemen, and welcome. The first question comes from Miss Pupkin."

A small woman stood up and said shyly, "Hello. A Terrible Thing was done by Somebody this week, and I'd like to ask the panel if they condemn this."

"A very good question," replied Webastow. "Mr. Kaine, perhaps you'd like to start the ball rolling?"

"Thank you, Tudor. Yes, I condemn utterly and completely the Terrible Thing in the strongest possible terms. We in the Whig Party are appalled by the way in which Terrible Things are done in this great nation of ours, with no retribution against the Somebody who did them. I would also like to point out that the current spate of Terrible Things being undertaken in our towns and cities is a burden we inherited from the Commonsense Party, and I am at pains to point out that in real terms the occurrence of Terrible Things has dropped by over twenty-eight percent since we took office."

There was applause at this, and Webastow then asked Mr. van de Poste for his comments.

"Well," said Redmond with a sigh, "quite clearly my learned friend has got his facts mixed up. According to the way *we* massage the figures, Terrible Things are actually on the increase. But I'd like to stop playing party politics for a moment and state for the record that although this is of course a great personal tragedy for those involved, condemning out of hand these acts does not allow us to understand why they occur, and more needs to be done to get to the root cause of—"

"Yet again," interrupted Kaine, "yet again we see the Commonsense Party shying away from its responsibilities and failing to act toughly on unspecified difficulties. I hope all the unnamed people who have suffered unclearly defined problems will understand—"

"I *did* say we condemned the Terrible Thing," put in van de Poste. "And I might add that we have been conducting a study into the entire range of Terrible Things, all the way from Just Annoying to Outrageously Awful, and will act on these findings—if we gain power."

"Trust the Commonsensers to do things by half measures!" scoffed Kaine, who obviously enjoyed these sorts of discussions. "By going only so far as 'Outrageously Awful,' Mr. van de Poste is selling his own nation short. We at the Whig Party have been looking at the Terrible Things problem and propose a zero-tolerance attitude to offenses as low as Mildly Inappropriate. Only in this way can the Somebodies who commit Terrible Things be stopped before they move on to acts that are Obscenely Perverse."

There was a smattering of applause again, presumably as the audience tried to figure out whether "Just Annoying" was worse than "Mildly Inappropriate."

"Succinctly put," announced Webastow. "At the end of the first round, I will award three points to Mr. Kaine for an excellent nonspecific condemnation, plus one bonus point for blaming the previous government and another for successfully mutating the question to promote the party line. Mr. van de Poste gets a point for a firm rebuttal, but only two points for his condemnation, as he tried to inject an impartial and intelligent observation. So at the end of the first round, it's Kaine leading with five points and van de Poste with three."

There was more applause as the numbers came up on the scoreboard.

"On to the next stage of the show, which we call the 'not answering the question' round. We have a question from Miss Ives."

A middle-aged woman put up her hand and asked, "Does the panel think that sugar should be added to rhubarb pie or the sweetness deficit made up by an additive, such as custard?"

"Thank you, Miss Ives. Mr. van de Poste, would you care to not answer this question first?"

"Well," said Redmond, eyeing the audience for any possible assassins, "this question goes straight to the heart of government, and I'd like to first point out that the Commonsense Party, when we were in power, tried more ways of doing things than any other party in living memory, and in consequence came closer to doing the right way of doing something, even if we didn't know it at the time."

There was applause, and Joffy and I exchanged looks.

"Does it get any better?" I whispered.

"Wait until they get on to Denmark."

"I utterly refute," began Kaine, "the implication that we aren't doing things the right way. To demonstrate this I'd like to wander completely off the point and talk about the Health Service overhaul that we will launch next year. We want to replace the outdated 'preventive' style of health care this country has relentlessly pursued with a 'wait until it gets really bad' system, which will target those most in need of medical treatment—the sick. Yearly health screenings for all citizens will end and be replaced by a 'tertiary' diagnostic regime that will save money and resources."

Again there was applause.

"Okay," announced Webastow, "I'm going to give van de Poste three points for successfully not answering that question at all, but five points to Kaine, who not only ignored the question but instead used it as a platform for his own political agenda. So with six rounds still to go, we have Kaine with ten points and van de Poste with six. Next question, please."

A young man with dyed red hair sitting in our row put his hand up. "I would like to suggest that the Danish are *not* our enemy, and this is nothing more than a cynical move by the Whigs to blame someone else for our own economic troubles."

"Ah!" said Webastow. "The controversial Danish question. I'm going to let Mr. van de Poste avoid this question first."

Van de Poste looked unwell all of a sudden and glanced nervously towards where Stricknene and Gayle were glaring at him.

"I think," he began slowly, "that if the Danish are as Mr. Kaine describes, I will offer my support to his policies."

He dabbed his forehead with a handkerchief as Kaine began: "When I came to power, England was a nation in the grip of economic decline and social ills. No one realized it at the time, and I took it upon myself to demonstrate by any means in my power the depths to which this great nation had fallen. With the support of my followers, I have managed to demonstrate reasonably clearly that things aren't as good as we thought they were, and what we imagined was peace and coexistence with our neighbors was actually a fool's paradise of delusion and paranoia. Anyone who thinks . . ."

I leaned over to Joffy. "Do people believe this garbage?"

"I'm afraid so. I think he's working on the 'people will far more readily believe a big lie than a small one' principle. Still surprises me, though."

". . . whoever disturbs this mission," rattled on Kaine, "is an enemy of the people, whether they be Danish or Welsh sympathizers, eager to overthrow our nation, or ill-informed lunatics who do not deserve the vote or a voice."

There was applause, but a few boos, too. I saw Colonel Gayle make notes on a scrap of paper as to who was shouting them, counting out the seat numbers as he did so.

"But why the Danish?" continued the man with the red hair. "They have a notoriously fair system of parliament, an impeccable record of human rights and a deserved reputation of upstanding charitable works in Third World nations. I think these are lies, Mr. Kaine!"

There were gasps and intakes of breath, but a few head noddings, too. Even, I think, from van de Poste.

"For the moment, at least," began Kaine in a conciliatory tone, "everyone is permitted an opinion, and I thank our friend for his candor. However, I would like to bring the audience's attention to an unrelated yet emotive issue that will bring the discussion away from embarrassing shortcomings of my administration and back into the arena of populist politics. Namely: the disgraceful record of puppy and kitten death when the Commonsense Party was in power."

At the mention of puppies and kittens dying, there were cries of alarm from the elder members of the audience.

Confident that he had turned the discussion, Kaine went on, "As things stand at the moment, over one thousand unwanted puppies and kittens are destroyed each year by lethal injections, which are freely available to veterinarians in Denmark. As committed humanitarians, the Whig Party has always condemned unwanted pet extermination."

"Mr. Van de Poste?" asked Webastow. "How do you react to Mr. Kaine's diversionary tactics regarding kitten death?"

"Clearly," began van de Poste, "kitten and puppy death is regrettable, but we in the Commonsense Party must bring it to everyone's attention that unwanted pets have to be destroyed in this manner. If people were more responsible with their pets, then this sort of thing wouldn't happen."

"Typical of the Commonsense approach!" barked Kaine. "Blaming the population as though they were feeble-minded fools with little personal responsibility! We in the Whig Party would never condone such an accusation and are appalled by Mr. van de Poste's outburst. I will personally pledge to you now that I will make the puppy-home-deficit problem my primary concern when I am made dictator."

There were loud cheers at this, and I shook my head sadly.

"Well," said Webastow happily, "I think I will give Mr. Kaine a full five points for his masterful misdirection, plus a bonus two points for obscuring the Danish issue rather than facing up to it. Mr. van de Poste, I'm sorry that I can only offer you a single point. Not only did you tacitly agree to Mr. Kaine's outrageous foreign policy, but you answered the unwanted-pet problem with an honest reply. So at the end of round three, Kaine is galloping ahead with seventeen points and van de Poste is bringing up the rear with seven. Our next question comes from Mr. Wedgwood."

"Yes," said a very old man in the third row, "I should like to know if the panel supports the Goliath Corporation's change to a faith-based corporate-management system."

And so it dragged on for nearly an hour, Kaine making outrageous claims and most of the audience failing to notice or, even worse, care. I was extremely glad when the program drew to a close, with Kaine leading thirty-eight points to van de Poste's sixteen, and we filed out of the door.

"What now?" asked Joffy.

I took my Jurisfiction TravelBook from my pocket and opened it at the page that offered a paragraph of *The Sword of the Zenobians,* one of the many unpublished works Jurisfiction used as a prison. All I had to do was grab Kaine's hand and read.

"I'm going to take Kaine back to the BookWorld with me. He's far too dangerous to leave out here."

"I agree," said Joffy, leading me around to where two large limousines were waiting for the Chancellor. "He'll want to meet his 'adoring' public, so you should have a chance."

We found the crowd waiting for him and pushed our way to the front. Most of the TV audience had turned up to see Kaine, but probably not for the same purpose as I. There was excited chatter as Kaine appeared. He smiled serenely and walked down the line, shook hands and was presented with flowers and babies to kiss. Close by his side was Colonel Gayle, with a phalanx of guards who stared into the crowd to make sure no one would try anything. Behind them all, I could see Stricknene still clinging onto the red briefcase. I partially hid myself behind a Kaine acolyte waving a Whig Party flag so Kaine didn't see me. We had crossed swords once before, and he knew what I was capable of, much as I knew what *he* was capable of—the last time we met, he had tried to have us eaten by the Glatisant, a sort of hell beast from the depths of mankind's most depraved imagination. If he could conjure up fictional beasts at will, I would have to be more careful.

But then, as the small group moved closer, I started to feel a curious impulse not to trap Kaine but to join in with the infectious enthusiasm. The atmosphere was electric, and being swept along with the crowd was something that just suddenly seemed *right.* Joffy had fallen under the spell already and was waving and whistling his support. I fought down a strong feeling to stop what I was doing and perhaps give Yorrick the benefit of the doubt when he and his entourage were upon us. His hand came out towards the crowd. I steadied myself, glanced at the opening lines of *Zenobians* and waited for the right moment. I would have to hold on tight as I read our way into the BookWorld, but that didn't bother me, as I'd done it many times before. What did worry me was the fact that my resolve was softening even faster.

Before the Kaine magnetism could take me over any further, I took a deep breath, grabbed the outstretched hand and muttered quickly, "It was a time of peace within the land of the Zenobians. . . ."

It didn't take long for me to jump into the BookWorld. Within a few moments, the bustling nighttime crowd in the car park of ToadNewsNetwork studios had vanished from view, to be replaced by a warm, verdant valley where herds of unicorns grazed peacefully under the summer sun. Grammasites wheeled in the blue skies, riding the thermals that rose from the warm grassland.

"So!" I said, turning to Kaine and receiving something of a shock. Beside me was not Yorrick but a middle-aged man holding a Whig Party flag and staring at the crystal-clear waters babbling through a gap in the rocks. I must have grabbed the wrong hand.

"Where am I?" asked the man, who was understandably confused.

"It's a near-death experience," I told him hastily. "What do you think?"

"It's beautiful!"

"Good. Don't get too fond of it. I'm taking you back."

I grasped him again, muttered the password under my breath and jumped out of fiction, something I had a lot less trouble with. We arrived behind some dustbins just as Kaine and his entourage were driving off. I ran up to Joffy, who was still waving good-bye, and told him to snap out of it.

"Sorry," he said, shaking his head. "What happened to you?"

"Don't ask. C'mon, let's go home."

We left the scene as a very excited and confused middle-aged man tried to tell anyone who would listen about his "near-death experience."

I went to bed past midnight, my head spinning from my experience of Kaine's almost hypnotic hold of the populace. Still, I wasn't out of ideas. I could try to grab him again and, failing that, use the eraserhead I had smuggled out of the BookWorld. Destroying him didn't bother me. I'd be no more guilty of murder than would an author with a delete key. But while Formby opposed him, Kaine would not become dictator, so I had a bit of time to work up a strategy. I could observe and plan. "Time spent doing renaissance," Mrs. Malaprop used to say, "is never wasted."

4.

A Town Like Swindon

Formby Denies Kaine

President-for-Life George Formby vetoed Chancellor Kaine's attempts to make himself dictator of England yesterday during one of the most heated exchanges this nation has ever seen. Kaine's Ultimate Executive Power Bill, already passed by parliament, requires only the presidential signature to become law. President Formby, speaking from the presidential palace in Wigan, told reporters, "Eeee, I wouldn't have a ***** like that run a grocer's, let alone a country!" Chancellor Kaine, angered by the President's remark, declared Formby "too old to have a say in this nation's future," "out of touch" and "a poor singer," the last of which he was forced to retract after a public outcry.

Article in *The Toad,* July 13, 1988

It was the morning following *Evade the Question Time,* and I had slept badly, waking up before Friday, which was unusual. I stared at the ceiling and thought about Kaine. I'd have to follow him to his next public engagement before he discovered that I had returned. I was just thinking about *why* Joffy and I had nearly been sucked into the whole Yorrick circus when Friday awoke and blinked at me in a breakfast sort of way. I dressed quickly and took him downstairs.

"Welcome to *Swindon Breakfast with Toad,*" announced the TV presenter as we walked in, "with myself, Warwick Fridge, and the lovely Leigh Onzolent—"

"Hello."

"—bringing you two hours of news and views, fun and competitions to see you into the day. *Breakfast with Toad* is sponsored by Arkwright's Doorknobs, the finest door furniture in Wessex."

Warwick turned to Leigh, who was looking way too glamorous for eight in the morning.

She smiled and continued, "This morning we'll be speaking to croquet captain Roger Kapok about Swindon's chances in the SuperHoop-88 and also to a man who claims to have seen unicorns in a near-death experience. Network Toad's resident dodo whisperer will be on hand for your pet's psychiatric problems, and our Othello backwards-reading competition reaches the quarterfinals. Later on we talk to Mr. Joffy Next about tomorrow's potential resurrection with St. Zvlkx, but first the news. The CEO of Goliath has announced contrition targets to be attainable within—"

"Morning, daughter," said my mother, who had just walked into the kitchen. "I never thought of you as an early riser."

"I wasn't until junior turned up," I replied, pointing at Friday, who was eyeing the porridge pot expectantly, "but if there's one thing he knows how to do, it's eat."

"It's what you did best when you were his age. Oh," added my mother absently, "I have to give you something, by the way."

She hurried from the room and returned with a sheaf of official-looking papers.

"Mr. Hicks left them for you."

Braxton Hicks was my old boss back at Swindon SpecOps. I had left abruptly, and from the look of his opening letter, it didn't look like he was very happy about it. I had been demoted to "Literary Detective Researcher," and it demanded my gun and badge back. The second letter was an outstanding warrant of arrest due to a trumped-up charge over possession of a small amount of illegally owned bootleg cheese.

"Is cheese still overpriced?" I asked my mother.

"Criminal!" she muttered. "Over five hundred percent duty. And it's not just cheese, either. They've extended the duty to cover all dairy products—even yogurt."

I sighed. I would probably have to go into SpecOps and explain myself. I could beg forgiveness, go to the stressperts and plead posttraumatic stress disorder or Xplkqulkiccasia or something and ask for my old job back. Perhaps if I were to get handy with a nine iron, it might swing things with my golf-mad boss. Outside SpecOps was not a good place to be if I wanted to hunt Yorrick Kaine or lobby the ChronoGuard for my husband back; it would help to have access to all the SpecOps and police databases.

I looked through the papers. I had apparently been found guilty of the cheese transgression and fined five thousand pounds plus costs.

"Did you pay this?" I asked my mother, showing her the court demand.

"Yes."

"Then I should pay you back."

"No need," she replied, adding before I could thank her, "I paid it out of *your* overdraft—which is quite big now."

"How . . . *thoughtful* of you."

"Don't mention it. Bacon and eggs?"

"Please."

"Coming up. Would you get the milk?"

I went to the front door to fetch the milk, and as I bent down to pick it up, there was a *whang-thop* noise as a bullet zipped past my ear and thudded into the doorframe next to me. I was about to slam the door and grab my automatic when an unaccountable stillness took hold, like a sudden becalming. Above me a pigeon hung frozen in the air, the wingtip feathers splayed as it reached the bottom of a downstroke. A motorcyclist on the road was balancing impossibly still, and passersby were now as stiff and unmoving as statues—even Pickwick had stopped in midwaddle. Time, for the moment at least, had frozen. I knew only one person who had a face that could stop a clock like this—my father. The question was, where was he?

I looked up and down the road. Nothing. Since I was about to be assassinated, I thought it might help to know who was doing the assassinating, so I walked down the garden path and across the road to the alley where de Floss had hidden himself so badly the previous day. It was here that I found my father looking at a small and very pretty blond woman no more than five foot high who was time frozen halfway through the process of disassembling a sniper's rifle. She was probably in her late twenties and her hair was pulled back into a pony tail held tight with a flower hair tie. I noted with a certain detached amusement that there was a lucky mascot attached to the trigger guard and the stock was covered with pink fur. Dad looked younger than I, but he was instantly recognizable. The odd nature of the time business tended to make their operatives live nonlinear lives—every time I met him, he was of a different age.

"Hello, Dad."

"You were correct," he said, comparing the woman's rigid features with those on a series of photographs, "it's an assassin, all right."

"Never mind that for the moment!" I cried happily. "How are you? I haven't seen you for years!"

He turned and stared at me. "My dear girl, we spoke only a few hours ago!"

"No we didn't."

"We did, actually."

"We did *not*."

He stopped, stared at me for a moment and then looked at his watch, shook it and listened to it, then shook it again.

"Here," I said, handing him the chronograph I was wearing, "take mine."

"Very nice—thank you. Ah! I stand corrected. Three hours *from* now. It's an easy mistake to make. Did you have any thoughts about that matter we discussed?"

"No, Dad," I said in an exasperated tone. "It hasn't happened yet, remember?"

"You're always so *linear,*" he muttered, returning to his job comparing the pictures to the assassin. "I think you ought to try and expand your horizons a bit— Bingo!"

He had found a picture that matched my assassin and read the label on the back.

"Expensive hit woman working in the Wiltshire-Oxford area. Looks petite and bijou but as deadly as the best of them. She trades under the name 'The Windowmaker.'" He paused. "Should be Widowmaker, shouldn't it?"

"But I heard that the Windowmaker was lethal," I pointed out. "A contract with her and you're deader than corduroy."

"I heard that, too," replied my father thoughtfully. "Sixty-seven victims—sixty-eight if she was the one that did Samuel Pring. She must have *meant* to miss. It's the only explanation. In any event, her real name is Cindy Stoker."

This was unexpected. Cindy was married to Spike Stoker, an operative over at SO-17 whom I had worked with a couple of times. I had even given him advice on how best to tell Cindy that he hunted down werewolves for a living—not the choicest profession for a potential husband.

"Cindy is my assassin? Cindy is the Windowmaker?"

"You know her?"

"*Of* her. Wife of a good friend."

"Well, don't get too chummy. She tries and fails to kill you three times. The second time with a bomb under your car on Monday, then next Friday at eleven in the morning—but she fails and you, ultimately, choose for her to die. I shouldn't really be telling you this, but like we discussed, we've got bigger fish to fry."

"What bigger fish to fry?"

"Sweetpea," he said, giving me his stern "Father knows best" voice, "I'm really not going to go through it all again. Now I have to get back to work—there's a timephoon brewing in the Dark Ages, and if we don't sort it out, we'll be picking anachronisms out of the time line for a century."

"Wait—you're working at the ChronoGuard?"

"I've told you all about this already! Do try and keep up—you're going to need all your wits about you over the next week. Now, get back to the house, and I'll start the world up again."

He wasn't in a very chatty mood, but since I would be seeing him later and would find out *then* what we had just discussed, there didn't seem a lot of point to talking anyway, so I bade him good-bye, and as I walked up the garden path, time returned to normal with a *snap*. The pigeon flew on, the traffic continued to move, and everything carried on as usual. Time had stopped so completely that everything my father and I had talked about occupied no time at all. Still, at least this meant I wouldn't have to be constantly looking over my shoulder if I knew when she would try to get rid of me. Mind you, I wasn't looking forward to her death. Spike would be severely pissed off.

I returned to the kitchen where Mum was still hard at work cooking my bacon and eggs. To her and Friday, I had been gone less than twenty seconds.

"What was that noise when you were at the door, Thursday?"

"Probably a car backfiring."

"Funny," she said, "I could have sworn it was a high-velocity bullet striking wood. Two eggs or one?"

"Two, please."

I picked up the newspaper, which was running a five-page exposé revealing that "Danish pastries" were actually brought to Denmark by displaced Viennese bakers in the sixteenth century. "In what other ways," thundered the article, "have the dishonest Danes made fools of us?" I shook my head sadly and turned to another page.

Mum said she could look after Friday until tea, something I got her to promise *before* she had fully realized the implications of nappy changing and seen just how bad his manners were at breakfast. He yelled, "Ut enim ad veniam!" which might have meant "Look how far I can throw my porridge!" as a spoonful of oatmeal flew across the kitchen, much to the delight of DH-82, who had learned pretty quickly that hanging around messy toddlers at mealtimes was an extremely productive pastime.

Hamlet came down to breakfast, followed, after a prudent gap, by Emma. They bade each other good morning in such an obvious way that only their serious demeanor kept me from laughing out loud.

"Did you sleep well, Lady Hamilton?" asked Hamlet.

"I did, thank you. *My* room faces east for the morning light, you know."

"Ah!" replied Hamlet. "Mine *doesn't*. I believe it was once the box room. It has pretty pink wallpaper and a bedside light shaped like Tweety Pie. Not that I noticed much, of course, being fast asleep—on my own."

"Of course."

"Let me show you something," said Mum after breakfast.

I followed her down to Mycroft's workshop. Alan had kept Mum's dodos trapped in the potting shed all night and even now threatened to peck anyone who so much as looked at him "in a funny way."

"Pickwick!" I said sternly. "Are you going to let your son bully those dodos?"

Pickwick looked the other way and pretended to have an itchy foot. To be honest, she couldn't control Alan any more than I could. Only half an hour previously, he had chased the postman out of the garden accompanied by an angry *plink-plink-plink* noise, something even the postman had to admit "was a first."

Mum opened the side door to the large workshop, and we entered. This was where my uncle Mycroft did all his inventing. It was here that he had demonstrated, amongst many other things, translating carbon paper, a sarcasm early-warning device, Nextian Geometry and, most important to me, the Prose Portal—the method by which I first entered fiction. Mother was always nervous in Mycroft's lab. Many years ago he'd developed some four-dimensional paper, the idea being that you could print on the same sheet of paper again and again, isolating the different overprintings in marginally different time zones that could be read by the use of temporal spectacles. By going to the nanosecond level, a million sheets of text or pictures could be stored on one sheet of paper in a single second. Brilliant—but the paper *looked* identical to a standard sheet of 8½-by-11—and it had been a long contentious family argument that my mother had used the irreplaceable prototype to line the compost bucket. It was no wonder she was careful near his inventions.

"What did you want to show me?"

She smiled and led me to the end of the workshop, and there, next to my stuff that she had rescued from my apartment, was the unmistakable shape of my Porsche 356 Speedster hidden beneath a dust sheet.

"I've run the engine every month and kept it MOTed for you. I even took it for a spin a couple of times."

She pulled the sheet off with a flourish. The car still looked slightly shabby after our various encounters, but just the way I liked it. I gently touched the bullet holes that had been made by Hades all those years ago, and the bent front wing where I had slid it into the river Severn. I opened the garage doors.

"Thanks, Mum. Sure you're all right with the boy Friday?"

"Until four this afternoon. But you have to promise me something."

"What's that?"

"That you'll come to my Eradications Anonymous group this evening."

"Mum—"

"It will do you good. You might enjoy it. Might *meet* someone. Might make you forget Linden."

"*Landen*. His name's *Landen*. And I don't need or want to forget him."

"Then the group will support you. Besides, you might learn something. Oh, and would you take Hamlet with you? Mr. Bismarck has a bee in his bonnet about Danes because of that whole silly Schleswig-Holstein thingummy."

I narrowed my eyes. Could Joffy be right?

"What about Emma? Do you want me to take her, too?"

"No. Why?"

" . . . er, no reason."

I picked up Friday and gave him a kiss. "Be good, Friday. You're staying with Nana for the day."

Friday looked at me, looked at Mum, stuck his finger up his nose and said, "Sunt in culpa qui officia id est laborum?"

I ruffled his hair, and he showed me a booger he had found. I declined the present, wiped his hand with a hanky, then went to look for Hamlet. I found him in the front garden demonstrating a thrust-and-parry swordfight to Emma and Pickwick. Even Alan had left off bullying the other dodos and was watching in silence. I called out to Hamlet, and he came running.

"Sorry," said the Prince as I opened the garage doors, "just showing them how that damn fool Laertes gets his comeuppance."

I showed him how to get into the Porsche, dropped in myself, started the engine and drove off down the hill towards the Brunel Centre.

"You seem to be getting on very well with Emma."

"Who?" asked Hamlet, unconvincingly vague.

"Lady Hamilton."

"Oh, *her.* Nice girl. We have a lot in common."

"Such as . . . ?"

"Well," said Hamlet, thinking hard, "we both have a good friend called Horatio."

We motored on down past the magic roundabout, and I pointed out the new stadium with its four floodlit towers standing tall amongst the low housing.

"That's our croquet stadium," I said. "Thirty thousand seats. Home of the Swindon Mallets croquet team."

"Croquet is a national sport out here?"

"Oh, yes," I replied, knowing a thing or two about it, since I used to play myself. "It has evolved a lot since the early days. For a start the teams are bigger—ten a side in World Croquet League. The players have to get their balls through the hoops in the quickest possible time, so it can be quite rough. A stray ball can pack a wallop, and a flailing mallet is potentially lethal. The WCL insists on body armor and Plexiglas barriers for the spectators."

I turned left into Manchester Road and parked up behind a Griffin-6 Lowrider.

"What now?"

"Haircut. You don't think I'm going to spend the next few weeks looking like Joan of Arc, do you?"

"Ah!" said Hamlet. "You hadn't mentioned it for a while, so I'd stopped noticing. If it's all right with you, I'll just stay here and write a letter to Horatio. Does 'pirate' have one *t* or two?"

"One."

I walked into Mum's hairdresser. The stylists looked at my hair with a sort of shocked numbness until Lady Volescamper, who along with her increasingly eccentric mayoral husband constituted Swindon's most visible aristocracy, suddenly pointed at me and said in a strident tone that could shatter glass:

"That's the style I want. Something new. Something retro— something to cause a sensation at the Swindon Mansion House Ball!"

Mrs. Barnet, who was both the chief stylist and official gossip laureate of Swindon, kept her look of horror to herself and then said diplomatically, "Of course. And may I say that Her Grace's boldness matches her sense of style."

Lady Volescamper returned to her *FeMole* magazine, appearing not to recognize me, which was just as well—the last time I went to Vole Towers, a hell beast from the darkest depths of the human imagination trashed the entrance lobby.

"Hello, Thursday," said Mrs. Barnet, wrapping a sheet around me with an expert flourish, "haven't seen you for a while."

"I've been away."

"In prison?"

"No—just away."

"Ah. How would you like it? I have it on good authority that the Joan of Arc look is set to be quite popular this summer."

"You know I'm not a fashion person, Gladys. Just get rid of the dopey haircut, would you?"

"As madame wishes." She hummed to herself for a moment, then asked, "Been on holiday this year?"

I got back to the car a half hour later to find Hamlet talking to a traffic warden, who seemed so engrossed in whatever he was telling her that she wasn't writing me a ticket.

"And that," said Hamlet as soon as I came within earshot and making a thrusting motion with his hand, "was when I cried, 'A rat, a rat!' and killed the unseen old man. Hello, Thursday—goodness—that's short, isn't it?"

"It's better than it was. C'mon, I've got to go and get my job back."

"Job?" asked Hamlet as we drove off, leaving a very indignant traffic warden who wanted to know what had happened next.

"Yes. Out here you need money to live."

"I've got lots," said Hamlet generously. "You should have some of mine."

"Somehow I don't think fictional kroner from an unspecified century will cut the mustard down at the First Goliath—and put the skull away. They aren't generally considered a fashion accessory here in the Outland."

"They're all the rage where I come from."

"Well, not here. Put it in this grocery bag."

"*Stop!*"

I screeched to a halt. "What?"

"That, over there. *It's me!*"

Before I could say anything, Hamlet had jumped out of the car and run across the road to a coin-operated machine on the corner of the street. I parked the Speedster and walked over to join him.

He was staring with delight at the simple box, the top half of which was glazed; inside was a suitably attired mannequin visible from the waist up.

"It's called a WillSpeak machine," I said, passing him a shopping bag. "Here—put the skull in the bag like I asked."

"What does it do?"

"Officially it's called a 'Shakespeare Soliloquy Vending Automaton,' " I explained. "You put in two shillings and get a short snippet from Shakespeare."

"Of me?"

"Yes," I said, "of you."

For it was, of course, a *Hamlet* WillSpeak machine, and the mannequin Hamlet sat looking blankly out at the flesh-and-blood Hamlet standing next to me.

"Can we hear a bit?" asked Hamlet excitedly.

"If you want. Here."

I dug out a coin and placed it in the machine. There was a whirring and clicking as the dummy came to life.

"*To be, or not to be,*" began the mannequin in a hollow, metallic voice. The machine had been built in the thirties and was now pretty much worn out. "*That is the question: Whether 'tis nobler in the mind—*"

Hamlet was fascinated, like a child listening to a tape recording of his own voice for the first time. "Is that really me?" he asked.

"The words are yours—but actors do it a lot better."

"*—Or to take arms against a sea of troubles—*"

"Actors?"

"Yes. Actors, playing Hamlet."

He looked confused.

"*—That flesh is heir to—*"

"I don't understand."

"Well," I began, looking around to check that no one was listening, "you know that you are Hamlet, from Shakespeare's *Hamlet*?"

"Yes?"

For it was, of course, a Hamlet WillSpeak machine, and the mannequin Hamlet sat looking blankly out at the flesh-and-blood Hamlet standing next to me.

"—*To die, to sleep, to sleep—perchance to dream—*"

"Well, that's a play, and out here in the Outland, people act out that play."

"With me?"

"Of you. *Pretending* to be you."

"But I'm the real me?"

"—*Who would fardels bear—*"

"In a manner of speaking."

"Ahhh, " he said after a few moments of deep thought, "I see. Like the whole *Murder of Gonzago* thing. I wondered how it all worked. Can we go and see me sometime?"

"I . . . *suppose*," I answered uneasily. "Do you really want to?"

"—*from whose bourn no traveler returns—*"

"Of course. I've heard that some people in the Outland think I am a dithering twit unable to make up his mind rather than a dynamic leader of men, and these 'play' things you describe will prove it to me one way or the other."

I tried to think of the movie in which he prevaricates the least. "We could get the Zeffirelli version out on video for you to look at."

"Who plays me?"

"Mel Gibson."

"—*Thus conscience does make cowards of us all—*"

Hamlet stared at me, mouth open. "But that's *incredible!*" he said ecstatically. "I'm Mel's biggest fan!" He thought for a moment. "So . . . Horatio must be played by Danny Glover, yes?"

"—*sicklied o'er with the pale cast of thought—*"

"No, no. Listen: the *Lethal Weapon* series is nothing like *Hamlet*."

"Well," replied the Prince reflectively, "in that I think you might be mistaken. The Martin Riggs character begins with self-doubt and contemplates suicide over the loss of a loved one but eventually turns into a decisive man of action and kills all the bad guys. Same as the *Road Warrior* series, really. Is Ophelia played by Patsy Kensit?"

"No," I replied, trying to be patient, "Helena Bonham Carter."

He perked up when he heard this. "This gets better and better! When I tell Ophelia, she'll flip—if she hasn't already."

"Perhaps," I said thoughtfully, "you'd better see the Olivier version instead. Come on, we've work to do."

"—*their currents turn awry / And lose the name of action.*"

The WillSpeak Hamlet stopped clicking and whirring and sat silent once more, waiting for the next florin.

5.

Ham(let) and Cheese

"Seven Wonders of Swindon" Naming Bureaucracy Unveiled
After five years of careful consideration, Swindon City Council has unveiled the naming procedure for the city's much vaunted "Seven Wonders" tourism plan. The twenty-seven-point procedure is the most costly and complicated piece of bureaucracy the city has ever devised and might even be included as one of the wonders itself. The plan will be be undertaken by the Swindon Special Committee for Wonders, which will consider applications prepared by the Seven Wonders Working Party from six separate name-selection subcommittees. Once chosen, the wonders will be further scrutinized by eight different oversight committees before being adopted. The byzantine and needlessly expensive system is already tipped to win the coveted Red Tape Award from *Bureaucracy Today*.
                              Article in *Swindon Globe News*, June 12, 1988

I drove to the car park above the Brunel Centre and bought a pay-and-display ticket, noting how they had almost tripled in price since I was here last. I looked in my purse. I had fifteen pounds, three shillings and an old Skyrail ticket.

"Short of cash?" asked Hamlet as we walked down the stairs to the street-level concourse.

"Let's just say I'm very 'receipt rich' at present."

Money had never been a problem in the BookWorld. All the details of life were taken care of by something called Narrative Assumption. A reader would *assume* you had gone shopping, or gone to the toilet, or brushed your hair, so a writer never needed to outline it—which was just as well, really. I'd forgotten all about the real-world trivialities, but I was actually quite enjoying them, in a mind-dulling sort of way.

"It says here," said Hamlet, who had been reading the newspaper, "that Denmark invaded England and put hundreds of innocent English citizens to death without trial!"

"It was the Vikings in 786, Hamlet. I hardly think that warrants the headline BLOODTHIRSTY DANES GO ON RAMPAGE. Besides, at the time they were no more Danish than we were English."

"So we're not the historical enemies of England?"

"Not at all."

"And eating rollmop herrings won't lead to erectile dysfunction?"

"No. And keep your voice down. All these people are real, not D-7 generic crowd types. Out here, you only exist in a play."

"Okay," he said, stopping at an electronics shop and staring at the TVs. "Who's she?"

"Lola Vavoom. An actress."

"Really? Has she ever played Ophelia?"

"Many times."

"Was she better than Helena Bonham Carter?"

"Both good—just *different*."

"Different? What do you mean?"

"They both brought different things to the role."

Hamlet laughed. "I think you're confusing the matter, Thursday. Ophelia is just Ophelia."

"Not out here. Listen, I'm just going to see how bad my overdraft is."

"How you Outlanders complicate matters!" he murmured. "If we were in a book right now, you'd be accosted by a solicitor who tells you a wealthy aunt has died and left you lots of money—and then we'd just start the next chapter with you in London making your way to Kaine's office disguised as a cleaning woman."

"Excuse me!" said a suited gentleman who looked suspiciously like a solicitor. "But are you Thursday Next?"

I glanced nervously at Hamlet.

"Perhaps."

"Allow me to introduce myself. My name is Mr. Wentworth of Wentworth, Wentworth and Wentworth, Solicitors. I'm the second Wentworth, if you're interested."

"And?"

"And . . . I wonder if I could have your autograph? I followed your *Jane Eyre* escapade with a great deal of interest."

I breathed a sigh of relief and signed his autograph book. Mr. Wentworth thanked me and hurried off.

"You had me worried for a moment there," said Hamlet. "I thought I was meant to be the fictitious one."

"You are." I smiled. "And don't you forget it."

"Twenty-two thousand pounds?" I said to the cashier. "Are you sure?"

The cashier looked at me with unblinking eyes, then at Hamlet, who was standing over me a bit indelicately.

"Quite sure. Twenty-two thousand, three hundred eight pounds and four shillings three pence ha'penny—*overdrawn*," she added, in case I had missed it. "Your landlord sued you for dodo-related tenancy violations and won five thousand pounds. Since you weren't here, we upped your credit limit when he demanded payment. Then we raised the limit again to pay for the additional interest."

"How very thoughtful of you."

"Thank you. Goliath First National Friendly always aims to please."

"Are you *sure* you wouldn't rather go with the 'wealthy aunt' scenario?" asked Hamlet, being no help at all.

"No. Shhh."

"We haven't had a single deposit from you for nearly two and a half years," continued the bank clerk.

"I've been away."

"Prison?"

"No. So the rest of my overdraft is . . . ?"

"Interest on the money we lent you, interest on the interest we lent you, letters asking for money that we know you haven't got, letters asking for an address that we knew wouldn't reach you, letters asking whether you got the letters we knew you hadn't received, further letters asking for a response because we have an odd sense of humor—you know how it all adds up! Can we expect a check in the near future?"

"Not really. Um . . . any chance of raising my credit limit?"

The cashier arched an eyebrow. "I can get you an appointment to see the manager. Do you have an address to which we can send expensive letters demanding money?"

I gave them Mum's address and made an appointment to see the manager. We walked past the statue of Brunel and the Booktastic shop, which I noted was still open, despite several closing-down sales—one of which I had witnessed with Miss Havisham.

Miss Havisham. How I had missed her guidance in my first few months heading Jurisfiction. With her I might have avoided that whole stupid sock episode in *Lake Wobegon Days*.

"Okay, I give up," said Hamlet quite suddenly. "How does it all turn out?"

"How does *what* all turn out?"

He spread his arms out wide.

"All this. You, your husband, Miss Hamilton, the small dodo, that SuperHoop thing and the big company—what's it called again?"

"Goliath?"

"Right. How does it all turn out?"

"I haven't the slightest idea. Out here our lives are pretty much an unknown quantity."

Hamlet seemed shocked by the concept. "How do you live here not knowing what the future might bring?"

"That's part of the fun. The pleasure of anticipation."

"There is no pleasure in anticipation," said Hamlet glumly. "Except perhaps," he added, "in killing that old fool Polonius."

"My point exactly," I replied. "Where you come from, events are preordained and everything that happens to you has some sort of relevance further on in the story."

"It's clear you haven't read *Hamlet* for a—*LOOK OUT!*"

Hamlet pushed me out of the way as a small steamroller—the size that works on sidewalks and paths—bore rapidly down upon us and crashed past into the window of the shop we had been standing outside. The roller stopped amongst a large display of electrical goods, the rear wheels still rotating.

"Are you okay?" asked Hamlet, helping me to my feet.

"I'm fine—thanks to you."

"Goodness!" said a workman, running up to us and turning a valve to shut off the roller. "Are you all right?"

"Not hurt in the least. What happened?"

"I don't know," replied the workman, scratching his head. "Are you sure you're okay?"

"Really, I'm fine."

We walked off as a crowd began to gather. The owner of the shop didn't look that upset; doubtless he was thinking about what he could charge to insurance.

"You see?" I said to Hamlet as we walked away.

"What?"

"This is *exactly* what I mean. A lot happens in the real world for no good reason. If this were fiction, this little incident would have relevance thirty or so chapters from now; as it is it means nothing—after all, not every incident in life *has* a meaning."

"Tell that to the scholars who study *me*," Hamlet snorted disdainfully, then thought for a moment before adding, "If the real world were a book, it would *never* find a publisher. Overlong, detailed to the point of distraction—and ultimately, without a major resolution."

"Perhaps," I said thoughtfully, "that's exactly what we like about it."

We reached the SpecOps Building. It was of a sensible Germanic design built during the occupation, and it was here that I, along with Bowden Cable and Victor Analogy, dealt with Acheron Hades' plot to kidnap Jane Eyre out of *Jane Eyre*. Hades had failed and died in the attempt. I wondered how many of the old gang would still be around. I had sudden doubts and decided to think for a moment before going in. Perhaps I should have a plan of action instead of charging in Zhark-like.

"Fancy a coffee, Hamlet?"

"Please."

We walked into the Café Goliathe opposite. The same one, in fact, that I had last seen Landen walking towards an hour before he was eradicated.

"Hey!" said the man behind the counter who seemed somehow familiar. "We don't serve those kind in here!"

"What kind?"

"The *Danish* kind."

Goliath was obviously working with Kaine on this particular nonsense.

"He's not Danish. He's my cousin Eddie from Wolverhampton."

"Really? Then why is he dressed like Hamlet?"

I thought quickly. "Because . . . he's insane. Isn't that right, Cousin Eddie?"

"Yes," said Hamlet, to whom feigning madness was not much of a problem. "When the wind is southerly, I know a hawk from a handsaw."

"See?"

"Well, that's all right, then."

I started as I realized why he seemed familiar. It was Mr. Cheese, one of the Goliath corporate bullies that Brik Schitt-Hawse had employed. He and his partner, Mr. Chalk, had made my life difficult before I left. He didn't have his goatee anymore, but it was definitely him. Undercover? I doubted it—his name was on his Café Goliathe badge with, I noted, two gold stars, one for washing up and the other for latte frothing. But he didn't show any sign of recognizing me.

"What will you have, Ham—I mean, Cousin Eddie?"

"What is there?"

"Espresso, mocha, latte, white mocha, hot chocolate, decaf, recaf, nocaf, somecaf, extracaf, Goliachino™ . . . what's the matter?"

Hamlet had started to tremble, a look of pain and hopelessness on his face as he stared wild-eyed at the huge choice laid out in front of him.

"To espresso or to latte, that is the question," he muttered, his free will evaporating rapidly. I had asked Hamlet for something he couldn't easily supply: a decision. "Whether 'tis tastier on the palate to choose white mocha over plain," he continued in a rapid garble, "or to take a cup to go. Or a mug to stay, or extra cream, or have nothing, and by opposing the endless choice, end one's heartache—"

"Cousin Eddie!" I said sharply. "Cut it out!"

"To froth, to sprinkle, perchance to drink, and in that—"

"He'll have a mocha with extra cream, please."

Hamlet stopped abruptly once the burden of decision was taken from him.

"Sorry," he said, rubbing his temples, "I don't know what came over me. All of a sudden I had this overwhelming desire to talk for a very long time without actually *doing* anything. Is that normal?"

"Not for me. I'll have a latte, Mr. *Cheese*," I said, watching his reaction carefully.

He still didn't seem to recognize me. He rang up the cost and then started making the coffees.

"Do you remember me?"

He narrowed his eyes and stared at me carefully for a moment or two. "No."

"Thursday Next?"

His face broke into a broad grin, and he put out a large hand for me to shake, welcoming me as an old workmate rather than a past nemesis. I faltered, then shook his hand slowly.

"Miss Next! Where have you been? Prison?"

"Away."

"Ah! But you're well?"

"I'm okay," I said suspiciously, retrieving my hand. "How are you?"

"Not bad!" he laughed, looking at me sideways for a moment and narrowing his eyes. "You've changed. What is it?"

"Almost no hair?"

"That's it. We were looking for you everywhere. You spent almost eighteen months in the Goliath top ten most wanted—although you never made it to the number-one slot."

"I'm devastated."

"No one has ever spent ten months on the list," carried on Cheese with a sort of dreamy, nostalgic look. "The next longest was three weeks. We looked *everywhere* for you!"

"But you gave up?"

"Goodness me, no," replied Cheese. "Perseverance is what Goliath does best. There was a restructuring of corporate policy, and we were *reallocated*."

"You mean fired."

"No one is ever fired from Goliath," said Cheese in a shocked tone. "Cots to coffins. You've heard the adverts."

"So just moved on from bullying and terrifying and into lattes and mochas?"

"Haven't you heard?" said Cheese, frothing up some milk. "Goliath has moved its corporate image away from the 'overbearing bully' and more towards 'peace, love and understanding.'"

"I heard something about it last night," I replied, "but you'll forgive me if I'm not convinced."

"Forgive is what Goliath does best, Miss Next. Faith is a difficult commodity to imbue—and that's why violent and ruthless bullies like me have to be reallocated. Our corporate seer, Sister Bettina,

79

foresaw a necessity for us to change to a faith-based corporate-management system, but the rules concerning new religions are quite strict—we have to make changes to the corporation that are meaningful and genuine. That's why the old Goliath Internal Security Service is now known as Goliath Is Seriously Sorry—you see, we even kept the old initials so we didn't have to divert money away from good causes to buy new headed notepaper."

"Or have to change them back when this charade has been played out."

"You know," said Cheese, waving a finger at me, "you always were just that teensy-weensy bit cynical. You should learn to be more trusting."

"Trusting. Right. And you think the public will believe this touchy-feely, good-Lord-we're-sorry-forgive-us-please crap after four decades of rampant exploitation?"

"Rampant exploitation?" echoed Cheese in a dismayed tone. "I don't think so. 'Proactive greater goodification' was more what we had in mind—and it's five decades, not four. Are you sure your cousin Eddie isn't Danish?"

"*Definitely* not."

I thought about Brik Schitt-Hawse, the odious Goliath agent who'd had my husband eradicated in the first place. "What about Schitt-Hawse? Where does he work these days?"

"I think he moved into some post in Goliathopolis. I really don't move in those circles anymore. Mind you, we should all get together for a reunion and have a drink! What do you think?"

"I think I'd rather have my husband back," I replied darkly.

"Oh!" said Cheese, suddenly remembering just what particular unpleasantness he and Goliath had done to me. Then he added slowly, "You must *hate* us!"

"Just a lot."

"We can't have that. Repent is what Goliath does best. Have you applied for a Goliath Unfair Treatment Reversal?"

I stared at him and raised an eyebrow.

"Well," he began, "Goliath has been allowing disgruntled citizens to apply to have reversed any unfair or unduly harsh measures taken against them—sort of a big apology, really. If Goliath is to become the opiate of the masses, we must first atone for our sins. We like to right any wrongs and then have a good strong hug to show we really mean it."

"Hence your demotion to coffee-shop attendant."

"Exactly so!"

"How do I apply?"

"We've opened an Apologarium in Goliathopolis; you can take the free shuttle from Tarbuck Graviport. They'll tell you what to do."

"Harmonious peace, eh?"

"Peace is what Goliath does best, Miss Next. Just fill out a form and see one of our trained apologists. I'm sure they can get your husband back in a jiffy!"

I took the mocha with extra cream and the latte and sat by the window, staring at the SpecOps Building in silence. Hamlet sensed my disquiet and busied himself on a list of things he wanted to tell Ophelia but didn't think he would be able to, then another list of things he should tell her but won't. Then a list of all the different lists he had written about Ophelia and, finally, a letter of appreciation to Sir John Gielgud.

"I'm going to sort out a few things," I said after a while. "Don't move from here, and don't tell anyone who you really are. Understand?"

"Yes."

"Who are you?"

"Hamlet, Prince of . . . just kidding. I'm your cousin Eddie."

"Good. And you have cream on your nose."

6.

SpecOps

The Special Operations Network was the agency that looked after areas too specialized to be undertaken by the regular police. There were over thirty SpecOps divisions. SO-1 policed us all, SO-12 was the ChronoGuard, and SO-13 dealt with reengineered species. SO-17 was the Vampire and Werewolf Disposal Operations and SO-32 the Horticultural Enforcement Agency. I had been SO-27, the Literary Detectives. Ten years authenticating Milton and tracking down forged Shakespeareana. After my work actually *within* fiction, it all seemed a bit tame. At Jurisfiction I could catch a horse as it bolted—in the Literary Detectives, it was like wandering around a very large field armed with only a halter and a photograph of a carrot.

Thursday Next, *Private Journals*

I pushed open the door to the station and walked in. The building was shared with Swindon's regular force and seemed slightly shabbier than I remembered. The walls were the same dismal shade of green, and I could smell the faint aroma of boiled cabbage from the canteen on the second floor. In truth, my stay here in late '85 had not actually been that long—most of my SpecOps career had been undertaken in London.

I walked over to the main desk, expecting to see Sergeant Ross. He had been replaced by someone who seemed too young to be a police officer, much less a desk sergeant.

"I'm here to get my old job back," I announced.

"Which was?"

"Literary Detective."

He chuckled. Unkindly, I thought.

"You'll need to see the commander," he replied without taking his gaze from the book he was scribbling in. "Name?"

"Thursday Next."

A hush descended slowly on the room, beginning with those closest to me and moving outwards with my whispered name like ripples in a pool. Within a few moments I was being stared at in silence by at least two dozen assorted police and SpecOps officers, a couple of Gaskell impersonators and an ersatz Coleridge. I gave an embarrassed smile and looked from blank face to blank face, trying to figure out whether to run, or to fight, or what. My heart beat faster as a young officer quite close to me reached into his breast pocket and pulled out—a notebook.

"Please," he said. "I wonder if I might have your autograph?"

"Well, no—of course not."

I breathed a sign of relief, and pretty soon I was having my back slapped and being congratulated on the whole *Jane Eyre* adventure. I'd forgotten the celebrity thing but also noticed that there were officers in the room who were interested in me for another reason—SO-1, probably.

"I need to see Bowden Cable," I said to the desk sergeant, realizing that if anyone could help, it was my old partner. He smiled, picked up a phone, announced me and wrote out a visitor's pass, then told me to go to Interview Suite 16 on the third floor. I thanked my newfound acquaintances, made my way to the elevators and ascended to the third floor. When the lift doors rattled open I walked with a hurried step towards Room 16. Halfway there I was accosted by Bowden, who slid his arm in mine and steered me into an empty office.

"Bowden!" I said happily. "How are you?"

He hadn't changed much in the past two years. Fastidiously neat, he was wearing the usual pinstripe suit but without jacket, so he must have been in a hurry to meet me.

"I'm good, Thursday, real good. But where the hell have you been?"

"I've been—"

"You can tell me later. Thank the GSD I got to you first! We don't have a lot of time. Goodness! What have you done to your hair?"

"Well, Joan of—"

"You can tell me later. Ever heard of Yorrick Kaine?"

"Of course! I'm here to—"

"No time for explanations. He's not fond of you at all. He has a personal adviser named Ernst Stricknene who calls us *every day* to ask if you've returned. But this morning—*he didn't call!*"

"So?"

"So he knows you're back. Why is the Chancellor interested in you, anyway?"

"Because he's fictional, and I want to take him back to the BookWorld where he belongs."

"That coming from anyone but you, I'd laugh. Is that really true?"

"As true as I'm standing here."

"Well, your life is in danger, that's all I know. Ever heard of the assassin known as the—"

"Windowmaker?"

"How did you know?"

"I have my sources. Any idea who took out the contract?"

"Well, they've killed sixty-seven people—sixty-eight if they did Samuel Pring—and they *definitely* did the number on Gordon Duff-Rolecks, whose death really only benefited—"

"Kaine."

"Exactly. You need to take particular care. More than that, we need you back as a full serving member of the Literary Detectives. We've got one or two problems that need ironing out in our department."

"So what do we do?"

"Well, you're AWOL at best and a cheese smuggler at worst. So we've concocted a cover story of such bizarre complexity and outrageous daring that it can only be true. Here it is: in a parallel universe ruled entirely by lobsters, you—"

But at that moment, the door opened and a familiar figure walked in. I say familiar, but not exactly welcome. It was Commander Braxton Hicks, head of SpecOps here in Swindon.

I could almost hear Bowden's heart fall—mine, too.

Hicks still had a job because of me, but I didn't expect that to count for much. He was a company man, a bean counter—more fond of his precious budget than anything else. He had never given me any quarter, and I didn't expect any now.

"Ah, found you!" said the Commander in a serious tone. "Miss Next. They told me you'd arrived. Been giving us the little runaround, haven't you?"

"She's been—" began Bowden.

"I'm sure Miss Next can explain for herself, hmmm?"

"Yes, sir."

"Good. Close the door behind you, eh?"

Bowden gave a sickly smile and slinked out of the interview room.

Braxton sat, opened my file and stroked his large mustache thoughtfully.

"Absent without leave for over two years, demoted eighteen months ago, nonreturn of SpecOps weapon, badge and ruler, pencil, eight pens and a dictionary."

"I can explain—"

"Then there is the question of the illegal cheese we found under a Hispano-Suiza at your picnic two and half years ago. I have sworn affidavits from everyone present that you were alone, met them up there, and that the cheese was yours."

"Yes, but—"

"And the traffic police said they saw you aiding and abetting a known serial dangerous driver on the A419 north of Swindon."

"That's—"

"But what's worse was that you lied to me systematically from the moment you came under my command. You said you would learn to play golf, and you never so much as picked up a putter."

"But—"

"I have proof of your lies, too. I personally visited every single golf club, and not one of them had ever let someone of your description play golf there—not even on the practice ranges. How do you explain *that,* eh?"

"Well—"

"You vanish from sight two and a half years ago. Not a word. Had to demote you. Star employee. Newspapers had a field day. Upset my swing for weeks."

"I'm sorry if it upset your golf, sir."

"You're rather in the soup, young lady."

He stared at me in exactly the sort of way my English teacher used to at school, and I had that sudden and dangerously overpowering urge to laugh out loud. Luckily, I didn't.

"What have you got to say for yourself?"

"I can explain, if you'll let me."

"My girl, I've been trying to get you to tell me for five—"

The door opened again, and in walked Colonel Flanker of SO-1. He ran Internal Affairs, the SpecOps Police. About as welcome as worms and another old bête noire of mine. If Hicks was bad, Flanker was worse. Braxton only wanted me to do some sort of disciplinary nonsense—Flanker would want to lock me up for good, *after* I had led them to my father.

"So!" he said as soon as he saw me. "It's true. Thank you, Braxton, my prisoner. Officer Jodrell, cuff her."

Jodrell walked over to me, took one of my wrists and placed it behind my back. There didn't seem to be much point of running; I could see at least three other SO-1 agents hovering near the door. I thought of Friday. If only Bowden had got to me a few minutes earlier!

"Just a minute, Mr. Flanker," said Braxton, closing my file. "What do you think you're doing?"

"Arresting Miss Next on charges of being AWOL, dereliction of duty and illegal possession of bootleg cheese—for starters."

"She was on assignment for SO-23," said Braxton, staring at him evenly, "undercover for the Cheese Squad."

I couldn't believe my ears. Braxton lying? For *me?*

"The Cheese Squad?" echoed Flanker with some surprise.

"Yes," replied Braxton, who, once started, clearly found the subterfuge and reckless use of his authority somewhat exciting. "She's been in deep cover in Wales for two years on a clandestine espionage operation monitoring illegal cheese factories. The cheeses with her fingerprints on them were part of an illegal cross-border shipment that she helped seize."

"Really?" said Flanker, his confidence rattled.

"On my word. She's not under arrest, she's being debriefed. It seems that the operation was under the control of Joe Martlet. Full details will be available from him."

"You know as well as I do that Joe was shot dead by the Cheese Mafia two weeks ago."

"It was a tragedy," admitted Braxton. "Fine man, Martlet—one of the best. Could play a three under par with ease and never swore when he drove it into the rough—and hence Miss Next's reappearance," he added without a pause. I'd never seen anyone lie so well before. Not even me. Not even Friday when I found he'd raided the cookie jar with Pickwick's help.

"Is this true?" asked Flanker. "Two years undercover in Wales?"

"*Ydy, ond dydy hi ddim wedi bwrw glaw pob dydd!*" I replied in my best Welsh.

He narrowed his eyes and stared at me for a moment without speaking.

"I was just reassigning her to the Literary Detectives when you walked in the door," added Braxton.

Flanker looked at Braxton, then at me, then at Braxton again. He nodded to Jodrell, who released me.

"Very well. But I want a full report on my desk Tuesday."

"You can have it Friday, Mr. Flanker. I'm a very busy man."

Flanker glared at me for a moment, then addressed Braxton: "Since Miss Next is back with the Literary Detectives perhaps you would be good enough to appoint her the SO-14 Danish Book Seizure Liaison Officer. My boys are pretty good at the seizure stuff, but to be honest, none of them can tell a Mark Twain from a Samuel Clemens."

"I'm not sure I want—" I began.

"I think you should be happy to assist me, Miss Next, don't you? A chance to make amends for past transgressions, yes?"

Braxton answered for me.

"I'm sure Miss Next would be happy to assist in any way she can, Mr. Flanker."

Flanker gave a rare smile.

"Good. I'll have my divisional head of SO-14 get in touch with you." He turned to Braxton. "But I'll still need that report on Tuesday."

"You'll get it," replied Braxton, ". . . on Friday."

Flanker glared at us both and without another word strode from the room, his minions at his heels. When the door closed I breathed a sigh of relief.

"Sir, I—"

"I don't want to hear anything more about it," replied Braxton sharply, gathering up his papers. "I retire in two months' time and wanted to do something that made my whole pen-pushing, play-it-safe, shiny-arse career actually be worth it. I don't know what's going to happen to the LiteraTec division with all this insane Danish book-burning stuff, but what I do know is that people like you need to stay in it. Lead them on a merry goose chase, young lady— I can keep Flanker wrapped up in red tape pretty much forever."

"Braxton," I said, giving him a spontaneous hug, "you're a darling!"

"Nonsense!" he said gruffly, and a tad embarrassed. "But I do expect a little something in return."

"And that is?"

"Well," he said slowly, his eyes dropping to the ground, "I wonder if you and I might—"

"Might what?"

"Might . . . play golf on Sunday. A few holes." His eyes gleamed. "Just for you to get the taste. Believe me, as soon as you grasp the handle of a golf club, you'll be hooked forever! Mrs. Hicks need never know. How about it?"

"I'll be there at nine," I told him, laughing.

"You'll be a long time waiting—I get there at eleven."

"Eleven it is."

I shook his hand and walked out of the door a free woman. Sometimes help arrives from the last place you expect it.

7.

The Literary Detectives

Goliath Corporation Publishes Broad Denial

The Goliath Corporation yesterday attempted to head off annoying and time-wasting speculation by issuing the broadest denial to date. "Quite simply, we deny everything," said Mr. Toedee, the Goliath head PR operative, "including any story that you might have heard now or in the future." Goliath's shock tactics reflected the growing unease with Goliath's unaccountability, especially over its advanced weapons division. "It's very simple," continued Mr. Toedee. "Until we have been elevated to a Faith when everything can be denied using the 'Goliath works in mysterious ways' excuse, we expressly deny possessing, or any involvement with, the Ovinator, Anti-Smite technology, Speedgrow tomatoes or Diatrymas running wild in the New Forest. In fact, we don't know what any of these things are." To cries of "What is an Ovinator?" and "Tomatoes?" Mr. Toedee declared the press conference over, blessed everyone and departed.

Article in The Toad on Sunday, July 3, 1988

I found Bowden fretting in the LiteraTec office and related what had happened.

"Well, well," he said at last, "I think old Braxton's got a crush."

"Oh, stop it!"

The office we were sitting in resembled a large library in a country house somewhere. It was two stories high, with shelves crammed full of books covering every square inch of wall space. A spiral staircase led to a catwalk that ran around the wall, enabling access to the upper galleries. It was neat and methodical—but somehow less busy than I remembered.

"Where is everyone?"

"When you were here last, we had a staff of eight. Now it's only Victor, me, and Malin. All the rest were reassigned or laid off."

"All SpecOps departments?"

Bowden laughed. "Of course not! The bullyboys at SO-14 are alive and well and answer to Yorrick Kaine's every order. SO-1 hasn't seen many cuts, either—"

"Thursday, what a delightful surprise!"

It was Victor Analogy, my old boss here at the Swindon Litera-Tecs. He was an elderly gentlemen with large muttonchop side-burns and was dressed in a neat tweed suit and bow tie. He had taken off his jacket due to the summer heat but still managed to cut a very dashing figure, despite his advanced age.

"Victor, you're looking very well!"

"And you, dear girl. What devilry have you been up to since last we met?"

"It's a long story."

"The best sort. Let me guess: *inside* fiction?"

"In one."

"What's it like?"

"It's quite good, really. Confusing at times and subject to moments of extreme imaginative overload, but varied, and the weather's generally pretty good. Can we talk safely in here?"

Victor nodded, and we sat down. I told them about Jurisfiction, the Council of Genres and everything else that had happened to me during my tenure as Bellman. I even told them loosely about my involvement in *The Solution of Edwin Drood*, which amused them both no end.

"I've always wondered about that," mused Victor thoughtfully. "But you're sure about Yorrick Kaine's being fictional?"

I told him that I was.

He stood up and walked to the window. "You'll have a hard time getting close," said Victor thoughtfully. "Does he know you're back?"

"Definitely," said Bowden.

"Then you could be threatening his position as absolute ruler of England almost as much as President Formby is. I should keep on your toes, my girl. Is there anything we can do to help?"

I thought for a moment. "There is, actually. We can't find which book Yorrick Kaine has escaped from. He could be using a false name, and we should contact any readers who might recognize the Chancellor's somewhat crazed antics from an obscure character they might have read somewhere. We at Jurisfiction have been going through the Great Library at our end, but we've still drawn a blank—every character in fiction has been accounted for."

"We'll do what we can, Thursday. When can you rejoin us?"

"I don't know," I answered slowly. "I have to get my husband back. Remember I told you he was eradicated by the Chrono-Guard?"

"Yes. *Lindane,* wasn't it?"

"Landen. If it weren't for him, I'd probably stay inside fiction." We all fell silent for a moment.

"So," I said cheerfully, "what's been happening in the world of the LiteraTecs?"

Victor frowned.

"We can't hold with the book-burning lark of Kaine's. You heard about the order to start incinerating Danish literature?"

I nodded.

"Kierkegaard's works are being rounded up as we speak. I told Braxton that if we were asked to do any of it we'd resign."

"Oh-ah."

"I'm not sure I like the way you said that," said Bowden.

I winced. "I agreed to be the SO-14 Danish Book Seizure Liaison Officer for Flanker—sorry. I didn't have much of a choice."

"I see that as *good* news," put in Bowden. "You can have them searching in places they won't find any Danish books. Just be careful. Flanker has been suspicious ever since we said we were too busy to find out who was planning to smuggle copies of *The Concept of Dread* to Wales for safekeeping."

Bowden laughed and lowered his voice. "It wasn't an excuse," he chuckled. "We actually *were* too busy—gathering copies of banned books ready for transportation to Wales!"

Victor grimaced. "I really don't want to hear this, Bowden. If you get caught, we'll all be for the high jump!"

"Some things are worth going to jail for, Victor," replied Bowden in an even tone. "As LiteraTecs we swore to uphold and defend the written word—not indulge a crazed politician's worst paranoic fantasies."

"Just be careful."

"Of course," replied Bowden. "It might come to nothing if we can't find a way to get the books out of England—the Welsh border shouldn't be a problem since Wales aligned itself with Denmark. I don't suppose you have any ideas how to get across the English border post?"

"I'm not sure," I replied. "How many copies of banned books do you want to smuggle anyway?"

"About four truckloads."

I whistled. Things—like cheese, for instance—were usually smuggled *in* to England. I didn't know how I'd get banned books *out.*

"I'll give it a shot. What else is going on?"

"Usual stuff," replied Bowden. "Faked Milton, Jonson, Swift . . . Montague and Capulet street gangs . . . someone discovered a first draft of *The Mill on the Floss* entitled *The Sploshing of the Weirs.* Also, the Daphne Farquitt Specialist Bookshop went up in smoke."

"Insurance scam?"

"No—probably anti-Farquitt protesters again."

Farquitt had penned her first bodice-ripping novel in 1932 and had been writing pretty much the same one over and over again ever since. Loved by many and hated by a vitriolic minority, Farquitt was England's leading romantic novelist.

"There's also been a huge increase in the use of performance-enhancing drugs by novelists," added Victor. "Last year's Booker speedwriting winner was stripped of his award when he tested positive for Cartlandromin. And only last week Handley Paige narrowly missed a two-year writing ban for failing a random dope test."

"Sometimes I wonder if we don't have too many rules," murmured Victor pensively, and we all three stood in silence, nodding thoughtfully for a moment.

Bowden broke the silence. He produced a piece of stained paper wrapped in a cellophane evidence bag and passed it across to me. "What do you make of this?"

I read it, not recognizing the words but recognizing the style. It was a sonnet by Shakespeare—and a pretty good one, too.

"Shakespeare, but it's not Elizabethan—the mention of Howdy Doody would seem to indicate that—but it *feels* like his. What did the Verse Meter Analyzer say about it?"

"Ninety-one percent probability of Will as the author," replied Victor.

"Where did you get it?"

"Off the body of a down-and-out by the name of Shaxtper killed on Tuesday evening. We think someone has been cloning Shakespeares."

"Cloning Shakespeares? Are you sure? Couldn't it just be a ChronoGuard 'temporal kidnap' sort of thing?"

"No. Blood analysis tells us they were all vaccinated at birth against rubella, mumps and so forth."

"Wait—you've got more than one?"

"Three," said Bowden. "There's been something of a spate recently."

"When can you come back to work, Thursday?" asked Victor solemnly. "As you can see, we need you."

I paused for a moment. "I'm going to need a week to get my life into gear first, sir. There are a few pressing matters that I have to attend to."

"What, may I ask," said Victor, "is more important than Montague and Capulet street gangs, cloned Shakespeares, smuggling Kierkegaard out of the country and authors using banned substances?"

"Finding reliable child care."

"Goodness!" said Victor. "Congratulations! You must bring the little squawker in sometime. Mustn't she, Bowden?"

"Absolutely."

"Bit of a problem, that," murmured Victor. "Can't have you dashing around the place only to have to get home at five to make junior's tea. Perhaps we'd better handle all this on our own."

"No," I said with an assertiveness that made them both jump. "No, I'm coming back to work. I just need to sort a few things out. Does SpecOps have a nursery?"

"No."

"Ah. Well, I suspect I shall think of something. If I get my husband back, there won't be a problem. I'll call you tomorrow."

There was a pause.

"Well, we have to respect that, I suppose," said Victor solemnly. "We're just glad that you're back. Aren't we, Bowden?"

"Yes," replied my ex-partner, "very glad indeed."

8.

Time Waits for No Man

SpecOps-12 is the ChronoGuard, the governmental department dealing with temporal stability. It is their job to maintain the integrity of the Standard History Eventline (SHE) and police the timestream against any unauthorized changes or usage. Their most brilliant work is never noticed, as changes in the past always seem to have been that way. It is not unusual in any one ChronoGuard work shift for history to flex dramatically before settling back down to the SHE. Planet-destroying cataclysms generally happen twice a week but are carefully rerouted by skilled ChronoGuard operatives. The citizenry never notices a thing—which is just as well, really.

Colonel Next, QT CG (nonexst.),
Upstream/Downstream (unpublished)

I wasn't done with SpecOps yet. I still needed to figure out what my father had told me on our first meeting. Finding a time traveler can be fraught with difficulties, but since I passed the Chrono-Guard office at almost exactly three hours from our last meeting, it seemed the obvious place to look.

I knocked at their door and, hearing no answer, walked in. When I was last working at SpecOps, we rarely heard anything from the mildly eccentric members of the time-traveling elite, but when you work in the time business, you don't waste it by nattering—it's much too precious. My father always argued that time was far and away the most valuable commodity we had and that temporal profligacy should be a criminal offense—which kind of makes watching *Celebrity Kidney Swap* or reading Daphne Far-quitt novels a crime straightaway.

The room was empty and from appearances had been so for a number of years. Although, that's what it *looked* like when I first peered in—a second later some painters were decorating it for the first time, the second after that it was derelict, then full, then empty again. It continued like this as I watched, the room jumping to various different stages in its history but never lingering for more than a few seconds on any one particular time. The Chrono-Guard operatives were merely smears of light that moved and whirled about, momentarily visible to me as they jumped from past to future and future to past. If I had been a trained member of the ChronoGuard, perhaps I could have made more sense of it, but I wasn't, and couldn't.

There was one piece of furniture that remained unchanged whilst all about raced, moved and blurred in a never-ending jum-ble. It was a small table with an old candlestick telephone upon it. I stepped into the room and lifted the receiver.

"Hello?"

"Hello," said a prerecorded voice. "You're through to the Swin-don ChronoGuard. To assist with your inquiry, we have a number of choices. If you have been the victim of temporal flexation, dial one. If you wish to report a temporal anomaly, dial two. If you feel you might have been involved in a timecrime . . ."

It gave me several more choices, but nothing that told me how to contact my father. Finally, at the end of the long list, it gave me the option for meeting an operative, so I chose that. In an instant the blurred movement in the room stopped and everything fell into place—but with furniture and fittings more suited to the sixties. There was an agent sitting at the desk. A tall and undeniably hand-some man in the blue uniform of the ChronoGuard, emblazoned at the shoulder with the pips of a captain. As he himself had pre-dicted, it was my father, three hours later and three hours younger. At first he didn't recognize me.

"Hello," he said. "Can I help you?"

"It's me, Thursday."

"Thursday?" he echoed, eyes wide open as he stood up. "My daughter Thursday?"

I nodded, and he moved closer.

"My goodness!" he exclaimed, scrutinizing me with great interest. "How wonderful to see you again! How long's it been? Six centuries?"

"Two years," I told him, not wanting to confuse a confusing matter even further by mentioning our conversation this morning, "but why are you working for the ChronoGuard again? I thought you went rogue?"

"Ah!" he said, beckoning me closer and lowering his voice. "There was a change of administration, and they said they would look very closely at my grievances if I'd come and work for them at the Historical Preservation Corps. I had to take a demotion, and I won't be reactualized until the paperwork is done, but it's working out quite well otherwise. Is your husband still eradicated?"

"I'm afraid so. Any chance . . . ?"

He winced. "I'd love to, Sweetpea, but I've really got to watch my p's and q's for a few decades. Do you like the office?"

I looked at the sixties decor in the tiny room. "Bit small, isn't it?"

"Oh, yes." My father grinned, clearly in an ebullient mood. "And over seven hundred of us work here. Since we could not *all* be here at one time, we simply stretch the usage out across the timestream, like a long piece of elastic."

He stretched his arms wide as if to demonstrate.

"We call it a timeshare."

He rubbed his chin and looked around. "What's the time out there?"

"It's July fourteenth, 1988."

"That's a stroke of good fortune," he said, lowering his voice still further. "It's a good job you've turned up. They've blamed me for the 1864 war between Germany and Denmark."

"Was it your fault?"

"No—it was that clot Bismarck. But it doesn't matter. They've transferred me to another division inside the Historical Preservation Corps for a second chance. My first assignment occurs in July 1988, so local knowledge right now is a godsend. Have you heard of anyone named Yorrick Kaine?"

"He's Chancellor of England."

"That figures. Did St. Zvlkx return tomorrow?"

"He might."

"Okay. Who won the SuperHoop?"

"That's Saturday week," I explained. "It hasn't happened yet."

"Not *strictly* true, Sweetpea. Everything that we do actually happened a long, long time ago—even this conversation. The future is already there. The pioneers that plowed the first furrows of history into virgin time line died eons ago—all we do now is try and keep it pretty much the way it should be. Have you heard of someone named Winston Churchill, by the way?"

I thought for a moment. "He was an English statesman who seriously blotted his copybook in the Great War, then was run over by a cab and killed in 1932."

"So no one of any consequence?"

"Not really. Why?"

"Ahh, no reason. Just a little pet theory of mine. Anyway, everything has already happened—if it hadn't, there'd be no need for people like me. But things go wrong. In the normal course of events, time flies back and forth from the end of and then until the beginning of now like a shuttle on a loom, weaving the threads of history together. If it encounters an obstacle, then it might just flex slightly and no change will be noticed. But if that obstacle is big enough—and Kaine is plenty big enough, believe me—then history will veer off at a tangent. And *that's* when we have to sort it out. I've been transferred to the Armageddon Avoidance Division, and we've got an apocalyptic disaster of life-extinguishing capability Level III heading your way."

There was a moment's silence.

"Does your mother know you wear your hair this short?"

"Is it meant to happen?"

"Your hair?"

"No, the Armageddon."

"Not at all. This one has an Ultimate Likelihood Index rating of only twenty-two percent: 'not very likely.' "

"Nothing like that incident with the Dream Topping, then," I observed.

"What incident?"

"Nothing."

"Right. Well, since I'm on probation—sort of—they thought they'd start me on the small stuff."

"I still don't understand."

"It's simple," began my father. "Two days after the SuperHoop, President Formby will die of natural causes. The following day Yorrick Kaine proclaims himself Dictator of England. Two weeks after that, following the traditional suspension of the press and summary executions of former associates, Kaine will declare war on Wales. Two days after a prolonged tank battle on the Welsh Marches, the United Clans of Scotland launch an attack on Berwick-on-Tweed. In a fit of pique, Kaine carpet-bombs Glasgow, and the Swedish Empire enters on Scotland's side. Russia joins Kaine after their colonial outpost of Fetlar is sacked—and the war moves to mainland Europe. It soon escalates to an apocalyptic shoot-out between the African and American superpowers. In less than three months, the earth will be nothing but a steaming radioactive cinder. Of course," he added, "that is a worst-case scenario. It'll probably never happen, and if you and I do our jobs properly, it won't."

"Can't you just kill Kaine?"

"Not that easy. Time is the glue of the cosmos, Sweetpea, and it has to be eased apart—you'd be surprised how strongly the Historical Time Line tends to look after despots. Why do you think dictators like Pol Pot, Bokassa and Idi Amin live such long lives and people like Mozart, Jim Henson and Mother Teresa are plucked from us when relatively young?"

"I don't think Mother Teresa could be thought of as *young*."

"On the contrary—she was *meant* to live until a hundred and twenty-eight.

There was a pause.

"Okay, Dad—so what's the plan?"

"Right. It's incredibly complex and also unbelievably simple. To stop Kaine gaining power, we have to seriously disrupt his sponsor, the Goliath Corporation. Without them his power is zero. To do that we need to ensure . . . that Swindon wins the SuperHoop."

"How is that going to work?"

"It's a causality thing. Small events have large consequences. You'll see."

"No, I mean, how am I going to get Swindon to win? Apart from Kapok and Aubrey Jambe and perhaps 'Biffo' Mandible, the players are . . . well, crap—not to put too fine a point on it. Especially when you compare them to their SuperHoop opponents, the Reading Whackers."

"I'm sure you'll think of something, but keep an eye on Kapok—they'll try to get to him first. You'll have to do this on your own, Sweetpea. I've got my own problems. It seems Nelson's getting killed at the beginning of the Battle of Trafalgar wasn't French History Revisionists after all. I talked to someone I know over at the ChronoGendarmerie, and they thought it amusing that the Revisionists should even *attempt* such a thing; advanced timestream models with Napoleon as emperor of all Europe bode very poorly for France—they're much better in the long run with things as they are meant to be."

"So who is killing Nelson?"

"Well, it's Nelson *himself*. Don't ask me why. Now, what did you want to see me about?"

I had to think carefully. "Well . . . nothing, *really*. I met you three hours ago and you said we'd spoken, so I came here to find you, so then I suppose I should ask you to figure out who's trying to kill me this morning, which you wouldn't have been able to do if I hadn't met you this morning, and I only met you this morning because I've just told you right now I might be assassinated. . . ."

Dad laughed. "It's a bit like having a tumble dryer in your head, Sweetpea. Sometimes I don't know whether I'm thening or nowing. But I'd better check this assassin out, just in case."

"Yes," I said, more confused than ever, "I suppose you should."

9.

Eradications Anonymous

Goliath Backs Kaine and Whig Party

The Goliath Corporation yesterday renewed its support for Chancellor Kaine at a party to honor England's leader. At a glittering dinner attended by over five hundred heads of commerce and governmental departments, Goliath pledged to continue its support of the Chancellor. In a reply speech, Mr. Kaine gratefully acknowledged their support and announced a package of measures designed to assist Goliath in the difficult yet highly desirable change to its faith-based corporate status, as well as funding for several ongoing weapons programs, details of which have been classified.

Article in *The Toad,* July 13, 1988

Hamlet and I arrived home to find a TV news crew from Swindon-5 waiting for me outside the house.

"Miss Next," said the reporter. "Can you tell us where you've been these past two years?"

"No comment."

"You can interview *me,*" said Hamlet, realizing he was something of a celebrity out here.

"And who are you?" asked the reporter, mystified.

I stared at him and his face fell.

I'm . . . I'm . . . her cousin Eddie."

"Well, Cousin Eddie, can *you* tell us where Miss Next has been for the past two years?"

"No comment."

And we walked up the garden path to the front door.

"Where have you been?" demanded my mother as we walked in the door.

"Sorry I'm late, Mum—how's the little chap?"

"Tiring. He says that his aunt Mel is a gorilla who can peel bananas with her feet while hanging from the light fixtures."

"He *talked?*"

Friday was using the time-honored international child signal to be picked up—raising his arms in the air—and when I did so, gave me a wet kiss and started to chatter away unintelligibly.

"Well, he didn't exactly *say* as much," admitted Mum, "but he drew me a picture of Aunt Mel, which is pretty conclusive."

"Aunt Mel a gorilla?" I laughed, looking at the picture, which was unequivocally of . . . well, a gorilla. "Quite an imagination, hasn't he?"

"I'd say. I found him standing on the sideboard ready to swing from the curtains. When I told him it wasn't allowed, he pointed to the picture of Aunt Mel, which I took to mean that she used to let him."

"Does she, now? I mean, did he, now?"

Pickwick walked in looking very disgruntled and wearing a bonnet made of cardboard and held together with sticky tape.

"Pickwick's a very tolerant playmate," said my mother, who was obviously not that skilled at reading dodo expressions.

"I really need to get him into a play group. Did you change his nappy?"

"Three times. It just goes straight through, doesn't it?"

I sniffed at the leg of his dungarees. "Yup. Straight through."

"Well, I've got my auto-body work group to attend to," she said, putting on her hat and taking her handbag and welding goggles from the peg, "but you'd better sort out some more reliable child care, my dear. I can do the odd hour here and there, but not whole days—and I certainly don't want to do any more nappies."

"Do you think Lady Hamilton would look after him?"

"It's possible," said my mother in the sort of voice that means the reverse. "You could always ask."

She opened the door and was plinked at angrily by Alan, who was in a bit of a bad mood and was pulling up flowers in the front garden. With unbelievable speed she grabbed him by the neck and, with a lot of angry plinking and scrabbling, deposited him unceremoniously inside the potting shed and locked the door.

"Miserable bird!" said my mother, giving me and Friday a kiss. "Have I got my purse?"

"It's in your bag."

"Am I wearing my hat?"

"Yes."

She smiled, told me that Bismarck was not to be disturbed and that I mustn't buy anything from a door-to-door salesman unless it was *truly* a bargain and was gone.

I changed Friday, then let him toddle off to find something to do. I made a cup of tea for myself and Hamlet, who had switched on the TV and was watching MOLE-TV's Shakespeare channel. I sat on the sofa and stared out the windows into the garden. It had been destroyed by a mammoth when I was last here, and I noted that my mother had replanted it with plants that are not very palatable to the Proboscidea tongue—quite wise, considering the migrations. As I watched, Pickwick waddled past, possibly wondering where Alan had gone. For the day's work, I had done very little. I was still a Literary Detective, but twenty thousand pounds in debt and no nearer getting Landen back.

My mother returned at about eight, and the first of her Eradications Anonymous friends began to appear at nine. There were ten of them, and they started to chatter about what they described as their "lost ones" as soon as they got through the door. Emma Hamilton and I weren't alone in having a husband with an existence problem. But although it seemed my Landen and Emma's Horatio were strong in our memories, many people were not so lucky. Some had only vague feelings about someone they felt who *should* be there but wasn't. To be honest, I really didn't want to be here, but I had promised my mother and I was living in her house, so that was the end of it.

"Thank you, ladies and gentlemen," said my mother, clapping her hands, "and if you'd all like to take a seat, we can allow this meeting to begin."

Everyone sat down, tea and Battenberg cake in hand, and looked expectant.

"Firstly I would like to welcome a new member to the group. As you know, my daughter has been away for a couple of years—not in prison, I'd like to make that clear!"

"Thank you, Mother," I murmured under my breath as there was polite laughter from the group, who instantly assumed that's exactly where I *had* been.

"And she has kindly agreed to join our group and say a few words. Thursday?"

I took a deep breath, stood up and said quickly, "Hello, everyone. My name's Thursday Next, and my husband doesn't exist."

There was applause at this, and someone said, "Way to go, Thursday," but I couldn't think of anything to add, nor wanted to, so sat down again. There was silence as everyone stared at me, politely waiting for me to carry on.

"That's it. End of story."

"I'll drink to that!" said Emma, gazing forlornly at the locked drinks cabinet.

"You're very brave," said Mrs. Beatty, who was sitting next to me. She patted my hand in a kindly manner. "What was his name?"

"Landen. Landen Parke-Laine. He was murdered by the ChronoGuard in 1947. I'm going to the Goliath Apologarium tomorrow to try to get his eradication reversed."

There was a murmuring.

"What's the matter?"

"You must understand," said a tall and painfully thin man who up until now had remained silent, "that for you to progress in this

"You mean to tell me, Mr. Holmes, that by a scientific oddity
we are in the wrong book?"

group, you must begin to accept that this is a problem of the memory—there is no Landen; you just *think* there is."

"It's very dry in here, isn't it?" muttered Emma unsubtly, still staring at the drinks cabinet.

"I was like you once," said Mrs. Beatty, who had stopped patting my hand and returned to her knitting. "I had a wonderful life with Edgar, and then one morning I wake up in a different house with Gerald lying next to me. He didn't believe me when I explained the problem, and I was on medication for ten years until I came here. It is only now, in the company of your good selves, am I coming to the realization that it is merely a malady of the head."

I was horrified. "Mother?"

"It's something that we must try and face, my dear."

"But Dad visits you, doesn't he?"

"Well, I *believe* he does," she said, thinking hard, "but of course when he's gone, it's only a memory. There isn't any *real* proof that he ever existed."

"What about me? And Joffy? Or even Anton? How were we born without Dad?"

She shrugged at the impossibility of the paradox. "Perhaps it was, after all," sighed my mother, "youthful indiscretions that I have expunged from my mind."

"And Emma? And Herr Bismarck? How do you explain them being here?"

"Well," said my mother, thinking hard, "I'm sure there's a rational explanation for it . . . somewhere."

"Is this what this group teaches you?" I replied angrily. "To deny the memories of your loved ones?"

I looked around at the gathering, who had, it seemed, given up in the face of the hopeless paradox that they lived every minute of their lives. I opened my mouth to try to describe eloquently just how I *knew* that Landen had once been married to me when I realized I was wasting my time. There was nothing, but *nothing,* to suggest that it was anything other than in my mind. I sighed. To be truthful, it *was* in my mind. It hadn't happened. I just had memories of how it *might* have turned out. The tall, thin man, the realist, was beginning to convince everyone they were not victims of a timeslip, but delusional.

"You want proof—"

I was interrupted by an excited knock at the front door. Whoever it was didn't waste any time; she just walked straight into the house and into the front room. It was a middle-aged woman in a floral dress who was holding the hand of a confused and acutely embarrassed-looking man.

"Hello, group!" she said happily. "It's Ralph! I got him back!"

"Ah!" said Emma. "This calls for a celebration!" Everyone ignored her.

"I'm sorry," said my mother, "have you got the right house? Or the right self-help group?"

"Yes, yes," she reasserted. "It's Julie, Julie Aseizer. I've been coming to this group every week for the past three years!"

There was silence in the group. All you could hear was the quiet click of Mrs. Beatty's knitting needles.

"Well, I haven't seen you," announced the tall, thin man. He looked around at the group. "Does *anyone* recognize this person?"

The group shook their heads blankly.

"I expect you think this is *really* funny, don't you?" said the thin man angrily. "This is a self-help group for people with severe memory aberrations, and I really don't think it is either amusing or constructive for pranksters to make fun of us! Now, please leave!"

She stood for a moment, biting her lip, but it was her husband who spoke.

"Come on, darling, I'm taking you home."

"But wait!" she said. "Now he's *back*, everything is as it *was*, and I wouldn't have needed to come to your group, so I *didn't*—yet I *remember* . . ."

Her voice trailed off, and her husband gave her a hug as she started to sob. He led her out, apologizing profusely all the while.

As soon as they had gone, the thin man sat down indignantly. "A sorry state of affairs!" he grumbled.

"Everyone thinks it's funny to do that old joke," added Mrs. Beatty. "That's the second time this month."

"It gave me a powerful thirst," added Emma. "Anyone else?"

"Maybe," I suggested, "they should start a self-help group for themselves—they could call it Eradications Anonymous *Anonymous*."

No one thought it was funny, and I hid a smile. Perhaps there would be a chance for me and Landen after all.

I didn't contribute much to the group after that, and indeed the conversation soon threaded away from eradications and onto more mundane matters, such as the latest crop of TV shows that seemed to have flourished in my absence. *Celebrity Name That Fruit!* hosted by Frankie Saveloy was a ratings topper these days, as was *Toasters from Hell* and *You've Been Stapled!*, a collection of England's funniest stationery incidents. Emma had given up all attempts at subtlety by now and was prying the lock off the drinks cabinet with a screwdriver when Friday wailed one of those ultrasonic cries that only parents can hear—makes you understand how sheep can know who's lamb is whose—and I mercifully excused myself. He was standing up in his cot rattling the bars, so I took him out and read to him until we were both fast asleep.

10.

Mrs. Tiggy-winkle

Kierkegaard Book-Burning Ceremony
Proves Danish Philosopher's Unpopularity

Chancellor Yorrick Kaine last night officiated at the first burning of Danish literature with the incineration of eight copies of *Fear and Trembling*, a quantity that fell far short of the expected "thirty or forty tons." When asked to comment on the apparent lack of enthusiasm among the public to torch their Danish philosophy, Kaine explained that "Kierkegaard is clearly less popular than we thought, and rightly so—next stop Hans Christian Andersen!" Kierkegaard himself was unavailable for comment, having inconsiderately allowed himself to be dead for a number of years.

Article in *The Toad*, July 14, 1988

I was dreaming that a large chain-saw-wielding elephant was sitting on me when I awoke at two in the morning. I was still fully dressed, with a snoring Friday fast asleep on my chest. I put him back in his cot and turned the bedside lamp to the wall to soften the light. My mother, for reasons known only to herself, had kept my bedroom pretty much as it was from the time I had left home. It was nostalgic, but also deeply disturbing, to see just what had interested me in my late teens. It seemed like it had been boys, music, Jane Austen and law enforcement, but not particularly in that order.

I undressed and slipped on a long T-shirt and stared at Friday's sleeping form, his lips making gentle sucky motions.

"Pssst!" said a voice close at hand. I turned. There, in the semidark, was a very large hedgehog dressed in a pinafore and bonnet. She was keeping a close lookout at the door and, after giving me a wan smile, crept to the window and peeked out.

"Whoa!" she breathed in wonderment. "Streetlights are *orange*. Never would have thought *that!*"

"Mrs. Tiggy-winkle," I said, "I've only been gone two days!"

"Sorry to bother you," she said, curtsying quickly and absently folding my shirt, which I had tossed over a chair back, "but there are one or two things going on that I thought you should know about—and you did say that if I had any questions, to ask."

"Okay—but not here; we'll wake Friday."

So we crept downstairs to the kitchen. I pulled down the blinds before turning the lights on, as a six-foot hedgehog in a bonnet might have caused a few eyebrows to be raised in the neighborhood—no one wore bonnets in Swindon these days.

I offered Mrs. Tiggy-winkle a seat at the table. Although she, Emperor Zhark and Bradshaw had been put in charge of running Jurisfiction in my absence, none of them had the leadership skills necessary to do the job on their own. And while the Council of Genres refused to concede that my absence was anything but "compassionate leave," a new Bellman was yet to be elected in my place.

"So what's up?" I asked.

"Oh, Miss Next!" she wailed, her spines bristling with vexation. "Please come back!"

"I have things to deal with out here," I explained. "You all know that!"

"I know," she sighed, "but Emperor Zhark threw a tantrum when I suggested he spend a little less time conquering the universe and a little more time at Jurisfiction. The Red Queen won't do anything post-1867, and Vernham Deane is tied up with the latest Daphne Farquitt novel. Commander Bradshaw does his own thing, which leaves me in charge—and someone left a saucer of bread and milk on my desk this morning."

"It was probably just a joke."

"Well, I'm not laughing," replied Mrs. Tiggy-winkle indignantly.

"By the way," I said as a thought suddenly struck me, "did you find out which book Yorrick Kaine escaped from?"

"I'm afraid not. The Cat is searching unpublished novels in the Well of Lost Plots at the moment, but it might take a little time. You know how chaotic things are down there."

"Only too well." I sighed, thinking about my old home in unpublished fiction with a mixture of fondness and relief. The Well was where books are actually constructed, where plotsmiths create the stories that authors *think* they write. You can buy plot devices at discount rates and verbs by the pint. An odd place, to be sure. "Okay," I said finally, "you'd better tell me what's going on."

"Well," said Mrs. Tiggy-winkle, counting the points out on her claw, "this morning a rumor of potential change in the copyright laws swept through the BookWorld."

"I don't know how these rumors get started," I replied wearily. "Was there any truth in it?"

"Not in the least."

This was a contentious subject to the residents of the Book-World. The jump to copyright-free Public Domain Status had always been a fearful prospect for a book character, and even with support groups and training courses to soften the blow, the Narrative Menopause could take some getting used to. The problem is that copyright laws tend to vary around the world, and sometimes characters are in public domain in one market and not in another, which is confusing. Then there is the possibility that the law might change and characters who had adjusted themselves to a Public Domain Status would find themselves in copyright again, or vice versa. Unrest in the BookWorld in these matters is palpable; it only takes a small spark to set off a riot.

"So all was well?"

"Pretty much."

"Good. Anything else?"

"Starbucks wants to open another coffee shop in the Hardy Boys series."

"Another one?" I asked with some surprise. "There's already sixteen. How much coffee do they think they can drink? Tell them they can open another in *Mrs. Dalloway* and two more in *The Age of Reason*. After that, no more. What else?"

"The Tailor of Gloucester needs three yards of cherry-colored silk to finish the Mayor's embroidered coat—but he's got a cold and can't go out."

"Who are we? Interlink? Tell him to send his cat, Simpkin."

"Okay."

There was a pause.

"You didn't come all this way to tell me bad news about Kaine, copyright panics and cherry-colored twist, now, did you?"

She looked at me and sighed. "There's a bit of a problem with Hamlet."

"I know. But he's doing a favor for my mother at the moment. I'll send him back in a few days."

"Um," replied the hedgehog nervously. "It's a bit more complex than that. I think it might be a good idea if you kept him out here for a bit longer."

"What's going on?" I asked suspiciously.

"It wasn't my fault!" she burst out, reaching for her pocket handkerchief. "I thought the Internal Plot Adjustment request was to sort out the seasonal anomalies! All that death in the orchard, then winter, then flowers—"

"What happened?" I asked again.

Mrs. Tiggy-winkle looked miserable.

"Well, you know there has been much grumbling unrest within *Hamlet* ever since Rosencrantz and Guildenstern got their own play?"

"Yes?"

"Well, just after you left, Ophelia attempted a coup de état in Hamlet's absence. She imported a B-6 Hamlet from *Lamb's Shakespeare* and convinced him to reenact some of the key scenes with a pro-Ophelia bias."

"And?"

"Well," said Mrs. Tiggy-winkle, "they retitled it: *The Tragedy of the Fair Ophelia, Driven Mad by the Callous Hamlet, Prince of Denmark.*"

"She's always up to something, isn't she? I'll give her 'Hey nonny, nonny.' Tell her to get back into line or we'll slap a Class II Fiction Infraction on her so fast it will make her head spin."

"We tried that, but Laertes returned from Paris and lent his voice to the revolution. Together they made some *more* changes, and it is now called *The Tragedy of the Noble Laertes, Who Avenges His Sister, the Fair Ophelia, Driven Mad by the Callous and Murderous Hamlet, Prince of Denmark.*"

I ran my fingers through what remained of my hair. "So . . . arrest them both?"

"Too late. Their father, Polonius, was in a 'have a go' mood and joined in. He *also* made changes, and together they renamed it: *The Tragedy of the Very Witty and Not Remotely Boring Polonius, Father of the Noble Laertes, Who Avenges His Fair Sister, Ophelia, Driven Mad by the Callous, Murderous and Outrageously Disrespectful Hamlet, Prince of Denmark.*"

"What was it like?"

"With Polonius? Very . . . *wordy*. We could replace them all," carried on Mrs. Tiggy-winkle, "but changing so many major players in one swoop might cause irreparable damage. The last thing we need right now is Hamlet coming back and sticking his oar in— you know how mad he gets when anybody even *suggests* a word change."

"Right," I said, "here's the plan. This is all happening in the 1623 folio edition, yes?"

Mrs. Tiggy-winkle nodded her head.

"Okay. Move *Hamlet*—or whatever it is called at present—to a disused Storycode Engine and fire up *The Penguin Modern Hamlet* so that is the one everyone in the Outland will read. It will give us some breathing space without anyone seeing the Polonized version. It won't be at its best, but it'll have to do. Horatio must still be on Hamlet's side, surely?"

"Most definitely."

"Then deputize him to Jurisfiction and try to get him to convince the Polonius family to attend an arbitration session. Keep me posted. I'll try to keep Hamlet amused out here."

She made a note.

"Is that all?" I asked.

"Not unless you need some washing done."

"I have a mother who will fight you for that. Now, please, please, Mrs. Tiggy-winkle, you must leave me to sort out Kaine and get my husband back!"

"You're right," she said after a short pause. "We're going to handle this all on our own."

"Good."

"Right."

"Well . . . good night, then."

"Yes," said the hedgehog, "good night."

She stood there on the kitchen linoleum, tapping her paws together and staring at the ceiling.

"Tiggy, what is it?"

"It's *Mr.* Tiggy-winkle!" she burst out at last. "He came home late last night in a state of shock and smelling of car exhaust, and I'm *so* worried!"

It was about three in the morning when I was finally left alone with my thoughts, a sleeping son and a pocket handkerchief drenched with hedgehog tears.

11.

The Greatness of St. Zvlkx

Goliath Corporation Implements
"Distraction Reduction" Program

Accusations were growing yesterday that the corporation's drive to increase productivity would result in the loss of civil liberties. This was strongly denied by Goliath, who commented, "We don't see bricking up the million or so windows in our ten thousand work facilities as anything less than a positive step forward. By removing windows we aim to help the worker who might be suffering from interest-in-work deficit disorder to higher levels of self-help and greater productivity. We also think that it will save thousands of gallons of Windex and the estimated six hundred deaths suffered by window cleaners every year." Accusations that the corporation was "nothing short of a bunch of bullies" were met with a three-hundred-page writ for defamation, delivered personally by very big men with tattoos.

Article in *The Toad on Sunday,* July 3, 1988

From humble beginnings in 1289 to a fiery end in the autumn of 1536, the towering beauty of the Great Cathedral of Swindon was once the equal of Canterbury or York, but no longer. Built over at least four times since then, the site of the cathedral was now occupied by a temple of another kind: Tesco's. Where monks once moved silently to prayer beneath vaulted cloisters, you can now buy Lola Vavoom workout videos, and where the exquisite stained-glass east window once brought forth tears from the coldest heart, there is now a refrigerated display boasting five different types of smoked sausage.

I took my seat and placed Friday on my lap, and he wriggled while I looked around. The car park was full of eager spectators. Some, like myself, were sitting on the especially constructed tiered seating, the rest standing behind barriers on the asphalt. But everyone, sitting or standing, was facing a small fenced-off area sandwiched between the shopping-trolley return point and the ATM machines. This small area contained a weathered arched doorway, the only visible remnant of Swindon's once great monastic settlement.

"How are you doing?" asked Joffy, who, as well as being a minister for the GSD and several other smaller denominations, was also head of the Idolatry Friends of St. Zvlkx.

"Fine. Isn't that Lydia Startright?"

I was pointing at a well-dressed female reporter readying herself for a broadcast.

"She's about to interview me. How do I look?"

"Very . . . ecclesiastical."

"Good. Excuse me."

He straightened his dog collar and walked over to join Lydia. She was standing next to her producer, a small and curiously unappealing man who was so unoriginal of thought that he still considered it cool and desirable for people in the media to wear black.

"What time is old Zvlkxy due to appear?" the producer asked Joffy.

"In about five minutes."

"Good. Lyds, we better go live."

Lydia composed herself, took one more look at her notes, awaited the count-in of the producer, gave a welcoming smile and began.

"Good afternoon, ladies and gentlemen, this is Lydia Startright for Toad News Network, reporting live from Swindon. In under five minutes, St. Zvlkx, the obscure and sometimes controversial thirteenth-century saint, is due to be resurrected here, live on regional TV."

She turned to indicate the weathered pieces of stone, previously ignored by thousands of shoppers but now the center of attention.

"On this spot once stood the towering Cathedral of Swindon, founded by St. Zvlkx in the thirteenth century. Where the wet fish counter now stands was where St. Zvlkx penned his Book of Revealments containing seven sets of prophecies, five of which have already come true. To help us through the quagmire of claims and counterclaims I have with me the Very Irreverent Joffy Next, head of the church of the Global Standard Deity here in Swindon, speaker at the the Idolatry Friends of St. Zvlkx and something of an expert in things Zvlkxian. Hello, Joffy, welcome to the show."

"Thank you, Lydia," said Joffy. "We're all big fans of yours at the GSD."

"Thank you. So tell me, what exactly are the revealments?"

"Well," he began, "details are understandably vague, but St. Zvlkx wrote a number of predictions in a small book before he vanished in a 'cleansing fire' in 1292. An incomplete copy of the revealments is in the Swindon City Library, but unlike the work of most of the other seers, who make vague and sweeping generalizations that are open to interpretation, St. Zvlkx's predictions are refreshingly specific."

"Perhaps you could give us an example?"

"Of course. Part of Zvlkx's Revealment the First tells us that 'a lowly butcher's son from the town of Ipswich will rise to be Lord Chancellor. His name shall be Tommy Wolsey, and he will be inaugurated the day before Christmas, and shall get only one present, not two, as should be his right. . . .' "

"That's uncannily accurate!" breathed Lydia.

"Indeed—existing letters from Cardinal Wolsey indicate most strongly that he was 'vexed and annoyed' at having to make do with only one present, something which he often spoke about and might have contributed, many years later, to his failure to persuade the Pope to grant Henry VIII an annulment of his marriage to Catherine of Aragon."

"Remarkable," said Lydia. "What else?"

"Well," continued Joffy, "Zvlkx's Revealment the Second told us that 'it shall be known as the "Sail of the Century"—an armada of over a hundred ships smelling of paella shall cross the Channel. Fire and wind will conspire to destroy them, England shall remain free.' "

"Not *quite* so good," said Lydia.

"I agree," replied Joffy. "Paella wasn't invented until *after* the Spanish Armada. There are the odd mistakes, but even so, his accuracy is astonishing. Not only do his revealments include names and dates but also, on one occasion, a reliable phone number for a good time in Leeds. By the end of the sixteenth century, St. Zvlkx had been afforded that rare hallmark of unbridled Elizabethan success—the commemorative plate. By the time of his next revealment a century and a half later, his supporters and followers had dwindled to only a handful. But when it arrived, this Revealment the Third catapulted Zvlkx back into the world's headlines: 'In seventeen hundred and seventy-six, a George King numbered three will lose his mind, his largest colony, and his socks. The colony would grow to be the greatest power in the world, but his mind and his socks will stay lost.' "

"And the fourth?"

" 'A man named after a form of waterproof shoe shall trounce a short Frenchman in Belgium.' "

"Clearly Waterloo—and the fifth?"

" 'The evil yet nattily dressed aggressors known as Nasis, whose fear has polarized the nation, will be ejected from these islands by—and I know this sounds really weird—the colony that was mentioned in prediction three. And Denis Compton will score 3,816 runs for Middlesex in a single season.' "

"Uncanny," murmured Lydia. "How would a thirteenth-century monk know that Compton batted for Middlesex?"

"He was, and indeed might be again, the greatest of seers," replied Joffy.

"We know that his Revealment the Sixth was a prediction of his own second coming, but it is the sports fans of Swindon who will really be bowled over by his Revealment the Seventh."

"Exactly so," replied Joffy. "According to the incomplete Codex Zvlkxus, it shall be 'There will be a home win on the playing fields of Swindonne in nineteen hundred and eighty-eight, and in consequence of . . .' There is more, but it's been lost. We can ask him about it when he reappears."

"Fascinating stuff, Irrev. Next! Just one question. Where is he?"

I looked at my watch as Friday stood on my lap and stared that unnerving sort of two-year-old stare at the couple behind us. St. Zvlkx was already three minutes late, and I saw Joffy bite his lip nervously. They had made much of the Great Man's predictions, and for him not to turn up would be just plain embarrassing—not to mention costly. Joffy had spent a great deal of Mum's savings learning Old English at the local adult-education center.

"Tell me, Irrev. Next," continued Lydia, trying to pad out the interview. "I understand that the Toast Marketing Board has secured a sponsorship deal with St. Zvlkx?"

"Indeed," replied Joffy. "We at the Idolatry Friends of St. Zvlkx have secured on his behalf a very favorable deal with Toast, who wanted to have exclusive rights to his likeness and wisdom, if he has any."

"Nevertheless, I understand that the Goliath Corporation was also said to be interested?"

"Not really. Goliath has been less than enthusiastic since their sportswear division paid over two hundred fifty thousand pounds for an exclusive sponsorship deal with St. Bernadette of Lincoln. But since her return six months ago, she has done nothing except brick herself up in a room and pray in silent retrospection, something that doesn't lend itself to selling running shoes. The Toast Marketing Board, on the other hand, made no such demands—they are happy just to see what Zvlkx himself would like to do for them."

Lydia turned back to the camera. "Astonishing. If you've just joined us, I'm speaking from the live telecast of the second coming of the thirteenth-century saint Thomas Zvlkx."

I looked at my watch again. Zvlkx was now five minutes late. Lydia carried on her live broadcast, interviewing several other people to soak up time. The crowd grew slightly impatient, and a low murmuring started to arise from the expectant silence. Lydia had just asked a style guru about the sort of clothes they might be expecting Zvlkx to be wearing when she was interrupted by a shout. Something was happening just outside Tesco's between the child's coin-in-the-slot flying-elephant ride and the letterbox. Joffy vaulted over the press enclosure and ran towards where a column of smoke was rising from a crack that had opened up in the mother-and-child parking area. The sky grew dark, birds stopped singing and shoppers coming out of the revolving doors stared in astonishment as a bolt of lightning struck the weathered stone arch and split it asunder. There was a collective cry of alarm as a wind sprang up from nowhere. Pennants advertising new Saver product lines that were hanging limply on the flagpoles opened with a crack, and a whirling mass of dust and wastepaper spread across the car park, making several people cough.

Within a few moments, it was all over. Sitting on the ground and dressed in a rough habit tied with a rope at the waist was a grubby man with a scraggy beard and exceptionally bad teeth. He blinked and looked curiously around at his new surroundings.

"𝔚𝔢𝔩𝔠𝔬𝔪𝔢," said Joffy, the first on the scene. "𝔍 𝔯𝔢𝔭𝔯𝔢𝔰𝔢𝔫𝔱 𝔱𝔥𝔢 𝔍𝔡𝔬𝔩-𝔞𝔱𝔯𝔶 𝔉𝔯𝔦𝔢𝔫𝔡𝔰 𝔬𝔣 𝔖𝔱. 𝔷𝔳𝔩𝔨𝔵 𝔞𝔫𝔡 𝔬𝔣𝔣𝔢𝔯 𝔶𝔬𝔲 𝔭𝔯𝔬𝔱𝔢𝔠𝔱𝔦𝔬𝔫 𝔞𝔫𝔡 𝔤𝔲𝔦𝔡𝔞𝔫𝔠𝔢."

The thirteenth-century monk looked at Joffy with his dark eyes, then at the crowds who had gathered closer to him, all of them talking and pointing and asking him if they could have their pictures taken with him.

"𝔜𝔬𝔲𝔯 𝔞𝔠𝔠𝔢𝔫𝔱 𝔦𝔰 𝔫𝔬𝔱 𝔟𝔞𝔡," replied St. Zvlkx slowly. "𝔍𝔰 𝔱𝔥𝔦𝔰 1988?"

"𝔍𝔱 𝔦𝔰, 𝔰𝔦𝔯. 𝔍'𝔳𝔢 𝔟𝔯𝔬𝔨𝔢𝔯𝔢𝔡 𝔞 𝔰𝔭𝔬𝔫𝔰𝔬𝔯𝔰𝔥𝔦𝔭 𝔡𝔢𝔞𝔩 𝔣𝔬𝔯 𝔶𝔬𝔲 𝔴𝔦𝔱𝔥 𝔱𝔥𝔢 𝔗𝔬𝔞𝔰𝔱 𝔐𝔞𝔯𝔨𝔢𝔱𝔦𝔫𝔤 𝔅𝔬𝔞𝔯𝔡."

"𝔠𝔞𝔰𝔥?"

Joffy nodded.

"Thank ?*&£@ for that," said Zvlkx. "Has the ale improved since I've been away?"

"Not much. But the choice is better."

"Can't wait. Hubba-hubba! Who's the moppet in the tight blouse?"

"Mr. Next," interjected Lydia, who had managed to push her way to the front, "perhaps you would be good enough to tell us what Mr. Zvlkx is saying?"

"I . . . um, welcomed him to the twentieth century and said we had much to learn from him as regards beekeeping and the lost art of brewing mead. He . . . um, said just then that he is tired after his journey and wants only world peace, bridges between nations and a good home for orphans, kittens and puppies."

The crowd suddenly parted to make way for the Mayor of Swindon. St. Zvlkx knew power when he saw it and smiled a greeting to Lord Volescamper, who walked briskly up and shook the monk's grimy hand.

"Look here, welcome to the twentieth century, old salt," said Volescamper, wiping his hand on his handkerchief. "How are you finding it?"

"Welcome to our age," translated Joffy. "How are you enjoying your stay?"

"Cushty, me old cocker babe," replied the saint simply.

"He says, 'Very well, thank you.' "

"Tell the worthy saint that we have a welcome pack awaiting him in the presidential suite at the Finis Hotel. Knowing his aversion to comfort, we took the liberty of removing all carpets, drapes, sheets and towels and replaced the bedclothes with hemp sacks stuffed with rocks."

"What did the old fart say?"

"You don't want to know."

"What about the incomplete Seventh Revealment?" asked Lydia. "Can St. Zvlkx tell us anything about that?"

Joffy swiftly translated, and St. Zvlkx rummaged in the folds of his blanket and produced a small leatherbound book. The crowd fell silent as he licked a grubby finger, turned to the requisite page and read:

" '𝕿𝖍𝖊𝖗𝖊 𝖜𝖎𝖑𝖑 𝖇𝖊 𝖆 𝖍𝖔𝖒𝖊 𝖜𝖎𝖓 𝖔𝖓 𝖙𝖍𝖊 𝖕𝖑𝖆𝖞𝖎𝖓𝖌 𝖋𝖎𝖊𝖑𝖉𝖘 𝖔𝖋 𝕾𝖜𝖎𝖓𝖉𝖔𝖓𝖓𝖊 𝖎𝖓 𝖓𝖎𝖓𝖊-teen hundred and eighty-eight, and in consequence of this, and only in consequence of this, a great tyrant and the company named Goliathe will fall.' "

All eyes switched to Joffy, who translated. There was a sharp intake of breath and a clamor of questions.

"Mr. Zvlkx," said a reporter from *The Mole* who up until that moment had been bored out of his skull, "do you mean to say that Goliath will be lost if Swindon wins the SuperHoop?"

"That is exactly what he says," replied Joffy.

There was a further clamor of questions from the assembled journalists as I carefully tried to figure out the repercussions of this new piece of intelligence. Dad had said that a SuperHoop win for Swindon would avert an Armageddon, and if what Zvlkx was saying came true, a triumph on Saturday would do precisely this. The question was, how? There was no connection as far as I could see. I was still trying to think how a croquet final could unseat a near dictator and destroy one of the most powerful multinationals on the planet, when Lord Volescamper intervened and silenced the noisy crowd of newsmen with a wave of his hand.

"Mr. Next, thank the gracious saint for his words. There is time enough to muse on his revealment, but right now I would like him to meet members of the Swindon Chamber of Commerce, which, I might add, is sponsored by St. Biddulph's® Hundreds and Thousands, the cake decoration of choice. After that we might take some tea and carrot cake. Would he be agreeable to that?"

Joffy translated every word, and Zvlkx smiled happily.

"Look here, St. Zvlkx," said Volescamper as they walked towards the marquee for tea and scones, "what was the thirteenth century like?"

"𝕿𝖍𝖊 𝕸𝖆𝖞𝖔𝖗 𝖜𝖆𝖓𝖙𝖘 𝖙𝖔 𝖐𝖓𝖔𝖜 𝖜𝖍𝖆𝖙 𝖙𝖍𝖊 𝖙𝖍𝖎𝖗𝖙𝖊𝖊𝖓𝖙𝖍 𝖈𝖊𝖓𝖙𝖚𝖗𝖞 𝖜𝖆𝖘 𝖑𝖎𝖐𝖊—and no lip, sunshine."

"𝕱𝖎𝖑𝖙𝖍𝖞, 𝖉𝖆𝖒𝖕, 𝖉𝖎𝖘𝖊𝖆𝖘𝖊-𝖗𝖎𝖉𝖉𝖊𝖓 𝖆𝖓𝖉 𝖕𝖊𝖘𝖙𝖎𝖑𝖊𝖓𝖙𝖎𝖆𝖑."

"He said it was like London, Your Grace."

St. Zvlkx looked at the weathered arch, the only visible evidence of his once great cathedral and asked, "𝔚𝔥𝔞𝔱 𝔥𝔞𝔭𝔭𝔢𝔫𝔢𝔡 𝔱𝔬 𝔪𝔶 𝔠𝔞𝔱𝔥𝔢𝔡𝔯𝔞𝔩?"

"𝔅𝔲𝔯𝔫𝔢𝔡 𝔡𝔲𝔯𝔦𝔫𝔤 𝔱𝔥𝔢 𝔡𝔦𝔰𝔰𝔬𝔩𝔲𝔱𝔦𝔬𝔫 𝔬𝔣 𝔱𝔥𝔢 𝔪𝔬𝔫𝔞𝔰𝔱𝔢𝔯𝔦𝔢𝔰."

"𝔥𝔬𝔱 𝔡𝔞𝔪𝔫," he muttered, eyebrows raised, "𝔰𝔥𝔬𝔲𝔩𝔡 𝔥𝔞𝔳𝔢 𝔰𝔢𝔢𝔫 𝔱𝔥𝔞𝔱 𝔠𝔬𝔪𝔦𝔫𝔤."

"Duis aute dolor in fugiat nulla pariatur," murmured Friday, pointing at St. Zvlkx's retreating form, rapidly vanishing in a crowd of well-wishers and newsmen.

"I have no idea, Sweetheart—but I've a feeling things are just beginning to get interesting."

"Well," said Lydia to the camera, "a revealment that could spell potential disaster for the Goliath Corporation and—"

Her producer was gesticulating wildly for her not to connect "Tyrant" with "Kaine" live on air.

"—an as-yet-unnamed tyrant. This is Lydia Startright, bringing you a miraculous event live for Toad News. And now a word from our sponsors, Goliath Pharmaceuticals, the makers of Hemmorrelief."

12.

Spike and Cindy

Operative Spike Stoker was with SO-17, the Vampire and Werewolf Disposal Operations. Undeniably employed in the loneliest of the SpecOps divisions, SO-17 operatives worked in the twilight world of the semidead, changelings, vampires, lycanthropes and those of a generally evil disposition. Stoker had been decorated more times than I had read *Three Men in a Boat,* but then he was the only staker in the southwest, and no one in his right mind would do what he did on a SpecOps wage, except me. And only then when I was desperate for the cash.

Thursday Next, Thursday Next: A Life in SpecOps

Deep in thought, I pushed Friday back towards my car. The stakes had just been raised, and any chance that I might somehow influence the outcome of the SuperHoop was suddenly made that much more impossible. With Goliath and Kaine both having a vested interest in making sure the Swindon Mallets lost, chances of our victory had dropped from "highly unlikely" to "nigh impossible."

"It explains," said a voice, "why Goliath is changing to a faith-based corporate-management system."

I turned to find my stalker, Millon de Floss, walking close behind me. It must have been important for him to contravene the blanket restraining order. I stopped for a moment. "Why do you think that?"

"Once they are a religion, they won't be a 'company named Goliathe' as stated in Zvlkx's prophecy," observed Millon, "and they can avoid the revealment's coming true. Sister Bettina, their own corporate precog, must have foreseen something like this and alerted them."

"Does that mean," I asked slowly, "that they're taking St. Zvlkx seriously?"

"He's too accurate not to be, Miss Next, however unlikely it may seem. Now that they know the complete Seventh Revealment, they'll try to do anything to stop Swindon's winning—and continue with the religion thing as a backup, just in case."

It made sense—sort of. Dad must have known this or something very like it. None of it boded very well, but my father had said the likelihood of this Armageddon was only 22 percent, so the answer must be somewhere.

"I'm going to visit Goliathopolis this afternoon," I said slowly. "Have you found out anything about Kaine?"

Millon rummaged in his pocket for a notepad, found it and flicked through the pages, which seemed to be full of numbers.

"It's here somewhere," he said apologetically. "I like to collect vacumn-cleaner serial numbers and was investigating a rare Hoover XB-23E when I got the call. Here it is. This Kaine fellow is a conspiracist's delight. He arrived on the scene five years ago with no past, no history, no parents—nothing. His national insurance number wasn't given to him until 1982, and it seems the only jobs he has ever held were with his publishing company and then as MP."

"Not a lot to go on, then."

"Not yet, but I'll keep digging. You might be interested to know that he has been seen on several occasions with Lola Vavoom."

"Who hasn't?"

"Agreed. You wanted to know about Mr. Schitt-Hawse? He heads the Goliath tech division."

"You sure?"

Millon looked dubious for a moment.

"In the conspiracy industry, the word 'sure' has a certain plasticity about it, but yes. We have a mole at Goliathopolis. Admittedly our mole only serves in the canteen, but you'd be surprised the sensitive information that one can overhear giving out shortbread fingers. Apparently Schitt-Hawse has been engaged in something called the Ovitron Project. We're not positive, but it might be a development of your uncle's Ovinator. Could it be something along the lines of *The Midwich Cuckoos*?"

"I sincerely hope not."

I made a few notes, thanked Millon for his time and pushed Friday back to my car, my head full of potential futures, Ovinators and Kaine.

Ten minutes later we were in my Speedster, heading north towards Cricklade. My father had told me that Cindy would fail to kill me three times before she died herself, but there was a chance the future didn't have to turn out that way—after all, I had once been shot dead by a SpecOps marksman in an alternative future, and I was still very much alive.

I hadn't seen Spike for more than two years but had been gratified to learn he had moved out of his dingy apartment to a new address in Cricklade. I soon found his street—it was on a newly built estate of Cotswold stone that shone a warm glow of ocher in the sunlight. As we drove slowly down the road checking door numbers, Friday helpfully pointed out things of interest.

"Ipsum," he said, pointing at a car.

I was hoping that Spike wasn't there so I could speak to Cindy on her own, but I was out of luck. I parked up behind his SpecOps black-and-white and climbed out. Spike himself was sitting on a deck chair on the front lawn, and my heart fell when I saw that not only had he married Cindy but they had also had a child—a one-year-old girl was sitting on the grass next to him playing under a parasol. I cursed inwardly as Friday hid behind my leg. I was going to have to make Cindy play ball—the alternative wouldn't be good for her and would be worse for Spike and their daughter.

"Yo!" yelled Spike, telling the person on the other end of the phone to hold it one moment and getting up to give me a hug. "How you doing, Next?"

"I'm good, Spike, you?"

He spread his arms, indicating the trappings of middle-England suburbia. The UPVC double glazing, the well-kept lawn, the drive, the wrought-iron sunrise gate.

"Look at all this, sister! Isn't it the best?"

"Ipsum," said Friday, pointing at a plant pot.

"Cute kid. Go on in. I'll be with you in a moment."

I walked into the house and found Cindy in the kitchen. She had an apron on and her hair tied up.

"Hello," I said, trying to sound as normal as possible, "you must be Cindy."

She stared me straight in the eye. She didn't look like a professional assassin who had killed sixty-seven times—sixty-eight if she did Samuel Pring—yet the really good ones never do.

"Well, well, Thursday Next," she said slowly, crouching down to pull some damp clothes out of the washing machine and tweaking Friday's ear. "Spike holds you in very high regard."

"Then you know why I'm here?"

She put down the washing and picked up a Fisher-Price Webster that was threatening to trip someone up, and passed it to Friday, who sat down to scrutinize it carefully.

"I can guess. Handsome lad. How old is he?"

"He was two last month. And I'd like to thank you for missing yesterday."

She gave a wan smile and walked out the backdoor. I caught up with her as she started to hang the washing on the line.

"Is it Kaine trying to have me killed?"

"I always respect client confidentiality," she said quietly, "and I can't miss forever."

"Then stop it right now," I said. "Why do you even need to do it at all?"

She pegged a blue romper on the line.

"Two reasons: first, I'm not going to give up work just because I'm married with a kid, and second, I always complete a contract, no matter what. When I don't deliver the goods, the clients want refunds. And the Windowmaker doesn't do refunds."

"Yes," I replied, "I was curious about that. Why the Windowmaker?"

She glared at me coldly. "The printers made a mistake on the notepaper, and it would have cost too much to redo. Don't laugh."

She hung up a pillowcase.

"I'll contract you out, Miss Next, but I won't try today—which gives you some time to get yourself together and leave town once and for all. Somewhere where I can't find you. And hide well—I'm very good at what I do."

She took a sideways glance towards the kitchen. I hung up a large SO-17 T-shirt on the line.

"He doesn't know, does he?" I asked.

"Spike is a fine man," replied Cindy, "just a little slow on the uptake. You're not going to tell him, and he's never going to know. Grab the other end of that sheet, will you?"

I took the end of a dry sheet, and we folded it together.

"I'm not going anywhere, Cindy," I told her, "and I'll protect myself in any way I can."

We stared at one another for a moment. It seemed like such a waste.

"Retire!"

"Never!"

"Why?"

"Because I *like* it and I'm *good* at it—would you like some tea, Thursday?"

Spike had entered the garden carrying the baby. "So how are my two favorite ladies?"

"Thursday was helping me with the washing, Spikey," said Cindy, her hard-as-nails professionalism replaced with a silly sort of girlie ditziness. "I'll put the kettle on—two sugars, Thursday?"

"One."

She skipped into the house.

"What do you think?" asked Spike in a low tone. "Isn't she just the cutest thing ever?"

He was like a fifteen-year-old in love for the first time.

"She's lovely, Spike. You're a lucky man."

"This is Betty," said Spike, waving the tiny arm of the infant with his huge hand. "One year old. You were right about being honest with Cindy—she didn't mind me doing all that vampire sh—I mean *stuff*. In fact, I think she's kinda proud."

"You're a lucky man," I repeated, wondering just how I was going to avoid making him a widower and the gurgling child motherless.

We walked back into the house, where Cindy was busying herself in the kitchen.

"Where have you been?" asked Spike, depositing Betty next to Friday, where they looked at one another suspiciously. "Prison?"

"No. Somewhere weird. Somewhere *other*."

"Will you be returning there?" asked Cindy innocently.

"She's only just got back!" exclaimed Spike. "We don't want to be shot of her quite yet."

"Shot of her—of course not," replied Cindy, placing a mug of tea on the table. "Have a seat. There are Hobnobs in that novelty dodo biscuit tin over there."

"Thank you."

"So," I continued, "how's the vampire business?"

"So-so. Been quiet recently. Werewolves the same. I dealt with a few zombies in the city center the other night, but Supreme Evil Being containment work has almost completely dried up. There has been a report of a few ghouls, bogeys and phantoms in Winchester, but it's not really my area of expertise. There is talk of disbanding the division and then taking me on freelance when they need something done."

"Is that bad?"

"Not really. I can charge what I want with vampires on the prowl—but in slack times I'd be a bit stuffed. Wouldn't want to send Cindy out to work full-time, now, would I?"

He laughed, and Cindy laughed with him, handing a rusk to Betty, who gave it an almighty toothless bite and then looked puzzled when there was no effect. Friday took it off her and showed how it was done.

"So what are you up to at present?" asked Spike.

"Not much. I was just dropping in before I went off up to Goliathopolis—my husband still isn't back."

"Did you hear about Zvlkx's revealment?"

"I was there."

"Then Goliath will want all the forgiveness they can get—you won't find a better time for forcing them to bring him back."

We chatted for ten minutes or more until it was time for me to leave. I didn't manage to speak to Cindy on her own again, but I had said what I wanted to say—I just hoped she would take notice, but somehow I doubted it.

"If I ever have any freelance jobs to do, will you join me?" asked Spike as he was seeing me out the door, Friday having nearly eaten all the rusks.

I thought of my overdraft. "Please."

"Good," replied Spike, "I'll be in touch."

I drove down the M4 to Saknussum International, where I had to run to catch the Gravitube to the James Tarbuck Graviport in Liverpool. Friday and I had a brief lunch before hopping on the shuttle to Goliathopolis. Goliath took my husband from me, and they could bring him back. And when you have a grievance with a company, you go straight to the top.

14.

The Goliath Apologarium

Danish Car a "Deathtrap," Claims Kainian Minister

Robert Edsel, the Kainian minister of road safety, hit out at Danish car manufacturer Volvo yesterday, claiming the boxy and unsightly vehicle previously considered one of the safest cars on the market to be the complete reverse—a death trap for anyone stupid enough to buy one. "The Volvo fared very poorly in the rocket-propelled grenade test," claimed Mr. Edsel in a press release yesterday, "and owners and their children risk permanent spinal injury when dropped in the car from heights as low as sixty feet." Mr. Edsel continued to pour scorn on the pride of the Danish motoring industry by revealing that the Volvo's air filters offered "scant protection" against pyroclastic flows, poisonous fumes and other forms of common volcanic phenomena. "I would very much recommend that anyone thinking of buying this poor Danish product should think again," said Mr. Edsel. When the Danish foreign minister pointed out that Volvos were, in fact, Swedish, Mr. Edsel accused the Danes of once again attempting to blame their neighbors for their own manufacturing weaknesses.

Article in *The Toad on Sunday*, July 16, 1988

The Isle of Man had been an independent corporate state within England since it was appropriated for the greater fiscal good in 1963. The surrounding Irish Sea was heavily mined to deter unwanted visitors and the skies above protected by the most technologically advanced antiaircraft system known to man. It had hospitals and schools, a university, its own fusion reactor and also, leading from Douglas to the Kennedy Graviport in New York, the world's only privately run Gravitube. The Isle of Man was home to almost two hundred thousand people who did nothing but support, or support the support, of the one enterprise that dominated the small island: the Goliath Corporation.

The old Manx town of Laxey was renamed Goliathopolis and was now the Hong Kong of the British archipelago, a forest of glassy towers striding up the hillside towards Snaefell. The largest of these skyscrapers rose higher even than the mountain peak behind and could be seen glinting in the sunlight all the way from Blackpool, weather permitting. In this building was housed the inner sanctum of the whole vast multinational, the cream of Goliath's corporate engineers. An employee could spend a lifetime on the island and never even get past the front desk. And it was on the ground floor of this building, right at the heart of the corporation, that I found the Goliath Apologarium.

I joined a small queue in front of a modern glass-topped table where two happy, smiling Goliath employees were giving out questionnaires and numbered tickets.

"Hello!" said the clerk, a youngish girl with a lopsided smile. "Welcome to the Goliath Corporation's Apology Emporium. Sorry you had to wait. How can we help you?"

"The Goliath Corporation murdered my husband."

"How simply dreadful!" she responded in a lame and insincere display of sympathy. "I'm *so* sorry to hear that. Goliath, as part of our move to a faith-based corporate-management system, is committed to reversing all the unpleasant matters we might have previously been engaged in. You need to fill in this form, and this form—and Section D of this one—and then take a seat. We'll get one of our highly trained apologists to see you just as soon as they can."

She handed me several long forms and a numbered ticket, then indicated a door to one side. I opened the door of the Apologarium and walked in. It was a large hall with floor-to-ceiling windows that gave a serene view of the Irish Sea. On one side was a row of perhaps twenty cubicles containing suited apologists, all listening intently to what they were being told with the same sad and contrite expression. On the other side were rows upon rows of wooden seating that held eager and once bullied citizens, anxiously clasping their numbered tickets and patiently waiting their turn. I looked at my ticket. It was number 6,174. I glanced up at the board, which told me that number 836 was now being interviewed.

"Dear, sweet people!" said a voice through a tannoy. "Goliath is deeply sorry for all the harm it might inadvertently have caused you in the past. Here at the Goliath Apologarium we are only too happy to assist in your problem, no matter how small—"

"You!" I said to a man who was hobbling past me towards the exit. "Has Goliath repented to your satisfaction?"

"Well, they didn't really need to," he replied blandly. "It was I who was at fault—in fact, I apologized for wasting their valuable time!"

"What did they do?"

"They bathed my neighborhood with ionizing radiation, then denied it for seventeen years, even after people's teeth fell out and I grew a third foot."

"And you forgave them?"

"Of course. I can see now that it was a genuine accident and the public has to accept equal risks if we are to have abundant clean energy, limitless food and household electrodefragmentizers."

He was carrying a sheaf of papers, not the application form that I had to fill out but leaflets on how to join New Goliath. Not as a consumer but as a *worshipper.* I had always been deeply distrustful of Goliath, but this whole "repentance" thing smelt worse than anything I had so far witnessed. I turned, tore up my numbered ticket and headed for the exit.

"Miss Next!" called out a familiar voice. "I say, Miss Next!"

A short man with pinched features and a rounded head covered with the fuzz of an aggresively short crew cut was facing me. He was wearing a dark suit and heavy gold jewelry and was arguably the person I liked least—this was Jack Schitt, once Goliath's top advanced-weapons guru and ex-convict of "The Raven." This was the man who had tried to prolong the Crimean War so he could make a fortune out of Goliath's latest superweapon, the Plasma Rifle.

Anger rose quickly within me. I turned Friday in the other direction so as not to give his young mind any wrong ideas about the use of violence and then grasped Schitt by the throat. He took a step back, stumbled and collapsed beneath me with a yelp. Sensing I had been in this position before, I released him and placed my hand on the butt of my automatic, expecting to be attacked by a host of Jack's minders. But there was nothing. Just sad citizens looking on sorrowfully.

"There is no one here to help me," said Jack Schitt, slowly getting to his feet. "I have been assaulted eight times today—I count myself fortunate. Yesterday it was twenty-three."

I looked at him and noticed, for the first time, that he had a black eye and a cut on his lip.

"No minders?" I echoed. "Why?"

"It is my absolution to face those I have bullied and harangued in the past, Miss Next. When we last met, I was head of Goliath's Advanced Weapons Division and corporate laddernumber 329." He sighed. "Now, thanks to your well-publicized denouncement of the failings of our Plasma Rifle, the corporation decided to demote me. I am an Apology Facilitation Operative Second Class, laddernumber 12,398,219. The mighty has fallen, Miss Next."

"On the contrary," I replied, "you have merely been moved to a level more fitting for your competence. It's a shame. You deserved much worse than this."

His eyes twitched as he grew angry. The old Jack, the homicidal one, returned for a moment. But the feelings were short-lived, and his shoulders fell as he realized that without the Goliath Security Service to back him up, his power over me was minimal.

"Maybe you are right," he said simply. "You will not have to wait your turn, Miss Next. I will deal with your case personally. Is this your son?" He bent down to look closer. "Cute fellow, isn't he?"

"Eiusmod tempor incididunt adipisicing elit," said Friday, glaring at Jack suspiciously.

"What did he say?"

"He said, 'If you touch me, my mum will break your nose.' "

Jack stood up quickly. "I see. Goliath and myself offer a full, frank and unreserved apology."

"What for?"

"I don't know. Have it on account. Would you care to come to my office?"

He beckoned me out the door, and we crossed a courtyard with a large fountain in the middle, past a few suited Goliath officials chattering in a corner, then through another doorway and down a wide corridor full of clerks moving backwards and forwards with folders tucked under their arms.

Jack opened a door, ushered me in, offered me a chair and then sat himself. It was a miserable little office, devoid of any decoration except a shabby Lola Vavoom calendar on the wall and a dead plant in a pot. The only window looked out onto a wall. He arranged some papers on his desk and spoke into the intercom.

"Mr. Higgs, would you bring the Thursday Next file in, please?"

He looked at me earnestly and set his head at a slight angle, as though trying to affect some sort of apologetic demeanor.

"None of us quite realized," he began in the sort of soft voice that undertakers use when attempting to persuade you to buy the deluxe coffin, "just how appalling we had been until we started asking people if they were at all unhappy with our conduct."

"Why don't we cut the cr—" I looked at Friday, who looked back at me. "Cut the . . . cut the . . . *nonsense* and go straight to the place where you atone for your crimes."

He sighed and stared at me for a moment, then said, "Very well. What did we do wrong again?"

"You can't remember?"

"I do lots of wrong things, Miss Next. You'll excuse me if I can't remember details."

"You eradicated my husband," I said through gritted teeth.

"Of course! And what was the name of the eradicatee?"

"Landen," I replied coldly. "Landen Parke-Laine."

At that moment a clerk arrived with a pile of papers and laid them on his desk. Jack opened the file, which was marked "Most Secret," and leafed through them.

"The record shows that at the time you say your husband was eradicated, your case officer was operative Schitt-Hawse. It says here that he pressured you to release operative Schitt—that's me—from within the pages of 'The Raven' by utilizing an unnamed ChronoGuard operative who *volunteered* his services. It says that you complied but our promise was revoked due to an unforeseen and commercially necessary overriding blackmail-continuance situation."

"You mean corporate greed, don't you?"

"Don't underestimate greed, Miss Next—it's commerce's greatest motivating force. In this context it was probably due to our plans to use the BookWorld to dump nuclear waste and sell our extremely high-quality goods and services to characters in fiction. You were then imprisoned in our most inaccessible vault, from where you escaped, methodology unknown."

He closed the file.

"What this means, Miss Next, is that we kidnapped you, tried to kill you, and then had you on our shoot-on-sight list for over a year. You may be in line for a generous cash settlement."

"I don't want cash, Jack. You had someone go back in time to kill Landen. Now you can just get someone to go back again and *unkill* him!"

Jack Schitt paused and drummed his fingers on the table for a moment.

"That's not how it works," replied Schitt testily. "The apology and restitution rules are very clear—for us to repent, we must agree as to what we have done wrong, and there's no mention of any Goliath-led illegal-time-related jiggery-pokery in our report. Since Goliath's records are time-audited on a regular basis, I think that proves conclusively that if there *was* any timefoolery, it was instigated by the ChronoGuard—Goliath's chronological record is above reproach."

I thumped the table with my fist, and Jack jumped. Without his henchmen around him, he was a coward, and every time he flinched, I grew stronger.

"This is complete and utter sh—" I looked at Friday again. "*Rubbish,* Jack. Goliath and the ChronoGuard eradicated my husband. You had the power to remove him—you can be the ones that put him back."

"That's not possible."

"Give me back my husband!"

The anger in Jack returned. He also rose and pointed an accusing finger at me. "Have you even the *slightest* idea how much it costs to bribe the ChronoGuard? More money than we care to spend on the sort of miserable, halfhearted forgiveness you can offer us. And another thing, I— Excuse me."

The phone had rung, and he picked it up, his eyes flicking instantly to me as he listened.

"Yes, it is. . . . Yes, she is. . . . Yes, we do. . . . Yes, I will."

His eyes opened wide, and he stood up.

"This is indeed an honor, sir. . . . No, that would not be a problem at all, sir. . . . Yes, I'm sure I can persuade her about that, sir. . . . No, it's what we all want. . . . And a very good day to you, sir. Thank you."

He put down the phone and fetched an empty cardboard box from the cupboard with a renewed spring in his step.

"Good news!" he exclaimed, taking some junk out of his desk and placing it in the box. "The CEO of New Goliath has taken a special interest in your case and will personally guarantee the return of your husband."

"I thought you said that timefoolery had nothing to do with you?"

"Apparently I was misinformed. We would be very happy to reactualize Libner."

"Landen."

"Right."

"What's the catch?" I asked suspiciously.

"No catch," replied Jack, picking up his desk nameplate and depositing it in the box along with the calendar. "We just want you to forgive us and *like* us."

"Like you?"

"Yes. Or pretend to anyway. Not so very hard, now, is it? Just sign this Standard Forgiveness Release Form at the bottom *here,* and we'll reactualize your hubby. Simple, isn't it?"

I was still suspicious.

"I don't believe you have any intention of getting Landen back."

"All right, then," said Jack, taking some files out of the filing cabinet and dumping them in his cardboard box, "don't sign and you'll never know. As you say, Miss Next—we got rid of him, so we can get him back."

"You stiffed me once before, Jack. How do I know you won't do it again?"

Jack paused in his packing and looked slightly apprehensive.

"Are you going to sign?"

"No."

Jack sighed and started to take things back out of the cardboard box and return them to their places.

"Well," he muttered, "there goes my promotion. But listen, whether you sign or not, you walk out of here a free woman. New Goliath has no argument with you any longer. Besides, what do you have to lose?"

"All I want," I replied, "is to get my husband back. I'm not signing anything."

Jack took his nameplate out of the cardboard box and put it back on his desk.

The phone rang again.

"Yes, sir. . . . No, she won't, sir. . . . I tried that, sir. . . . Very well, sir."

He put the phone down and picked up his nameplate again and hovered it over his box.

"That was the CEO. He wants to apologize to you personally. Will you go?"

I paused. Seeing the head honcho of Goliath was an almost unprecedented event for a non-Goliath official. If anyone could get Landen back, it was him. "Okay."

Jack smiled, dropped the nameplate in his box and then hurriedly threw everything else back in.

"Well," he said, "must dash—I've just been promoted up three laddernumbers. Go to the main reception desk, and someone will meet you. Don't forget your Standard Forgiveness Release Form, and if you could mention my name, I'd be really grateful."

He handed me my unsigned forms as the door opened and another Goliath operative walked in, also holding a cardboard box full of possessions.

"What if I don't get him back, Mr. Schitt?"

"Well," he said, looking at his watch, "if you have any grievances about the quality of our contrition, you had better take it up with your appointed Goliath apologist. I don't work here anymore."

And he smiled a supercilious smile, put on his hat and was gone.

"Well!" said the new apologist as he walked around the desk and started to arrange his possessions in the new office. "Is there anything you'd like us to apologize for?"

"Your corporation," I muttered.

"Fully, frankly and unreservedly," replied the apologist in the sincerest of tones.

15.

Meeting the CEO

Fifty years ago we were only a small multinational with barely 7,000 employees. Today we have over 38 million employees in 14,000 companies dealing in over 12 million different products and services. The size of Goliath is what gives us the stability to be able to say confidently that we will be looking after you for many years to come. By 1980 our turnover was equal to the combined GNP of 72 percent of the planet's nations. This year we see the corporation take the next great leap forward—to fully recognized religion with our own gods, demigods, priests, places of worship and prayerbook. Goliath shares will be exchanged for entry into our new faith-based corporate-management system, where you (the devotees) will worship us (the gods) in exchange for protection from the world's evils and a reward in the afterlife. I know you will join me in this endeavor as you have in all our past endeavors. A full leaflet explaining how you can help further the corporation's interest in this matter will be available shortly. *New* Goliath. For all you'll ever need. For all you'll ever want. *Ever.*

Extract from the Goliath Corporation CEO's 1988 Conference speech

I walked to the main desk and gave my name to the receptionist, who, raising her eyebrows at my request, called the 110th floor, registered some surprise and then asked me to wait. I pushed Friday towards the waiting area and gave him a banana I had in my bag. I sat and watched the Goliath officials walking briskly backwards and forwards across the polished marble floors, all looking busy but seemingly doing nothing.

"Miss Next?"

There were two individuals standing in front of me. One was

dressed in the dark Goliath blue of an executive; the other was a footman in full livery holding a polished silver tray.

"Yes?" I said, standing up.

"My name is Mr. Godfrey, the CEO's personal assistant's assistant. If you would be so kind?" He indicated the tray.

I understood his request, unholstered my automatic and laid it on the salver. The footman paused politely. I got the message and placed my two spare clips on it as well. He bowed and silently withdrew, and the Goliath executive led me silently towards a roped-off elevator at the far end of the concourse. I wheeled Friday in, and the doors hissed shut behind us.

It was a glass elevator that rose on the outside of the building and from our vantage point as we were whisked noiselessly heavenward, I could see all of Goliathopolis's buildings, reaching almost all the way down the coast to Douglas. The size of the corporation's holdings was never more demonstrably immense—all these buildings simply *administered* the thousands of companies and millions of employees around the world. If I had been in a charitable frame of mind, I might have been impressed by the scale and grandeur of Goliath's establishment. As it was, I saw only ill-gotten gains.

The smaller buildings were soon left behind as we continued on upwards, until even the other skyscrapers were dwarfed. I was staring with fascination at the spectacular view when without warning the exterior was suddenly obscured by a white haze. Water droplets formed on the outside of the elevator, and I could see nothing until we burst clear of the cloud and into bright sunshine and a deep blue sky a few seconds later. I stared across the tops of the clouds that stretched away unbroken into the distance. I was so enthralled by the spectacle that I didn't realize the elevator had stopped.

"Ipsum," said Friday, who was also impressed and pointed in case I had missed the view.

"Miss Next?"

I turned. To say the boardroom of the Goliath Corporation was impressive would not be doing it the justice it deserves. It was on the top floor of the building. The walls and roof were all tinted glass and, from where we stood, on a clear day you must be able to look down upon the world with the viewpoint of a god. Today it looked as though we were afloat on a cotton-wool sea. The building and its position, high above the planet both geographically and morally, perfectly reflected the corporation's dominance and power.

In the middle of the room was a long table with perhaps thirty suited Goliath board members all standing next to their seats, watching me in silence. No one said anything, and I was about to ask who was the boss when I noticed a large man staring out the window with his hands clasped behind his back.

"Ipsum!" said Friday.

"Allow me," began my escort, "to introduce the chief executive officer of the Goliath Corporation, John Henry Goliath V, great-great-grandson of our founder, John Henry Goliath."

The figure staring out the window turned to meet me. He must have been over six foot eight and was large with it. Broad, imposing and dominating. He was not yet fifty and had piercing green eyes that seemed to look straight through me, and he gave me such a warm smile that I was instantly put at my ease.

"Miss Next?" he said in a voice like distant thunder. "I've wanted to meet you for some time."

His handshake was warm and friendly; it was easy to forget just who he was and what he had done.

"They are standing for *you*," he announced, indicating the board members. "You have personally cost us over a billion pounds in cash and at least four times that in lost revenues. Such an adversary is to be admired rather than reviled."

The board members applauded for about ten seconds, then sat back down at their places. I noticed among them Brik Schitt-Hawse, who inclined his head to me in recognition.

"If I didn't already know the answer I would offer you a position on our board," said the CEO with a smile. "We're just finishing a board meeting, Miss Next. In a few minutes, I shall be at your disposal. Please ask Mr. Godfrey if you require any refreshments for you or your son."

"Thank you."

I asked Godfrey for an orange juice in a beaker for Friday and took Friday out of his stroller and sat with him on a nearby armchair to watch the proceedings.

"Item seventy-six," said a small man wearing a Goliath-issue cobalt blue suit, "Antarctica. There has been a degree of opposition to our purchase of the continent by a small minority of do-gooders who believe our use is anything but benevolent."

"And this, Mr. Jarvis, is a problem because . . . ?" demanded John Henry Goliath.

"Not a problem but an *observation,* sir. I propose that, to offset any possible negative publicity, we let it be known that we merely acquired the continent to generate new ecotourism-related jobs in an area traditionally considered a low point in employment opportunities."

"It shall be so," boomed the CEO. "What else?"

"Well, since we will take the role of 'ecocustodians' very seriously, I propose sending a fleet of ten warships to protect the continent against vandals who seek to harm the penguin population, illegally remove ice and snow and create general mischief."

"Warships eat heavily into profit margins," said another member of the board. But Mr. Jarvis had already thought of that. "Not if we subcontract the security issue to a foreign power eager to do business with us. I have formulated a plan whereby the United Caribbean Nations will patrol the continent in exchange for all the ice and snow they want. With the purchase of Antarctica, we can undercut snow exports from all the countries in the Northern Alliance. Their unsold snow will be bought by us at four pence a ton, melted and exchanged for building sand with Morocco. This will be exported to sand-deficient nations at an overall profit of twelve percent. You'll find it all in my report."

There was a murmur of assent around the table. The CEO nodded his head thoughtfully.

"Thank you, Mr. Jarvis, your idea finds favor with the board. But tell me, what about the vast natural resource that we bought Antarctica to exploit in the first place?"

Jarvis snapped his fingers, and the elevator doors opened to reveal a chef who wheeled in a trolley with a silver dinner cover. He stopped next to the CEO's chair, took off the cover and served the CEO a small plate with what looked like sliced pork on it. A footman laid a knife and a fork next to the plate, along with a crisp napkin, then withdrew.

The CEO took a small forkful and put it in his mouth. His eyes opened wide in shock, and he spit it out. The footman passed him a glass of water.

"Disgusting!"

"I agree, sir," replied Jarvis, "almost completely inedible."

"Blast! Do you mean to tell me we've bought an entire continent with a potential food yield of ten million penguin-units per year only to find we can't eat any of them?"

"Only a minor setback, sir. If you would all turn to page 72 of your agenda . . ."

All the board members simultaneously opened their files. Jarvis picked up his report and walked to the window to read it.

" 'The problem of selling penguins as the Sunday roast of choice can be split into two parts: one, that penguins taste like creosote, and two, that many people have a misguided idea that penguins are somewhat "cute" and "cuddly" and "endangered." To take the first point first, I propose that, as part of the launch of this abundant new foodstuff, there should be a special penguin-cookery show on GoliathChannel 16, as well as a highly amusing advertising campaign with the catchy phrase "P-p-p-prepare a p-p-p-penguin." ' "

The CEO nodded thoughtfully.

"I further suggest," continued Jarvis, "that we finance an independent study into the health-imbuing qualities of seabirds in general. The findings of this independent and wholly impartial study shall be that the recommended weekly intake of penguin per person should be . . . one penguin."

"And point two?" asked another board member. "The public's positive and noneatworthy perception of penguins in general?"

"Not insurmountable, sir. If you recall, we had a similar problem marketing baby-seal burgers, and that is now one of our most popular lines. I suggest we depict penguins as callous and unfeeling creatures who insist on bringing up their children in what is little more than a large chest freezer. Furthermore, the 'endangered' marketing problem can be used to our advantage by an advertising strategy along the lines of 'Eat them quick before they're all gone!' "

"Or," said another board member, " 'Place a penguin in your kitchen—have a snack before extinction.' "

"Doesn't rhyme very well, does it?" said a third. "What about 'For a taste that's a bit more distinct, eat a bird before it's extinct'?"

"I preferred mine."

Jarvis sat down and awaited the CEO's thoughts.

"It shall be so. Why not 'Antarctica—the New Arctic' as a byline? Have our people in advertising put a campaign together. The meeting is over."

The board members closed their folders in one single synchronized movement and then filed in an orderly way to the far end of the room, where a curved staircase led downstairs. Within a few minutes, only Brik Schitt-Hawse and the CEO remained. He placed his red-leather briefcase on the desk in front of me and looked at me dispassionately, saying nothing. For someone like Schitt-Hawse who loved the sound of his own voice, it was clear the CEO called every shot.

"What did you think?" asked Goliath.

"Think?" I replied. "How about 'Morally Reprehensible'?"

"I believe that you will find there is no moral good or bad, Miss Next. Morality can be asserted only from the safe retrospection of twenty years or more. Parliaments have far too short a life to do any long-term good. It is up to corporations to do what is best for everyone. The tenure of an administration may be five years—for us it can be several centuries, and none of that tiresome account-ability to get in the way. The leap to Goliath as a religion is the next logical step."

"I'm not convinced, Mr. Goliath," I told him. "I thought you were becoming a religion to evade the Seventh Revealment of St. Zvlkx."

He gazed at me with his piercing green eyes. "It's *avoid*, not evade, Miss Next. A trifling textual change but legally with great implications. We can legally attempt to avoid the future but not evade it. As long as we can demonstrate a forty-nine-percent chance that our future-altering attempts might fail, we are legally safe. The ChronoGuard is very strict on the rules and we'd be fools to try and break them."

"You didn't ask me up here to argue legal definitions, Mr. Goliath."

"No, Miss Next. I wanted to have this opportunity to explain ourselves to you, one of our most vociferous opponents. I have doubts, too, and if I can make you understand then I will have con-vinced myself that what we are doing is right, and good. Have a seat."

I sat, rather too obediently. Mr. Goliath had a strong personality.

"Humans are molded by evolution to be short-termists, Miss Next," he continued. His voice rumbled deeply and seemed to echo inside my head. "We need only to see our children to repro-ductive age to be successful in a biological sense. We have to move beyond that. If we see ourselves as residents on this planet for the long term, we need to plan for the long term. Goliath has a thousand-year plan for itself. The responsibility for this planet is far too important to leave to a fragmented group of governments, constantly bickering over borders and only looking towards their own self-interest. We at Goliath see ourselves not as a corporation or a government but as a force for good. A force for good in *wait-ing*. We have thirty-eight million employees at present; it isn't dif-ficult to see the benefit of having three billion. Imagine everyone on the planet working towards a single goal—the banishment of all governments and the creation of one business whose sole function it is to run the planet *for* the people on the planet, equally and sustainably for all—not Goliath, but *Earth,* Inc. A company with every member of the world holding a single, equal share."

"Is that why you're becoming a religion?"

"Let's just say that your friend Mr. Zvlkx has goaded us into a course of action that is long overdue. You used the word 'religion,' but we see it more as a one, unifying faith to bring all mankind together. One world, one nation, one people, one aim. Surely you can see the sense in that?"

The strange thing was, I began to see that it could work. Without nations there would be no border disputes. The Crimean War alone had lasted for nearly 132 years, and there were at least a hundred smaller conflicts going on around the planet. Suddenly Goliath seemed not so bad after all, and was indeed our friend. I was a fool not to realize it before.

I rubbed my temples.

"So," continued the CEO in a soft rumble, "I'd like to offer an olive branch to you right now and uneradicate your husband."

"In return," added Schitt-Hawse, speaking for the first time, "we would like for you to accept our full, frank and unreserved apology and sign our Standard Forgiveness Release Form."

I looked at them both in turn, then at the contract they had placed in front of me, then at Friday, who had put his fingers in his mouth and was looking up at me with an inquisitive air. I had to get my husband back, and Friday his father. There didn't seem any good reason not to sign.

"I want your word you'll get him back."

"You have it," replied the CEO.

I took the offered pen and signed the form at the bottom.

"Excellent!" muttered the CEO. "We'll reactualize your husband as soon as possible. Good day, Miss Next. It was a very great pleasure to meet you."

"And you," I replied, smiling and shaking both their hands. "I must say I'm very pleased with what I've heard here today. You can count on my support when you become a religion."

They gave me some leaflets on how to join New Goliath, which I eagerly accepted, and I was shown out a few minutes later, the shuttle to Tarbuck Graviport having been held on my account. By the time I had reached Tarbuck, the inane grin had subsided from my face; by the time I had arrived at Saknussum, I was confused; on the drive back to Swindon, I was suspicious that something wasn't quite right; by the time I had reached Mum's home, I was furious. I had been duped by Goliath—again.

16.

That Evening

Toast May Be Injurious to Health

That was the shock statement put out by a joint Kaine-Goliath research project undertaken last Tuesday morning. "In our research we have found that in certain circumstances eating toast may make the consumer writhe around in unspeakable agony, foaming at the mouth before death mercifully overcomes them." The scientists went on to report that although these findings were by no means complete, more work needed to be done before toast had a clean bill of health. The Toast Marketing Board reacted angrily and pointed out that the "at risk" slice of toast in the experiment had been spread with the deadly poison strychnine and these "scientific" trials were just another attempt to besmirch the board's good name and that of their sponsee, opposition leader Redmond van de Poste.

Report in Goliath Today!, July 17, 1988

How was your day?" asked Mum, handing me a large cup of tea. Friday had been tuckered out by all the activity and had fallen asleep into his cheesy bean dips. I had bathed him and put him to bed before having something to eat myself. Hamlet and Emma were out at the movies or something, Bismarck was listening to Wagner on his Walkman, so Mum and I had a moment to ourselves.

"Not good," I replied slowly. "I can't dissuade an assassin from trying to kill me; Hamlet isn't safe here, but I can't send him back; and if I don't get Swindon to win the SuperHoop, then the world will end. Goliath somehow duped me into forgiving them, I have my own stalker, and also have to figure out how to get the banned books I *should* be hunting for SO-14 out of the country. And Landen's still not back."

"Really?" she said, not having listened to me at all. "I think I've got a plan how we can deal with that annoying offspring of Pickwick's."

"Lethal injection?"

"Not funny. No, my friend Mrs. Beatty knows a dodo whisperer who can work wonders with unruly dodos."

"You're kidding me, right?"

"Not at all."

"I'll try anything, I suppose. I can't understand why he's so difficult—Pickers is a real sweetheart."

We fell silent for a moment.

"Mum?" I said at last.

"Yes?"

"What do you think of Herr Bismarck?"

"Otto? Well, most people remember him for his 'blood and iron' rhetoric, unification arguments, and the wars—but few give him credit for devising the first social security system in Europe."

"No, I mean . . . that is to say . . . you wouldn't—"

At that moment we heard some oaths and a slammed door. After a few thumps and bumps, Hamlet burst into the living room, stopped, composed himself, rubbed his forehead, looked heavenwards, sighed deeply and then said:

"O, that this too too solid flesh would melt, thaw and resolve itself into a dew!"[1]

"Is everything all right?" I asked

"Or that the Everlasting had not fix'd his canon 'gainst self-slaughter!"[2]

"I'll make a cup of tea," said my mother, who had an instinct for

---

[1] "Oh, how I wish my worthless body would melt into a liquid and then evaporate."

[2] "Or that God had not decreed suicide a complete no-no."

these sorts of things. "Would you like a slice of Battenberg, Mr. Hamlet?"

"O God! God! How weary, stale, flat and unprofitable—yes, please—seem to me all the uses of this world!"[3]

She nodded and moved off.

"What's up?" I asked Emma, who had entered with Hamlet, as he strutted around the living room, beating his head in frustration and grief.

"Well, we went to see *Hamlet* at the Alhambra."

"Crumbs!" I muttered. "It . . . er . . . didn't go down too well, I take it?"

"Well," reflected Emma, as Hamlet continued his histrionics around the living room, "the play was okay apart from Hamlet shouting out a couple of times that Polonius wasn't *meant* to be funny and Laertes wasn't remotely handsome. The management weren't particularly put out—there were at least twelve Hamlets in the audience, and they all had something to say about it."

"Fie on't! Ah, fie!" continued Hamlet. " 'Tis an unweeded garden that grows to seed; things rank and gross in nature possess it merely—!"[4]

"No," continued Emma, "it was when we and the twelve other Hamlets went to have a quiet drink with the play's company afterwards that things turned sour. Piarno Keyes—who was playing Hamlet—took umbrage at Hamlet's criticisms of his performance; Hamlet said his portrayal was far too indecisive. Mr. Keyes said Hamlet was mistaken, that Hamlet was a man racked by uncertainty. Then Hamlet said he *was* Hamlet so should know a thing or two about it; one of the other Hamlets disagreed and said *he* was

---

[3]. "Oh God, oh God! How tired, stale and boring life seems to me."

[4]. "Oh, damn and double blast! I feel like a garden that's been left to seed and has been overtaken by all those really annoying weeds, like Japanese knotweed or nettles, both of which can be destroyed by using a recommended herbicide, available from Jekyll Garden Centres."

Footnoterphone Simultaneous Translation sponsored by Jekyll Garden Centres.

Hamlet and thought Mr. Keyes was excellent. Several of the Hamlets agreed, and it might have ended there, but Hamlet said that if Mr. Keyes insisted on playing Hamlet, he should look at how Mel Gibson did it and improve his performance in light of that."

"Oh, dear."

"Yes," said Emma. "Oh, dear. Mr. Keyes flew right off the handle. 'Mel Gibson?' he roared. 'Mel ****ing Gibson? That's all I ever ****ing hear these days!' and he then tried to punch Hamlet on the nose. Hamlet was too quick, of course, and had his bodkin at Keyes's throat before you could blink, so one of the other Hamlets suggested a *Hamlet* contest. The rules were simple: they all had to perform the 'To be or not to be' soliloquy, and the drinkers in the tavern gave them points out of ten."

"And . . . ?"

"Hamlet came last."

"Last? How could he come last?"

"Well, he insisted on playing the soliloquy less like an existential question over life and death and the possibility of an afterlife, and more about a postapocalyptic dystopia where crossbow-wielding punks on motorbikes try to kill people for their gasoline."

I looked across at Hamlet who had quieted down a bit and was looking through my mother's video collection for Olivier's *Hamlet* to see if it was better than Gibson's.

"No wonder he's hacked off."

"Here we go!" said my mother, returning with a large tray of tea things. "There's nothing like a nice cup of tea when things look bad!"

"Humph," grunted Hamlet, staring at his feet. "I don't suppose you've got any of that cake, have you?"

"Especially for you!" My mother smiled, producing the Battenberg with a flourish. She was right, too. After a few cups and a slice of cake, Hamlet was almost human again.

I left Emma and Hamlet arguing with my mother over whether they should watch Olivier's *Hamlet* or *Great Croquet Sporting Moments* on the television and went to sort some washing in the kitchen. I stood there trying to figure out just what sort of brain-scrubbing technique Goliath had used on me to get me to sign their Forgiveness Release. Oddly, I was still getting pro-Goliath flashbacks. In absent moments I felt they weren't so bad, then had to consciously remind myself that they were. On the plus side, there was a possibility Landen might be reactualized, but I didn't know when it would be, or how.

I was just getting around to wondering if a cold soak might remove ketchup stains better than a hot wash when there was a light crackling sound in the air, like crumpled cellophane. It grew louder, and green tendrils of electricity started to envelop the Kenwood mixer, then grew stronger until a greenish glow like St. Elmo's fire was dancing around the microwave. There was a bright light and a rumble of thunder as three figures started to materialize into the kitchen. Two of them were dressed in body armor and holding ridiculously large blaster-type weapons; the other figure was tall and dressed in jet black high-collared robes that hung to the floor in one direction and buttoned tightly up to his throat in the other. He had a pale complexion, high cheekbones and a small and very precise goatee. He stood with his arms crossed and was staring at me with one eyebrow raised imperiously. This was truly a tyrant among tyrants, a cruel galactic leader who had murdered billions in his never-ending and inadequately explained quest for total galactic domination. This . . . was Emperor Zhark.

17.

Emperor Zhark

The eight Emperor Zhark novels were written throughout the seventies by Handley Paige, an author whose previous works included *Spacestation Z-5* and *Revenge of the Thraals*. With Zhark he hit upon a pastiche of everything a bad SF novel should ever be. Weird worlds, tentacled aliens, space travel and square-jawed fighter aces doing battle with a pantomime emperor who lived for no other reason than to cause evil and disharmony in the galaxy. His usual nemesis in the books was Colonel Brandt of the Space Corps assisted by his alien partner, Ashley. There have been two Zhark films starring Buck Stallion, *Zhark the Destroyer* and *Bad Day at Big Rock*, neither of which was any good.

Millon de Floss, *The Books of H. Paige*

Do you have to do that?" I asked.

"Do what?" replied the Emperor.

"Make such a pointlessly dramatic entrance? And what are those two goons doing here?"

"Who said that?" said a muffled voice from inside the opaque helmet of one of his minders. "I can't see a sodding thing in here."

"Who's a goon?" said the other.

"It's a contractual thing," explained the Emperor, ignoring them both. "I've got a new agent who knows how to properly handle a character of my quality. I have to be given a minimum of eighty words' description at least once in any featured book, and at least twice in a book a chapter has to end with my appearance."

"Do you get book-title billing?"

"We gave that one away in exchange for chapter-heading status. If this were a novel, you'd have to start a new chapter as soon as I appeared."

"Well, it's a good thing we're not," I replied. "If my mother was here, she'd probably have had a heart attack."

"Oh!" replied the Emperor, looking around. "Do *you* live with your mother, too?"

"What's up? Problems at Jurisfiction?"

"Take five, lads," said Zhark to the two guards, who felt around the kitchen until they found a chair and sat down. "Mrs. Tiggy-winkle sent me," he breathed. "She's busy at the Beatrix Potter Characters Annual General Meeting but wanted me to give you an update on what's happening at Jurisfiction."

"Who's that, darling?" called my mother from the living room.

"It's a homicidal maniac intent on galactic domination," I called back.

"That's nice, dear."

I turned back to Zhark. "So what's the news?"

"Max de Winter from *Rebecca*," said Zhark thoughtfully. "The BookWorld Justice Department has rearrested him."

"I thought Snell got him off the murder charge."

"He did. The department is still gunning for him, though. They've arrested him on—get this—*insurance fraud*. Remember the boat he sank with his wife in it?"

I nodded.

"Well, apparently he claimed the boat on insurance, so they think they might be able to get him on that."

It was not an untypical turn of events in the BookWorld. Our mandate from the Council of Genres was to keep fictional narrative as stable as possible. As long as it was how the author intended, murderers walked free and tyrants stayed in power—that was what we did. Minor infringements that weren't obvious to the reading public, we tended to overlook. However, in a masterstroke of inspired bureaucracy, the Council of Genres also empowered a Justice Department to look into individual transgressions. The conviction of David Copperfield for murdering his first wife was their biggest cause célèbre—before my time, I hasten to add—and Jurisfiction, unable to save him, could do little except train another character to take Copperfield's place. They had tried to get Max de Winter before, but we had always managed to outmaneuver them. Insurance fraud. I could scarcely believe it.

"Have you alerted the Gryphon?"

"He's working on Fagin's umpteenth appeal."

"Get him on it. We can't leave this to amateurs. What about Hamlet? Can I send him back?"

"Not . . . as such," replied Zhark hesitantly.

"He's becoming something of a nuisance," I admitted, "and Danes are liable to be arrested. I can't keep him amused by watching Mel Gibson's films forever."

"I'd like Mel Gibson to play me," said Zhark thoughtfully.

"I don't think Gibson does bad guys," I conceded. "You'd probably be played by Geoffrey Rush or someone."

"That wouldn't be so bad. Is that cake going begging?"

"Help yourself."

Zhark cut a large slice of Battenberg, took a bite and continued, "Okay, here's the deal: we managed to get the Polonius family to attend arbitration over their unauthorized rewriting of *Hamlet*."

"How did you achieve that?"

"Promised Ophelia her own book. All back to normal—no problem."

"So . . . I can send Hamlet back?"

"Not *quite* yet," replied Zhark, hiding his unease by pretending to find a small piece of fluff on his cape. "You see, Ophelia has now got her knickers in a twist about one of Hamlet's infidelities— someone she thinks is called Henna Appleton. Have you heard anything about this?"

"No. Nothing. Nothing at all. Not a thing. Don't even *know* anyone called Henna Appleton. Why?"

"I was hoping you could tell me. Well, she went completely nuts and threatened to drown herself in the first act rather than the fourth. We think we've got her straightened out. But whilst we were doing this—there was a hostile takeover."

I cursed aloud, and Zhark jumped. Nothing was ever straightforward in the BookWorld. Book mergers, where one book joined another to increase the collective narrative advantage of their own mundane plotlines, were thankfully rare but not unheard of. The most famous merger in Shakespeare was the conjoinment of the two plays *Daughters of Lear* and *Sons of Gloucester* into *King Lear*. Other potential mergers, such as *Much Ado About Verona* and *A Midsummer Night's Shrew,* were denied at the planning stage and hadn't taken place. It could take months to extricate the plots, if it could be done at all. *King Lear* resisted unraveling so strongly we just let it stand.

"So who merged with *Hamlet*?"

"Well, it's now called *The Merry Wives of Elsinore,* and features Gertrude being chased around the castle by Falstaff while being outwitted by Mistress Page, Ford and Ophelia. Laertes is the king of the fairies, and Hamlet is relegated to a sixteen-line subplot where he is convinced Doctor Caius and Fenton have conspired to kill his father for seven hundred pounds."

I groaned. "What's it like?"

"It takes a long time to get funny, and when it finally does, everyone dies."

"Okay," I conceded, "I'll try to keep Hamlet amused. How long do you need to unravel the play?"

Zhark winced and sucked in air through his teeth in the same manner heating engineers do when quoting on a new boiler. "Well, that's the problem, Thursday. I'm not sure that we can do it all. If this happened anywhere but in the original, we could have just deleted it. You know the trouble we had with *King Lear*? Well, I don't see that we're going to have any better luck with *Hamlet, Prince of Denmark*."

I sat down and put my head in my hands. No *Hamlet*. The loss was almost too vast to comprehend.

"How long have we got before *Hamlet* starts to change?" I asked without looking up.

"About five days, six at the outside," replied Zhark quietly. "After that, the breakdown will accelerate. In two weeks' time, the play as we know it will have ceased to exist."

"There must be *something* we can do."

"We've tried pretty much everything. We're stuffed—unless you've got a spare William Shakespeare up your sleeve."

I sat up. "What?"

"We're stuffed?"

"After that."

"A spare William Shakespeare up your sleeve?"

"Yes. How will that help?"

"Well," said Zhark thoughtfully, "since no original manuscripts of either *Hamlet* or *Wives* exist, a freshly penned script by the author would thus become the original manuscript—and we could use *those* to reboot the Storycode Engines from scratch. It's quite simple, really."

I smiled but Zhark looked at me with bewilderment. "Thursday, Shakespeare died in 1616!"

I stood up and patted him on the arm. "You get back to the office and make sure things don't get any worse. Leave the Shakespeare up to me. Now, has anyone figured out yet which book Yorrick Kaine is from?"

"We've got all available resources working on it," replied Zhark, still a bit confused, "but there are a lot of novels to go through. Can you give us any pointers?"

"Well, he's not very multidimensional, so I shouldn't go looking into anything too literary. I'd start at political thrillers and work your way towards spy."

Zhark made a note.

"Good. Any other problems?"

"Yes," replied the Emperor. "Simpkin is being a bit of a pest in *The Tailor of Gloucester*. Apparently the tailor let all his mice escape, and now Simpkin won't let him have the cherry-colored twist. If the Mayor's coat isn't ready for Christmas, there'll be hell to pay."

"Get the mice to make the waistcoat. They're not doing anything."

"Okay," he sighed, "I'll give it a whirl." He looked at his watch. "Well, better be off. I've got to annihilate the planet Thraal at four, and I'm already late. Do you think I should use my trusty Zharkian death-ray and fry them alive in a millisecond or nudge an asteroid into their orbit, thus unleashing at least six chapters of drama as they try to find an ingenious solution to defeat me?"

"The asteroid sounds a good bet."

"I thought so, too. Well, see you later."

I waved good-bye as he and his two guards were beamed out of my world and back into theirs, which was certainly the best place for them. We had quite enough tyrants in the real world as it was.

I was just wondering what *The Merry Wives of Elsinore* might be like when there was another buzzing noise and the kitchen was filled with light once more. There, imperious stare, high collar, etc., etc., was Emperor Zhark.

18.

Emperor Zhark Again

President George Formby Opens Motorcycle Factory
The President opened the new Brough-Vincent-Norton Motorcycle factory
yesterday in Liverpool, bringing much-welcomed jobs to the area. The
highly modernized factory, which aims to produce up to a thousand
quality touring and racing machines every week, was described by the
President as "Cracking stuff!" The President, a longtime advocate of mo-
torcycling, rode one of the company's new Vincent "Super Shadow" racers
around the test track, reportedly hitting over 120 MPH, much to his retinue's obvious concern for the octogenarian Formby's health. Our George
then gave a cheerful rendering of "Riding in the TT Races," reminding his
audience of the time he won the Manx Tourist Trophy on a prototype Rainbow motorcycle.

Article in *The Toad,* July 9, 1988

F orget something?" I asked.

"Yes. What was that cake of your mother's?"

"It's called Battenberg."

He got a pen and made a note on his cuff. "Right. Well, that's it,
then."

"Good."

"Right."

"Is there something else?"

"Yes."

"And . . . ?"

"It's . . . it's . . ."

"What?"

Emperor Zhark bit his lip, looked around nervously and drew closer. Although I'd had good reason for reprimanding him in the past—and even suspended his Jurisfiction badge for "gross incompetence" on two occasions—I actually liked him a great deal. Within the amnesty of his own books, he was a sadistic monster who murdered millions with staggering ruthlessness, but out here he had his own fair share of worries, demons and peculiar habits—many of which seemed to have stemmed from the strict upbringing undertaken by his mother, the Empress Zharkeena.

"Well," he said, unsure of quite how to put it, "you know the sixth in the Emperor Zhark series is being written as we speak?"

"*Zhark: End of Empire*? Yes, I'd heard that. What's the problem?"

"Well, I've just read the advanced plotline, and it seems that I'm going to be vanquished by the Galactic Freedom Alliance."

"I'm sorry, Emperor, I'm not sure I see your point—are you concerned about losing your empire?"

He moved closer. "If the story calls for it, I guess not. But it's what happens to me at the end that I have a few problems with. I don't mind being cast adrift in space on the imperial yacht or left marooned on an empty planet, but my writer has planned . . . *a public execution.*"

He stared at me, shocked by the enormity of it all.

"If that's what he has planned—"

"Thursday, you don't understand. I'm going to be killed off—*written out!* I'm not sure I can take that kind of rejection."

"Emperor," I said, "if a character has run its course, then it's run its course. What do you want me to do? Go and talk the author out of it?"

"Would you?" replied Zhark, opening his eyes wide. "Would you really do that?"

"No. You can't have characters trying to tell their authors what to write in their books. Besides, within your books you are truly evil and need to be punished."

Zhark pulled himself up to his full height. "I see," he said at length. "Well, I might decide to take *drastic* action if you don't at least *attempt* to persuade Mr. Paige. And besides, I'm not *really* evil—I'm just written that way."

"If I hear any more of this nonsense," I replied, beginning to get annoyed, "I will have you placed under book arrest and charged with incitement to mutiny for what you've just told me."

"Oh, crumbs," he said, suddenly deflated. "You can, can't you?"

"I can. I won't because I can't be bothered, but if I hear anything more about this, I will take steps—do you understand?"

"Yes," replied Zhark meekly and, without another word, vanished.

19.

Cloned Will Hunting

Opposition Leader Mildly Criticizes Kaine

Opposition leader Mr. Redmond van de Poste lightly attacked Yorrick Kaine's government yesterday over the possible failure to adequately address the nation's economic woes. Mr. van de Poste suggested that the Danish were "no more guilty of attacking this country than the Swedes" and then went on to question Kaine's independence due to his close sponsorship ties with the Goliath Corporation. In reply Chancellor Kaine thanked van de Poste for alerting him to the Swedes, who were "doubtless up to something," and pointed out that Mr. van de Poste himself was sponsored by the Toast Marketing Board.

Article in *The Gadfly,* July 17, 1988

*S*unday was meant to be a day off but it didn't really seem like it. I played golf with Braxton in the morning and outside work he was as amiable a gent as I could possibly hope to meet. He delighted in showing me the rudiments of golf and once or twice I hit the ball quite well—when it made the *thwack* noise and flew away as straight as a die I suddenly realized what all the fuss was about. It wasn't all fun and games, though—Braxton had been leaned on by Flanker who, I assume, had been leaned on by somebody else higher up. In between putting practice and attempting to get my ball out of the bunker, Braxton confided that he couldn't hold off Flanker forever with his empty promise of a report on my alleged Welsh cheese activities, and if I knew what was good for me I would have to at least *try* and look for banned books with SO-14. I promised I would and then joined him for a drink at the nineteenth hole where we were regaled with stories by a large man with a red nose who was, apparently, the Oldest Member.

I was awakened Monday morning by a burbling noise from Friday. He was standing up in his cot and trying to grasp the curtain, which was out of his reach. He said that now that I was awake I could do a lot worse than take him downstairs, where he could play whilst I made some breakfast. Well, he didn't use those *precise* words, of course—he said something more along the lines of, "Reprehenderit in voluptate velit id est mollit," but I knew what he meant.

I couldn't think of any good reason not to, so I pulled on my dressing gown and took the little fellow downstairs, pondering on quite who, if anyone, was going to look after him today. After I nearly got into a fight with Jack Schitt in front of Friday, I wasn't sure he should witness all that his mum got up to.

My own mother was already up.

"Good morning, Mother," I said cheerfully, "and how are you today?"

"I'm afraid not during the morning," she said, divining my unasked question instantly, "but I can probably manage from teatime onwards."

"I'd appreciate it," I replied, looking at *The Mole* as I put on the porridge. Kaine had given an ultimatum to the Danish: either the government in Denmark ended all its efforts to destabilize England and undermine our economy, or England would have no choice but to recall our ambassador. The Danish had replied that they didn't know what Kaine was talking about and demanded that the trade ban on Danish goods be lifted. Kaine responded angrily, made all sorts of counterclaims, put a 200 percent tariff on Danish bacon imports and closed all avenues of communication.

"Duis aute irure dolor est!" yelled Friday.

"Keep your hair on," I replied, "it's coming."

"Plink!" said Alan angrily, gesturing towards his supper dish indignantly.

"Wait your turn," I told him.

"Plink, *PLINK!*" he replied in a threatening tone, taking a step closer and opening his beak threateningly.

"Try to bite me," I told him, "and you'll be finding a new owner from the front window of Pete & Dave's!"

Alan figured out this was a threat and closed his beak. Pete & Dave's was the local reengineered-pet store, and I was serious. He'd already tried to bite my mother, and even the local dogs were giving him a wide berth.

At that moment Joffy opened the back door and walked in. But he wasn't alone. He was with something that I can only describe as an untidy bag of thin bones covered in dirty skin and a rough blanket.

"Ah!" said Joffy. "Mum and Sis. Just the ticket. This is St. Zvlkx. Your Grace, this is my mother, Mrs. Next, and my sister, Thursday."

St. Zvlkx looked at me suspiciously from behind a heavy curtain of oily black hair.

"Welcome to Swindon, Mr. Zvlkx," said my mother, curtsying politely. "Would you like some breakfast?"

"He only speaks 𝔒𝔩𝔡 𝔈𝔫𝔤𝔩𝔦𝔰𝔥," put in Joffy. "Here, let me translate."

"𝔒i, pigface—are you going to eat or what?"

"𝔄hh!" said the monk, and sat down at the table. Friday stared at him a little dubiously, then started to jabber Lorem Ipsum at him while the monk stared at *him* dubiously.

"How's it all going?" I asked.

"Pretty good," replied Joffy, pouring some coffee for himself and St. Zvlkx. "He's shooting a commercial this morning for the Toast Marketing Board and will be on *The Adrian Lush Show* at four. He's also guest speaker at the Swindon Dermatologists' Convention at the Finis; apparently some of his skin complaints are unknown to science. I thought I'd bring him around to see you—he's full of wisdom, you know."

"It's barely eight in the morning!" said Mum.

"St. Zvlkx rises with the dawn as a penance," Joffy explained. "He spent all of Sunday pushing a peanut around the Brunel Centre with his nose."

"I spent it playing golf with Braxton Hicks."

"How did you do?"

"Okay, I think. My croquet-playing skills stopped me making a complete arse of myself. Did you know that Braxton had six kids?"

"Well, how about some wisdom, then?" asked my mother brightly. "I'm very big on thirteenth-century sagacity."

"Okay," said Joffy. "𝔒𝔦! 𝔐𝔞𝔨𝔢 𝔶𝔬𝔲𝔯𝔰𝔢𝔩𝔣 𝔲𝔰𝔢𝔣𝔲𝔩 𝔞𝔫𝔡 𝔤𝔦𝔳𝔢 𝔲𝔰 𝔰𝔬𝔪𝔢 𝔴𝔦𝔰𝔡𝔬𝔪, 𝔶𝔬𝔲 𝔬𝔩𝔡 𝔣𝔞𝔯𝔱."

"𝔓𝔬𝔨𝔢 𝔦𝔱 𝔲𝔭 𝔶𝔬𝔲𝔯 𝔞𝔯𝔰𝔢."

"What did he say?"

"Er . . . he said he would meditate upon it."

"Well," said my mother, who was nothing if not hospitable and could just about make breakfast without consulting the recipe book, "since you are our guest, Mr. Zvlkx, what would you like for breakfast?"

St. Zvlkx stared at her.

"Eat," repeated my mother, making biting gestures. This seemed to do the trick.

"𝔜𝔬𝔲𝔯 𝔪𝔬𝔱𝔥𝔢𝔯 𝔥𝔞𝔰 𝔣𝔦𝔯𝔪 𝔟𝔯𝔢𝔞𝔰𝔱𝔰 𝔣𝔬𝔯 𝔞 𝔪𝔦𝔡𝔡𝔩𝔢-𝔞𝔤𝔢𝔡 𝔴𝔬𝔪𝔞𝔫, 𝔬𝔯𝔟𝔩𝔦𝔨𝔢 𝔞𝔫𝔡 𝔡𝔢-𝔣𝔶𝔦𝔫𝔤 𝔤𝔯𝔞𝔳𝔦𝔱𝔶. 𝔍 𝔰𝔥𝔬𝔲𝔩𝔡 𝔩𝔦𝔨𝔢 𝔱𝔬 𝔭𝔩𝔞𝔶 𝔴𝔦𝔱𝔥 𝔱𝔥𝔢𝔪, 𝔞𝔰 𝔞 𝔟𝔞𝔨𝔢𝔯 𝔭𝔩𝔞𝔶𝔰 𝔴𝔦𝔱𝔥 𝔡𝔬𝔲𝔤𝔥."

"What did he say?"

"He says he'd be very grateful for bacon and eggs," replied Joffy quickly, turning to St. Zvlkx and saying, "𝔄𝔫𝔶 𝔪𝔬𝔯𝔢 𝔠𝔯𝔞𝔭 𝔬𝔲𝔱 𝔬𝔣 𝔶𝔬𝔲, 𝔰𝔲𝔫𝔰𝔥𝔦𝔫𝔢, 𝔞𝔫𝔡 𝔍'𝔩𝔩 𝔩𝔬𝔠𝔨 𝔶𝔬𝔲 𝔦𝔫 𝔱𝔥𝔢 𝔠𝔢𝔩𝔩𝔞𝔯 𝔱𝔬𝔪𝔬𝔯𝔯𝔬𝔴 𝔫𝔦𝔤𝔥𝔱 𝔞𝔰 𝔴𝔢𝔩𝔩."

"What did you say to him?"

"I thanked him for his attendance in your home."

"Ah."

Mum put the big frying pan on the cooker and broke some eggs into it, followed by large rashers of bacon. Pretty soon the smell of bacon pervaded the house, something that attracted not only a sleepwalking DH-82 but also Hamlet and Lady Hamilton, who had given up pretending they weren't sleeping together.

"𝕳ubba hubba," said St. Zvlkx as soon as Emma entered. "𝖂ho's the bunny with the scrummy hooters?"

"He wishes you . . . um . . . both good morrow," said Joffy, visibly shaken. "𝕊t. 𝖅vlkx, this is 𝕷ady 𝕳amilton and 𝕳amlet, 𝕻rince of 𝕯enmark."

"𝕴f you're giving away one of those puppies," continued St. Zvlkx, staring at Emma's cleavage, "𝕴'll have the one with the brown nose."

"Good morning," said Hamlet without smiling. **"Any more bad language against the good Lady Hamilton and I'll take you outside and make your quietus with a bare bodkin."**

"𝖂hat did the 𝕻rince say?" asked St. Zvlkx.

"Yes," said Joffy, "what did he say?"

"It's **Courier Bold**," I told him, "the traditional language of the BookWorld. He said that he would be failing in his duty as a gentleman if he allowed Zvlkx to show any disrespect to Lady Hamilton."

"𝖂hat did your sister say?" asked St. Zvlkx.

"𝕾he said that if you insult 𝕳amlet's bird again, your nose will be two foot wide across your face."

"𝕺h."

"Well," said my mother, "this is turning out to be a *very* pleasant morning!"

"In that case," asked Joffy, sensing that the time was just right, "could St. Zvlkx stay here until midday? I've got to give a sermon to the Sisters of Eternal Punctuality at ten, and if I'm late, they throw their prayer books at me."

"No can do, oh, son-my-son," said my mother, flipping the bacon. "Why not take St. Zvlkx with you? I'm sure the nuns will be impressed by his piety."

"𝕯id someone mention nuns?" asked St. Zvlkx, looking around eagerly.

"How you got to be a saint I have no idea," chided Joffy. "Another peep out of you and I'll personally kick your vulgar arse all the way back to the thirteenth century."

St. Zvlkx shrugged, wolfed down his bacon and eggs with his hands and then burped loudly. Friday did the same and collapsed into a fit of giggles.

They all left soon after. Joffy wouldn't mind Friday, and Zvlkx certainly couldn't, so there was nothing for it. As soon as Mum had found her hat, coat and keys and gone out, I rushed upstairs, dressed, then read myself into *Bradshaw Defies the Kaiser* to ask Melanie if she would look after Friday until teatime. Mum said she would be out the whole day, and since Hamlet already knew that Melanie was a gorilla and neither Emma nor Bismarck could *exactly* complain since they were long-dead historical figures themselves, I thought it a safe bet. It was against regulations, but with Hamlet and the world facing an uncertain future, I was past caring.

Melanie happily agreed, and once she had changed into a yellow polka-dot dress, I brought her out of the BookWorld to my mother's front room, which she thought very smart, especially the festoon curtains. She was pulling the cord to watch the curtains rise and fall when Emma walked in.

"Lady Hamilton," I announced, "this is Melanie Bradshaw."

Mel put out a large hand, and Emma shook it nervously, as though expecting Melanie to bite her or something.

"How . . . how do you do?" she stammered. "I've never been introduced to a monkey before."

"Ape," corrected Melanie helpfully. "Monkeys generally have tails, are truly arboreal and belong to the families Hylobatidae, Cebidae and Ceropithecidae. You and I and all the great apes are Pongidae. I'm a gorilla. Well, *strictly* speaking, I'm a mountain gorilla—*Gorilla gorilla beringei*—which lives on the slopes of the Virunga volcanoes—we used to call it British East Africa, but I'm not sure what it is now. Have you ever been there?"

"No."

"Charming place. That's where Trafford—my husband—and I met. He was with his gun bearers hacking his way through the undergrowth during the backstory to *Bradshaw Hunts Big Game* (Collins, 1878, 4/6, illustrated), and he slipped from the path and fell twenty feet into the ravine below, where I was taking a bath."

She picked up Friday in her massive arms, and he chortled with delight.

"Well, I was most *dreadfully* embarrassed. I mean, I was sitting there in the running water without a stitch on, but—and I'll always remember this—Trafford politely apologized and turned his back so I could nip into the bushes and get dressed. I came out to ask him if he might want directions back to civilization—Africa was quite unexplored then, you know—and we got to chatting. Well, one thing led to another, and before I knew it, he had asked me out to dinner. We've been together ever since. Does that sound silly to you?"

Emma thought about how her relationship with Admiral Lord Nelson was lampooned mercilessly in the press. "No, I think that sounds really quite romantic."

"Right," I said, clapping my hands, "I'll be back at three. Don't go out, and if anyone calls, get Hamlet or Emma to answer the door. Okay?"

"Certainly," replied Melanie. "Don't go out, don't answer the door. Simple."

"And no swinging on the curtains or lamp fixtures—they won't stand it."

"Are you saying I'm a bit large?"

"Not at all," I replied hastily. "Things are just *different* in the real world. There is lots of fruit in the bowl and fresh bananas in the refrigerator. Okay?"

"No problemo. Have a nice day."

I drove into town and, avoiding several newspapermen who were still eager to interview me, entered the SpecOps Building, which I noted had been freshly repainted since my last visit. It looked a bit more cheery in mauve, but not much.

"Agent Next?" said a young and extremely keen SO-14 agent in a well-starched black outfit, complete with Kevlar vest, combat boots, and highly visible weaponry.

"Yes?"

He saluted.

"My name is Major Drabb, SO-14. I understand you have been assigned to us to track down more of this pernicious Danish literature."

He was so keen to fulfill his duties I felt chilled. To his credit he would be as enthusiastic helping flood victims; he was just following orders unquestioningly. Worse acts than destroying Danish literature had been perpetrated by men like this. Luckily, I was prepared.

"Good to see you, Major. I had a tip-off that this address might hold a few copies of the banned books."

I passed him a scrap of paper and he read it eagerly.

"The Albert Schweitzer Memorial Library? We'll be on it right away."

And he saluted smartly once again, turned on his heel and was gone.

I made my way up to the LiteraTec office and found Bowden in the process of packing Karen Blixen's various collections of stories into a cardboard box.

"Hi!" he said, tying up the box with string. "How are things with you?"

"Pretty good. I'm back at work."

Bowden smiled, put down the scissors and string and shook my hand.

"That's very good news indeed! Heard the latest? Daphne Farquitt has been added to the list of banned Danish writers."

"But . . . Farquitt isn't Danish!"

"Her father's name was Farquittsen, so it's Danish enough for Kaine and his idiots."

172

It was an interesting development. Farquitt's books were pretty dreadful but burning was still a step too far. Just.

"Have you found a way to get all these banned books out of England?" asked Bowden, running some tape across a box of *Out of Africa*s. "With Farquitt's books and all the rest of the stuff that's coming in, I think we'll need closer to ten trucks."

"It's certainly on my mind," I replied, having not done anything about it at all.

"Excellent! We'd like to take a convoy through as soon as you say the word. Now, what do you want me to brief you on first? The latest Capulet v. Montague drive-by shooting or which authors are next up for a random dope test?"

"Neither," I replied. "Tell me *everything* you know about cloned Shakespeares."

"We've had to put that on low priority. It's intriguing to be sure, but ultimately pointless from a law-and-order point of view—anyone involved in their sequencing will be too dead or too old to go to trial."

"It's more of a BookWorld thing," I replied, "but important, I promise."

"Well, in *that* case," began Bowden, who knew me too well to think I'd waste his time or my own, "we have three Shakespeares on the slab at the moment, all aged between fifty and sixty—put those Hans Christian Andersen books in that box, would you? If they *were* cloned, it was way back in the poorly regulated days of the thirties, when there was all sorts of nonsense going on, when people thought they could engineer Olympic runners with four legs, swimmers with real fins, that sort of thing. I've had a brief trawl through the records. The first confirmed WillClone surfaced in 1952 with the accidental shooting of a Mr. 'Shakstpear' in Tenbury Wells. Then there's the unexplained death of a Mr. 'Shaxzpar' in 1958, Mr. 'Shagxtspar' in 1962 and a Mr. 'Shogtspore' in 1969. There are others, too—"

"Any theories why?"

"I think," said Bowden slowly, "that perhaps someone was

trying to synthesize the great man so they could have him write some more great plays. Illegal and morally reprehensible, of course, but potentially of huge benefit to Shakespearean scholars everywhere. The lack of any *young* Shakespeares turning up makes me think this was an experiment long since abandoned."

There was a pause as I mulled this over. Genetic cloning of entire humans was *strictly* forbidden—no commercial bioengineering company would dare try it, and yet no one but a large bioengineering company would have the facilities to undertake it. But if these Shakespeare clones had survived, chances are there were more. And with the real one long dead, his reengineered other self was the only way we could unravel *The Merry Wives of Elsinore*.

"Doesn't this come under the jurisdiction of SO-13?" I said at last.

"Officially, yes," conceded Bowden, "but SO-13 is as underfunded as we are, and Agent Stiggins is far too busy dealing with mammoth migrations and chimeras to have anything to do with cloned Elizabethan playwrights."

Stiggins was the neanderthal head of the cloning police. Legally reengineered by Goliath, he was the ideal person to run SO-13.

"Have you spoken to him?" I asked.

"He's a neanderthal," Bowden replied. "They don't talk at all unless it's absolutely necessary. I've tried a couple of times, but he just stares at me in a funny way and eats live beetles from a paper bag—yuck."

"He'll talk to me," I said. He would, too. I still owed him a favor for when he got me out of a jam with Flanker. "Let's see if he's about."

I picked up the phone, consulted the internal directory and dialed a number.

I watched as Bowden boxed up more banned books. If he was caught, he'd be finished. The irony of a LiteraTec's being jailed for protecting Farquitt's *Canon of Love*. I liked him all the more for it. No one in the Literary Detectives would knowingly harm a book. We'd all resign before torching a single copy of anything.

"Right," I said, replacing the phone. "His office said there was a chimera alert in the Brunel Centre—we should be able to find him there."

"Whereabouts in the Brunel Centre?"

"If it's a chimera alert, we just follow the screams."

20.

Chimeras and Neanderthals

The neanderthal experiment was conceived in order to create the eu-
phemistically entitled "medical test vessels," living creatures that were as
close as possible to humans without actually *being* human within the context of the law. The experiment was an unparalleled success—and failure.
The neanderthal was everything that could be hoped for. A close cousin,
but not human, physiologically almost identical—and legally with fewer
rights than a dormouse. But, sadly for Goliath, even the hardiest of medical technicians balked at experiments conducted upon intelligent and
speaking entities, so the first batch of neanderthals were trained instead as
"expendable combat units," a project that was shelved as soon as the lack
of aggressive instincts in the neanderthal was noted. They were subsequently released into the community as cheap labor and became a celebrated tax write-off. It was *Homo sapien* at his least sapient.

Gerhard von Squid, Neanderthals—Back After a Short Absence

The Brunel Centre was packed, as usual. Busy shoppers moved
from chain store to chain store, trying to find bargains in places
whose identical goods were price-fixed by the head office several
months in advance. It didn't stop them trying, though.

"So why the interest in photocopied bards?" asked Bowden as
we crossed the canal.

"We've got a crisis in the BookWorld."

I outlined what was happening within the play formerly known
as *Hamlet,* and he opened his eyes wide.

"Whoa!" he said after a pause. "And I thought *our* work was unusual!"

We didn't have to wait long to find Mr. Stiggins. Within a few moments, there was a bloodcurdling cry of terror from a startled shopper. A second scream followed, and all of a sudden there was a mad rush of people moving away from the junction of Canal Walk and Bridge Street. We moved against the flow, stepping over discarded shopping and the odd shoe. The cause of the panic was soon evident. Rifling through a rubbish bin for a tasty snack was a bizarre hybrid of a creature—in SO-13 slang a chimera. The genetic revolution that gave us unlimited replacement organs and the power to create dodos and other extinctees from home cloning kits had a downside: perverse pastiches of animals who were borne not on the shoulders of evolution but by hobby gene splicers who didn't know any better than to try to play God in the comfort of their own potting sheds.

As the crowds rapidly departed, Bowden and I stared at the strange creature that lurched and slavered as it rooted through the waste bin. It was about the size of a goat and had the rear legs of one, but not much else. The tail and the forelegs were lizard, the head almost feline. It had several tentacles, and it sucked noisily on a chip-soaked newspaper, the saliva from its toothless mouth dribbling copiously onto the pavement. In general, hybrid birds were the most common product of illegal gene splicing, as birds were closely enough related to one another to come out pretty well no matter how ham-fisted the amateur splicer. You could even create a passable dogfoxwolf or a domestic catleopard with no greater knowledge than a biology O level. No, it was the cross-class abominations that had led to the total ban on home cloning, the lizard-mammal switcheroos that really pushed the limits on what was socially acceptable. It didn't stop the sport, just pushed it underground.

The creature rummaged with its one good arm in the bin, found the remains of a SmileyBurger, stared at it with its five eyes, then pushed it into its mouth. It then flopped to the ground and moved, half shuffling and half slithering to the next bin, all the while hissing like a cat and slapping its tentacles together.

"Oh, my God," said Bowden, "it's got a human arm!"

And so it had. It was when there were bits of recognizable human in them that chimeras were most repellant—a failed attempt to replace a deceased loved one, or hobby gene splicers trying to make themselves a son.

"Repulsive?" said a voice close at hand. "The creature . . . or the creator?" I turned to find myself looking at a squat, beetle-browed neanderthal in a pale suit with a homburg hat perched high on his domed head. I had met him several times before. This was Bartholomew Stiggins, head of SO-13 here in Wessex.

"Both," I replied.

Stiggins nodded imperceptibly as a blue SO-13 Land Rover pulled up with a squealing of brakes. A uniformed officer jumped out and started to try to push us back.

Stiggins said, "We are together."

The neanderthal took a few steps forward, and we joined him at the creature, which was close enough to touch.

"Reptile, goat, cat, human," murmured the neanderthal, crouching down and staring intently at the creature as it ran a thin, pink, forked tongue across a crisps packet.

"The eyes look insectoid," observed the SO-13 agent, dart gun in the crook of his arm.

"Too big. More like the eyes we found on the chimera up at the bandstand. You remember, the one that looked like a giant hamster?"

"Same splicer?"

The neanderthal shrugged. "Same eyes. You know how they like to trade."

"We'll take a sample and compare. Might lead us to them. That looks like a human arm, doesn't it?"

The creature's arm was red and mottled and no bigger than a

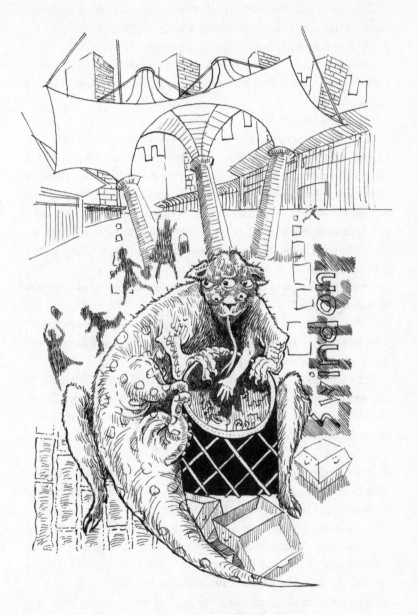

The cause of the panic was soon evident. Rifling through a rubbish bin for a tasty snack was a bizarre hybrid of a creature—in SO-13 slang a chimera.

child's. To grasp anything, the fingers grabbed and twisted randomly until they found something and then clung on tight.

"Gives it an age," said Stiggins. "Perhaps five years."

"Do you want to take it alive, sir?" asked the SO-13 agent, breaking the barrel of his gun and pausing. The neanderthal shook his head.

"No. Send him home."

The agent inserted a dart and snapped the breech shut. He took careful aim and fired it into the creature. The chimera didn't flinch—a fully functioning nervous system is a complicated piece of design and well beyond the capabilities of even the most gifted of amateur splicers—but it stopped trying to chew the bark off a tree and twitched several times before lying down and breathing more slowly. The neanderthal moved closer and held the creature's grubby hand as its life ebbed away.

"Sometimes," said the neanderthal softly, "sometimes the innocent must suffer."

"Dennis!" came a panicked voice from the gathering crowd, who had fallen silent as the creature's breathing grew slower. "Dennis, Daddy's worried! Where are you?"

The whole sad, sorry scene had just got a lot worse. A man with a beard and in a sleeveless white shirt had run into the empty circle around the rapidly dying creature and stared at us with a look of numb horror on his face.

"Dennis?"

He dropped to his knees next to his creation, which was now breathing in short gasps. The man opened his mouth and made such a wail of heartbroken grief that it made me feel quite odd inside. Such an outpouring cannot be feigned; it comes from the soul, one's very being.

"You didn't have to kill him!" he wailed, wrapping his arms around the dying beast. *"You didn't have to kill him . . . !"*

The uniformed agent moved to pull Dennis's creator away, but the neanderthal stopped him. "No," he said gravely. "Leave him for a moment."

The agent shrugged and walked to the Land Rover to fetch a body bag.

"Every time we do this, it's like killing one of our own," said Stiggins softly. "Where have you been, Miss Next? In prison?"

"Why does everyone think I've been in prison?"

"Because you were heading towards either death or prison when we last met—and you are not dead."

Dennis's maker was rocking backwards and forwards, bemoaning the loss of his creation.

The agent returned with a body bag and a female colleague, who gently pried the man from the creature and told his unhearing ears his rights.

"Only one signature on a piece of paper keeps neanderthals from being destroyed, the same as him," said Stiggins, indicating the creature. "We can be added to the list of banned creatures and designated a chimera without even an act of parliament."

We turned from the scene as the other two agents laid out the body bag and then rolled the corpse of the chimera onto it.

"You remember Bowden Cable?" I asked. "My partner at the LiteraTecs."

"Of course," replied Stiggins, "we met at your reception."

"How have you been?" asked Bowden.

Stiggins stared back at him. It was a pointless human pleasantry that neanderthals never trouble themselves with.

"We have been fine," replied Stig, forcing the standard answer from his lips. Bowden didn't know it, but he was only rubbing Stiggins's nose deeper in *sapien*-dominated society.

"He means nothing by it," I said matter-of-factly, which is how neanderthals like all their speech. "We need your help, Stig."

"Then we will be happy to give it, Miss Next."

"Mean nothing by *what?*" asked Bowden as we walked across to a bench.

"Tell you later."

Stig sat down and watched as another SO-13 Land Rover turned up, followed by two police cars to disperse the now curious crowd. He pulled out a carefully wrapped package of greaseproof paper and unfolded it to reveal his lunch—two windfall apples, a small bag of live bugs and a chunk of raw meat.

"Bug?"

"No thanks."

"So what can we do for the Literary Detectives?" he asked, attempting to eat a beetle that didn't really want him to and was chased twice around Stig's hand until caught and devoured.

"What do you make of this?" I asked as Bowden handed him a picture of the Shaxtper cadaver.

"It is a dead human," replied Stig. "Are you sure you won't have a beetle? They're very crunchy."

"No thanks. What about this?"

Bowden handed him another picture of one of the other dead clones, and then a third.

"The same dead human from a different viewpoint?"

"They're all different corpses, Stig."

He stopped chewing the uncooked lamb chop and stared at me, then wiped his hands on a large handkerchief and looked more carefully at the photographs. "How many?"

"Eighteen that we know of."

"Cloning entire humans has always been illegal," murmured Stig. "Can we see the real thing?"

The Swindon morgue was a short walk from the SpecOps office. It was an old Victorian building, which in a more enlightened age would have been condemned. It smelt of formaldehyde and damp, and all the morgue technicians looked unhappy and probably had odd hobbies that I would be happier not knowing about.

The lugubrious head pathologist, Mr. Rumplunkett, looked avariciously at Mr. Stiggins. Since killing a neanderthal wasn't technically a crime, no autopsy was ever performed on one—and Mr. Rumplunkett was by nature a curious man. He said nothing, but Stiggins knew precisely what he was thinking.

"We're pretty much the same inside as you, Mr. Rumplunkett.

That was, after all, the reason we were brought into being in the first place."

"I'm sorry—" began the embarrassed chief pathologist.

"No, you're *not*," replied Stig. "Your interest is purely professional and in the pursuit of knowledge. We take no offense."

"We're here to look at Mr. Shaxtper," said Bowden.

We were led to the main autopsy room, where several bodies were lying under sheets with tags on their toes.

"Overcrowding," said Mr. Rumplunkett, "but they don't seem to complain too much. This the one?"

He threw back a sheet. The cadaver had a high-domed head, deep-set eyes, a small mustache and goatee. It looked a lot like William Shakespeare from the Droeshout engraving on the title page of the First Folio.

"What do you think?"

"Okay," I said slowly, "he *looks* like Shakespeare, but if Victor wore his hair like that, so would he."

Bowden nodded. It was a fair point.

"And this one wrote the Howdy Doody sonnet?"

"No, that particular sonnet was written by *this* one."

With a flourish, Bowden pulled back the sheet from another cadaver to reveal an identical corpse to the first, only a year or two younger. I stared at them both as Bowden revealed yet another.

"So how many Shakespeares did you say you had?"

"Officially, none. We've got a Shaxtper, a Shakespoor and a Shagsper. Only two of them had any writing on them, all have ink-stained fingers, all are genetically identical, and all died of disease or hypothermia brought on by self-neglect."

"Down-and-outs?"

"Hermits is probably nearer the mark."

"Aside from the fact they all have two left eyes and one size of toe," said Stig, who had been examining the cadavers at length, "they are very good indeed. We haven't seen this sort of craftsmanship for years."

"They're copies of a playwright named William Shakes—"

183

"We know of Shakespeare, Mr. Cable," interupted Stig. "We are particularly fond of Caliban from *The Tempest*. This is a deep recovery job. Brought back from a piece of dried skin or a hair in a death mask or something."

"When and where, Stig?"

He thought for a moment.

"They were probably built in the mid-thirties," he announced. "At the time there were perhaps only ten biolabs in the world who could have done this. We think we can safely say we are looking at one of the three biggest genetic-engineering labs in England."

"Not possible," said Bowden. "The manufacturing logs of York, Bognor Regis and Scunthorpe are a matter of public record; it would be inconceivable that a project of this magnitude could have been kept secret."

"And yet they exist," replied Stig, pointing to the corpses and bringing Bowden's argument to a rapid close. "Do you have the genome logs and trace-element spectroscopic evaluations?" he added. "More careful study might reveal something."

"That's not standard autopsy procedure," replied Rumplunkett. "I have my budget to think of."

"If you do a molar cross-section as well, we will donate our body to this department when we die."

"I'll do them for you while you wait," said Mr. Rumplunkett.

Stig turned back to us. "We'll need forty-eight hours to have a look at them. Shall we meet again at my house? We would be honored by your presence." He looked me in the eye and would know if I lied.

"I'd like that very much."

"We, too. Wednesday at midday?"

"I'll be there."

The neanderthal raised his hat, gave a small grunt and moved off.

"Well," said Bowden as soon as Stig was out of earshot, "I hope you like eating beetles and dock leaves."

"You and me both, Bowden—you're coming, too. If he wanted

me and me alone, he would have asked me in private. But I'm sure he'll make something more palatable for us."

I frowned as we walked blinking back out into the sunlight. "Bowden?"

"Yup?"

"Did Stig say anything that seemed unusual to you?"

"Not really. Do you want to hear my plans for infil—"

Bowden stopped talking in midsentence as the world ground to a halt. Time had ceased to exist. I was trapped between one moment and the next. It could only be my father.

"Hello, Sweetpea," he said cheerfully, giving me a hug. "How did the SuperHoop turn out?"

"That's next Saturday."

"Oh!" he said, looking at his watch and frowning. "You won't let me down, will you?"

"How will I not let you down? What's the connection between the SuperHoop and Kaine?"

"I can't tell you. Events *must* unfold naturally or there'll be hell to pay. You'll just have to trust me."

"Did you come all this way just to not tell me anything?"

"Not at all. It's a Trafalgar thing. I've been trying all sorts of plans, but Nelson stubbornly resists surviving. I *think* I've figured it out, but I need your help."

"Will this take long?" I asked. "I've got a lot to do, and I have to get home before my mother finds I've left a gorilla in charge of Friday."

"I think I am right in saying," replied my father with a smile, "that this will take no time at all—if you'd prefer, even less!"

21.

Victory on the *Victory*

Raunchy Admiral in Love Child Shock
Our sources can reveal exclusively in this paper that Admiral Lord Nelson, the nation's darling and much-decorated war hero, is the father of a daughter with Lady Emma Hamilton, wife of Sir William Hamilton. The affair has been going on for some time, apparently with the full knowledge of both Sir William and Lady Nelson, from whom the hero of the Nile is now estranged. Full story, page two; leader, page three; lurid engravings, pages four, seven, and nine; hypocritical moralistic comment, page ten; bawdy cartoon featuring an overweight Lady Hamilton, pages twelve and fourteen. Also in this issue: reports of the French and Spanish defeat at Cape Trafalgar, page thirty-two, column four.

Article in *The Portsmouth Penny Dreadful*, October 28, 1805

There was a succession of flickering lights, and we were on the deck of a fully rigged battleship that heaved in a long swell as the wind gathered in its sails. The deck was scrubbed for action, and a sense of expectancy hung over the vessel. We were sailing abreast with two other men-of-war, and to landward a column of French ships sailed on a course that would bring us into conflict. Men shouted, the ship creaked, the sails heaved and pennants fluttered in the breeze. We were on board Nelson's flagship, the *Victory*.

I looked around. High on the quarterdeck stood a group of men, uniformed officers in navy blue, with cream breeches and cockaded hats. Amongst them was a smaller man with one arm of his uniform tucked neatly into a jacket festooned with medals and decorations. He couldn't have been a better target if he'd tried.

"It would be hard to miss him," I breathed.

"We keep telling him that, but he's pretty pigheaded about it and won't budge—just says they are military orders and he does not fear to show them to the enemy. Would you like a jawbreaker?"

He offered me a small paper bag, which I declined. The vessel healed over again, and we watched in silence as the distance between the two ships steadily closed.

"I never get bored of this. See them?"

I followed his gaze to where three people were huddled the other side of a large coil of rope. One was dressed in the uniform of the ChronoGuard, another was holding a clipboard, and the third had what looked like a TV camera on his shoulder.

"Documentary filmmakers from the twenty-second century," explained my father, hailing the other ChronoGuard operative. "Hello, Malcolm, how's it going?"

"Well, thanks!" replied the agent. "Got into the soup a bit when I lost that cameraman at Pompeii. Wanted an extra close-up or something."

"Hard cheese old man, hard cheese. Golf after work?"

"Righto!" replied Malcolm, returning to his charges.

"It's nice being back at work, actually," confessed my father, turning back to me. "Sure you won't have a jawbreaker?"

"No, thanks."

There was a flash and a burst of smoke from the closest French warship. A second later two cannon shots plopped harmlessly into the water. The balls didn't move as fast as I supposed—I could actually see them in flight.

"Now what?" I asked. "Take out the snipers so they can't shoot Nelson?"

"We'd never get them all. No, we must cheat a little. But not yet. Time is of the essence at moments like this."

So we waited patiently on the main deck while the battle heated up. Within minutes seven or eight warships were firing at the *Victory,* the cannonballs tearing into the sails and rigging. One even cut a man in half on the quarterdeck, and another dispatched a small gang of what I took to be marines, who dispersed rapidly. All through this the diminutive admiral, his captain and a small retinue paced the quarterdeck as the smoke from the guns billowed around us, the heat of the muzzle flashes hot on our faces, the concussion almost deafening. The ship's wheel disintegrated as a shot went through it, and as the battle progressed, we moved about the deck, following the safest path in the light of my father's superior and infinitely precise knowledge of the battle. We moved to one side as a cannonball flew past, moved to another area of the deck as a heavy piece of wood fell from the rigging, then to a third place when some musket balls whizzed past where we had been crouched.

"You know the battle very well!" I shouted above the noise.

"I should do!" he shouted back. "I've been here over sixty times."

The French and British warships drew nearer and nearer until the *Victory* was so close behind the *Bucentaure* that I could see the faces of the staff in the staterooms as we passed. There was a deafening broadside from the guns, and the stern of the ship was torn apart as the British cannonballs ripped through it and down the length of the gun deck. In the lull of the cannon fire as the crews reloaded, I could hear the multilingual cries of injured men. I had seen warfare in the Crimea, but nothing like this. Such close fighting with such devastating weapons reduced men to nothing more than tatters in an instant, the plight of the survivors made worse by the almost certain knowledge that the medical attention they would receive was of the most rudimentary and brutal kind.

I nearly fell over as the *Victory* collided with a French ship just astern of the *Bucentaure,* and as I recovered my balance, I realized just how close the ships were to one another in these sorts of battles. It wasn't a cable's length—they were actually touching. The smoke of the guns made me cough, and the *wheeezip* of musket shot close by made me realize that the danger here was very real. There was another deafening concussion as the *Victory*'s guns spoke, and the French ship seemed to tremble in the water. My father leaned back to allow a large metal splinter to pass between us, then handed me a pair of binoculars.

"Dad?"

He was reaching into his pocket and pulling out, of all things— a slingshot. He loaded it with a lead ball that was rolling along the deck and pulled the elastic back tight, aiming through the swirling smoke at Nelson.

"See the sharpshooter on the most for'ard platform in the French rigging?"

"Yes?"

"As soon as he puts his finger on the trigger, count two and then say 'fire.' "

I stared up at the French rigging, found the sharpshooter and kept a close eye on him. He was less than fifty feet from Nelson. It was the easiest shot in the world. I saw his finger touch the trigger and—

"*Fire!*"

The lead ball flew from the slingshot and caught Nelson painfully on the knee; he collapsed on the deck while the shot that would have killed him buried itself harmlessly in the deck behind.

Captain Hardy ordered his men to take Nelson below, where he would be detained for the rest of the battle. Hardy would face his wrath come the morning and for disobeying orders would not serve with him again. My father saluted Captain Hardy, and Captain Hardy saluted him back. Hardy had marred his career but saved his admiral. It was a good trade.

"Well," said my father, placing the slingshot back in his pocket, "we all know how this turns out—come on!"

He took my hand as we started to accelerate through time. The battle quickly ended, and the ship's deck was scrubbed clean; day rapidly followed night as we sailed swiftly back to England to a riotous welcome of crowds lining the docks. Then the ship moved again, but this time to Chatham, moldered, lost its rigging, gained it and then moved again—but this time to Portsmouth, whose buildings rose around us as we moved into the twentieth century at breakneck speed.

When we decelerated, we were back in the present time but still in the same position on the deck, by now in dry dock and crowded with schoolchildren holding exercise books and in the process of being led around by a guide.

"And it was at this spot," said the guide, pointing to a plaque on the deck, "that Admiral Nelson was hit on the leg by a ricochet that probably saved his life."

"Well, that's that job taken care of," said Dad, standing up and dusting off his hands. He looked at his watch.

"I've got to go. Thanks for helping out, Sweetpea. Remember: Goliath may try to nobble the Swindon Mallets—especially the team captain—to rig the outcome of the SuperHoop, so be on your toes. Tell Emma—I mean, Lady Hamilton—that I'll pick her up at 0830 her time tomorrow—and send my love to your mother."

He smiled, there was another rapid flashing of lights, and I was back in the SpecOps Building, walking down the corridor with Bowden who was just finishing the sentence he had begun when Dad arrived.

"—trating the Montagues?"

"Sorry?"

"I said, 'Do you want to hear my plans for infiltrating the Montagues?'" He wrinkled his nose. "Is that you smelling of cordite?"

"I'm afraid so. Listen, you'll have to excuse me—I think Goliath may try to nobble Roger Kapok, and without him we have even *less* chance of winning the SuperHoop."

He laughed.

"Photocopied bards, Swindon Mallets, eradicated husbands. You like impossible assignments, don't you?"

22.

Roger Kapok

Contrition Rates Not High Enough to Meet Targets

That was the shocking report from Mr. Tork Armada, the spokesman for OFGOD, the religious-institution-licensing authority. "Despite continual and concerted efforts by Goliath to meet the levels of repentance demanded by this authority," said Mr. Armada at a press conference yesterday, "they have not managed to reach even halfway to the minimum divinity requirements of this office." Mr. Armada's report was greeted with surprise by Goliath, who had hoped their application would be swift and unopposed. "We are changing tactics to target those to whom Goliath is anathema," said Mr. Brik Schitt-Hawse, a Goliath spokesman. "We have recently secured forgiveness from someone who had despised us deeply, something that counts twentyfold in OFGOD's own contrition-target goals. More like her will soon follow." Mr. Armada was clearly not impressed and simply said, "Well, we'll see."

Report in Goliath News, *July 17, 1988*

I trotted up the road to the thirty-thousand-seat croquet stadium, deep in thought. Goliath's contrition rate had been published that morning, and thanks to me and the Crimean Mass-Apology Project, switching to a religion was now not only possible but probable. The only plus side was that in all likelihood it wouldn't happen until after the SuperHoop, which raised the possibility—confirmed by my father—that Goliath would try and nobble the Swindon team. And getting to the captain, Roger Kapok, was probably the best way to do it.

I passed the VIP car park, where a row of expensive automobiles was on display, and showed my SpecOps pass to the bored security guard. I entered the stadium and walked up one of the public-access tunnels to the terraces and from there looked down upon the green. From this distance the hoops were almost invisible, but their positions were marked by large white circles painted on the turf. The ten-yard lines crossed the green from side to side, and the "natural hazards"—the Italian Sunken Garden, rhododendron bushes and herbaceous flower beds—stood out from within their positions on the green itself. Each "obstruction" was scrupulously constructed to World Croquet League specifications. The height of the rhododendrons was carefully measured before each game, the herbaceous border stocked with identical shrubs, the sunken garden with its lilies and lead fountain of Minerva was the same on every green the world over, from Dallas to Poona, Nairobi to Reykjavik.

Below me I could see the Swindon Mallets indulging in a tough training session. Roger Kapok was amongst them, barking orders as his team ran backwards and forwards, whirling their mallets dangerously close to one another. Four-ball croquet could be a dangerous sport, and close-quarters stickwork that managed not to involve severe physical injury was considered a skill unique to the Croquet League.

I ran down the steps between the tiered seating, which was nearly my undoing; halfway down I slipped on some carelessly deposited banana skins and if it hadn't have been for some deft footwork I might have plunged headfirst onto the concrete steps. I muttered a curse under my breath, glared at one of the groundsmen and stepped out onto the green.

"So," I heard Kapok say as I drew closer, "we've got the big match on Saturday, and I don't want anyone thinking that we will automatically win just because St. Zvlkx said so. Brother Thomas of York predicted a twenty-point victory for the Battersea Chargers last week, and they were beaten hollow, so stay on your toes. I won't have the team relying on destiny to win this match—we do it on teamwork, application and tactics." There was a grunting and nodding of heads from the assembled team, and Kapok continued. "Swindon has never won a SuperHoop, so I want this to be our first. Biffo, Smudger and Aubrey will lead the offensive as usual, and I don't want anyone tumbling into the sunken garden like at last Tuesday's practice. The hazards are there to lose opponents' balls on a clean and legal roquet, and I don't want them used for any other purpose."

Roger Kapok was a big man with closely cropped hair and a badly broken nose, which he wore with pride. He had taken a croquet ball in the face five years ago, before helmets and body armor were compulsory. At thirty-five he had reached the upper age limit for pro croquet and had been with Swindon for over ten years. He and the rest of the team were local legends and hadn't needed to buy a drink in Swindon's pubs for as long as anyone could remember—but *outside* Swindon they were barely known at all.

"Thursday Next," I said, walking closer and introducing myself, "SpecOps. Can I have a word?"

"Sure. Take five, guys."

I shook Roger's hand, and we walked off towards the herbaceous border, which was aligned on the forty-yard line, just next to the garden roller, which, due to a horrific accident at the Pan-Pacific Cup last year, was now padded.

"I'm a big fan, Miss Next," said Roger, smiling broadly to reveal several missing teeth. "Your work on *Jane Eyre* was astounding. I love Charlotte Brontë's novels. Don't you think the Ginerva Fanshawe character from *Villette* and Blanche Ingram from *Jane Eyre* are sort of similar?"

I had noticed of course, because they actually *were* the same person, but I didn't think Kapok or anyone else out should know about the economics of the BookWorld.

"Really?" I said. "I'd not noticed. I'll come straight to the point, Mr. Kapok. Has anyone tried to dissuade you from playing this Saturday?"

"No. And you probably just heard me telling the team to ignore the Seventh Revealment. We aim to win for our own sakes and that of Swindon. And we *will* win, you have my word on that!"

He smiled that dazzling reconstructed Roger Kapok smile that I had seen so many times on billboards throughout Swindon, advertising everything from toothpaste to floor paint. His confidence was infectious, and suddenly our chances of beating the Reading Whackers seemed to move from "totally impossible" to "deeply improbable."

"And what about you?" I asked, remembering my father's warning that he would be the first one Goliath would try to nobble.

"What about me?"

"Would you stay with the team no matter what?"

"Of course!" he replied. "Wild horses couldn't drag me away from leading the Mallets to victory."

"Promise?"

"On my honor. The code of the Kapoks is at stake. Only death will keep me off the green on Saturday."

"You should be on your guard, Mr. Kapok," I murmured. "Goliath will try anything to make sure Reading wins the SuperHoop."

"I can look after myself."

"I don't doubt it, but you should be on your guard."

I paused as a sudden childish urge came over me. "Would you mind . . . if I had a whack?"

I pointed at his mallet, and he dropped a blue ball to the ground.

"Did you used to play?"

"For my university."

"Roger!" called one of the players from behind us. He excused himself, and I squared up to the ball. I hadn't played for years, but only through a lack of spare time. It was a fast and furious game, quite unlike its ancient predecessor, although the natural hazards such as rhododendrons and other garden architecture had remained from when it was simply a polite garden sport. I rolled the ball with my foot to plant it firmly on the grass. My old croquet coach had been an ex-league player named Alf Widdershaine, who always told me that concentration made the finest croquet players—and Alf should know, as he had been a pro for the Slough Bombers and retired with 7,892 career hoops, a record yet to be beaten. I looked down the green at the forty-yard right-back hoop. From here it was no bigger than my fingertip. Alf had hooped from up to fifty yards away, but my personal best was only twenty. I concentrated as my fingers clasped the leather grip, and then I raised the mallet and followed through with a hard swing. There was a satisfying *crack,* and the ball hurtled off in a smooth arc—straight into the rhododendrons. Blast. If this had been a match, I would have lost the ball until the next third. I turned around to see if anyone had been watching, but fortunately no one had. Instead an altercation seemed to be going on between the team members. I dropped the mallet and hurried up.

"You can't leave!" cried Aubrey Jambe, hoop defense. "What about the SuperHoop?"

"You'll do fine without me," implored Kapok, "really you will!"

He was standing with two men in suits who didn't appear as though they were in the sports business. I showed them my ID.

"Thursday Next, SpecOps. What's going on?"

The two men looked at one another, but it was the tall one who spoke.

"We're scouts for the Gloucester Meteors, and we think Mr. Kapok would like to come play for us."

"Less than a week before a SuperHoop?"

"I'm due for a change, Miss Next," said Kapok, glancing about nervously. "I think that Biffo would lead the team far better than me. Don't you think so, Biffo?"

"What about all that 'wild horses' and 'code of the Kapoks' stuff?" I demanded. "You promised!"

"I need to spend more time with my family," muttered Kapok, shrugging his shoulders and clearly not keen to remain in the stadium one second longer than he had to. "You'll be fine—hasn't St. Zvlkx predicted it?"

"Seers aren't always a hundred percent accurate—you said so yourself!" I retorted. "Who are you two really?"

"Leave us out of it," said the tall suited man. "All we did was make an offer—Mr. Kapok decides if he stays or goes."

Kapok and the two men turned to leave.

"Kapok, for God's sake!" yelled Biffo. "The Whackers will knock the stuffing out of the team if you're not here to lead us!"

But Kapok continued walking; his former teammates looked on in disgust and grumbled and swore for a while before the Mallets' manager, a reedy-looking character with a thin mustache and a pale complexion, walked on the green and asked what was going on.

"Ah!" he said when he heard the news. "I'm very sorry to hear that, but since you are all present, I think it's probably the right time to announce that I'm retiring on grounds of ill health."

"When?"

"Right now," said the manager, and ran off. Goliath was working overtime this morning.

"Well," said Aubrey as soon as he had gone, "what now?"

"Listen," I said, "I can't tell you why, but it is historically imperative that we win this SuperHoop. You *will* win this match because you *have* to. It's that simple. Can you captain?" I asked, turning to a burly croquet player named Biffo. I had seen him do "blind passes" across the rhododendron bushes with uncanny accuracy, and his classic "pegging out" shot from the sixty-yard line during the league game against Southampton was undeniably one of the Top Ten Great Croquet Moments of history. Of course, that was over ten years ago and before a bad tackle had twisted his knee. These days he played defense, guarding the hoops against opposition strikers.

"Not me," he replied with a resigned air.

"Smudger?"

Smudger played attack and had made midair roquets something of a trademark. His celebrated double hoop in the Swindon-

Gloucester playoff of 1978 was still talked about, even if it hadn't won us the match.

"Nope," he answered.

"Anyone?"

"I'll captain, Miss Next."

It was Aubrey Jambe. He had been captain once before until a media-led campaign had had him ousted following allegations about him and a chimp.

"Good."

"But we'll need a new manager," said Aubrey slowly, "and since you seem to be so passionate about it, I think you'd better take it on."

Before I knew what I was saying, I had agreed, which went down pretty well with the players. Morale of a sort had returned. I took Aubrey by the arm, and we walked into the middle of the green for our first strategy meeting.

"Okay," I said, "tell me truthfully, Jambe, what are our chances?"

"Borderline impossible," answered Aubrey candidly. "We had to sell our best player to Glasgow to be able to meet the changes that the World Croquet League insisted we do to the green. Then our top defender, Laura de Rematte, won a once-in-a-lifetime trip to Africa on one of those junk-mail prize-draw things. With Kapok gone, we're down to ten players, no reserve, and lost the best striker. Biffo, Smudger, Snake, George and Johnno are all good players, but the rest are second-raters."

"So what do we need to win?"

"If all the players on the Reading team were to die overnight and be replaced by unfit nine-year-olds, then we might be in with a chance."

"Too difficult and probably illegal. What else?"

Aubrey stared at me glumly. "Five quality players and we might have a chance."

It was a tall order. If they could get to Kapok, they could offer "inducements" to any other player who might want to join us.

"Okay," I said, "leave it to me."

"You have a plan?"

"Of course," I lied, feeling the managerial mantle falling about my shoulders. "Your new players are as good as signed. Besides," I added, with a certain amount of faux conviction, "we've got a revealment to protect."

23.

Granny Next

Reading Whackers Confident to Win SuperHoop

Following the surprise resignation of both Roger Kapok and Gray Ferguson from the Swindon Mallets croquet team this afternoon, the Whackers seem almost certain to win next Sunday's SuperHoop, despite the prophecy by St. Zvlkx. Betting shops were being cautious despite the news and lowered the Mallets' odds to 700–1. Miss Thursday Next, the new manager of the Mallets, derided any talk of failure and told waiting reporters that Swindon would triumph. When pressed how that might be so, she declared the interview over.

Article in the Swindon Evening Blurb, July 18, 1988

You're the manager of the Mallets?" asked Bowden with incredulity. "What happened to Gray Ferguson?"

"Bought out, bribed, frightened—who knows?"

"You like being busy, don't you? Does this mean you won't be able to help me get banned books out of England?"

"Have no fear of that," I reassured him. "I'll find a way."

I wished I could share in my own confidence. I told Bowden I'd see him tomorrow and walked out, only to be waylaid by the overzealous Major Drabb, who told me with great efficiency that he and his squad had searched the Albert Schweitzer Memorial Library from top to bottom but had not unearthed a single Danish book. I congratulated him for his diligence and told him to check in with me again tomorrow. He saluted smartly, presented me with a thirty-two-page written report and was gone.

Gran was in the garden of the Goliath Twilight Homes when I stopped by on the way home. She was dressed in a blue gingham frock and was attending to some flowers with a watering can.

"I just heard the news on the wireless. Congratulations!"

"Thanks," I replied without enthusiasm, slumping myself into a large wicker chair. "I have no idea why I volunteered to run the Mallets—I don't know the first thing about running a croquet team!"

"Perhaps," replied Gran, reaching forward to deadhead a rose, "all that is required is faith and conviction—two areas in which, I might add, I think you excel."

"Faith isn't going to conjure up five world-class croquet players, now, is it?"

"You'd be surprised what faith can do, my dear. You have St. Zvlkx's revealment on your side, after all."

"The future isn't fixed, Gran. We *can* lose—and probably will."

She tut-tutted. "Well! Aren't you the Moaning Minnie today! What does it matter if we do lose? It's only a game, after all!"

I slumped even lower. "If it *was* only a game, I wouldn't be worried. This is how my father sees it: Kaine proclaims himself dictator as soon as President Formby dies next Monday. Once he wields ultimate executive power, he will embark on a course of warfare that results in an Armageddon of life-extinguishing capability Level III. We can't stop the President from dying, but we can, my father insists, avoid the world war by simply winning the SuperHoop."

Gran sat down in a wicker chair next to me.

"And then there's Hamlet," I continued, rubbing my temples. "His play has been subjected to a hostile takeover from *The Merry Wives of Windsor,* and if I don't find a Shakespeare clone pronto, there won't be a *Hamlet* for Hamlet to return to. Goliath tricked me yet again. I don't know what they did, but it felt as though my free will was being sucked out through my eyeballs. They said they'd get Landen back, but, quite frankly, I have my doubts. And I have to illegally smuggle ten truckloads of banned books out of England."

Tirade over, I sighed and was silent. Gran had been thoughtful for a while and, after appearing to come to some sort of a momentous decision, announced, "You know what you should do?"

"What?"

"Take Smudger off defense and make him the midhoop wingman. Jambe should be the striker as usual, but Biffo—"

"Gran! You haven't listened to a word I've said, have you?"

She patted my hand. "Of course I did. Hamlet was having his merry wives smuggled out of England by sucking out his eyeballs, which leads to an Armageddon and the death of the President. Right?"

"Never mind. How are things with you? Found the ten most boring books?"

"Indeed I have," she replied, "but I am loath to finish reading them, as I feel there is one last epiphanic moment to my life that will be revealed just before I die."

"What sort of epiphanic moment?"

"I don't know. Do you want to play Scrabble?"

So Gran and I played Scrabble. I thought I was winning until she got "cazique" on a triple-word score, and it was downhill from there. I lost, 503 points to 319.

24.

Home Again

Denmark Blamed for Dutch Elm Disease

"Dutch elm disease was nothing of the sort," was the shock claim from leading arborealists last week. "For many years we had blamed Dutch elm disease on the Dutch," declared Jeremy Acorn, head spokesman of the Knotty Pine Arboreal Research Facility. "So-called Dutch elm disease, a tree virus that killed off nearly all England's elms in the mid-seventies, was thought to have originated in Holland—hence the name." But new research has cast doubt on this long-held hypothesis. "Using techniques unavailable to us in the seventies, we have uncovered new evidence to suggest that Dutch elm disease originated in Denmark." Mr. Acorn went on to say, "We have no direct evidence to suggest that Denmark is engaged in the design and proliferation of arborealogical weapons, but we have to maintain an open mind. There are many oaks and silver birches in England at present unprotected against attack." Arboreal Warfare—Should We Be Worried? Full report, page 9.

Article in the *Arboreal Times,* July 17, 1988

I hurried home to get there before my mother, as I wasn't sure how she'd react to finding that Friday was being looked after by a gorilla. It was possible that she might not have any problems with this, but I didn't really want to put it to the test.

To my horror Mum had got there before me—and not just her, either. A large crowd of journalists had gathered outside her house, awaiting the return of the Mallets' new manager, and it was only after I had run the gauntlet of a thousand "no comments" that I caught her, just as she was putting her key in the front door.

"Hello, Mother," I said, somewhat breathlessly.

"Hello, daughter."

"Going inside?"

"That's what I usually do when I get home."

"Not thinking of going shopping?" I suggested.

"What are you hiding?"

"Nothing."

"Good."

She pushed the key in the lock and opened the door, giving me a funny look. I ran past her and into the living room, where Melanie was asleep on the sofa, feet up on the coffee table, with Friday snoring happily on her chest. I quickly shut the door.

"He's sleeping!" I hissed to my mother.

"The little lamb! Let's have a look."

"No, better let him be. He's a very light sleeper."

"I can look very quietly."

"Maybe *not* quietly enough."

"I'll look through the serving hatch, then."

"No!"

"Why not?"

"It's jammed. Stuck fast. Meant to tell you this morning, but it slipped my mind. Remember how Anton and I used to climb through it? Got any oil?"

"The serving hatch has never been stuck—"

"How about tea?" I asked brightly, attempting a form of misdirection that I knew my mother would find irresistible. "I want to talk to you about an emotional problem—that *you* might be able to help me with!"

Sadly, she knew me only too well.

"Now I know you're hiding something. Let me in!"

She attempted to push past, but I had a brain wave.

"No, Mother, you'll embarrass them—and yourself."

She stopped. "What do you mean?"

"It's Emma."

"Emma? What about her?"

"Emma . . . and Hamlet."

She looked shocked and covered her mouth with her hand. "In there? On my sofa?"

I nodded.

"Doing . . . you know? Both of them—together?"

"And *very* naked—but they folded the antimacassars first," I added, so as not to shock her too much.

She shook her head sadly. "It's not good, you know, Thursday."

"I know."

"Highly immoral."

"Very."

"Well, let's have that cup of tea, and you can tell me about that emotional problem of yours—is it about Daisy Mutlar?"

"No. I don't have any emotional problems."

"But you said . . . ?"

"Yes, Mother, that was an excuse to stop you barging in on Emma and Hamlet."

"Oh," she said, realization dawning. "Well, let's have a cup of tea anyway."

I breathed a sigh of relief, and Mother walked into the kitchen—to find Hamlet and Emma talking as they did the washing up. Mother stopped dead and stared at them.

"It's disgusting!" she said at last.

"Excuse me?" inquired Hamlet.

"What you're doing in the living room—on *my* sofa."

"What are we doing, Mrs. Next?" asked Emma.

"What are you doing?" flustered my mother, her voice rising. "I'll tell you what you're doing. Well, I won't because it's too— Here, have a look for yourself."

And before I could stop her, she opened the door to the living room to reveal—Friday, alone, asleep on the sofa.

My mother looked confused and stared at me.

"Thursday, just what is going on?"

"I can't even begin to explain it," I replied, wondering where Melanie had gone. It's a big room, but not nearly large enough to hide a gorilla. I leaned in and saw that the French windows were ajar. "Must have been a trick of the light."

"Trick of the light?"

"Yes. May I?"

I closed the door and froze as I noticed Melanie tiptoeing across the lawn, fully visible through the kitchen windows.

"How can it be a trick of the light?"

"I'm . . . not really sure," I stammered. "Have you changed the curtains in here? They look kind of different."

"No. Why didn't you want me to look in the living room?"

"Because . . . because . . . I asked Mrs. Beatty to look after Friday, and I knew you didn't approve, but now she's gone and everything is okay."

"Ah!" said my mother, satisfied at last. I breathed a sigh of relief. I'd got away with it.

"Goodness!" said Hamlet, pointing. "Isn't that a gorilla in the garden?"

All eyes swiveled outside, where Melanie stopped in midstride over the sweet williams. She paused for a moment, gave an embarrassed smile and waved her hand in greeting.

"Where?" said my mother. "All I can see is an unusually hairy woman tiptoeing through my sweet williams."

"That's Mrs. Bradshaw," I murmured, casting an angry glance at Hamlet. "She's been doing some child care for me."

"Well, don't be so rude and let her wander around the garden, Thursday—ask her in!"

Mum put down her shopping and filled the kettle. "Poor Mrs. Bradshaw must think us dreadfully inhospitable. Do you suppose she'd fancy a slice of Battenberg?"

Hamlet and Emma stared at me, and I shrugged. I beckoned Melanie into the house and introduced her to my mother.

"Pleased to meet you," said Melanie. "You have a very lovely grandchild."

"Thank you," Mum replied, as though the effort had been entirely hers. "I do my best."

"I've just come back from Trafalgar," I said, turning to Lady Hamilton. "Dad's restored your husband, and he said he'd pick you up at eight-thirty tomorrow."

"Oh!" she said, with not quite as much enthusiasm as I had hoped. "That's . . . that's wonderful news."

"Yes," added Hamlet more sullenly, "wonderful news."

They looked at one another.

"I'd better go and pack," said Emma.

"Yes," replied Hamlet, "I'll help you."

And they both left the kitchen.

"What's wrong with them?" asked Melanie, helping herself to a slice of the proffered cake and sitting down on one of the chairs, which creaked ominously.

"Lovesick," I replied. And I think they genuinely were.

"So, Mrs. Bradshaw," began my mother, settling into business mode, "I have recently become an agent for some beauty products, many of which are *completely unsuitable* for people who are bald—if you get my meaning."

"Ooooh!" exclaimed Melanie, leaning closer. She *did* have a problem with facial hair—hard not to, being a gorilla—and had never had the benefit of talking to a cosmetics consultant. Mum would probably end up trying to sell her some Tupperware, too.

I went upstairs, where Hamlet and Emma were arguing. She seemed to be saying that her "dear Admiral" needed her more than anything, and Hamlet said that she should come and live with him at Elsinore and "to hell with Ophelia." Emma replied that this really wasn't practical and then Hamlet made an extremely long and intractable speech which I *think* meant that nothing in the real world was simple or slick and he lamented the day he ever left his play, and that he was sure Ophelia had discussed country matters with Horatio when his back was turned. Then Emma got confused and thought he was impugning *her* Horatio, and when he explained that it was *his* friend Horatio she changed her mind and said she would come with him to Elsinore, but then Hamlet thought perhaps this wasn't such a good idea after all and he made

. . . Melanie stopped in midstride over the sweet williams.
She paused for a moment, gave an embarrassed smile and
waved her hand in greeting.

another long speech until even Emma got bored and she crept downstairs for a beer and returned before he'd even noticed she had gone. After a while he just talked himself to a standstill without having made any decision—which was just as well as there wasn't a play for him to return to.

I was just pondering whether finding a cloned Shakespeare was actually going to be possible when I heard a tiny wail. I went back downstairs to find Friday blinking at me from the door to the living room, looking tousled and a little sleepy.

"Sleep well, little man?"

"Sunt in culpa qui officia deserunt mollit," he replied, which I took to mean, "I have slept very well and now require a snack to see me through the next two hours."

I walked back into the kitchen, something niggling away at my mind. Something that Mum had said. Something that Stiggins had said. Or maybe Emma? I made Friday a Nutella sandwich, which he proceeded to smear about his face.

"I think you'll find I have just the color for you," said my mother, picking out a shade of gray varnish that suited Melanie's black fur. "Goodness—what strong nails!"

"I don't dig as much as I used to," replied Melanie with an air of nostalgia. "Trafford doesn't like it. He thinks it makes the neighbors talk."

My heart missed a beat, and I shouted out, quite spontaneously, "AHHHHHHHHH!"

My mother jumped and painted a line of nail varnish up Melanie's hand and upset the bottle onto her polka-dot dress.

"Look what you've made me do!" she scolded. Melanie didn't look very happy either.

"Posh, Murray Posh, Daisy Posh, Daisy Mutlar— Why did you . . . mention Daisy Mutlar a few minutes ago?"

"Well, because I thought you'd be annoyed she was still around."

Daisy Mutlar, it must be understood, was someone whom Landen nearly married during our ten-year enforced separation. But that wasn't important. What *was* important is that without Landen there had never been any Daisy. And if Daisy was around, then Landen must be, too—

I looked down at my hand. On my ring finger was . . . a ring. A *wedding* ring. I pulled it forward to the knuckle to reveal a white ridge. It looked as though it had always been there. And if it had . . .

"Where's Landen now?"

"At his house, I should imagine," said my mother. "Are you staying here for supper?"

"Then . . . he's *not* eradicated?"

She looked confused. "Good Lord, no!"

I narrowed my eyes. "Then I didn't ever go to Eradications Anonymous?"

"Of course not, darling. You know that myself and Mrs. Beatty are the only people who ever attend—and Mrs. Beatty is just there to comfort me. What on earth are you talking about? And come back! Where do you—"

I opened the door and was two paces down the garden path when I remembered I had left Friday behind, so went back to get him, found he had got chocolate all over his front despite the bib, put on his sweatshirt over his T-shirt, found he had glibbed down the front of it, got a clean one, changed his nappy, and—no socks.

"What are you doing, darling?" asked my mother as I rummaged in the laundry basket.

"It's Landen," I babbled excitedly. "He was eradicated, and now he's back, and it's as though he'd never gone, and I want him to meet Friday, but Friday is way way too sticky right now to meet his father."

"Eradicated? Landen? When?" asked my mother incredulously. "Are you sure?"

"Isn't that the point about eradication?" I replied, having found six socks, none of them matching. "No one *ever* knows. It might surprise *you* to know that Eradications Anonymous once had forty or more attendees. When I came, there were fewer than ten. You did a wonderful job, Mother. They'd all be really grateful—if only they could remember."

"Oh!" said my mother in a rare moment of complete clarity. "Then . . . when eradicatees are brought back, it was as if they had never gone. Ergo: the past automatically rewrites itself to take into account the noneradication."

"Well, yes—more or less."

I slipped some odd socks on Friday's feet—he didn't help matters by splaying his toes—then found his shoes, one of which was under the sofa and the other right on top of the bookcase— Melanie *had* been climbing on the furniture after all. I found a brush and tidied his hair, trying desperately to get an annoying crusty bit that smelt suspiciously of baked beans to lie flat. It didn't and I gave up, then washed his face, which he didn't like one bit. I eventually managed to make it out of the door when I saw myself in the mirror and dashed back upstairs. I plonked Friday onto the bed, put on a clean pair of jeans and T-shirt and tried to do something—*anything*—with my short hair.

"What do you think?" I asked Friday, who was sitting on the dressing table staring at me.

"Aliquippa ex consequat."

"I hope that means 'You look adorable, Mum.' "

"Mollit anim est laborum."

I pulled on my jacket, walked out of my room, came back to brush my teeth and fetch Friday's polar bear, then was out the door again, telling Mum that I might not be back tonight. My heart was still racing as I walked outside, ignored the journalists and popped Friday into the passenger seat of the Speedster, put down the hood—might as well arrive in style—and strapped him in. I put the key in the ignition and then—

"Don't drive, Mum."

Friday *spoke*. I was speechless for a second, hand poised on the ignition.

"Friday?" I said. "You're talking . . . ?"

And then my heart grew cold. He was looking at me with the

most serious look I have ever seen on a two-year-old, before or since. And I knew the reason why. Cindy. It was the day of the second assassination attempt. In all the excitement, I had completely forgotten. I slowly and very carefully took my hands off the key and left it where it was, turn signal blinking, oil and generator warning lights burning. I carefully unstrapped Friday, and then, not wanting to open any of the doors, I climbed carefully out of the open top and took him with me. It was a close call.

"Thanks, baby, I owe you—but why did you wait until now to say anything?"

He didn't answer, just put his fingers in his mouth and sucked them innocently.

"Strong silent type, eh? Come on, wonder boy, let's call SO-14."

The police closed the road and the bomb squad arrived twenty minutes later, much to the excitement of the journalists and TV crews. They went live to the networks almost immediately, linking the bomb squad with my new job as the Mallets' manager, filling up any gaps in the story with speculation or, in one case, colorful invention.

The four pounds of explosives had been connected to the starter-motor relay. One more second and Friday and I would have been knocking on the pearly gates. I was jumping up and down with impatience by the time I had given a statement. I didn't tell them this was the second of three assassination attempts, nor did I tell them there would be another attempt at the end of the week. But I wrote it on *my* hand so I wouldn't forget.

"*Windowmaker,*" I told them. "Yes, with an *n*—I don't know why. Well, yes—but sixty-eight if you count Samuel Pring. Reason? Who knows? I was the Thursday Next who changed the ending of *Jane Eyre*. Never read it? Preferred *The Professor*? Never mind. It'll be in my files. No, I'm with SO-27. Victor Analogy. His name's Friday. Two years old. Yes, he's very cute, isn't he? You do? Congratulations. No, I'd love to see the pictures. His aunt? Really? Can I go now?"

After an hour they said I could leave, so I plonked Friday into his buggy and pushed him rapidly up to Landen's place. I arrived a bit puffed and had to stop and regain my breath and my thoughts. The house was back to how I remembered it. The tub of *Tickia orologica* on the porch had vanished, along with the pogo stick. Beyond the more tasteful curtains, I could see movement within. I straightened my shirt, attempted to smooth Friday's hair, walked up the garden path and rang the doorbell. My palms felt hot and sweaty, and I couldn't control a stupid grin that had spread all over my face. I was carrying Friday for greater dramatic effect and moved him to the other hip, as he was a bit of a lump. After what seemed like several hours but was, I suspect, less than ten seconds, the door opened to reveal . . . *Landen,* every bit as tall and handsome and as large as life as I had wished to see him all these past years. He wasn't as I remembered him—he was way better than that. My love, my life, the father of my son—made *human.* I felt the tears start to well up in my eyes and tried to say something, but all that came out was a stupid snorty cough. He stared at me, and I stared at him, and then he stared at me some more, and I stared at *him* some more, and then I thought perhaps he didn't recognize me with the short hair, so I tried to think of something really funny and pithy and clever but couldn't, so I shifted Friday to the other hip, as he was becoming even more of a lump with every passing second, and said, rather stupidly:

"It's Thursday."

"I know who it is," he said unkindly. "You've got a bloody nerve, haven't you?"

And he shut the door in my face.

I was stunned for a moment and had to recover my thoughts before I rang the doorbell again. There was another pause that seemed to last an hour but I suspect was only fractionally longer—thirteen seconds, tops—and the door opened again.

"Well," said Landen, "if it isn't Thursday Next."

"And Friday," I replied, "your son."

"My son," replied Landen, deliberately not looking at him, "right."

"What's the matter?" I asked, tears starting to well up again in my eyes. "I thought you'd be pleased to see me!"

He let out a long breath and rubbed his forehead. "It's difficult—"

"What's difficult? How can anything be difficult?"

"Well," he began, "you disappear from my life two and a half years ago. I haven't seen hide nor hair of you. Not a postcard, not a letter, not a phone call—nothing. And then you just turn up at my doorstep as though nothing has happened and I should be pleased to see you!"

I sort of breathed a sigh of relief. Sort of. Somehow I'd always imagined Landen's being uneradicated as just a simple sort of meeting each other after a long absence. I hadn't ever thought that Landen wouldn't *know* he had been eradicated. When he was gone, no one had known he had ever existed, and now that he was back, no one knew he had gone. Not even him.

"Ever heard of an eradication?" I asked.

He shook his head.

I took a deep breath. "Well, two and a half years ago, a chronupt member of SO-12 had you killed at the age of two in an accident. It was a blackmail attempt by a Goliath Corporation member called Brik Schitt-Hawse."

"I remember him."

"Right. And he wanted me to get his half brother out of 'The Raven,' where Bowden and I had trapped him."

"I remember that, too."

"O-kay. So all of a sudden you didn't exist. Everything we had done together hadn't happened. I tried to get you back by going with my father to your accident in 1947, was thwarted and chose to live inside fiction while little Friday was born and return when I was ready. Which was now. End of story."

We stared at each other for another long moment that might

also have been an hour but was probably only twenty seconds. I moved Friday to the other hip again, and then finally he said, "The trouble is, Thursday, that things are different now. You vanished from my life. Gone. I've had to carry on."

"What do you mean?" I asked, suddenly feeling very uneasy.

"Well, the thing is," he went on slowly, "I didn't think you were coming back. *So I married Daisy Mutlar.*"

25.

Practical Difficulties
Regarding Uneradications

Danish Person Sought

A man of Danish appearance was sought yesterday in connection with an armed robbery at the First Goliath Bank in Banbury. The man, described as being "of Danish appearance," entered the bank at 9:35 and demanded the teller hand over all the money. Five hundred pounds in sterling and a small amount of Danish kroner held in the foreign-currencies department were stolen. Police described this small sum of kroner as of "particular significance" and pledged to wipe out the menace of Danish criminality as soon as possible. The public has been warned to be on the lookout for anyone of Danish appearance, and to let the police know of any Danes acting suspiciously, or failing that, any Danes at all.

Article in *The Toad*, July 15, 1988

You did *what?*"

"Well, you did vanish without a trace—what was I meant to do?"

I couldn't believe it. The little scumbag had sought solace in the arms of a miserable cow who wasn't good enough to carry his bag, let alone be his wife. I stared at him, speechless. I think my mouth might even have dropped open at that point, and I was just wondering whether I should burst into tears, kill him with my bare hands, slam the door, scream, swear or all of the above at the same time when I noticed that Landen was doing that thing he does when he's trying not to laugh.

"You one-legged piece of crap," I said at last, smiling with relief, "you did no such thing!"

"Had you going though, didn't I?" He grinned.

Now I *was* angry.

"What do you want to go and do that stupid joke for? You know I'm armed and unstable!"

"It's no more stupid than your dopey yarn about me being eradicated!"

"It's *not* a dopey yarn."

"It *is*. If I *had* been eradicated, then there wouldn't be any little boy. . . ."

His voice trailed off, and suddenly all our remonstrations vanished as Friday became the center of attention. Landen looked at Friday, and Friday looked at Landen. I looked at both of them in turn. Then, taking his fingers out of his mouth, Friday said:

"𝔅𝔲𝔪."

"What did he say?"

"I'm not sure. Sounds like a word he picked up from St. Zvlkx." Landen pressed Friday's nose. "Beep," said Landen.

"𝔅𝔲𝔟𝔟𝔦𝔢𝔰," said Friday.

"Eradicated, eh?"

"Yes."

"That must be the most preposterous story I have ever heard in my life."

"I have no argument with that."

He paused. "Which I guess makes it too weird not to be true."

We moved towards each other at the same time, and I bumped into his chin with my head. There was a crack as his teeth snapped together, and he yelped in pain—I think he had bitten his tongue. It was as Hamlet said. Nothing is ever slick and simple in the real world. He hated it for that reason—and I loved it.

"What's so funny?" Landen demanded.

"Nothing," I replied. "It's just something Hamlet said."

"Hamlet? Here?"

"No—at Mum's. He was having an affair with Emma Hamilton,

whose boyfriend, Admiral Nelson, seems to be trying to commit suicide."

"By what means?"

"The French navy."

"No . . . *no*," said Landen, shaking his head. "Let's just stick with one ludicrously preposterous story at a time. Listen, I'm an author and *I* can't think up the sort of cr—I mean, *nonsense* you get yourself into."

Friday managed to squeeze off one shoe despite the best attention of my double knots and was now tugging at his sock.

"Handsome fellow, isn't he?" said Landen after a pause.

"He takes after his father."

"Nah—his mother. Is his finger stuck permanently up his nose?"

"Most of the time. It's called 'The Search.' An amusing little pastime that has kept small children amused since the dawn of time. Enough, Friday."

He took his finger out with an almost audible *pop* and handed Landen his polar bear.

"Ullamco laboris nisi ut aliquip."

"What did he say?"

"I don't know," I replied. "It's something called Lorem Ipsum—a sort of quasi Latin that typesetters use to make up blocks of realistic-looking type."

Landen raised an eyebrow. "You're not joking, are you?"

"They use it a lot in the Well of Lost Plots."

"The *what*?"

"It's a place where all fiction is—"

"Enough!" said Landen, clapping his hands together. "We can't have you telling ridiculous stories here on the front step. Come on in and tell me them inside."

I shook my head and stared at him.

"What?"

"My mother said Daisy Mutlar was back in town."

"She has a job here, apparently."

"Really?" I asked suspiciously. "How do you know?"

"She works for my publisher."

"And you haven't been seeing her?"

"Definitely not!"

"Cross your heart, hope to die?"

He held up his hand.

"Scout's honor."

"Okay," I said slowly, "I believe you." I tapped my lips. "I don't come inside until I get one right here."

He smiled and took me in his arms. We kissed very tenderly, and I shivered.

"Consequat est *laborum,*" said Friday, joining in with the hug.

We walked into the house, and I put Friday on the floor. His sharp eyes scanned the house for anything he could pull on top of himself.

"Thursday?"

"Yes?"

"Let's just say for reasons of convenience that I *was* eradicated."

"Yuh?"

"Then everything that happened since the last time we parted outside the SpecOps Building didn't *really* happen?"

I hugged him tightly.

"It did happen, Land. It shouldn't have had, but it did."

"Then the pain I felt was real?"

"Yes. I felt it, too."

"Then I missed you getting bulgy—got any pictures, by the way?"

"I don't think so. But play your cards right and I may show you the stretch marks."

"I can hardly wait." He kissed me again and stared at Friday while an inane grin spread across his face.

"Thursday?"

"What?"

"I have a son!"

I decided to correct him.

"No—*we* have a son!"

"Right. Well," he said, rubbing his hands together. "I suppose you better have some supper. Do you still like fish pie?"

There was a crash as Friday found a vase in the living room to knock over. So I mopped it up while apologizing, and Landen said it was okay but shut the doors of his office anyway. He made us both supper, and I caught up with what he was doing whilst he wasn't eradicated—if that makes any sense at all—and I told him about Mrs. Tiggy-winkle, WordStorms, Melanie and all the rest of it.

"So a grammasite is a parasitic life-form that lives inside books?"

"Pretty much."

"And if you don't find a cloned Shakespeare, then we lose *Hamlet*?"

"Yup."

"And the SuperHoop is inextricably linked to the avoidance of a thermonuclear war?"

"It is. Can I move back in?"

"I kept the sock drawer just how you liked it."

I smiled. "Alphabetically, left to right?"

"No, rainbow. Violet to the right—or was that how Daisy liked— Ah! Just kidding! You have no sense of— Ah! Stop it! Get off! No! Ow!"

But it was too late. I had pinned him to the floor and was attempting to tickle him. Friday sucked his fingers and looked on, disgusted, while Landen managed to get out of my hands, roll around and tickle *me*, which I didn't like at all. After a while we just collapsed into a silly, giggling mess.

"So, Thursday," he said as he helped me off the floor, "are you going to spend the night?"

"No."

"No?"

"No. I'm moving in and staying forever."

We put Friday to bed in the spare room after making up a sort of cot for him. He was quite happy sleeping almost anywhere as long as he had his polar bear with him. He'd stayed over at Melanie's house and once at Mrs. Tiggy-winkle's, which was warm and snug and smelt of moss, sticks and washing powder. He had even slept on *Treasure Island* during a visit there I made last year to sort out the Ben Gunn goat problem—Long John had talked him to sleep, something he was very good at.

"Now, then," said Landen as we went across to our room, "a man's needs are many—"

"Let me guess! You want me to rub your back?"

"Please. Right there in the small where you used to do it so well. I've really missed that."

"Nothing else?"

"No, nothing. Why, did you have something in mind?"

I giggled as he pulled me closer. I breathed in his scent. I could remember pretty well what he looked like and how he sounded, but not his smell. That was something that was instantly recognizable as soon as I pressed my face into the folds of his shirt, and it brought back memories of courting, and picnics, and passion.

"I like your short hair," said Landen.

"Well, I don't," I replied, "and if you ruffle it once more like that, I may feel inclined to poke you in the eye."

We lay back on the bed, and he pulled my sweatshirt very slowly over the top of my head. It caught on my watch, and there was an awkward moment as he tugged gently, trying to keep the romance of the moment. I couldn't help it and started giggling.

"Oh, do please be serious, Thursday!" he said, still pulling at the sweatshirt. I giggled some more, and he joined in, then asked if I had any scissors and finally removed the offending garment. I started to undo the buttons of his shirt, and he nuzzled my neck, something that gave me a pleasant tingly sensation. I tried to flip off my shoes, but they were lace-ups, and when one finally came off, it shot across the room and hit the mirror on the far wall, which fell off and smashed.

"Bollocks!" I said. "Seven years' bad luck."

"That was only a two-year mirror," explained Landen. "You don't get the full seven-year jobs from the pound shop."

I tried to get the other shoe off and slipped, striking Landen's shin—which wasn't a problem, as he had lost a leg in the Crimea and I'd done it several times before. But there wasn't a hollow *bong* sound as usual.

"New leg?"

"Yeah! Do you want to see?"

He removed his trousers to reveal an elegant prosthesis that looked as though it had come from an Italian design studio—all curves, shiny metal and rubber absorption joints. A thing of beauty. A leg amongst legs.

"Wow!"

"Your uncle Mycroft made it for me. Impressed?"

"You bet. Did you keep the old one?"

"In the garden. It has a hibiscus in it."

"What color?"

"Blue."

"Light blue or dark blue?"

"Light."

"Have you redecorated this room?"

"Yes. I got one of those wallpaper books and couldn't make up my mind which one to use, so I just took the samples out of the book and used them instead. Interesting effect, don't you think?"

"I'm not sure that the Regency Flock matches Bonzo the Wonder Hound."

"Perhaps," he conceded, "but it was very economical."

I was nervous as hell, and so was he. We were talking about everything but what we really wanted to talk about.

"Shh!"

"What?"

"Was that Friday?"

"I didn't hear anything."

"A mother's hearing is finely attuned. I can hear a half-second wail across ten shopping aisles."

I got up and went to have a look, but he was fast asleep, of course. The window was open, and a cooling breeze moved the muslin curtains ever so slightly, causing shadows of the streetlights to move across his face. How much I loved him, and how small and vulnerable he was. I relaxed and once more regained control of myself. Apart from a stupid drunken escapade that luckily went nowhere, my romantic involvement with anyone had been the sum total of zip over the past two and a half years. I had been waiting for this moment for ages. And now I was acting like a lovesick sixteen-year-old. I took a deep breath and turned to go back to our bedroom, taking off my T-shirt, trousers, remaining shoe and socks as I walked, half hobbled and hopped down the corridor. I stopped just outside the bedroom door. The light was off, and there was silence. This made things easier. I stepped naked into the bedroom, padded silently across the carpet, slipped into bed and snuggled up to Landen. He was wearing pajamas and smelt different. The light switched on, and there was a startled scream from the man lying next to me. It wasn't Landen but Landen's *father*—and next to him, his wife, Houson. They looked at me, I looked back, stammered "Sorry, wrong bedroom," and ran out of the room, grabbing my clothes from the heap outside the bedroom door. But I wasn't in the wrong room, and the lack of a wedding ring confirmed what I feared. Landen had been returned to me—only to be taken away again. Something had gone wrong. The uneradication hadn't held.

"Don't I recognize you?" said Houson, who came out of the bedroom and stared at me as I retrieved Friday from the spare bedroom, where he was tucked up next to Landen's aunt Ethel.

"No," I replied, "I've just walked into the wrong house. Happens all the time."

I left my shoes and trotted downstairs with Friday tucked under my arm, picked up my jacket from where it was hanging on the back of a different chair in a differently furnished front room and ran into the night, tears streaming down my face.

26.

Breakfast with Mycroft

Feathered Friend Found Tarred

Swindon's mysterious seabird asphalt-smotherer has struck again, this time a stormy petrel found in an alleyway off Commercial Road. The unnamed bird was discovered yesterday covered in a thick glutinous coating that forensic scientists later confirmed as crude oil. This is the seventh such attack in less than a week and the Swindon police are beginning to take notice. "This has been the seventh attack in less than a week," declared a Swindon policeman this morning, "and we are beginning to take notice." The inexplicable seabird tarrer has so far not been seen, but an expert from the NSPB told the police yesterday that the suspect would probably have a displacement of 280,000 tons, be covered in rust and be floundering on a nearby rock. Despite numerous searches by police in the area, a suspect of this description has not yet been found.

Article in the *Swindon Daily Eyestrain,* July 18, 1988

It was the following morning. I was sitting at the kitchen table staring at my ring finger and the complete absence of a wedding band. Mum walked in wrapped in a dressing gown and with her hair in curlers, fed DH-82, let Alan out of the broom cupboard, where we had to keep him these days, and pushed the delinquent dodo outside with a mop. He made an angry plinking noise, then attacked the bootscraper.

"What's wrong, sweetheart?"

"It's Landen."

"Who?"

"My husband. He was reactualized last night, but only for about two hours."

"My poor darling! That must be *very* awkward."

"Awkward. Extremely. I climbed naked into bed with Mr. and Mrs. Parke-Laine."

My mother went ashen and dropped a saucer. "Did they recognize you?"

"I don't think so."

"Thank the GSD for that!" she gasped, greatly relieved. Being embarrassed in public was something she cared to avoid more than anything else, and having a daughter climbing into bed with patrons of the Swindon Toast League was probably the biggest faux pas she could think of.

"Good morning, pet," said Mycroft, shuffling into the kitchen and sitting down at the breakfast table. He was my extraordinarily brilliant inventor uncle and apparently had just returned from the 1988 Mad Scientists' Conference, or MadCon-88, as it was known.

"Uncle," I said, probably with less enthusiasm than I should, "how good to see you again!"

"And you, my dear," he said kindly. "Back for good?"

"I'm not sure," I replied, thinking about Landen. "Aunt Polly well?"

"The very best of health. We've been to MadCon—I was given a Lifetime Achievement Award for something, but for the life of me I can't think what, or why."

It was a typically Mycroft statement. Despite his undoubted brilliance, he never thought he was doing anything particularly clever or useful—he just liked to tinker with ideas. It was his Prose Portal invention that got me inside books in the first place. He had set up home in the Sherlock Holmes canon to escape Goliath but had remained stuck there until I rescued him about a year ago.

"Did Goliath ever bother you again?" I asked. "After you came back, I mean?"

"They tried," he replied softly, "but they didn't get anything from me."

"You wouldn't tell them anything?"

"No. It was better than that. I *couldn't*. You see, I can't remember a single thing about any of the inventions they wanted me to talk about."

"How is that possible?"

"Well," replied Mycroft, taking a sip of tea, "I'm not sure, but, logically speaking, I must have invented a memory-erasure device or something and used it selectively on myself and Polly—what we call the Big Blank. It's the only possible explanation."

"So you can't remember how the Prose Portal actually works?"

"The what?"

"The Prose Portal. A device for entering fiction."

"They were asking me about something like that, now you mention it. It's very intriguing to try to redevelop it, but Polly says I shouldn't. My lab is full of devices, the purpose of which I haven't the foggiest notion about. An Ovinator, for example—it's clearly something to do with eggs—but what?"

"I don't know."

"Well, perhaps it's all for the best. These days I only work for peaceful means. Intellect is worthless if it isn't for the betterment of us all."

"I'll agree with you on that one. What work were you presenting to MadCon-88?"

"Theoretical Nextian Mathematics, mostly," replied Mycroft, warming to the subject dearest to his heart—his work. "I told you all about Nextian Geometry, didn't I?"

I nodded.

"Well, Nextian Number Theory is very closely related to that, and in its simplest form allows me to work *backwards* to discover the original sum from which the product is derived."

"Eh?"

"Well, say you have the numbers 12 and 16. You multiply them together and get 192, yes? Well, in conventional maths, if you were given the number 192, you would not know how that number was arrived at. It might just as easily have been 3 times 64 or 6 times 32 or even 194 minus 2. But you couldn't tell just from *looking* at the number alone, now, could you?"

"I suppose not."

"You suppose wrong," said Mycroft with a smile. "*Nextian* Number Theory works in an inverse fashion from ordinary maths—it allows you to discover the precise *question* from a stated *answer.*"

"And the practical applications of this?"

"Hundreds." He pulled a scrap of paper from his pocket and passed it over. I unfolded it and found a simple equation written upon it: $2^{216,091}$ minus 1, or 2 raised to the power of 216,091, minus 1.

"It looks like a big number."

"It's a *medium*-size number," he corrected.

"And?"

"Well, if I were to give you a short story of ten thousand words, instructed you to give a value for each letter and punctuation mark and then wrote them down, you'd get a number with sixty-five thousand or so digits. All you need to do then is to find a simpler way of expressing it. Using a branch of Nextian Maths that I call FactorZip, we can reduce any size number to a short, notated style."

I looked at the equation in my hand again. "So this is . . . ?"

"A FactorZipped *Sleepy Hollow*. I'm working on reducing all the books ever written to an equation less than fifty digits long. Makes you think, eh? Instead of buying a newspaper every day, you'd simply jot down today's equation and pop it in your Nexpanding Calculator to read it."

"Ingenious!" I breathed.

"It's still early days, but I hope one day to be able to predict a cause simply by looking at the event. And after that, trying to construct unknown questions from known answers."

"Such as?"

"Well, the answer 'Good Lord no, *quite* the reverse.' I've always wanted to know the question to *that.*"

"Right," I replied, still trying to figure out how you'd know by looking at the number nine that it had got there by being three squared or the square root of eighty-one.

"Isn't it just?" he said with a smile, thanking my mother for the bacon and eggs she had just put down in front of him.

Lady Hamilton's departure at eight-thirty was really sad only for Hamlet. He went into a glowering mood and made up a long soliloquy about his heart that was aching fit to break and how cruel a fate life's hand had dealt him. He said that Emma was his one true love and her departure made his life bereft; a life that had little meaning and would be better ended—and so on and so forth until eventually Emma had to interrupt him and thank him but she really *must* go or else she'd be late for something she couldn't specify. So he then screamed abuse at her for five minutes, told her she was a whore and marched out, muttering something about being a chameleon. With him gone we could all get on with our good-byes.

"Good-bye, Thursday," said Emma, holding my hand. "You've always been very kind to me. I hope you get your husband back. Would you permit me to afford you a small observation that I think might be of help?"

"Of course."

"Don't let Smudger dominate the forward hoop positions. He works best in defense, especially if backed up by Biffo—and play offensively if you want to win."

"Thank you," I said slowly, "you're very kind."

I gave her a hug, and my mother did, too—a tad awkwardly, as she had never fully divested herself of the suspicion that Emma had been carrying on with Dad. Then, a moment later, Emma vanished—which must be what it was like when Father arrives and stops the clock for other people.

"Well," said my mother, wiping her hands on her apron, "that's her gone. I'm glad she got her husband back."

"Yes," I agreed somewhat diffidently, and walked off to find

Hamlet. He was outside, sitting on the bench in the rose garden, deep in thought.

"You okay?" I asked, sitting down next to him.

"Tell me truthfully, Miss Next. Do I dither?"

"Well—not really."

"Truthfully now!"

"Perhaps . . . a *bit*."

Hamlet gave a groan and buried his face in his hands.

"Oh what a rogue and peasant slave am I! A slave to this play with contradictions so legion that scholars write volumes attempting to explain me. One moment I love Ophelia, the next I treat her cruelly. I am by turns a petulant adolescent and a mature man, a melancholy loner and a wit telling actors their trade. I cannot decide whether I'm a philosopher or a moping teenager, a poet or a murderer, a procrastinator or a man of action. I might be truly mad or sane *pretending* to be mad or even mad pretending to be sane. By all accounts my father was a war-hungry monster—was Claudius's act of assassination so bad after all? Did I *really* see a ghost of my father or was it Fortinbras in disguise, trying to sow discord within Denmark? How long did I spend in England? How old am I? I've watched sixteen different film adaptations of *Hamlet* and two plays, read three comic books and listened to a wireless adaptation. Everything from Olivier to Gibson to Barrymore to William Shatner in *Conscience of the King*."

"And?"

"Every single one of them is different."

He looked around in quiet desperation for his skull, found it, and then stared at it meditatively for a few moments before continuing. "Do you have any idea the pressure I'm under being the world's leading dramatic enigma?"

"It must be intolerable."

"It is. I'd feel worse if anyone else had figured me out—but they haven't. Do you know how many books there are about me?"

"Hundreds?"

"Thousands. And the slanders they write! The Oedipal thing is by far the most insulting. The good-night kiss with Mum has got longer and longer. That Freud fellow will have a bloody nose if ever I meet him. My play is a complete and utter mess—four acts of talking and one of action. Why does anyone trouble to watch it?"

His shoulders sagged and he appeared to sob quietly to himself. I rested a hand on his shoulder.

"It is your *complexity* and philosophical soul-searching that we pay money to see—you are the quintessential tragic figure, questioning everything, dissecting all life's shames and betrayals. If all we wanted was action, we'd watch nothing but Chuck Norris movies. It is your journey to resolving your demons that makes the play the prevaricating tour de force that it is."

"All four and a half hours of it?"

"Yes," I said, wary of his feelings, "all four and a half hours of it."

He shook his head sadly.

"I wish I could agree with you but I need more answers, Horatio."

"Thursday."

"Yes, her, too. More answers and a new facet to my character. Less talk, more action. So I have secured the services . . . of a conflict-resolution consultant."

This didn't sound good at all.

"Conflict resolution? Are you sure that's wise?"

"It might help me resolve matters with my uncle—and that twit Laertes."

I thought for a moment. An all-action Hamlet might not be such a good idea, but since he had no play to return to, it at least gave me a few days' breathing space. I decided not to intervene for the time being.

"When are you talking to him?"

He shrugged. "Tomorrow. Or perhaps the day after. Conflict-resolution advisers are pretty busy, you know."

I breathed a sigh of relief. True to form, Hamlet was still dithering. But he had brightened up, having come to a decision of sorts, and continued in a more cheery tone. "But that's enough about me. How goes it with you?"

I gave him a brief outline, beginning with Landen's reeradication and ending with the importance of finding five good players to help Swindon win the SuperHoop.

"Hmm," he replied as soon as I had finished. "I've got a plan for you. Want to hear it?"

"As long as it's not about where Biffo should play."

He shook his head, looked around carefully and then lowered his voice. "Pretend to be mad and talk a lot. Then—and this is the important bit—do *nothing at all* until you absolutely have to and then make sure everyone dies."

"Thanks," I said at length, "I'll remember that."

"Plink!" said Alan, who had been padding grumpily around the garden.

"I think that bird is looking for trouble," observed Hamlet.

Alan, who clearly didn't like Hamlet's attitude, decided to attack and made a lunge at Hamlet's shoe. It was a bad move. The Prince of Denmark leapt up, drew his sword and, before I could stop him, made a wild slash in Alan's direction. He was a skilled swordsman and did no more damage than to pluck the feathers off the top of Alan's head. The little dodo, who now had a bald patch, opened his eyes wide and looked around him with a mixture of horror and awe at the small feathers that were floating to the ground.

"Any more from *you,* my fine feathered friend," announced Hamlet, replacing his sword, "and you'll be in the curry!"

Pickwick, who had been watching from a safe corner near the compost heap, boldly strode out and stood defiantly between Alan and Hamlet. I'd never seen her acting brave before, but I suppose Alan was her son, even if he was a hooligan. Alan, either terrified or incensed, stood completely motionless, beak open.

*   *   *

"Telephone for you," my mother called out. I walked into the house and picked up the receiver. It was Aubrey Jambe. He wanted me to speak to my old coach Alf Widdershaine to get him out of retirement and also to know if I had found any new players yet.

"I'm working on it," I said, rummaging through the Yellow Pages under "Sports Agents." "I'll call you back. Don't lose hope, Aubrey."

He harrumphed and rang off. I called Wilson Lonsdale & Partners, England's top sports agents, and was delighted to hear there were any number of world-class croquet players available; sadly, the interest evaporated when I mentioned which team I represented.

"Swindon?" said one of Lonsdale's associates. "I've just remembered—we don't have anyone on our books at all."

"I thought you said you had?"

"It must have been a clerical error. Good day."

The phone went dead. I called several others and received a similar response from all of them. Goliath and Kaine were obviously covering all their bases.

Following that, I called Alf Widdershaine and, after a long chat, managed to persuade him to go down to the stadium and do what he could. I called Jambe back to tell him the good news about Alf, although I thought it prudent to hide the lack of new players from him for the time being.

I thought about Landen's existence problem for a moment and then found the number of Julie Aseizer, the woman at Eradications Anonymous who had got her husband back. I called her and explained the situation.

"Oh, yes!" she said helpfully. "My Ralph flickered on and off like a faulty lightbulb until his uneradication held!"

I thanked her and put the phone down, then checked my finger for a wedding ring. It still wasn't there.

I glanced into the garden and saw Hamlet walking on the lawn, deep in thought—with Alan following him at a safe distance. As I watched, Hamlet turned to him and glared. The small dodo went

231

all sheepish and laid his head on the ground in supplication. Clearly Hamlet wasn't just a fictional Prince of Denmark but also something of an alpha dodo.

I smiled to myself and wandered into the living room where I found Friday building a castle out of bricks with Pickwick helping. Of course, "helping" in this context meant "watching." I glanced at the clock. Time for work. Just when I could do with some relaxing brick-building therapy. Mum agreed to look after Friday and I gave him a kiss good-bye.

"Be good."

"𝔄𝔯𝔰𝔢."

"What did you say?"

"𝔓𝔦𝔨𝔢𝔰𝔱𝔞𝔣𝔣."

"If those are rude 𝔒𝔩𝔡 𝔈𝔫𝔤𝔩𝔦𝔰𝔥 words, St. Zvlkx is in a lot of trouble—and so are you, my little fellow. Mum, sure you're okay?"

"Of course. We'll take him to the zoo."

"Good. No, wait—*we?*"

"Bismarck and I."

"Mum!?"

"What? Is there any reason a more or less widowed woman can't have a bit of male company from time to time?"

"Well," I stammered, feeling unnaturally shocked for some reason. "I suppose no reason at all."

"Good. Be off with you. After we've gone to the zoo we might drop in at the tea rooms. And then the theater."

She had started to go all dreamy so I left, shocked not only that Mother might be even *considering* some sort of a fling with Bismarck, but that Joffy might have been right.

27.

Weird Shit on the M4

George Formby was born George Hoy Booth in Wigan in 1904. He followed his father into the music-hall business, adopted the ukulele as his trademark, and by the time the war broke out, he was a star of variety, pantomime and film. During the first years of the war, he and his wife Beryl toured extensively for ENSA, entertaining the troops as well as making a series of highly successful movies. When invasion of England was inevitable, many influential dignitaries and celebrities were shipped out to Canada. Moving underground with the English resistance and various stalwart regiments of the Local Defence Volunteers, Formby manned the outlawed "Wireless St. George" and broadcast songs, jokes and messages to secret receivers across the country. The Formbys used their numerous contacts in the north to smuggle Allied airmen to neutral Wales and form resistance cells that harried the Nazi invaders. In postwar republican England, he was made nonexecutive President for Life.

John Williams, *The Extraordinary Career of George Formby*

I avoided the news crews who were staking out the SpecOps Building and parked at the rear. Major Drabb was waiting for me as I walked into the entrance lobby. He saluted smartly but I detected a slight reticence about him this morning. I handed him another scrap of paper. "Good morning, Major. Today's assignment is the Museum of the American Novel in Salisbury."

"Very . . . good, Agent Next."

"Problems, Major?"

"Well," he said, biting his lip nervously, "yesterday you had me searching the library of a famous Belgian and today the Museum of the American Novel. Shouldn't we be searching more, well, *Danish* facilities?"

I pulled him aside and lowered my voice. "That's *precisely* what they would be expecting us to do. These Danes are clever people. You wouldn't expect them to hide their books in somewhere as obvious as the Wessex Danish Library, now would you?"

He smiled and tapped his nose.

"Very astute, Agent Next."

Drabb saluted again, clicked his heels and was gone. I smiled to myself and pressed the elevator call button. As long as Drabb didn't report to Flanker I could keep this going all week.

Bowden was not alone. He was talking to the last person I would expect to see in a LiteraTec office: Spike.

"Yo, Thursday," Spike said.

"Yo, Spike."

He wasn't smiling. I feared it might be something to do with Cindy, but I was wrong.

"Our friends in SO-6 tell us there's some seriously weird shit going down on the M4," he announced, "and when someone says 'weird shit' they call—"

"You."

"Bingo. But the weird shit merchant can't do it on his own, so he calls—"

"Me."

"Bingo."

There was another officer with them. He wore a dark suit typical of the upper SpecOps divisions, and he looked at his watch in an unsubtle manner.

"Time is of the essence, Agent Stoker."

"What's the job?" I asked.

"Yes," returned Spike, whose somewhat laid-back attitude to

life-and-death situations took a little getting used to. "What *is* the job?"

The suited agent looked impassively at us both.

"Classified," he announced. "But I am authorized to tell you this: unless we get ****** back in under ******-**** hours, then ***** will seize ultimate executive ***** and you can **** goodbye to any semblance of *******."

"Sounds pretty ****ing serious," said Spike, turning back to me. "Are you in?"

"I'm in."

We were driven without explanation to the roundabout at Junction 16 of the M4 motorway. SO-6 were national security, which made for some interesting conflicts of interest. The same department protecting Formby also protected Kaine. And for the most part the SO-6 agents looking after Formby did so against Kaine's SO-6 operatives who were more than keen to see him gone. SpecOps factions always fought, but rarely from within the same department. Kaine had a lot to answer for.

In any case, I didn't like them and neither did Spike, and whatever it was they wanted it would have to be pretty weird. No one calls Spike until every avenue has been explored. He was the last line of defense before rationality started to crumble.

We pulled onto the verge, where two large black Bentley limousines were waiting for us. Parked next to them were six standard police cars, with the occupants looking bored and waiting for orders. Something pretty big was going down.

"Who's she?" demanded a tall agent with a humorless demeanor as soon as we stepped from the car.

"Thursday Next," I replied, "SO-27."

"Literary Detectives?" he sneered.

"She's good enough for me," said Spike. "If I don't get my own people, you can do your own weird shit."

The SO-6 agent looked at the pair of us in turn. "ID."

I showed him my badge. He took it, looked at it for a moment, then passed it back.

"My name is Colonel Parks," said the agent. "I'm head of Presidential Security. This is Dowding, my second in command."

Spike and I exchanged looks. The President. This really *was* serious.

Dowding, a laconic figure in a dark suit, nodded his greeting as Parks continued:

"Firstly, I must point out to you both that this is a matter of great national importance, and I am asking for your advice only because we are desperate. We find ourselves in a head-of-state-deficit condition by virtue of a happenstance of a high-otherworldliness-possibility situation—and we hoped you might be able to reverse-engineer us out of it."

"Cut the waffle," said Spike. "What's going on?"

Parks's shoulders slumped, and he took off his dark glasses. "We've lost the President."

My heart missed a beat. This was *bad* news. Really bad news. The way I saw it, the President wasn't due to die until next Monday, *after* Kaine and Goliath had been neutered. Formby's going missing or dying early allowed Kaine to gain power and start World War III a week before he was meant to—and that was certainly *not* in the game plan.

Spike thought for a moment and then said, "Bummer."

"Quite."

"Where?"

Parks swept his arm towards the busy traffic speeding past on the motorway. "Somewhere out there."

"How long ago?"

"Twelve hours. Chancellor Kaine has got wind of it, and he's pushing a parliamentary vote to establish himself dictator at six o'clock this evening. That gives us less than eight hours."

Spike nodded thoughtfully. "Show me where you last saw him."

Parks snapped his fingers, and a black Bentley drew up alongside. We climbed in, and the limo joined the M4 in a westerly direction, the police cars dropping in behind to create a rolling road-block. Within a few miles, our lane of the busy thoroughfare was deserted and quiet. As we drove on, Parks explained what had happened. President Formby was being driven from London to Bath along the M4, and somewhere between Junctions 16 and 17—where we now were—he vanished.

The Bentley glided to a halt on the empty asphalt.

"The President's car was the center vehicle in a three-car motorcade," explained Parks as we got out. "Saundby's car was behind, I was with Dowding in front, and Mallory was driving the President. At this precise point, I looked behind and noticed that Mallory was indicating to turn off. I saw them move onto the hard shoulder, and we pulled over immediately."

Spike sniffed the air. "And then what happened?"

"We lost sight of the car. We thought it had gone over the embankment, but when we got there—nothing. Not a bramble out of place. The car just vanished."

We walked to the edge and looked down the slope. The motorway was carried above the surrounding countryside on an earth embankment; there was a steep slope that led down about fifteen feet through ragged vegetation to a fence. Beyond this was a field, a concrete bridge over a drainage ditch and beyond that, about half a mile distant, a row of white houses.

"Nothing *just* vanishes," said Spike at last. "There is always a reason. Usually a simple one, sometimes a weird one—but always a reason. Dowding, what's your story?"

"Pretty much the same. His car started to pull over, then just . . . well, vanished from sight."

"Vanished?"

"More like *melted,* really," said a confused Dowding. Spike rubbed his chin thoughtfully and bent down to pick up a handful of roadside detritus. Small granules of toughened glass, shards of metal and wires from the lining of a car tire. He shivered.

"What is it?" asked Parks.

"I think President Formby's gone . . . deadside."

"Then where's the body? In fact, where's the car?"

"There are three types of dead," said Spike, counting on his fingers. "Dead, undead and semidead. Dead is what we call in the trade 'spiritually bereft'—the life force is extinct. Those are the lucky ones. Undead are the 'spiritually challenged' that I seem to spend most of my time dealing with. Vampires, zombies, bogeys and what have you."

"And the semidead?"

"Spiritually *ambiguous*. Those that are moving on from one state to another or in a spiritual limbo—what you and I generally refer to as *ghosts*."

Parks laughed out loud, and Spike raised an eyebrow, the only outward sign of indignation I had ever seen him make.

"I didn't ask you along so I could listen to some garbage about ghoulies and ghosties and long-legged beasties, Officer Stoker."

"Don't forget 'things that go bump in the night,'" countered Spike. "You won't believe how bad a thing can bump if you don't deal with it quick."

"Whatever. As far as I can see, there is one state of dead and that's 'not living.' Now, do you have anything useful to add to this investigation or not?"

Spike didn't answer. He stared hard at Parks for a moment and then scrambled down the embankment towards a dead and withered tree. It had leafless branches that looked incongruous amongst the summer greenery, and the plastic bags that had caught in its branches moved lazily in the breeze. Parks and I looked at one another, then slid down the bank to join him. We found Spike examining the short grass with great interest.

"If you have a theory, you should tell us," said Parks, leaning against the tree. "I'm getting a bit bored with all this New Age mumbo jumbo."

"We *all* visit the realm of the semidead at some point," continued Spike, picking at the ground with his fingers like a chimp checking a partner for fleas, "but for most of us it is only a millisecond as we pass from one realm to the next. Blink and you'll miss it. But there are *others*. Others who loiter around in the world of the semidead for years. The 'spiritually ambiguous' who don't know they are dead, or, in the case of the President, there by accident."

"And . . . ?" asked Parks, who was becoming less keen on Spike with each second that passed. Spike carried on rummaging in the dirt, so the SO-6 agent shrugged resignedly and started to walk back up the embankment.

"He didn't stop for a leak at Membury or Chievley services, did he?" announced Spike in a loud voice. "I wonder if he even went at Reading."

Parks stopped, and his attitude changed abruptly. He slid clumsily back down the embankment and rejoined us.

"How did you know that?"

Spike looked around at the empty fields. "There is a motorway services here."

"There *was* going to be one," I corrected, "but after Kington St— I mean, Leigh Delamare was built, it wasn't considered necessary."

"It's here all right," replied Spike, "just occluded from our view. This is what happened: The President needs a leak and tells Mallory to pull over at the next services. Mallory is tired, and his mind is open to those things usually hidden from our sight. He sees what he *thinks* are the services and pulls over. For a fraction of a second, the two worlds touch—the presidential Bentley moves across— and then part again. I'm afraid, ladies and gentlemen, that President Formby has accidentally entered a gateway to the underworld—a living person adrift in the abode of the dead."

There was deathly quiet.

"That is the most insanely moronic story I have ever been forced to listen to," announced Parks, not wanting to lose sight of reality for even one second. "If I listened to a gaggle of lunatics for a month, I'd not hear a crazier notion."

"There are more things in heaven and earth, Parks, than are dreamt of in *your* philosophy."

There was a pause as the SO-6 agent weighed up the facts.

"Do you think you can get him back?" he asked at last.

"I fear not. The spirits of the semidead will be flocking to him like moths to a light, trying to feed off his life force and return *themselves* to the land of the living. Such a trip would almost certainly be suicidal."

Parks sighed audibly. "All right. How much?"

"Ten grand. Realm-of-the-dead-certain-to-die work pays extra."

"Each?"

"Since you mention it, why not?"

"Okay then," said Parks with a faint grin, "you'll get your blood money—but only on results."

"Wouldn't have it any other way."

Spike beckoned me to follow him, and we climbed back over the fence, the SO-6 agents staring at us, unsure of whether to be impressed or have us certified or what.

"That really put the wind up them!" hissed Spike as we scrambled to the top of the embankment, across bits of broken bumpers and shards of plastic moldings. "Nothing like a bit of that wooo-wooo crossing-over-into-the-spirit-world stuff to scare the crap out of them!"

"You mean you were making all that up?" I asked, not without a certain degree of nervousness in my voice. I had been on two jobs with Spike before. On the first I was nearly fanged by a vampire, on the second almost eaten by zombies.

"I wish," he replied, "but if we make it look too easy, then they don't cough up the big moola. It'll be a cinch! After all, what do we have to lose?"

"Our lives?"

"Dahhhh! You must loosen up a bit, Thursday. Look upon it as an experience—part of death's rich tapestry. You ready?"

"No."

"Good. Let's hit those semideads where it hurts!"

By the fifth time we had driven the circuit between Junctions 16 and 17 and without so much as a glimpse of anything other than bored motorists and a cow or two, I was beginning to wonder whether Spike really knew what he was doing.

"Spike?"

"Mmm?" he replied, concentrating on the empty field that he thought might contain the gateway to the dead.

"What *exactly* are we looking for?"

"I don't have the foggiest idea, but if the President can make his way in without dying, so can we. Are you sure you won't put Biffo on midhoop attack? He's wasted on defense. You could promote Johnno to striker and use Jambe and Snake to build up defense."

"If I don't find another five players, it might not matter anyway," I replied. "I managed to get Alf Widdershaine out of retirement to coach, though. You used to play county croquet, didn't you?"

"No way, Thursday."

"Oh, go on."

"No."

There was a long pause. I stared out the window at the traffic, and Spike concentrated on driving, every now and then looking expectantly into the fields by the side of the road. I could see this was going to be a long day, so it seemed as good a time as any to broach the subject of Cindy. I wasn't keen to kill her, and Spike, I knew, would be less than happy to see her dead.

"So . . . when did you and Cindy tie the knot?"

"About eighteen months ago. Have you ever visited the realm of the dead?"

"Orpheus told me about the Greek version of it over coffee once—but only the highlights. Does she . . . er . . . have a job?"

"She's a librarian," replied Spike, "part-time. I've been there a couple of times; it's not half as creepy as you'd have thought."

"The library?"

"The abode of the dead. Orpheus would have paid the ferry-man, but, you know, that's just a scam. You can easily do it yourself; those inflatable boats from Wal-Mart work a treat."

I tried to visualize Spike paddling his way to the underworld on a brightly colored inflatable boat but quickly swept it aside.

"So . . . which library does Cindy work in?"

"The one in Highclose. They have day care, so it's very convenient. I want to have another kid, but Cindy's not sure. How's your husband, by the way—still eradicated?"

"Wavering between 'to be' and 'not to be' at the moment."

"So there's hope, then?"

"There's always hope."

"My sentiments entirely. Ever had a near-death experience?"

"Yes," I replied, recalling the time I was shot by a police marksman in an alternative future.

"What was it like?"

"Dark."

"That sounds like a plain old common or garden-variety death experience," replied Spike cheerfully. "I get them all the time. No, we need something a bit better than that. To pass over into the dark realm, we need to just come within spitting distance of the Grim Reaper and hover there, tantalizingly just out of his reach."

"And how are we going to achieve that?"

"Haven't a clue."

He turned off the motorway at Junction 17 and took the entrance ramp back onto the opposite carriageway to do another circuit.

"What did Cindy do before you were married?"

"She was a librarian then, too. She comes from a long line of dedicated Sicilian librarians—her brother is a librarian for the CIA."

"The CIA?"

"Yes, he spends the time traveling the world—cataloging their books, I presume."

It seemed as though Cindy was wanting to tell him what she really did but couldn't pluck up the courage. The truth about Cindy might easily shock him, so I thought I'd better plant a few seeds of doubt. If he could figure it all out himself, it would be a great deal less painful.

"Does it pay well, being a librarian?"

"Certainly does!" exclaimed Spike. "Sometimes she is called away to do freelance contract work—emergency card-file indexing or something—and they pay her in used notes, too—in suitcases. Don't know how they manage it, but they do."

I sighed and gave up.

We drove around twice more. Parks and the rest of the SO-6 spooks had long since got bored and driven off, and I was beginning to get a little tired of this myself.

"How long do we have to do this for?" I asked as we drove onto the Junction 16 roundabout for the seventh time, the sky darkening and small spots of rain appearing on the windshield. Spike turned on the wipers, which squeaked in protest.

"Why, am I keeping you from something?"

"I promised Mum she wouldn't have to look after Friday past five."

"What are grannies for? Anyway, you're working."

"Well, that's not the point, is it?" I answered. "If I annoy her, she may decide not to look after him again."

"She should be grateful for it. My parents love looking after Betty, although Cindy doesn't have any—they were both shot by police marksmen while being librarians."

"Doesn't that strike you as unusual?"

He shrugged. "In my line of work, it's difficult to know what unusual is."

"I know the feeling. Are you sure you don't want to play in the SuperHoop?"

"I'd sooner attempt root-canal work on a werewolf." He pressed his foot hard on the accelerator and weaved around the traffic that was waiting to return to the westbound M4. "I'm bored with all this. Death, drape your sable coat upon us!"

Spike's car shot forward and rapidly gathered speed down the slip road as a deluge of summer rain suddenly dumped onto the motorway, so heavy that even with the wipers on full speed, it was difficult to see. Spike turned on the headlights, and we joined the motorway at breakneck speed, through the spray of a passing juggernaut, before pulling into the fast lane. I glanced at the speedometer. The needle was just touching ninety-five.

"Don't you think you'd better slow down?" I yelled, but Spike just grinned maniacally and overtook a car on the inside.

We were going almost a hundred when Spike pointed out the window and yelled, "Look!"

I gazed out my window to the empty fields; there was nothing but a curtain of heavy rain falling from a leaden sky. As I stared, I suddenly glimpsed a sliver of light as faint as a will-o'-the-wisp. It might have been anything, but to Spike's well-practiced eye, it was just what we'd been looking for—a chink in the dark curtain that separates the living from the dead.

"Here we go!" yelled Spike, and he pulled the wheel hard over. The side of the M4 greeted us in a flash, and I had just the barest glimpse of the embankment, the white branches of the dead tree and rain swirling in the headlights before the wheels thumped hard on the drainage ditch and we left the road. There was a sudden smoothness as we were airborne, and I braced myself for the heavy landing. It didn't happen. A moment later we were driving slowly into a motorway services in the dead of night. The rain had stopped, and the inky black sky had no stars. We had arrived.

28.

Dauntsey Services

Art is long, and Time is fleeting,
And our hearts, though stout and brave,
Still, like muffled drums, are beating
Funeral marches to the grave.
Henry Wadsworth Longfellow,
"A Psalm of Life"

We motored slowly in and parked next to where Formby's Bentley was standing empty with the keys in the ignition.

"Looks like we're still in time. What sort of plan do you suggest?"

"Well, I understand a lyre seems to work quite well—and not looking back has something to do with it."

"Optional, if you ask me. My strategy goes like this: We locate the President and get the hell out. Anyone who tries to stop us gets bashed. What do you think?"

"Wow!" I muttered. "You planned this down to the smallest detail, didn't you?"

"It has the benefit of simplicity."

Spike looked around at the number of people entering the motorway services building. "This gateway isn't just for road accidents," he muttered, opening the boot of the car and taking out a pump-action shotgun. "From the numbers, I reckon this portal must service most of Wessex and a bit of Oxfordshire as well. Years ago there was no need for this sort of place. You just croaked, then went up or down. Simple."

"So what's changed?"

Spike tore open a box of cartridges and pushed them one by one into the shotgun. "The rise of secularism has a hand in it, but mostly it's down to CPR. Death takes a hold—you come here, someone resuscitates you, you leave."

"Right. So what's the President doing here?"

Spike filled his pockets with cartridges and placed the sawn-off shotgun in a long pocket on the inside of his duster. "An accident. He's not meant to be here at all—like us. Are you packing?"

I nodded.

"Then let's see what's going on. And act dead—we don't want to attract any attention."

We strode slowly down the parking lot towards the motorway services. Tow trucks that pulled the empty cars of the departed souls drove past, vanishing into the mist that swathed the exit ramp.

We opened the doors to the services and stepped in, ignoring a Royal Automobile Club man who tried in a desultory manner to sell us membership. The interior was well lit, airy, smelt vaguely of disinfectant and was pretty much identical to every other motorway services I had ever been in. The visitors were the big difference. Their talking was muted and low and their movements languorous, as though the burden of life was pressing heavily on their shoulders. I noticed also that although many people were walking *in* the main entrance, not so many people were walking *out*.

We passed the phones, which were all out of order, and then walked towards the canteen, which smelt of stewed tea and pizza. People sat around in groups, talking softly, reading out-of-date newspapers or sipping coffee. Some of the tables had a number on a stand that designated some unfulfilled food order.

"Are all these people dead?" I asked.

"Nearly. This is only a gateway, remember. Have a look over

there." Spike pulled me to one side and pointed out the bridge that connected us—the Southside services—to the other side, the Northside. I looked out the grimy windows at the pedestrian bridge that stretched in a gentle arc across the carriageways towards nothingness.

"No one comes back, do they?"

" 'The undiscover'd country from whose bourn no traveler returns,' " replied Spike. "It's the last journey we ever make."

The waitress called out a number. "Thirty-two?"

"Here!" said a couple quite near us.

"Thank you, the Northside is ready for you now."

"Northside?" echoed the woman. "I think there's been some sort of mistake. We ordered fish, chips and peas for two."

"You can take the pedestrian footbridge over there. Thank you!"

The couple grumbled and muttered a bit to themselves but got up nonetheless and walked slowly up the steps to the footbridge and began to cross. As I watched, their forms became more and more indistinct until they vanished completely. I shivered and looked by way of comfort towards the living world and the motorway. I could dimly make out the M4 streaming with rush-hour traffic, the headlights shining and sparkling on the rain-soaked asphalt. The living, heading home to meet their loved ones. What in God's name was I doing here?

I was interrupted from my thoughts by Spike, who nudged me in the ribs and pointed. On the far side of the canteen was a frail old man who was sitting by himself at a table. I'd seen President Formby once or twice before, but not for about a decade. According to Dad, he would die of natural causes in six days, and it wouldn't be unkind to say that he looked it. He was painfully thin, and his eyes seemed sunken into his sockets. His teeth, so much a trademark, more protruding than ever. A lifetime's entertaining can be punishing, a half lifetime in politics doubly so. He was hanging on to keep Kaine from power, and by the look of it, he was losing and knew it.

I moved to get up but Spike murmured:

"We might be too late. Look at his table."

There was a "Number 33" sign in front of him. I felt Spike tense and lower his shoulders, as though he had seen someone he recognized but didn't want them to see him.

"Thursday," he whispered, "get the President to my car by whatever means you can before the waitress comes back. I have to take care of something. I'll see you outside."

"What? Hey, Spike!"

But he was away, moving slowly amongst the lost souls milling around the newsagent until he was gone from sight. I took a deep breath, got up and crossed to Formby's table.

"Hullo, young lady!" said the President. "Where are me bodyguards?"

"I've no time to explain, Mr. President, but you need to come with me."

"Oh, well," he said agreeably, "if you say so—but I've just ordered pie and chips. Could eat a horse and probably will, too!" He grinned and laughed weakly.

"We must go," I urged. "I will explain everything, I promise!"

"But I've already paid—"

"Table 33?" said the waitress, who had crept up behind me.

"That's us," replied the President cheerfully.

"There's been a problem with your order. You're going to have to leave for the moment, but we'll keep it hot for you."

I breathed a sigh of relief. He wasn't meant to be dead, and the staff knew it.

"Now can we go?"

"I'm not leaving until I get a refund," he said stubbornly.

"Your life is in danger, Mr. President."

"Been in danger many times, young lady, but I'm not leaving till I get my ten bob back."

"*I* will pay it," I replied. "Now, let's get out of here."

I heaved him to his feet and walked him to the exit. As we pushed open the doors and stumbled out, three disreputable-looking men appeared from the shadows. They were all armed.

"Well, well!" said the first man, who was dressed in a very tired and battered SpecOps uniform. He had stubble, oily hair and was pale to the point of cadaverousness. With one hand he held an aged SpecOps-issue revolver, and the other was planted firmly on the top of his head. "Looks like we've got some live ones here!"

"Drop your gun," said the second.

"You'll live to regret this," I told him, but realized the stupidity of the comment as soon as I had said it.

"Way too late for that!" he replied. "Your gun, if you please."

I complied, and he grabbed Formby and took him back inside while the first man picked up my gun and put it in his pocket.

"Now you," said the first man again, "inside. We've got a little trading to do, and time is fleeting."

I didn't know where Spike was, but he had sensed the danger, that much was certain. I supposed he had a plan, and if I delayed, perhaps it would help.

"What do you want?"

"Nothing much," laughed the man who had his hand pressed firmly on his head, "just . . . your *soul*."

"Looks like a good one, too," said the third man, who was holding some sort of humming meter and was pointing it in my direction. "*Lots* of life in this one. The old man has only six days to run—we won't get much for that."

I didn't like the sound of this, not one little bit.

"Move," said the first man, indicating the doors.

"Where to?"

"Northside."

"Over my dead body."

"That's the poi—"

The third man didn't finish his sentence. His upper torso exploded into a thousand dried fragments that smelt of moldy vegetables. The first man whirled around and fired in the direction of the cafeteria, but I seized the opportunity and ran back into the car park to take cover behind a car. After a few moments, I peered out cautiously. Spike was inside, trading shots with the first man, who was pinned behind the presidential Bentley, still with his hand on his head. I cursed myself for giving up my weapon, but as I stared at the scene—the nighttime, the motorway services—a strong sense of déjà vu welled up inside me. No, it was stronger than that—I *had* been here before—during a leap through time nearly three years ago. I had witnessed the jeopardy I was in and left a gun for myself. I looked around. Behind me a man and a woman—Bowden and myself, in point of fact—were jumping into a Speedster—*my* Speedster. I smiled and dropped to my knees, feeling under the car tire for the weapon. My hands closed around the automatic and I flicked off the safety and moved from the car, firing as I went. The first man saw me and ran for cover amongst the milling crowds, who scattered, terrified. I cautiously entered the now seemingly deserted services and rejoined Spike just inside the doorway of the shop. We had a commanding position of the stairs to the connecting bridge; no one was going Northside without passing us. I dropped the magazine out of my automatic and reloaded.

"The tall guy is Chesney, my ex-partner from SO-17," announced Spike as he reloaded his shotgun. "The necktie covers the decapitation wound I gave him. He has to hold his head to stop it falling off."

"Ah. I wondered why he was doing that. But losing his head—that makes him dead, right?"

"Usually. He must be bribing the gateway guardians or something. It's my guess he's running some sort of soul-reclamation scam."

"Wait, wait," I said, "slow down. Your ex-partner, Chesney—who is dead—is now running a service pulling souls out of the netherworld?"

"Looks like it. Death doesn't care about personalities—he's more interested in meeting quotas. After all, one departed soul is very like another."

"So . . ."

"Right. Chesney swaps the soul of someone deceased for the soul of someone healthy and living."

"I'd say, 'You're shitting me,' but I've got a feeling you're not."

"I wish I was. Nice little earner, I'm sure. It looks like that's where Formby's driver, Mallory, went. Okay, here's the plan: we'll do a hostage swap for the President, and once you're in their custody, I'll get Formby to safety and return for you."

"I've got a better idea," I replied. "How about we swap *you* for Formby and *I* go to get help?"

"I thought you knew all about the underworld from your bosom pal Orpheus?" countered Spike with a trace of annoyance.

"It was highlights over coffee—and anyway, you've done it before. What was that about an inflatable boat from Wal-Mart to paddle yourself to the underworld?"

"Well," said Spike slowly, "that was more of a hypothetical journey, really."

"You haven't a clue what you're doing, do you?"

"No. But for ten grand, I'm willing to take a few risks."

We didn't have time to argue further, as several shots came our way. There was a frightened scream from a customer as one of the bullets reduced a magazine shelf to confetti. Before I knew it, Spike had fired his shotgun into the ceiling, where it destroyed a light fixture in a shower of bright sparks.

"Who shot at us?" asked Spike. "Did you see?"

"I think it's fair to say that it wasn't the light fixture."

"I had to shoot at something. Cover me."

He jumped up and fired. I joined him, fool that I was. I had thought that my being out of my depth was okay because Spike vaguely knew what he was doing. Now that I was certain this was *not* the case, escape seemed a very good option indeed. After firing several shots ineffectively down the corridor, we stopped and dropped back behind the corner.

"Chesney!" shouted Spike. "I want to talk to you!"

"What do you want here?" came a voice. "This is my patch!"

"Let's have a head-to-head," replied Spike, stifling a giggle. "I'm sure we can come to some sort of arrangement!"

There was a pause, and then Chesney's voice rang out again:

"Hold your fire. We're coming out."

Chesney stepped out into the open, just next to the children's helicopter ride and a *Coriolanus* WillSpeak machine. His remaining henchman joined him, holding the President.

"Hello, Spike," said Chesney. He was a tall man, who looked as though he didn't have a drop of liquid blood in his entire body. "I haven't forgiven you for killing me."

"I kill vampires for a living, Dave. You became one—*I had to.*"

"Had to?"

"Sure. You were about to sink your teeth into an eighteen-year-old virgin's neck and turn her into a lifeless husk willing to do your every bidding."

"Everyone should have a hobby."

"Train sets, I tolerate," Spike replied. "Spreading the seed of vampirism, I do not."

He nodded towards Chesney's neck. "Nasty scratch you have there."

"Very funny. What's the deal?"

"Simple. I want President Formby back."

"And in return?"

Spike turned the shotgun towards me. "I give you Thursday. She's got bags of life left in her. Give me your gun, sweetheart."

"What?" I yelled in a well-feigned cry of indignation.

"Do as I say. The President must be protected at all costs—you told me so yourself."

I handed the gun over.

"Good. Now move forward."

I walked slowly up the concourse, the cowering visitors watching us with a sort of morbid fascination. We stopped ten yards apart just near the game-arcade area.

"Send the President to me."

Chesney nodded to his henchman who let him go. Formby, a little confused by now, tottered up to us.

"Now send me Thursday."

"Whoa!" said Spike. "Still using that old SpecOps-issue revolver? Here, have her automatic—she won't need it anymore."

And he tossed my gun towards his ex-partner. Chesney, in an unthinking moment, went to catch the gun—but with the hand he used to keep his head on. Unrestrained, his head wobbled dangerously. He tried to grab it, but this made matters worse, and his head tumbled off to the front, past his flailing hands, where it hit the floor with the sound of a large cabbage. This unseemly situation had distracted Chesney's number two, who was then disarmed by a blast from Spike's shotgun. I didn't see why Spike should have all the fun, so I ran forward and caught Chesney's head on the bounce and expertly booted it through the door of the arcade, where it scored a direct hit into the SlamDunk! basketball game, earning three hundred points. Spike had thumped the now confused and headless Chesney in the stomach and retrieved both my automatics. I grabbed the President, and we legged it for the car park while Chesney's head screamed obscenities from where he was stuck upside down in the SlamDunk! basket.

"Well . . ." Spike smiled as we reached his car. "Chesney really lost his—"

"No," I said, "don't say it. It's too corny."

"Is this some sort of theme park?" asked Formby as we bundled him into Spike's car.

"Of a sort, Mr. President," I replied as we reversed out of the parking lot with a squealing of tires and tore towards the exit ramp. No one tried to stop us, and a couple of seconds later, we were blinking in the daylight—and the rain—of the M4 westbound. The time, I noticed, was 5:03—lots of time to get the President to a phone and oppose Kaine's vote in parliament. I put out my hand to Spike, who shook it happily and returned my gun, which was still covered in the desiccated dust of Chesney's hoodlum friend.

"Did you see the look on his face when his head started to come off?" Spike asked, chuckling. "Man, I live for moments like that!"

29.

The Cat Formerly Known
as Cheshire

Danish King in Tidal Command Fiasco

In another staggering display of Danish stupidity, King Canute of Denmark attempted to use his authority to halt the incoming tide, our reporters have uncovered. It didn't, of course, and the dopey monarch was soaked. Danish authorities were quick to deny the story and rushed with obscene haste to besmirch the excellent and unbiased English press with the following lies: "For a start it wasn't Canute—it was *Cnut*," began the wild and wholly unconvincing tirade from the Danish minister of propaganda. "You English named him Canute to make it sound less like you were ruled by foreigners for two hundred years. And Cnut didn't try to command the sea—it was to demonstrate to his overly flattering courtiers that the tide wouldn't succumb to his will. And it all happened nine hundred years ago—if it happened at all." King Canute himself was unavailable for comment.

Article in The Toad, July 18, 1988

We told the President that yes, he was right—the whole thing was some sort of motorway services theme park. Dowding and Parks were genuinely pleased to get their President back, and Yorrick Kaine canceled the vote in parliament. Instead he led a silent prayer to thank providence for returning Formby to our midst. As for Spike and me, we were each given a postdated check and told we would be sure to receive the Banjulele with Oak Clusters for our steadfast adherence to duty.

Spike and I parted after the tiring day's work and I returned to the SpecOps office where I found a slightly annoyed Major Drabb waiting for me near my car.

"No Danish books found again, Agent Next!" he said through clenched teeth, handing me his report. "More failure and I will have to take the matter to higher authority."

I glared at him, took a step closer and prodded him angrily in the chest. I needed Flanker off my back until the SuperHoop at the very least.

"You blame me for your failings?"

"Well," he said, faltering slightly and taking a nervous step backwards as I moved even closer, "that is to say—"

"Redouble your efforts, Major Drabb, or I will have you removed from your command. Do you understand?"

I shouted the last bit, which I didn't want to do—but I was getting desperate. I didn't want Flanker on my back in addition to everything else that was going on.

"Of course," croaked Drabb. "I take full responsibility for my failure."

"Good," I said, straightening up, "tomorrow you are to search the Australian Writers' Guild in Wooten Bassett."

Drabb dabbed his brow and made another salute.

"As you say, Miss Next."

I tried to drive past the mixed bag of journalists and TV news crews, but they were more than insistent so I stopped to say a few words.

"Miss Next," said a reporter from ToadSports, jostling with the five or six other TV crews trying to get the best angle, "what is your reaction to the news that five of the Mallets team members have withdrawn following death threats?"

This was news to me but I didn't show it.

"We are in the process of signing new players to the team—"

"Miss Manager, with only five players in your team, don't you think it better to just withdraw?"

"We'll be playing, I assure you."

"What is your response to the rumor that the Reading Whackers have signed ace player Bonecrusher McSneed to play forward hoop?"

"The same as always—the SuperHoop will be a momentous victory for Swindon."

"And what about the news that you have been declared 'unfit to manage' given your highly controversial move of putting Biffo on defense?"

"Positions on the field are yet to be decided and are up to Mr. Jambe. Now if you'll excuse me . . ."

I started the engine again and drove away from the SpecOps Building, the news crews still shouting questions after me. I was big news again, and I didn't like it.

I arrived home just in time to rescue Mother from having to make more tea for Friday.

"Eight fish fingers!" she muttered, shocked by his greed. "Eight!"

"That's nothing," I replied, putting my paycheck into a novelty teapot and tickling Friday on the ear. "You wait until you see how many beans he can put away."

"The phone's been ringing all day. Aubrey somebody-or-other about death threats or something?"

"I'll call him. How was the zoo?"

"Ooh!" she cooed, touched her hair and tripped out of the kitchen. I waited until she was gone then knelt down close to Friday.

"Did Bismarck and Gran . . . kiss?"

"Tempor incididunt ut labore," he replied enigmatically, "et dolore magna aliqua."

"I hope that's a 'definitely not,' darling," I murmured, filling up his beaker. As I did so, I caught my wedding ring on the lip of the cup, and I stared at it in a resigned manner. Landen was back again. I clasped it tightly and picked up the phone.

"Hello?" came Landen's voice.

"It's Thursday."

"Thursday!" he said with a mixture of relief and alarm. "What happened to you? I was waiting for you in the bedroom, and then I heard the front door close! Did I do something wrong?"

"No, Land, nothing. You were eradicated again."

"Am I still?"

"Of course not."

There was a long pause. Too long, in fact. I looked at my hand. My wedding ring had gone again. I sighed, replaced the receiver and went back to Friday, heavy in heart. I called Aubrey as I was giving Friday his bath and tried to reassure him about the missing players. I told him to keep training and I'd deliver. I wasn't sure how, but I didn't tell him that. I just said it was "in hand."

"I have to go," I told him at last. "I've got to wash Friday's hair and I can't do it with one hand."

That evening, as I was reading *Pinocchio* to Friday, a large tabby cat appeared on the wardrobe in my bedroom. He didn't appear instantly, either—he faded in from the tip of his tail all the way up to his very large grin. When he first started working in *Alice in Wonderland,* he was known as the Cheshire Cat, but the authorities moved the Cheshire county boundaries, and he thus became the Unitary Authority of Warrington Cat, but that was a bit of a mouthful, so he was known more affectionately as the Cat formerly known as Cheshire or, more simply, the Cat. His real name was Archibald, but that was reserved for his mother when she was cross with him.

He worked very closely with us at Jurisfiction, where he was in charge of the Great Library, a cavernous and almost infinite depository of every book ever written. But to call the Cat a librarian would be an injustice. He was an überlibrarian—he knew about all the books in his charge. When they were being read, by whom—everything. Everything, that is, except where Yorrick Kaine was a featured part. Friday giggled and pointed as the Cat stopped appearing and stared at us with a grin etched on his features, eagerly listening to the story.

"Hello!" he said as soon as I had finished, kissed Friday and put out the bedside light. "I've got some information for you."

"About?"

"Yorrick Kaine."

I took the Cat downstairs, where he sat on the microwave as I made some tea.

"So what have you found out?" I asked.

"I've found out that an alligator isn't someone who makes allegations—it's a large reptile a bit like a crocodile."

"I mean about Kaine."

"Ah. Well, I've had a careful trawl, and he doesn't appear anywhere in the character manifests, either in the Great Library or the Well of Lost Plots. Wherever he's from, it isn't from published fiction, poetry, jokes, nonfiction or knitting patterns."

"I didn't think you'd come out here to tell me you've failed, Chesh," I said. "What's the good news?"

The Cat's eyes flashed, and he twitched his whiskers. "Vanity publishing!" he announced with a flourish.

It was an inspired guess. I'd never even considered he might be from there. The realm of the self-published book was a bizarre mix of quaint local histories, collections of poetry, magnum opuses of the truly talentless—and the occasional gem. The thing was, if such books became officially published, they were welcomed into the Great Library with open arms—and that hadn't happened.

"You're sure?"

The Cat handed me an index card. "I knew this was important to you, so I called in a few favors."

I read the card aloud. " 'At Long Last Lust. 1931. Limited-edition run of one hundred. Author: Daphne Farquitt.' "

I looked at the Cat. Daphne Farquitt. Writer of nearly five hundred romantic novels and darling of the romance genre.

"Before she got famous writing truly awful books, she used to write truly awful books that were self-published," explained the Cat. "In *At Long Last Lust,* Yorrick plays a local politician eager for advancement. He isn't a major part either. He's only mentioned twice and doesn't even warrant a description."

"Can you get me into the vanity-publishing library?" I asked.

"There is no vanity library," he said with a shrug. "We have figures and short reviews gleaned from vanity publishers' manifests and *Earnest Scribbler Monthly,* but little else. Still, we need only to find one copy and he's ours."

He grinned again, but I didn't join him.

"Not that easy, Cat. Take a look at this."

I showed him the latest issue of *The Toad.* The Cat carefully put on his spectacles and read, " 'Danish book-burning frenzy reaches new heights, with Copenhagen-born Farquitt's novels due to be consigned to flames.' "

"I don't get it," said the Cat, placing a longing paw on a Moggi-licious Cat Food advert. "What's he up to, burning all her books?"

"Because," I said, "he obviously can't find all the original copies of *At Long Last Lust* and in desperation has whipped up anti-Danish feeling as a cover. With luck his book-burning idiots will do the job for him. I'm a fool not to have realized. After all, where would you hide a stick?"

There was a long pause.

"I give up," said the Cat. "Where would you hide a stick?"

"In a forest."

I stared out the window thoughtfully. *At Long Last Lust.* I didn't know how many of the hundred copies still remained, but with Farquitt's books still being consigned to the furnaces, I figured there had to be at least one. An unpublished Farquitt novel the key to destroying Kaine. I couldn't make this stuff up.

"Why would you hide a stick in a forest?" asked the Cat, who had been pondering over this question for some moments in silence.

"It's an analogy," I explained. "Kaine needs to get rid of every copy of *At Long Last Lust* but doesn't want us to get suspicious, so he targets the Danes—the *forest,* rather than Farquitt—the *stick.* Get it?"

"Got it."

"Good."

"Well, I'd better be off then," announced the Cat and he vanished.

I was not much surprised at this for the Cat usually left in this manner. I poured the tea, added some milk, and then put some mugs on a tray. I was just pondering where I might find a copy of *At Long Last Lust* and, more important, calling Julie again to ask her how long her husband flicked on and off "like a lightbulb," when the Cat reappeared balanced precariously on the Kenwood mixer.

"By the by," he said, "the Gryphon tells me that the sentencing for your Fiction Infraction is due in two weeks' time. Do you want to be present?"

This related to the time I changed the ending of *Jane Eyre.* They found me guilty at my trial but the law's delay in the BookWorld just dragged things on and on.

"No," I said after a pause. "No, tell him to come and find me and let me know what my sentence will be."

"I'll tell him. Well, toodle-oo," said the Cat, and vanished, this time for good.

I pushed open the door of Mycroft's workshop with my toe, held it open for Pickwick to follow me in, then closed it before Alan could join us and placed the tray on a worktop. Mycroft and Polly were staring intently at a small and oddly shaped geometric solid made of brass.

"Thank you, pet," said Polly. "How are things with you?"

"Fair to not very good at all, Auntie."

Polly was Mycroft's wife of some forty-two years and, although seemingly in the background, was actually almost as brilliant as her husband. She was a bouncy seventy and managed Mycroft's often irascible and forgetful nature with a patience that I found inspiring. "The trick," she told me once, "is to regard him like a five-year-old with an IQ of two hundred sixty." She picked up her tea and blew on it.

"Still thinking about whether to put Smudger on defense?"

"I was thinking of Biffo, actually."

"Smudger and Biffo would both be wasted on defense," muttered Mycroft, making a fine adjustment on one face of the brass polyhedron with a file. "You ought to put Snake on defense. He's untried, I admit, but he plays well and has youth on his side."

"Well, I'm really leaving team strategy to Aubrey."

"I hope he's up to it. What do you make of this?"

He handed me the solid, and I turned the grapefruit-size object over in my hands. Some of the faces were odd-sided and some even-sided—and some, strangely enough, appeared to be *both*, and my eyes had trouble making sense of it.

"Very . . . pretty," I replied. "What does it do?"

"Do?" Mycroft smiled. "Put it on the worktop, and you'll see what it do!"

I placed it on the surface, but the oddly shaped solid, unstable on the face I had placed it upon, tipped onto another. Then, after a moment's pause, it wobbled again and fell onto a third. It carried on in this jerky fashion across the worktop until it fell against a screwdriver, where it stopped.

"I call it a Nextahedron," announced Mycroft, picking up the solid and placing it on the floor, where it continued its random perambulations, watched by Pickwick, who thought it might be chasing her and ran away to hide. "Most irregular solids are only unstable on one or two faces. The Nextahedron is unstable on *all* its faces—it will continue to fall and tip until a solid object impedes its progress."

"Fascinating!" I murmured, always surprised by the ingenuity of Mycroft's inventions. "But what's the point?"

"Well," explained Mycroft, warming to the subject, "you know those inertial-generator things that self-wind a wristwatch?"

"Yes?"

"If we have a larger one of those inside a Nextahedron weighing six hundred tons, I calculate we could generate as much as a hundred watts of power."

"But . . . but that's only enough for a lightbulb!"

"Considering the input is nil, I think it's a remarkable achievement," replied Mycroft somewhat sniffily. "To generate significant quantities of power, we'd have to carve something of considerable mass—Mars, say—into a huge Nextahedron with a flat plate falling around the exterior, held firm by gravity. The power could be transmitted to Earth using Tesla beams and . . ."

His voice trailed off as he started to sketch ideas and equations in a small notebook. I watched the Nextahedron fall and rock and jiggle across the floor until it fell against a roll of wire.

"On a more serious note," confided Polly, putting down her tea, "you could help us identify some of the devices in the workshop. Since both Mycroft and I have taken the Big Blank, you might be able to help."

"I'll try," I said, looking around the room at the bizarre devices. "That one over there guesses how many pips there are in an unopened orange, the one with the horn is an Olfactrograph for measuring smells, and the small box thing there can change gold into lead."

"What's the point in that?"

"I'm not entirely sure."

Polly made notes against her inventory, and I spent the next ten minutes trying to name as many of Mycroft's inventions as I could. It wasn't easy. He didn't tell me everything.

"I'm not sure what this one is either," I said, pointing at a small machine about the size of a telephone directory lying on a workbench.

"Oddly enough," replied Polly, "this is one we do have a name for. It's an Ovinator."

"How do you know if you can't remember?"

"Because," said Mycroft, who had finished his notes and now

rejoined us, "it has 'Ovinator' engraved on the case just there. We think it's either a device for making eggs without the need of a chicken or for making chickens without the need of an egg. Or something else entirely. Here, I'll switch it on."

Mycroft flicked a switch and a small red light came on.

"Is that it?"

"Yes," replied Polly, staring at the small and very unexciting metallic box thoughtfully.

"No sign of any eggs or chickens," I observed.

"None at all," sighed Mycroft. "It might just be a machine for making a red light come on. Drat my lost memory! Which reminds me: any idea which device actually *is* the memory eraser?"

We looked around the workshop at the odd and mostly anonymous contraptions. Any one of them might have been used to erase memories, but then any one of them might have been a device for coring apples, too.

We stood in silence for a moment.

"I still think you ought to have Smudger on defense," said Polly, who was probably the biggest croquet fan in the house.

"You're probably right," I said, suddenly feeling that it would be easier just to go with the flow. "Uncle?"

"Polly knows best," he replied. "I'm a bit tired. Who wants to watch *Name That Fruit!* on the telly?"

We all agreed that it would be a relaxing way to end the day, and I found myself watching the nauseating quiz show for the first time in my life. Halfway through, I realized just how bad it was and went to bed, temples aching.

30.

Neanderthal Nation

Neanderthals "of Use" at Politicians' Training College
Neanderthals, the reengineered property of the Goliath Corporation, found unexpected employment at the Chipping Sodbury College for Politicians yesterday when four selected individuals were inducted as part of the Public Office Veracity Economics class. Neanderthals, whose high facial-acuity skills make them predisposed to noticing an untruth, are used by students to hone their lying skills—something that trainee politicians might find useful once in a position of office. "Man, those thals can spot everything!" declared Mr. Richard Dixon, a first-year student. "Nothing gets past them—even a mild embellishment or a tactical omission!" The lecturers at the college declared themselves wholly pleased with the neanderthals and privately admitted that "if the proletariat were even half as good at spotting lies, we'd really be in the soup!"

Article in The Toad (political section), July 4, 1988

The hunt for *At Long Last Lust* had been going on all morning, but with little success. Kaine had almost two years' head start on us. Of the one hundred copies in the print run, sixty-two of them had changed hands within the past eighteen months. Initially they had been sold for modest sums of £1,000 or so, but there is nothing like a mystery buyer with deep pockets to push up the price, and the last copy sold was for £720,000 at Agatha's Auction House—an unprecedented sum, even for a prewar Farquitt.

The likelihood of finding a copy of *Lust* was looking increasingly desperate. I called Farquitt's agent, who said that the author's entire library had been confiscated and the septuagenarian author questioned at length about pro-Danish political activism before being released. Even a visit to the Library of Farquitt in Didcot didn't bear any fruit—both their original manuscript of *At Long Last Lust* and a signed copy had been seized by "government agents" nearly eighteen months before. The librarian met us in the sculpted marble hall and after telling us not to talk so loudly, reported that representative copies of all Farquitt's works were packed and ready for removal "as soon as we wanted." Bowden responded that we'd be heading towards the border just as soon as we finalized the details. He didn't look at me as he said it, but I knew what he was thinking—I still needed to figure out a way to get us across the border.

We drove back to the LiteraTec office in silence, and as soon as we got in, I called Landen. My wedding ring, which had been appearing and disappearing all morning, had been solid for a good twenty minutes.

"Yo, Thursday!" he said enthusiastically. "What happened to you yesterday? We were talking, and you just went quiet."

"Something came up."

"Why don't you come around for lunch? I've got fish fingers, beans and peas—with mashed banana and cream for pudding."

"Have you been discussing the menu with Friday?"

"Whatever made you think that?"

"I'd love to, Land. But you're still a bit existentially unstable at the moment, so I'd only end up embarrassing myself in front of your parents again—and I've got to go and meet someone to talk about Shakespeares."

"Anyone I know?"

"Bartholomew Stiggins."

"The neanderthal?"

"Yes."

"Hope you like beetles. Call me when I exist next. I lo—"

The phone went dead. My wedding ring had gone again, too.

I listened to the dial tone for a moment, tapping the receiver thoughtfully on my forehead. "I love you too, Land," I said softly.

"Your Welsh contact?" asked Bowden, walking up with a fax from the Karen Blixen Appreciation Society.

"Not exactly."

"New players for the SuperHoop, then?"

"If only. Goliath and Kaine have frightened every player in the country except Penelope Hrah, who'll play for food and doesn't care what anyone says, thinks or does."

"Didn't she have a leg torn off during the Newport Strikers v. Dartmoor Wanderers semifinal a few years back?"

"I'm in no position to be choosy, Bowd. If I put her on back-hoop defense, she can just growl at anyone who comes close. Ready for lunch?"

The neanderthal population of Swindon numbered about three hundred, and they all lived in a small village to the west known as the Nation. Because of their tool-using prowess, they were just given six acres of land, water and sewage points and told to get on with it, as if they needed to be asked, which they didn't.

The neanderthals were not humans nor descendants of ours, but cousins. They had evolved at the same time as us, then been forced into extinction when they failed to compete successfully with the more aggressive human. Brought back to life by Goliath BioEngineering in the late thirties and early forties, they were as much a part of modern life as dodos or mammoths. And since they had been sequenced by Goliath, each individual was actually owned by the corporation. A less-than-generous "buyback" scheme to enable one to purchase oneself hadn't been well received.

We parked a little way down from the Nation and got out of the car.

"Can't we just park inside?" asked Bowden.

"They don't like cars," I explained. "They don't see the point in traveling any distance. According to neanderthal logic, anywhere that can't be reached in a day's walk isn't worth visiting. Our nean-

derthal gardener used to walk the four miles to our hous
Tuesday and then walk back again, resisting all offers o
Walking was, he maintained, 'the only decent way to travel—
drive, you miss the conversations in the hedgerows.' "

"I can see his point," replied Bowden, "but when I need
somewhere in a hurry—"

"That's the difference, Bowd. You've got to get off the h
way of thinking. To neanderthals nothing is so urgent that i
be done another time—or not done at all. By the way, did y
member not to wash this morning?"

He nodded. Because scent is so important to neanderthal
munications, the soapy cleanliness of humans reads more like s
form of suspicious subterfuge. Speak to a neanderthal while w
ing scent and he'll instantly think you have something to hide.

We walked into the grassy entrance of the Nation and enco
tered a lone neanderthal sitting on a chair in the middle of
path. He was reading the large-print *Neanderthal News*. He fol
up the paper and sniffed the air delicately before staring at us fo
moment or two and then asking, "Whom do you wish to visit?"

"Next and Cable, lunch with Mr. Stiggins."

The neanderthal stared at us for moment or two, then point
us towards a house on the other side of a grassed open area th
surrounded a totem representing I-don't-know-what. There wer
five or six neanderthals playing a game of street croquet on th
grass area, and I watched them intently for a while. They weren'
playing in teams, just passing the ball around and hooping where
possible. They were excellent, too. I watched one player hoop from
at least forty yards away off a roquet. It was a pity neanderthals
were aggressively noncompetitive—I could have done with them
on the team.

"Notice anything?" I asked as we walked across the grassed area,
the croquet players moving past us in a blur of well-coordinated
limbs.

"No children?"

"The youngest neanderthal is fifty-two," I explained. "The

males are infertile. It's probably their biggest source of disagreement with their owners."

"I'd be pissed off, too."

We found Stiggins's house, and I opened the door and walked straight in. I knew a bit about neanderthal customs, and you would never go into a neanderthal home unless you were expected—in which case you treated it as your own and walked in unannounced. The house was built entirely of scrap wood or recycled rubbish and was circular in shape, with a central hearth. It was comfortable and warm and cozy, but not the sort of basic cave I think Bowden expected. There was a TV and proper sofas, chairs and even a hi-fi. Standing next to the fire was Stiggins, and next to him was a slightly smaller neanderthal.

"Welcome!" said Stig. "This is Felicity—we are a partnership."

His wife walked silently up to us and hugged us both in turn, taking an opportunity to smell us, first in the armpit and then in the hair. I saw Bowden flinch, and Stig gave a small, grunty cough that was a neanderthal laugh.

"Mr. Cable, you are uncomfortable," observed Stig.

Bowden shrugged. He *was* uncomfortable, and he knew neanderthals well enough to know that you can't lie to them.

"I am," he replied. "I've never been in a neanderthal house before."

"Is it any different to yours?"

"Very," said Bowden, looking up at the construction of the roof beams, which had been made by gluing oddments of wood together and then planing them into shape.

"Not a single wood screw or bolt, Mr. Cable. Have you heard the noise wood makes when you turn a screw into it? Most uncharitable."

"Is there anything you don't make yourself?"

"Not really. You are insulting the raw material if you do not extract all possible use from it. Any cash we earn has to go to our buyback scheme. We may be able to afford our ownership papers by the time we are due to leave."

"Then what, if you'll excuse me, is the point?"

"To die free, Mr. Cable. Drink?"

Mrs. Stiggins appeared with four glasses that had been cut from the bottom of wine bottles and offered them to us. Stig drank his straight down, and I tried to do the same and nearly choked—it was not unlike drinking petrol. Bowden *did* choke, and clasped his throat as if it were on fire. Mr. and Mrs. Stiggins stared at us curiously, then collapsed into an odd series of grunty coughs.

"I'm not sure I see the joke," said Bowden, eyes streaming.

"It is the neanderthal custom to humiliate guests," announced Stig, taking our glasses from us. "Yours was potato gin—ours was merely water. Life is good. Have a seat."

We sat down on the sofa, and Stig poked at the embers in the fire. There was a rabbit on a stick, and I gave a deep sigh of relief it wasn't going to be beetles for lunch.

"Those croquet players outside," I began, "do you suppose anything could induce them to play for the Swindon Mallets?"

"No. Only humans define themselves by conflict with other humans. Winning or losing has no meaning to us. Things just are as they are meant to be."

I thought about offering some money. After all, a month's salary for an averagely rated player would easily cover a thousand buyback schemes. But neanderthals are funny about money—especially money that they don't think they've earned. I kept quiet.

"Have you had any more thoughts about the cloned Shakespeares?" asked Bowden.

Stig thought for a moment, twitched his nose, turned the rabbit and then went to a large rolltop bureau and returned with a manila folder—the genome report he had got from Mr. Rumplunkett.

"Definitely clones," he said, "and whoever built them covered their tracks—the serial numbers are scrubbed from the cells, and the manufacturer's information is missing from the DNA. On a molecular level, they might have been built anywhere."

"Stig," I said, thinking of *Hamlet,* "I can't stress how important it is that I find a WillClone—and soon."

"We haven't finished, Miss Next. See this?"

He handed me a spectroscopic evaluation of Mr. Shaxtper's teeth, and I looked at the zigzag graph uncomprehendingly.

"We do this test to monitor long-term health patterns. By taking a cross-section of Shaxtper's teeth, we can trace the original manufacturing area solely from the hardness of the water."

"For what purpose?"

"We recognize this pattern," he said, jabbing a stubby finger at the chart. "In particular the high concentration of calcium just here. We can usually trace a chimera's original manufacturing area solely from the hardness of the water."

"I see," said Bowden. "So where do we find this sort of water?"

"Simple: Birmingham."

Bowden clapped his hands happily. "You mean to tell me there's a secret bioengineering lab in the Birmingham area? We'll find it in a jiffy!"

"The lab isn't in Birmingham," said Stig.

"But you said . . . ?"

I knew exactly what he was driving at.

"Birmingham imports its water," I said in a low voice, "from the Elan Valley—in the *Socialist Republic of Wales*."

The job had just got that much worse. Goliath's biggest biotech facility used to be on the banks of the Craig Goch Reservoir, deep in the Elan, before they moved to the Presellis. They had built across the border due to the lax bioengineering regulations; they shut down as soon as the Welsh parliament caught up. The lab in the Presellis did only legitimate work.

"Impossible!" scoffed Bowden. "They closed down decades ago!"

"And yet," retorted Stig slowly, "your Shakespeares were built there. Mr. Cable, you are not a natural friend to the neanderthal, and you do not have the strength of spirit of Miss Next, yet you *are* impassioned."

Bowden was unconvinced by Stig's précis. "How can you know me that well?"

There was a silence for a moment as Stig turned the rabbit on the spit.

"You live with a woman whom you don't truly love, but need for stability. You are suspicious that she is seeing someone else, and that anger and suspicion hangs heavily on your shoulders. You feel passed over for promotion, and the one woman whom you truly love is inaccessible to you—"

"All right, all right," he said sullenly, "I get the picture."

"You humans radiate emotions like a roaring fire, Mr. Cable. We are astounded how you are able to deceive each other so easily. We see all deception, so have evolved to have no need for it."

"These labs," I began, eager to change the subject, "you are sure?"

"We are sure," affirmed Stig, "and not only Shakespeares were built there. All neanderthals up to Version 2.3.5, too. We wish to return. We have an urgent wish for that which we have been denied."

"And that is?" asked Bowden.

"Children," breathed Stig. "We have planned for just such an expedition, and your *sapien* characteristics will be useful. You have an impetuosity that we can never have. A neanderthal considers each move before taking it and is genetically predisposed towards caution. We need someone like you, Miss Next—a human with drive, a propensity towards violence and the ability to take command— yet someone governed by what is *right*."

I sighed. "We're not going to get into the Socialist Republic," I said. "We have no jurisdiction, and if we're caught, there will be hell to pay."

"What about your plan to take all those books across, Thursday?" asked Bowden in a quiet voice.

"There is no plan, Bowd. I'm sorry. And I can't risk being banged up in some Welsh slammer during the SuperHoop. I *have* to make sure the Mallets win. I *have* to be there."

Stig frowned at me. "Strange!" he said at last. "You do not want to win for a deluded sense of hometown pride—we see a greater purpose."

"I can't tell you, Stig, but what you read is true. It is vital to *all* of us that Swindon wins the SuperHoop."

Stig looked across to Mrs. Stiggins, and the two of them held a conversation for a good five minutes—using only facial expressions and the odd grunt.

After they had finished, Stig said, "It is agreed. You, Mr. Cable, and ourself will break into the abandoned Goliath reengineering labs. You to find your Shakespeares, we to find a way to seed our females."

"I can't—"

"Even if we fail," continued Stig, "the Neanderthal Nation will field five players to help you win your SuperHoop. There can be no payment and no glory. Is this the deal?"

I stared at his small brown eyes. By the quality I had seen of the players outside and my knowledge of neanderthals in general, we would be in with a chance—even with me locked up in a Welsh jail.

I shook his outstretched hand. "This is the deal."

"Then we must eat. Do you like rabbit?"

We both nodded.

"Good. This is a speciality of ours. In Neanderlese it is called *rabite'n'bitels*."

"Sounds excellent," replied Bowden. "What's it served with?"

"Potatoes and a . . . tangy, greeny-brown, crunchy sauce."

I can't be sure, but I think Stig winked at me. I needn't have worried. The meal was excellent, and neanderthals are quite correct—beetles are severely underrated.

31.

Planning Meeting

Common Cormorants' Numbers Decline

A leading ornithologist claimed yesterday that bear-bird incompatibility is to blame for the cormorant decline in recent years. "We have known for many years that cormorants lay eggs in paper bags to keep the lightning out," explained Mr. Daniel Chough, "but the reintroduction of bears to England has placed an intolerable strain on the birds' breeding habits. Even though bears and birds rarely compete for food and resources, it seems that wandering bears with buns steal the cormorants' paper bags in order, according to preliminary research, to hold the crumbs." That the bears are of Danish origin is suspected but not yet substantiated.

Article in *Flap!* magazine, July 20, 1988

So what do you know about the Elan?" asked Bowden as we drove back into the town.

"Not much," I replied, looking at the charts of Mr. Shaxspoor's teeth. Stig reckoned he had lived in the Elan for a lot longer than the others—perhaps until only a few years ago. If he had survived that long, why not some of the others? I wasn't going to raise any false hopes quite yet, but at least it seemed *possible* we could save *Hamlet* after all.

"Were you serious about not being able to think of a way in?"

"I'm afraid so. We could always pretend to be water officials from Birmingham or something."

"Why would water officials have ten truckloads of banned Danish books?" asked Bowden, not unreasonably.

"Something to read while doing water-officially things?"

"If we don't get these books to safety, they'll be burned, Thursday—we've *got* to find a way into the Republic."

"I'll think of something."

I spent the rest of the afternoon fielding calls from numerous sports reporters, eager to get a story and find out who would be playing in what position on the field. I called Aubrey and told him that he would have five new players—but I didn't tell him they'd be neanderthals. I couldn't risk the press's finding out.

By the time I returned to Mum's house, my wedding ring was firmly back on my finger again. I pushed Friday around to Landen's house and, noticing that everything seemed to be back to normal, knocked twice. There was an excited scrabble from within, and Landen opened the door.

"There you are!" he said happily. "When you hung up on me, I got kinda worried."

"I didn't hang up, Land."

"I was eradicated again?"

"I'm afraid so."

"Will I be again?"

"I'm hoping not. Can I come in?"

I put Friday on the floor, and he immediately started to try to climb the stairs.

"Bedtime already, is it, young man?" asked Landen, following him as he clambered all the way up. I noticed that in the spare room there were two as-yet-unpacked stair gates, which put my mind at rest. He had bought a cot, too, and several toys.

"I bought some clothes."

He opened the drawer. It was stuffed with all kinds of clothes for the little chap, and although some looked a bit small, I didn't say anything. We took Friday downstairs, and Landen made some supper.

"So you knew I was coming back?" I asked as he cut up some broccoli.

"Oh, yes," he replied, "as soon as you got all that eradication nonsense sorted out. Make us a cup of tea, would you?"

I walked over to the sink and filled the kettle.

"Any closer to a plan for dealing with Kaine?" asked Landen.

"No," I admitted, "I'm really banking on Zvlkx's Seventh Revealment coming true."

"What I don't understand," said Landen, chopping some carrots, "is why everyone except Formby seems to agree with everything Kaine says. Bloody sheep, the lot of them."

"I must say I'm surprised by the lack of opposition to Kaine's plans," I agreed, staring absently out the kitchen window. I frowned as the germ of an idea started to ferment in my mind. "Land?"

"Yuh?"

"When was the last time Formby went anywhere near Kaine?"

"Never. He avoids him like the plague. Kaine wants to meet him face-to-face, but the President won't have anything to do with him."

"That's it!" I exclaimed, suddenly having a flash of inspiration.

"What's it?"

"Well . . ."

I stopped because something at the bottom of the garden had caught my eye.

"Do you have nosy neighbors, Land?"

"Not really."

"It's probably my stalker, then."

"You have a stalker?"

I pointed. "Sure. Just there, in the laurels, beckoning to me."

"Do you want me to do the strong male thing and chase him off with a stick?"

"No. I've got a better idea."

"Hello, Millon. How's the stalking going? I brought you a cup of tea and a bun."

"Pretty well," he said, marking down in his notebook the time

I had stopped to talk to him and budging aside to make room for me in the laurel bush. "How are things with you?"

"They're mostly good. What were you waving at me for?"

"Ah!" he said. "We were going to run a feature about thirteenth-century seers in *Conspiracy Theorist* magazine, and I wanted to ask you a few questions."

"Go ahead."

"Do you think it's odd that no fewer than twenty-eight Dark Ages saints have chosen this year for their second coming?"

"I'd not really given it that much thought."

"O-kay. Do you not also find it strange that of these twenty-eight supposed seers, only two of them—St. Zvlkx and Sister Bettina of Stroud—have actually made any prophecies that have come remotely true?"

"What are you saying?"

"That St. Zvlkx might not be a thirteenth-century saint at all, but some sort of time-traveling criminal. He takes an illicit journey to the Dark Ages, writes up what he can remember of history and then, at the appropriate time, he is catapulted forward to see his last revealment come true."

"Why?" I asked. "If the ChronoGuard gets wind of what he's up to, he's never been born—literally. Why risk nonexistence for at most a few years' fame as a washed-up visitor from the thirteenth century with a host of unpleasant skin complaints?"

Millon shrugged. "I don't know. I thought you might be able to help *me*." He lapsed into silence.

"Tell me, Millon—is there any connection between Kaine and the Ovinator?"

"Of course! You should read *Conspiracy Theorist* magazine more often. Although most of our links between secret technology and those in power are about as tenuous as mist, this one really is concrete: his personal assistant, Stricknene, used to work with Schitt-Hawse at the Goliath tech division. If Goliath has an Ovinator, then Kaine might very well have one, too. Do you know what it does, then?"

I laughed. This was *exactly* the news I wanted to hear.

"You'll see. Tell me," I added, my hopes rising by the second, "what do you know about the old Goliath BioEngineering labs?"

"Hoooh!" he said, making a noise like any enthusiast invited to comment on his particular field of interest. "Now you're talking! The old Goliath BioE is still standing in what we call Area 21—the empty quarter in Mid-Wales, the Elan."

"Empty metaphorically or empty literally?"

"Empty as in no one goes there except water officials—and we have wholly uncorroborated evidence that we peddle as fact that an unspecified number of officials have vanished without a trace. In any event, it's all off-limits to everyone, surrounded by an electrified fence."

"To keep people out?"

"No," said Millon slowly, "to keep whatever genetic experiments Goliath was working on *in*. The whole of Area 21 is infested with chimeras. I've got files and files of dubious stories about people breaking in, allegedly never to be seen again. What's your interest in the Elan BioE plant anyway?"

"Illegal genetic experiments on humans undertaken covertly by an apparently innocent multinational."

Millon nearly passed out with the conspiracy overload. When he had recovered, he asked how he could help.

"I need you to find any pictures, plans, layout drawings—anything that might be of use for a visit."

Millon opened his eyes wide and scribbled in his notepad. "You're going to go into Area 21?"

"No," I replied, "we both are. Tomorrow. Leaving here at seven in the morning, *sharp*. Can you find what I asked for?"

He narrowed his eyes. "I can get you your information, Miss Next," he said slowly and with a gleam in his eye, "but it will cost. Let me be your official biographer."

I put out a hand and he shook it gratefully. "Deal."

*   *   *

I walked back inside to find Landen talking to a man dressed in slightly punky clothes, with brightly colored spectacle frames, bleached-blond hair and an infinitesimally small goatee firmly planted just under his lower lip.

"Darling," Landen said, grasping the hand that I had just rested on his shoulder, "this is my very good friend Handley Paige."

I shook Paige's hand. He seemed pretty much the same as any other SF writers I had ever met. Slightly geeky, but pleasant enough.

"You write the Emperor Zhark books," I observed.

He winced slightly. "No one ever talks about the decent stuff I write," he moaned. "They just ask me for more and more Zhark stuff. I did it as a joke—a pastiche of bad science fiction—and blow me down if it isn't the most popular thing I've ever done."

I remembered what Emperor Zhark had told me. "You're going to kill him off, aren't you?"

Handley started. "How did you know that?"

"She works for SO-27," explained Landen. "They know *every-thing*."

"I thought you guys were more hooked on the classics?"

"We deal with all genres," I explained. "For reasons that I can't reveal, I advise you to maroon Zhark on an uninhabited planet rather than expose him to the humiliation of a public execution."

Handley laughed. "You talk about him as if he were a real person!"

"She takes her work very seriously, Handley," said Landen without the glimmer of a smile. "I'd advise you to consider very seriously anything she happens to say. Wheels within wheels, Handley."

But Handley was adamant. "I'm going to kill him off so utterly and completely that no one will ever ask me for another Zhark novel again. Thanks for lending me the book, Land. I'll see myself out."

"Is Handley in danger?" asked Landen as soon as he had gone.

"Quite possibly. I'm not sure the Zharkian death-ray works

in the real world, and I'd hate for Handley to be the one who finds out."

"This is a BookWorld thing, isn't it? Let's just change the subject. What did your stalker want?"

I smiled. "You know, Landen, things are beginning to look up. I must call Bowden."

I quickly dialed his number.

"Bowd? It's Thursday. I've figured out how we're going to get across the border. Set everything up for tomorrow morning. We'll muster at Leigh Delamare at eight. . . . I can't tell you. . . . Stig and Millon. . . . See you there. Bye."

I called Stig and told him the same, then kissed Landen and asked him if he'd mind feeding Friday on his own. He didn't, of course, and I dashed off to speak to Mycroft.

I was back in time to help Landen scrub the food off Friday, read the boy a story and put him to bed. It wasn't late, but we went to bed ourselves. Tonight there was no shyness or confusion, and we undressed quickly. He pushed me backwards onto the bed and with his fingertips—

"Wait!" I cried out.

"What?"

"I can't concentrate with all those people!"

Landen looked around the empty bedroom. "What people?"

"Those people," I repeated, waving a hand in the general direction of everywhere, "the ones *reading* us."

Landen stared at me and raised an eyebrow. I felt stupid, then relaxed and gave out a nervous giggle.

"Sorry. I've been living inside fiction for too long; sometimes I get this weird feeling that you, me and everything else are just . . . well, characters in a book or something."

"Plainly, that is ridiculous."

"I know, I know. I'm sorry. Where were we?"

"Just here."

32.

Area 21: The Elan

Freedom of ▮▮▮▮▮▮▮ **Act a Step Closer,**
Announces Mr. ▮▮▮▮

Open government came one step closer yesterday with the announcement that Mr. ▮▮▮▮ would lend his weight to the Freedom of ▮▮▮▮▮▮▮▮ Act. The act, which aims to bring once top-▮▮▮▮ information from ▮▮▮▮▮▮▮ into the hands of the ▮▮▮▮, was hailed as a "great leap forward" by Mr. ▮▮▮▮, the Department of ▮▮▮▮▮▮▮'s senior ▮▮▮▮▮▮. The chief opponent to the draft bill, Mr. ▮▮▮▮, gave his assurance that "as long as my name is ▮▮▮, I won't allow this ▮ to be passed."

Article in The ▮▮, July ▮, 19▮

So what's the plan?" asked Bowden as we drove towards the Welsh border town of Hay-on-Wye. It was about ten in the morning, and we were traveling in Bowden's Welsh-built Griffin Sportina with Millon de Floss and Stig in the backseat. Behind us was a convoy of ten lorries, all loaded with banned Danish books.

"Well," I said, "ever thought it odd that parliament just rolls over and does anything that Kaine asks?"

"I've given up with even *trying* to understand parliament," said Bowden.

"They're all sniveling toadies," put in Millon.

"If you even *need* a government," added Stig, "you are a life-form flawed beyond redemption."

"I was confused, too," I continued. "A government wholly

280

agreeable to the worst excesses of Kaine could mean only one thing: some form of short-range mind control wielded by unscrupulous power brokers."

"Now, that's *my* kind of theory!" exclaimed Millon excitedly.

"I couldn't figure it out at first, but then when I was up at Goliathopolis, I felt it myself. A sort of mind-numbing go-with-the-flow feeling, where I just wanted to follow the path of least resistance, no matter how pointless or wrong. I had seen its effect at the *Evade the Question* TV show, too—the front row was eating out of Kaine's hand, no matter what he said."

"So what's the connection?"

"I felt it again in Mycroft's lab. It was only when Landen made a sarcastic comment that it twigged. The Ovinator. We all thought the 'ovi' part of it was to do with eggs, but it's not. Think 'ovine.' It's to do with *sheep*. The Ovinator transmits subalpha brain waves that inhibit free will and instill sheeplike tendencies into the minds of anyone close by. It can be tuned to the user so he is unaffected; it's possible that Goliath might have developed a long-range version called the Ovitron and an antiserum. Mycroft thinks he probably invented it to transmit public health messages, but he can't remember. Goliath gets hold of it, Stricknene gives it to Kaine—bingo. Parliament does everything Kaine asks. The only reason Formby is still anti-Yorrick is because he refuses to go anywhere near him."

There was silence in the car.

"What can we do about it?"

"Mycroft's working on an Ovi-negator that should cancel it out, but our plans carry on as before. The Elan—and win the SuperHoop."

"Even I'm finding this hard to believe," murmured Millon, "and that's a first for me."

"How does it get us out of England?" asked Bowden.

I patted the briefcase that was sitting on my lap. "With the Ovinator on our side, no one will want to oppose us."

"I'm not sure that's morally acceptable," said Bowden. "I mean, doesn't that make us as bad as Kaine?"

"I think we should stop and talk this through," added Millon. "It's one thing making up stories about mind-control experiments but quite another actually *using* them."

I opened the briefcase and switched the Ovinator on.

"Who's with me to go to the Elan, guys?"

"Well, all right then," conceded Bowden, "I guess I'm with you on this."

"Millon?"

"I'll do whatever Bowden does."

"It really does work, doesn't it?" observed Stig, giving a short, snorty cough. I chuckled slightly myself, too.

Getting through the English checkpoint at Clifford was even easier than I had imagined. I went ahead with the Ovinator in my brief-case and stood for some time at the border station, chatting to the duty guard and giving him and the small garrison a good soaking with Ovinator rays for half an hour before Bowden drove up with the ten trucks behind him.

"What's in those trucks?" asked the guard with a certain degree of torpidity in his voice.

"You don't need to look in the trucks," I told him.

"We don't need to look in the trucks," echoed the border guard.

"We can go through unimpeded."

"You can go through unimpeded."

"You're going to be nicer to your girlfriend."

"I'm *definitely* going to be nicer to my girlfriend. . . . Move along."

He waved us through, and we drove across the demilitarized zone to the Welsh border guards who called their colonel as soon as we explained that we had ten truckloads of Danish books that required safekeeping. There was a long and convoluted phone call with someone from the Danish consulate, and after about an hour, we and the trucks were escorted to a disused hangar at the Llandrindod Wells airfield park. The colonel in charge offered us free passage back to the border, but I switched on the Ovinator again and told him that he could take the truck drivers back but to let us go on our way, a plan that he quickly decided was probably the best thing.

Ten minutes later we were on the road north towards the Elan, Millon directing us all the way according to a 1950s tourist map. By the time we were past Rhayder, the countryside became more rugged and the farms less and less frequent and the road more and more potholed until, as the sun reached its zenith and started its downward track, we arrived at a tall set of gates, strung liberally with rusty barbed wire. There was an old stone-built guardhouse with two very bored guards who needed only a short burst from the Ovinator to switch off the electrified fence, allowing us to pass. Bowden drove the car through and stopped at another internal fence twenty yards inside the first. This was unelectrified, and I pushed it open to let the car pass.

The road was in worse repair on the Area 21 side of the gates. Tussocky grass was growing from the cracks in the concrete roadway, and on occasion trees that had fallen across the road impeded our progress.

"Now can you tell me what we're doing here?" asked Millon, staring intently out the window and taking frequent photographs.

"Two reasons," I said, looking at the map that Millon had obtained from his conspiracy buddies. "First, because we think someone's been cloning Shakespeares and I need one as a matter of some urgency, and second, to find vital reproductive information for Stig."

"So it's true you can't have children?"

Stig liked Millon because he asked such direct questions.

"It is true," he replied simply, loading up his dart gun with tranqs the size of Havana cigars.

"Take a left here, Bowd."

He changed gear, pulled the wheel around, and we entered a stretch of road with dark woodland on either side. We drove up a hill, took a left-hand turn past an outcrop of rock, then stopped. There was a rusty car upside down on the road in front of us, blocking the way.

"Stay in the car, keep it running," I said to Bowden. "Millon, stay put. Stig—with me."

Stig and I climbed out of the car and cautiously approached the upturned vehicle. It was a custom-made Studebaker, probably about ten years old. I peered in. Vandals never came here. The glass in the speedometer was unbroken, the rusty keys still in the ignition, the leather from the seats hanging in rotten strands. There was a sun-bleached briefcase lying on the ground, and it was full of water-related technical stuff, now all mushy and faded by the wind and rain. Of the occupants there was no sign. I had thought Millon was overcooking it with all his "chimeras running wild" stuff, but suddenly I felt nervous.

"Miss Next!"

It was Stig. He was about ten yards ahead of the car and was squatting down, rifle across his knees. I walked slowly up to him, looking anxiously into the deep woodland on either side of the road. It was quiet. Rather *too* quiet. The sound of my own footfalls felt deafening.

"What's up?"

He pointed to the ground. There was a human ulna lying on the road. Whoever had been in this accident, one of them never left.

"Hear that?" asked Stig.

I listened. "No."

"Exactly. No noise at all. We think it advisable to leave."

We pivoted the car on its roof to give us room to pass and drove on, this time much slower, and in silence. There were three other cars on that stretch of road, two on their sides and one pushed into the verge. None of them had the least sign of the occupants, and the woods to either side seemed somehow even darker and deeper and more impenetrable as we drove past. I was glad when we reached the top of the hill, cleared the forest and drove down past a small dam and a lake before a rise in the road brought us within sight of the old Goliath BioEngineering labs. I asked Bowden to stop. He pulled up silently, and we all got out to observe the old factory through binoculars.

It was in a glorious location, right on the edge of the reservoir. But from what we had been led to expect from Millon's hyperactive imagination and a tatty photograph taken in its heyday, it was something of a disappointment. The plant had once been a vast, sprawling complex, built in the art deco style popular for factories in the thirties, but now it looked as though a hurried and not entirely successful effort had been made to demolish it a long time ago. Although much of the building had been destroyed or collapsed, the east wing looked as though it had survived relatively unscathed. Even so, it didn't appear that anyone had been there for years, if not decades.

"What was that?" said Millon.

"What was what?"

"A sort of *yummy* noise."

"Hopefully just the wind. Let's have a closer look at the plant."

We motored down the hill and parked in front of the building. The front facade was still imposing, though half collapsed, and even retained much of the ceramic tile exterior and decoration. Clearly Goliath had great things planned for this place. We picked our way amongst the rubble that lay strewn across the steps and approached the main doors. They had both been pushed off their hinges, and one of them had large gouge marks, something that Millon was most interested in. I stepped inside. Broken furniture and fallen masonry lay everywhere in the oval lobby. The once fine suspended glass ceiling had long since collapsed, bringing natural light to an otherwise gloomy interior. The glass squeaked and cracked as we stepped across it.

"Where are the main labs?" I asked, not wanting to be here a minute longer than I had to.

Millon unfolded a blueprint.

"Where do you get all this stuff?" asked Bowden incredulously.

"I swapped it for a Cairngorm yeti's foot," he replied, as though talking about bubble-gum cards. "It's this way."

We walked through the building, amongst more fallen masonry and partially collapsed ceilings towards the relatively undamaged east wing. The roof was more intact here, and our torches flicked into offices and incubating rooms where rows upon rows of abandoned glass amniojars were lined up against the wall. In many of them, the liquefied remnant of a potential life-form had pooled in the bottom. Goliath had left in a hurry.

"What was this place?" I asked, my voice barely louder than a whisper.

"This was," muttered Millon, consulting his blueprint, "the main saber-toothed tiger manufacturing facility. The neanderthal wing should be through there and the first on the left."

The door was locked and bolted, but it was dry and rotten, and it didn't take much to force it open. There were papers scattered everywhere, and a halfhearted attempt had been made to destroy them. We stopped at the doorway and let Stiggins walk in alone. The room was about a hundred feet long and thirty feet wide. It was similar to the tiger facility next door, but the amniojars were larger. The glass nutrient pipes were still in evidence, and I shivered. To me the room was undeniably creepy, but to Stig it was his first home. He, along with many thousands of his fellow extinctees, had been grown here. I had sequenced Pickwick at home using nothing more complex than average kitchen utensils and cultivated her in a denucleated goose egg. Birds and reptiles were one thing, umbilical cultivation of mammals quite another. Stig trod carefully amongst the twisted pipes and broken glass to a far door and found the decanting room, where the infant neanderthals were taken out of their amniojars and breathed for the first time. Beyond this the nursery, where the young had been brought up. We followed Stig through, and he stood at the large window that overlooked the reservoir.

"When we dream, it is of this," he said quietly. Then, obviously feeling that he was wasting time, he strode back to the incubating room and started rummaging in filing cabinets and desk drawers. I told him we'd meet him outside and rejoined Millon, who was trying to make sense of his floor plan.

After walking in silence through several more rooms with even more ranks of amniojars, we arrived at a steel-gated secure area. The gate was open, and we stepped through, entering what had once been the most secret area of the entire plant.

A dozen or more paces farther on, the corridor led into a large hall, and we knew we had found what we had been looking for. Built within the large room was a full-scale copy of the Globe Theatre. The stage and groundling area were strewn with torn-out pages of Shakespeare's plays, heavily annotated in black ink. In a room leading off, we found a dormitory that might have contained two hundred beds. All the bedding was upended in a corner, the bedsteads broken and lying askew.

"How many do you think went through here?" asked Bowden in a whisper.

"Hundreds and hundreds," replied Millon, holding up a battered copy of *The Two Gentlemen of Verona* with the name "Shaxpreke, W, 769" written on the inside front cover. He shook his head sadly.

"What happened to them all?"

"Dead," said a voice, "dead as a ducat!"

33.

Shgakespeafe

"All the World's a Stage," Claims Playwright
That was the analogy of life offered by Mr. William Shakespeare yesterday
when his latest play opened at the Globe. Mr. Shakespeare went on to further compare plays with the seven stages of life by declaring "all the men
and women merely players: They have their exits and their entrances; and
one man in his time plays many parts." Mr. Shakespeare's latest offering, a
comedy entitled *As You Like It,* opened to mixed reviews with the *fouth-
wark Gazette* calling it "a rollicking comedy of the highest order," while the
Westminster Evening News described it as "tawdry rubbish from the War-
wickshire shithouse." Mr. Shakespeare declined to comment, as he is already penning a follow-up.

Article in *Blackfriars News,* September 1589

We turned to find a small man with wild, unkempt hair standing at the doorway. He was dressed in Elizabethan clothes that had seen far better days, and his feet were bound with strips of cloth as makeshift shoes. He twitched nervously, and one eye was closed—but beyond this the similarity to the Shakespeares Bowden had found was unmistakable. A survivor. I took a step closer. His face was lined and weathered, and those teeth he still possessed were stained dark brown and worn. He must have been at least seventy, but it didn't matter. The genius that had been Shakespeare had died in 1616, but genetically speaking, he was with us right now.

"William Shakespeare?"

"I *am* a William, sir, and my name is Shgakespeafe," he corrected.

"Mr. Shgakespeafe," I began again, unsure of how to explain exactly what I wanted, "my name is Thursday Next, and I have a Danish prince urgently in need of your help."

He looked from me to Bowden to Millon and back to me again. Then a smile broke across his weathered features.

"O wonder!" he said at last. "How beauteous mankind is! O brave new world that has such people in't!"

He stepped forward and shook our hands warmly; it didn't look as though he had seen anyone for a while.

"What happened to the others, Mr. Shgakespeafe?"

He beckoned us to follow him and then was off like a gazelle. We had a hard job keeping up with him as he darted down the labyrinthine corridors, nimbly avoiding the rubbish and broken equipment. We caught up with him when he stopped at a smashed window that overlooked what had once been a large exercise compound. In the middle were two grassy mounds. It didn't take a huge amount of imagination to guess what was underneath them.

"O heart, heavy heart, why sigh'st thou without breaking?" murmured Shgakespeafe sorrowfully. "After the slaughter of so many peers by falsehood and by treachery, when will our great regenitors be conquered?"

"I only wish I could say your brothers would be avenged," I told him sadly, "but in all honesty, the men who did this are now dead themselves. I can only offer yourself and those who survive my protection."

He took in every word carefully and seemed impressed by my candor. I looked beyond the mass graves of the Shakespeares to several other mounds beyond. I had thought they might have cloned two dozen or so, not hundreds.

"Are there any other Shakespeares here?" asked Bowden.

"Only myself—yet the night echoes with the cries of my *cousins*," replied Shgakespeafe. "You will hear them anon."

As if in answer, there was a strange cry from the hills. We had heard something like it when Stig dispatched the chimera back in Swindon.

"We are not safe, Clarence, we are not safe," he said, looking around nervously. "Follow me and give me audience, friends."

Shgakespeafe led us along the corridor and into a room that was full of desks set neatly in rows, each with a typewriter upon it. Only one typewriter was anything like still functioning; around it stood stacks and stacks of typewritten sheets of paper—the product of Shgakespeafe's outpourings. He led us across and gave us some of his work to read, looking on expectantly as our eyes scanned the writing. It was, disappointingly, nothing special at all—merely scraps of existing plays cobbled together to give new meaning. I tried to imagine the whole room full of Shakespeare clones clattering away at their typewriters, their minds filled with the Bard's plays, and scientists moving amongst them trying to find one, just *one*, who had even one half the talent of the original.

Shgakespeafe beckoned us to the office next to the writing room, and there he showed us mounds and mounds of paperwork, all packaged in brown paper with the name of the Shakespeare clone who had written it printed on a label. As the production of writing outstripped the ability to evaluate it, the people working here could only file what had been written and then store it for some unknown employee in the future to peruse. I looked again at the piles of paperwork. There must have been twenty tons or more in the storeroom. There was a hole in the roof, and the rain had got in; much of this small mountain of prose was damp, moldy and unstable.

"It would take an age to sort through it for anything of potential brilliance," mused Bowden, who had arrived by my side. Perhaps, ultimately, the experiment had succeeded. Perhaps there *was* an equal of Shakespeare buried in the mass grave outside, his work somewhere deep within the mountain of unintelligible prose facing us. It was unlikely we would ever know, and if we did, it would teach us nothing new—except that it could be done and others might try. I hoped the mound of paperwork would just slowly rot.

In the pursuit of great art, Goliath had perpetrated a crime that far outstripped anything I had so far seen.

Millon took pictures, his flashgun going off in the dim interior of the scriptorium. I shivered and decided I needed to get away from the oppressiveness of the interior. Bowden and I walked to the front of the building and sat amongst the rubble on the front steps, just next to a fallen statue of Socrates that held a banner proclaiming the value of the pursuit of knowledge.

"Do you think we'll have trouble persuading Shgakespeafe to come with us?" he asked.

As if in answer, Shgakespeafe walked cautiously from the building. He carried a battered suitcase and blinked in the harsh sunlight. Without waiting to be asked, he got into the back of the car and started to scribble in a notebook with a pencil stub.

"Does that answer your question?"

The sun dropped below the hill in front of us, and the air suddenly felt colder. Every time there was a strange noise from the hills, Shgakespeafe jumped and looked around nervously, then continued to scribble. I was just about to fetch Stig when he appeared from the building carrying three enormous leatherbound volumes.

"Did you find what you needed?"

He passed me the first book, which I opened at random. It was, I discovered, a Goliath BioTech manual for building a neanderthal. The page I had selected gave a detailed description of the neanderthal hand.

"A complete manual," he said slowly. "With it we can make children."

I handed back the volume, and he placed it with the others in the boot of the car just as there was another unearthly wail in the distance.

"A deadly groan," muttered Shgakespeafe, sitting lower in his seat, "like life and death's departing!"

"We had better get going," I said. "There is something out there, and I've a feeling we should leave before it gets too inquisitive."

"Chimera?" asked Bowden. "To be honest, we've seen the grand total of none from the moment we came in here."

"We do not see them because they do not wish to be seen," observed Stig. "There is chimera here. *Dangerous* chimera."

"Thanks, Stig," said Millon, dabbing his brow with a handkerchief, "that's a real help."

"It is the truth, Mr. de Floss."

"Well, keep the truth to yourself in future."

I shut the rear door as soon as Stig had wedged himself in next to Shgakespeafe, and then I climbed into the front passenger seat. Bowden drove off as rapidly as the car would allow.

"Millon, is there any other route out that doesn't take us through that heavily wooded area where we found the other cars?"

He consulted the map for a moment. "No. Why?"

"Because it looked like a good place for an ambush."

"This really gets better and better, doesn't it?"

"On the contrary," replied Stig, who took all speech on face value, "this is not good at all. We find the prospect of being eaten by chimeras extremely awkward."

"Awkward?" echoed Millon. "Being eaten is *awkward?*"

"Indeed," said Stig, "the neanderthal instruction manuals are far more important than we."

"That's *your* opinion," retorted Millon. "Right now there is nothing more important than me."

"How very *human,*" replied Stig simply.

We sped up the road, drove back through the rock cutting and headed towards the wood.

"By the pricking of my thumbs," remarked Shgakespeafe in an ominous tone of voice, "something wicked this way comes!"

"There!" yelled Millon, pointing a quivering finger out the window. I caught a glimpse of a large beast before it vanished behind a fallen oak, then another jumping from one tree to another. They didn't hide themselves anymore. We could all see them as we drove down the wooded road, past the abandoned cars. Lolloping beasts of a ragged shape flitted through the woods, experimental creations of an industry before regulation. We heard a thump as one leapt out of the woods, sprung upon the steel roof of the car and then disappeared with a whoop into the forest. I looked out of the rear window and saw something unspeakably nasty scrabble across the road behind us. I drew my automatic, and Stig wound down the window to have his tranquilizer gun at the ready. We rounded the next corner, and Bowden stomped on the brakes. A row of chimeras had placed themselves across the road. Bowden threw the car into reverse, but a tree came crashing down behind us, cutting off our escape. We had driven into the trap, the trap was sprung—and all that remained was for the *trappers* to do with the *trapped* whatever they wished.

"How many?" I asked.

"Ten up front," said Bowden.

"Two dozen behind," answered Stig.

"Lots either side!" quivered Millon, who was more used to making up facts to fit his bizarre conspiracy theories than actually witnessing any firsthand.

"What a sign it is of evil life," murmured Shgakespeafe. "Where death's approach is seen so terrible!"

"Okay," I muttered, "everyone stay calm, and when I say, open fire."

"We will not survive," said Stig in a matter-of-fact tone. "Too many of them, not enough of us. We suggest a different strategy."

"And that is?"

Stig was momentarily lost for words. "We do not know. Just *different*."

The chimeras slavered and emitted low moans as they moved closer. Each one was a kaleidoscope of varying body parts, as though the beasts' creators had been indulging in some sort of perverse genetic mix-and-match one-upmanship.

"When I count to three, rev up and drop the clutch," I instructed Bowden. "The rest of you open up with everything we've got." I handed Bowden's gun to Floss. "Know how to use one of these?"

He nodded and flipped off the safety.

"One . . . two . . ."

I stopped counting because a cry from the woods had startled the chimeras. Those that had ears pricked them up, paused, then began to depart in fright. It wasn't an occasion for relief. Chimeras are bad, but something that frightened chimeras could only be worse. We heard the cry again.

"It sounds human," murmured Bowden.

"*How* human?" added Millon.

There followed several more cries from more than one individual, and as the last of the terrified chimeras vanished into the brush, I breathed a sigh of relief. A group of men appeared out of the undergrowth to our right. They were all extremely short and wore the faded and tattered uniform of what appeared to be the French army. Some wore shabby cockaded hats, others had no jackets at all, and some wore only a dirty white linen shirt. My relief was short-lived. They stood at the edge of the forest and regarded us suspiciously, heavy cudgels in their hands.

"*Qu'est-ce que c'est?*" said one, pointing at us.

"*Anglais?*" said another.

"*Les rosbifs? Ici, en France?*" said a third in a shocked tone.

"*Non, ce n'est pas possible!*"

It didn't take a genius to figure out who they were.

"A gang of *Napoleons,*" hissed Bowden. "Looks like Goliath wasn't just trying to eternalize the Bard. The military potential of cloning a Napoleon in his prime would be considerable."

The Napoleons stared at us for a moment and then talked amongst themselves in low tones, had an argument, gesticulated wildly, raised their voices and generally disagreed with one another.

"Let's go," I whispered to Bowden.

But as soon as the car clunked into gear, the Napoleons leapt into action with cries of *"Au secours! Les rosbifs s'échappent! N'oubliez pas Agincourt! Vite! Vite!"* and then rushed the car. Stig got off a shot and managed to tranq a particularly vicious-looking Napoleon in the thigh. They smashed their cudgels against the car, broke the windows and sent a cascade of broken glass all over us. I thumped the central door-locking mechanism with my elbow as a Napoleon grappled with my door handle. I was just about to fire at point-blank range into the face of another Napoleon when there was a tremendous explosion thirty yards in front. The car was rocked by the blast and enveloped momentarily in a drifting cloud of smoke.

"Sacre bleu!" shrieked a Napoleon, breaking off the attack. *"Le Grand Nez! Avancez, mes amis! Mort aux ennemis de la République!"*

"Go!" I shouted to Bowden, who, despite having been struck a glancing blow by a Napoleon, was still just about conscious. The car juddered away, and I grabbed the steering wheel to avoid a band of twenty or so Wellingtons of varying shabbiness who were streaming past the car in their haste to dispose of Napoleons.

"Up, guards, and at them!" I heard a Wellington shout as we gathered speed down the road, past a smoking artillery piece and the abandoned cars we had seen on the way in. Within a few minutes, we were clear of the wood and the battling factions, and Bowden slowed down.

"Everyone okay?"

Although not unscathed, they all answered in the affirmative. Millon was still ashen, and I took Bowden's gun off him just in case. Stig had a bruise coming up on his cheek, and I had several cuts on my face from the glass.

"Mr. Shgakespeafe," I asked, "are you okay?"

"Look about you," he said grimly. "Security gives way to conspiracy."

We drove to the gates, out of Area 21 and through the darkening evening sky to the Welsh border and home.

34.

St. Zvlkx and Cindy

Kaine "Fictional," Claims Bournemouth Man

Retired gas-fitter Mr. Martin Piffco made the ludicrous comment yesterday, claiming that the beloved leader of the nation was simply a fictional character "come to life." Speaking from the Bournemouth Home for the Exceedingly Odd where he has been committed "for his own protection," Mr. Piffco was more specific and likened Mr. Yorrick Kaine to a minor character with an over-inflated opinion of himself in a Daphne Farquitt book entitled *At Long Last Lust.* The Chancellor's office dubbed the report "a coincidence," but ordered the Farquitt book be confiscated nonetheless. Mr. Piffco, who faces unspecified charges, made news last year when he made a similar outrageous claim regarding Kaine and Goliath investing in "mind-control experiments."

Article in the Bournemouth Bugle, March 15, 1987

I awoke and gazed at Landen in the early-morning light that had started to creep around the bedroom. He was snoring ever so softly, and I gave him a long hug before I got up, wrapped myself in a dressing gown and tiptoed past Friday's room on my way downstairs to make some coffee. I walked into Landen's study as I waited for the kettle to boil, sat down at the piano and played a very quiet chord. The sun crept above the roof of the house across the way at that precise moment and cast a finger of orange light across the room. I heard the kettle click off and returned to the kitchen to make the coffee. As I poured the hot water on the grounds, there was a small wail from upstairs. I paused to see if another would follow it. A single wail might be only a stirring, and Friday could be left alone. Two wails or more would be Hungry Boy, eager for a gallon or two of porridge. There was a second wail ten seconds later, and I was just about to go and get him when I heard a thump and a scraping as Landen pulled on his leg and then walked along the corridor to Friday's room. There were more footsteps as he returned to his room, then silence. I relaxed, took a sip of coffee and sat at the kitchen table, deep in thought.

The SuperHoop was tomorrow and I had my team—the question was, would it make a difference? There was a chance we might find a copy of *At Long Last Lust,* too—but I wasn't counting on this, either. Of equal chance and equal risk of failure was Shgakespeafe's being able to unravel *The Merry Wives of Elsinore,* and Mycroft's coming up with an Ovi-negator at short notice. But none of these pressing matters was foremost in my mind: most important to me was that at eleven o'clock this morning Cindy would try to kill me for the third and final time. She would fail, and she would die. I thought of Spike and Betty and picked up the phone. I figured he'd be a heavy sleeper, and I was right—Cindy answered the phone.

"It's Thursday."

"This is professionally very unethical," said Cindy in a sleepy voice. "What's the time?"

"Half six. Listen, I rang to suggest that it'd be a good idea if you stayed at home today and didn't go to work."

There was a pause. "I can't do that," she said at last. "I've arranged child care and everything. But there's nothing to stop you getting out of town and never returning."

"This is my town, too, Cindy."

"Leave now, or the Next family crypt will be up for a dusting."

"I won't do that."

"Then," replied Cindy with a sigh, "we've got nothing else to discuss. I'll see you later—although I doubt you'll see me."

The phone went dead, and I gently replaced the receiver. I felt sick. The wife of a good friend would die, and it didn't feel good.

"What's the matter?" said a voice close at hand. "You seem upset."

It was Mrs. Tiggy-winkle.

"No," I replied, "everything's just as it should be. Thanks for dropping round; I've found us a William Shakespeare. He's not the original, but close enough for our purposes. He's in this cupboard."

I opened the cupboard door, and a very startled Shgakespeafe looked up from where he'd been scribbling by the light of a candle end he had stuck upon his head. The wax had begun to run down his face, but he didn't seem to mind.

"Mr. Shgakespeafe, this is the hedgehog I was telling you about."

He shut his notebook and stared at Mrs. Tiggy-winkle. He wasn't the slightest bit afraid or surprised—after the abominations he'd dodged on an almost daily basis in Area 21, I suspect a six-foot-high hedgehog was something of a relief.

Mrs. Tiggy-winkle curtsied gracefully. "Delighted to make your acquaintance, Mr. Shgakespeafe," she said politely. "Will you come with me, please?"

"Who was that?" Landen called out as he walked downstairs a little later.

"It was Mrs. Tiggy-winkle picking up a William Shakespeare clone in order to save *Hamlet* from permanent destruction."

"You can't ever be serious, can you?" he laughed as he gave me a hug. I had smuggled Shgakespeafe into the house without Landen's seeing. I know you're meant to be honest and truthful to your spouse, but I thought there might be a limit, and if there was, I didn't want to reach it too soon.

Friday came down to breakfast ten minutes later. He looked tousled, sleepy and a bit grumpy.

"Quis nostrud laboris," he moaned. "Nisi ut aliquip ex consequat."

I gave him some toast and rummaged in the cupboard under

the stairs for my bulletproof vest. All my stuff was now back in Landen's house as if I had never moved out. Sideslips are confusing, but you can get used to almost anything.

"Why are you wearing a bulletproof vest?"

It was Landen. Drat. I should have put it on at the station.

"What bulletproof vest?"

"The one you're trying to put on."

"Oh, *that* one. No reason. Listen, if Friday gets hungry you can always give him a snack. He likes bananas—you may have to buy some more, and if a gorilla calls, it's only that Mrs. Bradshaw I was telling you about."

"Don't change the subject. How can you go to work wearing a vest for 'no reason'?"

"It's a precaution."

"Insurance is a precaution. A vest means you're taking unnecessary risks."

"I'd be taking a bigger one without it."

"What's going on, Thursday?"

I waved a hand vaguely in the air and tried to make light of it. "Just an assassin. A small one. Barely worth thinking about."

"Which one?"

"I can't remember. Window . . . *something*."

"The Windowmaker? A contract with her and stick to reading short stories? Sixty-seven known victims?"

"Sixty-eight if she did Samuel Pring."

"That's not important. *Why didn't you tell me?*"

"I . . . I . . . didn't want you to worry."

He rubbed his face with his hands and stared at me for a moment, then sighed deeply. "This is the Thursday Next I married, isn't it?"

I nodded my head.

He wrapped his arms around me and held me tightly. "Will you be careful?" he whispered in my ear.

"I'm always careful."

"No, *really* careful. The sort of careful that you should be when you have a husband and son who'd be supremely pissed off if they were to lose you?"

"Ah," I whispered back, "*that* sort of careful. Yes, I will."

We kissed and I Velcroed up the vest, put my shirt over the top of it and my shoulder holster on top of this. I kissed Friday and told him to be good, then kissed Landen again.

"I'll see you this evening," I told him, "and that's a promise."

I drove to Wanborough to find Joffy. He was officiating at a GSD civil-union ceremony, and I had to wait in the back of the temple until he had finished. I had some time before I had to deal with Cindy, and looking more closely into St. Zvlkx seemed like a good way to fill it. Millon's idea that Zvlkx wasn't a seer but a rogue member of the ChronoGuard involved in some sort of timecrime seemed, on the face of it, unlikely. You couldn't hide from the ChronoGuard. They would *always* find you. Perhaps not here and now, but then and there—when you least expected it. Long before you even *thought* about doing something wrong. Plus, the Chrono-Guard left no trace. With the perpetrator gone, then the timecrime never happened either. Very neat, very clever. But with the historical record so closely scrutinized and the ChronoGuard itself giving Zvlkx the seal of approval, how on earth did Zvlkx—if he *was* a fake—get around the system?

"Hello, Doofus!" said Joffy as the happy couple kissed outside the temple to a shower of confetti. "What brings you here?"

"St. Zvlkx—where is he?"

"He got the bus into Swindon this morning. Why?"

I outlined my suspicions.

"Zvlkx a rogue member of the ChronoGuard? But why? What's he up to? Why risk permanent eradication for dubious fame as a thirteenth-century seer?"

"How much did he get from the Toast Marketing Board?"

"Twenty-five grand."

"Hardly a fortune. Can we look in his room?"

"Outrageous!" replied Joffy. "I would be guilty of a shameful breach of trust if I were to allow a room search in his absence. I have a spare key here."

Zvlkx's room was much as you would suppose a monk's cell to be. Spartan in the extreme. He slept on a mattress stuffed with straw and had only a table and chair as furniture. On the table was a Bible. It was only after we started searching that we found a CD Walkman under the mattress, along with a few copies of *Big & Bouncy* and *Fast Horse*.

"A betting man?" I asked.

"Drinking, betting, smoking, wenching—he did it all."

"The magazines show he can read English, too. What are you looking for, Joff?"

Joffy had been opening the drawers of his desk and looking under the pillow.

"His Book of Revealments. He usually hides it here."

"So! You've searched his room before. Suspicious?"

Joffy looked sheepish. "I'm afraid so. His behavior is less like a saint's and more like . . . well, a cheap vulgarian's—when I translate, I have to make certain . . . *adjustments.*"

I pulled out his desk drawer and turned it over. Stuck to the bottom was an envelope. "Bingo!"

It contained a single one-way Gravitube ticket all the way to Bali. Joffy raised his eyebrows, and we exchanged nervous glances. Zvlkx was definitely up to something.

Joffy accompanied me into Swindon, and we drove up and down the streets trying to find the wayward saint. We visited the site of his old cathedral at Tesco's but couldn't find him, so went on a circuit that took in the law courts, the SpecOps Building and the theater before driving past the university and down Commercial Road. Joffy spotted him outside Pete & Dave's, lumbering up the street.

"There!"

"I see him."

We abandoned the car and trotted to keep up with the scruffy figure dressed in only a blanket. It was just bad luck that he glanced furtively behind and spotted us. He darted across the street. I don't know whether his lank and uncut hair had got in his eyes or he had forgotten about traffic during his stay in the Dark Ages, but he didn't look where he was going and ran straight in front of a bus. His head cracked the windscreen, and his bony body was thrown sideways onto the pavement with a thump. Joffy and I were first on the scene. A younger man might have survived relatively unscathed, but Zvlkx, his body weakened through poor diet and disease, didn't stand much of a chance. He was coughing and crawling with all the strength he could muster to the entrance of the nearest shop.

"𝔈𝔞𝔰𝔶, 𝔜𝔬𝔲𝔯 𝔊𝔯𝔞𝔠𝔢," murmured Joffy, laying a hand on his shoulder and stopping him moving. "𝔜𝔬𝔲'𝔯𝔢 𝔤𝔬𝔦𝔫𝔤 𝔱𝔬 𝔟𝔢 𝔞𝔩𝔩 𝔯𝔦𝔤𝔥𝔱."

"𝔅𝔬𝔩𝔩𝔬𝔠𝔨𝔰," said Zvlkx in a state of exasperation, "𝔟𝔬𝔩𝔩𝔬𝔠𝔨𝔰, 𝔟𝔬𝔩𝔩𝔬𝔠𝔨𝔰, 𝔟𝔬𝔩𝔩𝔬𝔠𝔨𝔰. 𝔖𝔲𝔯𝔳𝔦𝔳𝔢𝔡 𝔱𝔥𝔢 𝔭𝔩𝔞𝔤𝔲𝔢 𝔱𝔬 𝔤𝔢𝔱 𝔥𝔦𝔱 𝔟𝔶 𝔞 𝔰𝔬𝔡𝔡𝔦𝔫𝔤 𝔑𝔲𝔪𝔟𝔢𝔯 𝔗𝔴𝔢𝔫𝔱𝔶-𝔱𝔥𝔯𝔢𝔢 𝔟𝔲𝔰. 𝔅𝔬𝔩𝔩𝔬𝔠𝔨𝔰."

"What did he say?"

"He's annoyed."

"Who are you?" I said. "Are you ChronoGuard?"

His eyes flicked across to mine, and he groaned. Not only dying, but dying and rumbled.

He made another attempt to reach the doorway and collapsed.

"Someone call for an ambulance!" yelled out Joffy.

"𝔍𝔱'𝔰 𝔱𝔬𝔬 𝔩𝔞𝔱𝔢 𝔣𝔬𝔯 𝔱𝔥𝔞𝔱," he muttered. "𝔗𝔬𝔬 𝔩𝔞𝔱𝔢 𝔣𝔬𝔯 𝔪𝔢, 𝔱𝔬𝔬 𝔩𝔞𝔱𝔢 𝔣𝔬𝔯 𝔞𝔩𝔩 𝔬𝔣 𝔲𝔰. 𝔗𝔥𝔦𝔰 𝔴𝔞𝔰𝔫'𝔱 𝔥𝔬𝔴 𝔦𝔱 𝔴𝔞𝔰 𝔪𝔢𝔞𝔫𝔱 𝔱𝔬 𝔱𝔲𝔯𝔫 𝔬𝔲𝔱; 𝔱𝔦𝔪𝔢 𝔦𝔰 𝔬𝔲𝔱 𝔬𝔣 𝔧𝔬𝔦𝔫𝔱—𝔞𝔫𝔡 𝔦𝔱 𝔴𝔬𝔫'𝔱 𝔟𝔢 𝔣𝔬𝔯 𝔪𝔢 𝔱𝔬 𝔰𝔢𝔱 𝔦𝔱 𝔯𝔦𝔤𝔥𝔱. 𝔄𝔥, 𝔴𝔢𝔩𝔩. 𝔍𝔬𝔣𝔣𝔶, 𝔱𝔞𝔨𝔢 𝔱𝔥𝔦𝔰 𝔞𝔫𝔡 𝔲𝔰𝔢 𝔦𝔱 𝔴𝔦𝔰𝔢𝔩𝔶, 𝔞𝔰 𝔍 𝔴𝔬𝔲𝔩𝔡 𝔫𝔬𝔱 𝔥𝔞𝔳𝔢 𝔡𝔬𝔫𝔢. 𝔅𝔲𝔯𝔶 𝔪𝔢 𝔦𝔫 𝔱𝔥𝔢 𝔤𝔯𝔬𝔲𝔫𝔡𝔰 𝔬𝔣 𝔪𝔶 𝔠𝔞𝔱𝔥𝔢𝔡𝔯𝔞𝔩—𝔞𝔫𝔡 𝔡𝔬𝔫'𝔱 𝔱𝔢𝔩𝔩 𝔱𝔥𝔢𝔪 𝔴𝔥𝔬 𝔍 𝔴𝔞𝔰. 𝔍 𝔩𝔦𝔳𝔢𝔡 𝔞 𝔰𝔦𝔫𝔫𝔢𝔯, 𝔟𝔲𝔱 𝔍'𝔡 𝔩𝔦𝔨𝔢 𝔱𝔬 𝔡𝔦𝔢 𝔞 𝔰𝔞𝔦𝔫𝔱. 𝔒𝔥, 𝔞𝔫𝔡 𝔦𝔣 𝔞 𝔣𝔞𝔱 𝔰𝔩𝔞𝔭𝔭𝔢𝔯 𝔫𝔞𝔪𝔢𝔡 𝔖𝔥𝔦𝔯𝔩𝔢𝔶 𝔱𝔢𝔩𝔩𝔰 𝔶𝔬𝔲 𝔍 𝔭𝔯𝔬𝔪𝔦𝔰𝔢𝔡 𝔥𝔢𝔯 𝔞 𝔱𝔥𝔬𝔲𝔰𝔞𝔫𝔡 𝔮𝔲𝔦𝔡, 𝔰𝔥𝔢'𝔰 𝔞 𝔟𝔩𝔬𝔬𝔡𝔶 𝔩𝔦𝔞𝔯."

He coughed again, shivered for a moment and stopped moving. I placed my hand on his grimy neck but could feel no pulse.

"What did he say?"

"Something about an overweight lady named Shirley, time being out of joint—and using his revealments as I see fit."

"What did he mean by that? That his revealment is *not* going to come true?"

"I don't know—but he handed me this."

It was Zvlkx's Book of Revealments. Joffy flicked through the yellowed pages, which outlined in Old English every supposed prophecy he had made, next to an arithmetic sum of some sort. Joffy closed Zvlkx's eyes and placed his jacket over the dead saint's head. A crowd had assembled, including a policeman, who took charge. Joffy hid the book, and we stood to one side as the blare of an ambulance started up in the distance. The owner of the shop had come out and told us that having tramps dying on his doorstep was bad for business but changed his mind when he found out who it was.

"My goodness!" he said with a respectful tone. "Imagine a real live saint honoring us with his death on our doorstep!"

I nudged Joffy and pointed to the shop front. It was a betting shop.

"Typical!" snorted Joffy. "If he didn't die trying to get to the bookies, it would have been the brothel. The only reason I knew he wouldn't be at the pub is because it's not opening time."

Startled, I looked at my watch. It was 10:50. Cindy. I had been thinking about St. Zvlkx so much I had forgotten all about her. I backed into the doorway and glanced around. No sign of her, of course, but then she was the best. I thought the fact that a crowd had gathered was good, as she would be unlikely to want to kill innocent people, but then changed my mind when I realized that Cindy's creed of respect for innocent life could be written in very large letters on the back of a matchbox. I had to get away from the crowd in case someone else was hurt. I dashed off up Commercial Road and was approaching the corner with Granville Street when I stopped abruptly. Cindy had walked around the corner. My hand reflexively closed around the butt of my gun, but then I stopped, all of a sudden uncertain. She was not alone. She had Spike with her.

"Well!" said Spike, looking beyond me to the melee on the street behind. "What's going on here?"

"The death of Zvlkx, Spike."

I was staring at Cindy, who stared back at me. I could see only one of her hands. The other was hidden in her handbag. She had failed twice—how far would she go to kill me? In broad daylight, with her husband as witness? I was standing awkwardly with my hand on my automatic, but it was still in its holster. I had to trust my father. He had been right about Cindy on the previous attempt. I pulled out my gun and pointed it at her. There was a gasp from several passersby, who scattered.

"Thursday?" yelled Spike. "What the hell is going on? Put that down!"

"No, Spike. Cindy isn't a librarian, she's the Windowmaker."

Spike looked at me, then at his petite wife and laughed. "Cindy, an assassin? You're joking!"

"She's delusional, and I'm frightened, Spikey," whimpered Cindy, in her best pathetic-girlie voice. "I don't know what she's talking about. I've never even held a gun!"

"*Very* slowly take your hand out of your handbag, Cindy."

But it was Spike who made the next move. He pulled out his gun and pointed it—at *me*.

"Put the gun down, Thurs. I've always liked you, but I have no problem making this choice."

I bit my lip but didn't stop staring at Cindy. "Ever wondered why she was paid cash to do those freelance library jobs? Why her brother works for the CIA? Why her parents were killed by police marksmen? Have you ever heard of librarians being killed by the police?"

"There's an explanation for it all, Spikey!" whined Cindy. "Kill her! She's mad!"

I saw her game now. She wasn't even going to do the job herself. In broad daylight, her husband pulls the trigger, and it's all legal: a good man defending his wife. She was good. She was the best. She was the Windowmaker. A contract with her and you're deader than corduroy.

"She has a contract out on me, Spike. Already tried to kill me on two occasions!"

"Put down the gun, Thursday!"

"Spikey, I'm frightened!"

"Cindy, I want to see both your hands!"

"*Drop the gun,* Thursday!"

We had reached an impasse. As I stood there with Spike pointing a gun at my head and with me pointing a gun at Cindy's, I realized this was quite possibly the worst situation to be in. If I lowered my gun, Cindy would kill me. If I didn't lower my gun, Spike would kill me. If I killed Cindy, Spike would kill me. Try as I might, I couldn't think of a scenario that didn't end in my own death. Tricky, to say the least. And it was then that the grand piano fell on her.

I'd never heard a piano falling thirty feet onto concrete before, but it was exactly as I imagined. A sort of musical concussion that reverberated around the street. As chance would have it, the piano—a Steinway baby, I learned later—missed us all. It was the *stool* that hit Cindy and she went down like a sack of coal. One look at her and we both knew it was bad. A serious head wound and a badly broken neck.

It was a time of mixed emotions for Spike. Grief and shock at the accident but also realization that I had been right—still clasped in Cindy's hand was a silenced .38 revolver.

"No!" yelled Spike, placing his hand gently upon her pale cheek. "Not again!"

Cindy groaned weakly as the policeman who had been dealing with St. Zvlkx rushed up with two paramedics at his side.

"You should have told me," Spike muttered, refusing to look at me, his powerful shoulders quivering slightly as tears rolled down his cheeks.

"I'm so sorry, Spike."

He didn't reply but moved aside so the paramedics could try to stabilize her.

"Who is she?" asked the policeman. "In fact, who are you two?"

"SpecOps," we said in unison, producing our badges.

"And this is Cindy Stoker," said Spike sadly, "the assassin known as the Windowmaker—and my wife."

35.

What Thursday Did Next

Kainian Government to Fund "Anti-Smite Shield"
Mr. Yorrick Kaine yesterday announced plans to set up a defensive network to counter the growing threat of God's wrath unto His creations. Specific details of the "Anti-Smite Shield" are still classed top secret, but defense experts and top theologians have both agreed that a system might be in place within five years. Kaine's followers point to the smiting of the small town of Oswestry with a "rain of cleansing fire" last October and the Rutland plague of toads. "Both Oswestry and Rutland are wake-up calls to our nation," said Mr. Kaine. "They may have been sinful, but ultimate retribution without due process of law is something that I will not tolerate. In today's modern world where the accepted definition of sin has become blurred, we need to protect ourselves against an overzealous deity keen to promote an outdated set of rules. It is for this reason that we are investing in Anti-Smite technology." The £14 billion contract will be awarded exclusively to Goliath Weapons, Inc.

Article in The Mole, July 1988

The news networks had a field day. The death of St. Zvlkx so soon after his resurrection raised a few eyebrows, but the Windowmaker's somewhat bizarre accident while "on assignment" became a sensation, supplanting even the upcoming SuperHoop from the front pages. Incredibly, despite severe internal injuries and a devastating head wound, she didn't die. She was taken to St. Septyk's Hospital, where they battled to stabilize her. Not from any great sense of moral duty, you understand, but for the fact that she could finger the sixty-seven or sixty-eight clients who had paid her to carry out her foul trade, and this was a prize the prosecutors were keen to claim. Within an hour of her coming out of surgery, three attempts by underworld bosses had been made to silence her for good. She was moved to the secure ward at the Kingsdown Home for the Criminally Insane, and there she stayed, comatose, attached to a ventilator.

"Spike was right. I should have told him earlier," I said to Gran, "or tipped off the authorities or something!"

Granny Next was feeling a lot better today. Although greatly enfeebled by her advanced years, she had actually walked around for a bit that morning. When I arrived, she had her reading glasses on and was surrounded by stacks of well-read tomes. The kind of things one generally reads for study, and rarely for pleasure.

"But you didn't," she replied, looking over the top of her spectacles, "and your father *knew* you wouldn't when he told you."

"He also said that I would decide whether she lived or died, but he was wrong—it's out of my hands now." I rubbed my scalp and sighed. "Poor Spike. He's taking it very badly."

"Where is he?"

"Still being interviewed by SO-9. They got an agent down from London who's been after her for more than ten years. I'd be there yet but for Flanker."

"Flanker?" queried Gran. "What did he do?"

"He came to thank me for leading SO-14 to a huge stockpile of hidden Danish literature."

"I thought you were trying *not* to help them?"

I shrugged.

"So did I. How was I to know the Danish underground really *was* using the Australian Writers' Guild as a depository?"

"Did you tell them it was Kaine who had paid her to kill you?"

"No," I said, looking down. "I don't know who I can trust and the last thing I need is to be taken into protective custody or something. If I'm not at the touchline tomorrow for the SuperHoop, the neanderthals won't play."

"But there is good news, surely?"

"Yes," I said, brightening somewhat, "we got some Danish books out of the country, *Hamlet* is on the mend—and I got Landen back."

Gran stared at me and lifted my face with her hand.

"For good?"

I looked down at my wedding ring.

"Twenty-four hours and counting."

"They did the same to me," sighed Gran, taking off her glasses and rubbing her eyes with a bony hand. "We were very happy for over forty years, until he was taken away again—this time in a more natural and inevitable way. And that was over thirty years ago."

She fell silent for a moment, and to distract her I told her about St. Zvlkx and his death and his revealments and how little of it made any sense. Time-traveling paradoxes tended to make my head spin.

"Sometimes," said Gran, holding up the cover of the *Swindon Evening Globe,* "the facts are all in front of us—we just have to get them in the right order."

I took the picture and stared at it. It had been taken a few seconds after the piano fell on Cindy. I hadn't realized how far the wreckage of the Steinway had scattered. A little way down the road, the lonely figure of Zvlkx was still lying on the pavement, abandoned in the drama.

"Can I keep this?"

"Of course. Be careful, my dear—remember that your father can't warn you of every single one of your potential demises. Invulnerability is reserved only for superheroes. The croquet final is far from won and anything can happen in the next twenty-four hours."

"A neanderthal defense?" repeated Aubrey and Alf when I found them taking "pegging out" at the croquet stadium. They had threatened to fire me if I didn't tell them what I was up to. "Of course, any team would spend millions trying to get a neanderthal to join—but they just won't do it."

"I've already got them. You can't pay them, and I really don't know how they will work as a team with humans—I get the feeling that they'll be a team of their own *within* your team."

"I don't care," said Aubrey, leaning on his mallet and sweeping a hand in the direction of the squad. "I was fooling myself. Biffo's too old, Smudger has a drink problem, and Snake is mentally unstable. George is okay, and I can handle myself, but a fresh crop of talent has infused the Whackers' team. They'll be fielding people like Bonecrusher McSneed."

He wasn't kidding. A mysterious benefactor—probably Goliath—had given a vast amount of money to the Whackers. Enough for them to buy almost anyone they wanted. Goliath was taking no chances that the Seventh Revealment would be fulfilled.

"So we're still in the game with five thals?"

"Yes," said Aubrey with a smile, "we're still in the game."

I dropped in to see Mum on the way home, ostensibly to take Hamlet and the dodos round to Landen's place. I found my mother in the kitchen with Bismarck, who seemed to be in the middle of telling her a joke.

". . . and then the white horse he says, 'What, Erich?' "

"Oh, Herr B!" said my mother, giggling and slapping him on the shoulder. "You are a wag!"

She noticed me standing there.

"Thursday! Are you okay? I heard on the radio there was some sort of accident involving a piano. . . ."

"I'm fine, Mum, really." I stared coldly at the Prussian Chancellor who, I had decided, was taking liberties with my mother's affections. "Good afternoon, Herr Bismarck. So, you haven't sorted out the Schleswig-Holstein question yet?"

"I am waiting still for the Danish prime minister," replied Bismarck, rising to greet me. "But I am growing impatient."

"I expect him very soon, Herr Bismarck," said my mother, putting the kettle on the stove. "Would you like a cup of tea while you're waiting?"

He bowed politely again. "Only if Battenberg cake we will be having."

"I'm sure there's a bit left over if that naughty Mr. Hamlet hasn't eaten it!" Her face dropped when she discovered that, indeed, naughty Mr. Hamlet *had* eaten it. "Oh dear! Would you like an almond slice instead?"

Bismarck's eyebrows twitched angrily.

"Everywhere I turn, the Danish are mocking my person and the German Confederation," he intoned angrily, smacking his fist into his open palm. "The incorporation of the Duchy of Schleswig into Danish state overlooked I might have, but personal Battenberg insult I will not. It is war!"

"Hang on a minute, Otto," said my mother, who, having brought up a large family almost single-handedly, was well placed to sort out the whole Battenberg-Schleswig-Holstein issue. "I thought we'd agreed that you weren't going to invade Denmark."

"That was then, this is now," muttered the Chancellor, puffing out his chest so aggressively that one of his brass buttons shot across the room and struck Pickwick a glancing blow on the back of the head. "Choice: Mr. Hamlet for his behavior apologizes on behalf of Danish people, or we go to war!"

"He's talking to that nice conflict-resolution man at the moment," replied my mother in an anxious tone.

"Then it *is* war," announced Bismarck, sitting down at the table and having an almond slice anyway. "More talk is pointless. Return I wish to 1863."

But then the door opened. It was Hamlet. He stared at us all and looked . . . well, *different.*

"Ah!" he said, drawing his sword. "Bismarck! Your aggressive stance against Denmark is at an end. Prepare . . . to die!"

The conflict-resolution talk had obviously affected him deeply. Bismarck, unmoved by the sudden threat to his life, drew a pistol.

"So! Battenberg you finish behind my back, yes?"

And they might have killed one another there and then if Mum and I hadn't intervened.

"Hamlet!" I said. "Killing Bismarck won't get your father back, now, will it?"

"Otto!" said Mum. "Killing Hamlet won't alter the feelings of the Schleswigers, now, will it?"

I took Hamlet into the hall and tried to explain why sudden retributive action might not be such a good idea after all.

"I disagree," he said, swishing his sword through the air. "The first thing I shall do when I get home is kill that murdering uncle of mine, marry Ophelia and take on Fortinbras. Better still, I shall invade Norway in a preemptive bid, and then Sweden, and—what's the one next to that?"

"Finland?"

"That's the one."

He placed his left hand on his hip and lunged aggressively with his sword at some imaginary foe. Pickwick made the mistake of walking into the corridor at that precise moment and made a startled *plooock* noise as the point of Hamlet's rapier stopped two inches from her head. She looked unsteady for a moment, then fainted clean away.

"That conflict-management specialist really taught me a thing or two, Miss Next. Apparently my problem was an unresolved or latent conflict—the death of my father—that persists and festers in an individual—me. To face up to problems, we must meet those conflicts head-on and resolve them to the best of our ability!"

It was worse than I thought.

"So you won't pretend to be mad and talk a lot, then?"

"No need," replied Hamlet, laughing. "The time for talking is over. Polonius will be for the high jump, too. As soon as I marry his daughter, he'll be fired as adviser and made chief librarian or something. Yes, we're going to have some changes around my play, I can tell *you*."

"What about building tolerance between opponents for a long-standing peaceful and ultimately rewarding coexistence between the conflicting parties?"

"I think he was going to cover that in the second session. It doesn't matter. By this time tomorrow, *Hamlet* will be a dynamic tale of one man's revenge and rise to power as the single greatest king Denmark has ever seen. It's the end of Hamlet the ditherer and the beginning of Hamlet the man of action! There's something rotten in the state of Denmark, and Hamlet says . . . it's payback time!"

This was bad. I couldn't send him back until Mrs. Tiggy-winkle and Shgakespeafe had sorted out his play, and in this condition there was no saying *what* he was capable of. I had to think fast.

"Good idea, Hamlet. But *before* that, I think you might like to know that Danish people are being insulted and maligned here in England, and that Kierkegaard, Andersen, Branner, Blixen and Farquitt are having their books burned."

He went quiet and stared at me with dumbstruck horror in his eyes.

"I am doing what I can to stop this," I went on, "but—"

"Daphne's books are being burned?"

"You know of her?"

"Of course. I'm a big fan. We have to have *something* to do during those long winters at Elsinore. Mum's a big fan, too—although my uncle prefers Catherine Cookson. But enough talk," he carried on, his postprevarication, nonhesitative brain clicking over rapidly, "what shall we do about it?"

"Everything hinges on us winning the SuperHoop tomorrow, but we need a show of force in case Kaine tries anything. Can you get together as many Danish supporters as you can?"

"Is it very important?"

"It could be vital."

Hamlet's eyes flashed with steely resolution. He picked his skull off the hall table, placed a hand on my shoulder and struck a dramatic pose.

"By tomorrow morning, my friend, you will have more Danes than you know what to do with. But stay this idle chitter-chatter— I must away!"

And without another word, he was out the door. From all-talk-no-action, he was now all-action-no-talk. I should *never* have brought him into the real world.

"By the way," said Hamlet who had popped his head back around the door, "you won't tell Ophelia about Emma, will you?"

"My lips are sealed."

I gathered up the dodos and popped them in the car, then drove home. I had called Landen soon after Cindy's accident to say I was unhurt. He said he knew all along I'd come to no harm, and I promised that I'd avoid assassins where possible from now onwards. I couldn't pull up outside the house as there were at least three news vans, so I parked round the back, walked through the alleyway, nodded a greeting to Millon and walked across the back lawn to the French windows.

"Lipsum!" said Friday, running up to give me a hug. I picked him up as Alan sized up his new home, trying to work out the areas of highest potential mischief.

"There's a telegram for you on the table," said Landen, "and if you're feeling masochistic the press would love you to reiterate how the Mallets will win tomorrow."

"Well, I'm not," I replied, tearing open the telegram. "How was your . . ."

My voice trailed off as I read the telegram. It was clear and to the point. WE HAVE UNFINISHED BUSINESS. COME ALONE, NO TRICKS, HANGAR D, SWINDON AIRPARK—KAINE.

"Darling?" I called out.

"Yes?" came Landen's voice from upstairs.

"I have to go out."

"Assassins?"

"No—megalomaniac tyrants keen on global domination."

"Do you want me to wait up?"

"No, but Friday needs a bath—and don't forget behind the ears."

36.

Kaine v. Next

Anti-Smite Technology Faces Criticism

Leading churchmen were not keen on Mr. Kaine's use of Anti-Smite technology. "We're not sure Mr. Kaine can place his will above that of God," said a nervous bishop who preferred not to be named, "but if God decides to smite something, then we think He had probably very good reason to do so." Atheists weren't impressed by Kaine's plans, nor that the cleansing of Oswestry was anything but an unlucky hit by a meteorite. "This smacks of the usual Kainian policy of keeping us cowed and afraid," said Rupert Smercc of Ipswich. "While the population worries about nonexistent threats from a product of mankind's need for meaning in a dark and brutal world, Kaine is raising taxes and blaming the Danes for everything." Not everyone was so forthright in condemnation. Mr. Pascoe, official spokesman of the Federated Agnostics, claimed, "There might be something in the whole smiting thing, but we're not sure."

Article in *The Mole*, July 1988

It was night when I arrived at Swindon Airpark's maintenance depot. Although airships still droned out into the night sky from the terminal opposite, this side of the field was deserted and empty, the workers long since punched out for the day. I showed my badge to security then followed the signs along the perimeter road and passed a docked airship, its silvery flanks shimmering with the reflected moon. The eight-story-high main doors of the gargantuan Hangar D were shut tight but I soon found a black Mercedes sports car near an open side door, so I stopped a little way short and killed my engine and lights. I replaced the clip in my automatic with the spare that I had loaded with five eraserheads—all I had managed to smuggle out of the BookWorld. I got out of the car, paused to listen and, hearing nothing, made my way quietly into the hangar.

Since the transcontinental "thousand-footer" airships were built these days at the Zeppelinwerks in Germany, the only airship within the cathedral-sized hangar was a relatively small sixty-seater, halfway through construction and looking like a metallic basket, its aluminum ribs held together with a delicate filigree of interconnecting struts each riveted carefully to the next. It looked overly complex for something in essence so simple. I glanced around the lofty interior but of Kaine there was no sign. I pulled out my automatic, chambered the first eraserhead and released the safety.

"Kaine?"

No answer.

I heard a noise and whipped my gun towards where a partly completed engine nacelle was resting on some trestles. I cursed myself for being so jumpy and suddenly realized that I wished Bradshaw was with me. Then I felt it—or at least, I *smelt* it. The lazy stench of death borne on a light breeze. I turned as a dark fetid shape loomed rapidly towards me. I had a brief vision of some unearthly terror before I pulled the trigger and the hollow thud of my first eraserhead hit home and the hellbeast evaporated into a flurry of the individual letters that made up its existence. They fell about me with the light tinkling sound of Christmas decorations shattering.

I heard the sound of a single slow handclap and noticed the silhouette of Kaine standing behind the partly finished control gondola. I didn't pause for a moment and let fly a second eraserhead. In an instant Kaine invoked a minor character—a small man with glasses—right in the path of the projectile and he, not Kaine, was erased.

Yorrick moved into the light. He hadn't aged a day since I had seen him last. His complexion was unblemished and he didn't have a hair out of place. Only the finest described characters were indistinguishable from real people; the rest—and Kaine was among them—had a vague plasticity that belied their fictional origins.

"Enjoying yourself?" I asked him sarcastically.

"Oh yes," he replied, giving me a faint smile.

He was a B character in an A role and had been elevated far beyond his capabilities—a child in control of a nation. Whether by virtue of Goliath or the Ovinator or simply by his fictional roots I wasn't sure, but what I did know was that he was dangerous in the real world and dangerous in the BookWorld. Anyone who could invoke hellbeasts at will was not to be ignored.

I fired again and the same thing happened. The character was different—from a costume drama, I think—but the effect was identical. Kaine was using expendable bit parts as shields. I glanced nervously around, sensing a trap.

"You forget," said Kaine as he stared at me with his unblinking eyes, "that I have had many years to hone my powers, and as you can see, nobodies from the Farquitt canon are ten a penny."

"Murderer!"

Kaine laughed.

"You can't murder a fictional person, Thursday. If you could, every author would be behind bars!"

"You know what I mean," I growled, beginning to move forwards. If I could just grasp hold of him I could jump into fiction and take him with me. Kaine knew this and kept his distance.

"You're something of a pest, you know," he carried on, "and I really thought the Windowmaker would have been able to dispose of you so I wouldn't have to. Despite the woefully poor odds on Swindon winning tomorrow, I really can't risk Zvlkx's revealment coming true, no matter how unlikely. And my friends at Goliath agree with me."

"This place is not your place," I told him, "and you are messing with real people's lives. You were created to entertain, not to rule."

"Have you any idea," he carried on as we slowly circled one another about the airship's unfinished control gondola, "just what it's like being stuck as a B-9 character in a self-published novel? Never

317

being read, having two lines of dialogue and constantly being bettered by my inferiors?"

"What's wrong with the character exchange program?" I asked, stalling for time.

"I tried. Do you know what the Council of Genres told me?"

"I'm all ears."

"They told me to do the best with what I had. Well, I'm doing exactly that, Miss Next!"

"I have some swing with the council, Kaine. Surrender and I'll do the best I can for you."

"Lies!" spat Kaine. "Lies, lies, and more lies! You have no intention of helping me!"

I didn't deny it.

"Well," he carried on. "I said I needed to speak to you, and here it is: you've found out where I'm from, and despite my best efforts to retain all copies of *At Long Last Lust,* there is still a possibility you might find a copy and delete me from within. I can't have that. So I wanted to give you the opportunity of entering into a mutually agreeable partnership. Something that will benefit both of us. Me in the corridors of power and you as head of any SpecOps division you want—or SpecOps itself, come to that."

"I think you underestimate me," I said quietly. "The only deal I'm listening to tonight will be your unconditional surrender."

"Oh, I didn't underestimate you at all," continued the Chancellor with a slight smile. "I only said that to give a Gorgon friend of mine enough time to creep up behind you. Have you met . . . Medusa, by the way?"

I heard a hissing noise behind me. The hairs on my neck rose and my heart beat faster. I looked down as I twisted and jumped to the side, resisting any temptation to look at the naked and repellent creature that had been slinking towards me. It's difficult to hit a target that you are trying not to look at and my fourth eraserhead impacted harmlessly on a gantry on the other side of the hangar. I stepped back, caught my foot on a piece of metal and collapsed over backwards, my gun skittering across the floor towards some packing cases. I swore and attempted to scramble away from the mythological horror, only to have my ankle grasped by Medusa, whose head snakes were now hissing angrily. I tried to kick off her grasp but she had a grip like a vise. Her free hand grabbed my other ankle and then, cackling wildly, she crept her way up my body as I struggled in vain to push her away, her sharply nailed claws biting into my flesh and making me cry out in pain.

"Stare into my face!" screamed the Gorgon as we wrestled in the dust. "Stare into my face and accept your destiny!" I kept my eyes averted as she pinned me against the cold concrete and then, when her bony and foul-smelling body was sitting on my chest, she cackled again and took hold of my head in both hands. I screamed and shut my eyes tight, gagging at her putrid breath. It was no escape. I felt her hands move on my face, her fingertips on my eyelids.

"Come along, Thursday my love," she screeched, the hissing of the snakes almost drowning her out, "gaze into my soul and feel your body turn to stone—!"

I strained and cried out as her fingers pulled my eyelids open. I swiveled my eyes as low in their sockets as I could, desperate to stave off the inevitable, and was just beginning to see glimmers of light and the lower part of her body when there was the sound of steel being drawn from a scabbard and a soft *whoop* noise. Medusa fell limp and silent on my chest. I opened my eyes and pushed the severed head of the Gorgon into the shadows. I jumped up, slipped once in the pool of blood issuing from her headless corpse and ran backwards, stumbling in my panic to get away.

"Well," said a familiar voice. "Looks like I got here just in time!"

It was the Cheshire Cat. He was sitting on an unfinished airship rib and was grinning wildly. He wasn't alone. Next to him stood a man. But it wasn't any ordinary man. He was, firstly, tall—at least seven foot six and broad with it. He was dressed in rudimentary armor and grasped in his powerful hands a shield and sword that appeared to weigh almost nothing. He was a frightening warrior to behold; the sort of hero for whom epics are written—the likes of which we have no need of in our day and age. He was the most alpha of males—he was Beowulf. He made no sound, knees slightly bent in readiness, bloody sword moving elegantly in a slow figure-eight pattern.

"Good move, Mr. Cat," said Kaine sardonically, stepping from behind the gondola and facing us across the only open area in the hangar.

"You can end this right now, Mr. Kaine," said the Cat. "Go back to your book and stay there—or face the consequences."

"I choose not to," he replied with an even smile, "and since you have raised the stakes by invoking an eighth-century hero, I challenge you to a one-on-one invocation contest pitting my fictional champions against yours. You win and I stay forever in *At Long Last Lust;* I win and you leave me unmolested."

I looked at the Cheshire Cat who was, for once, not smiling.

"Very well, Mr. Kaine. I accept your challenge. Usual rules? One beast at a time and *strictly* no kraken?"

"Yes, yes," replied Kaine impatiently. He closed his eyes and with a wild shriek Grendel appeared and flew towards Beowulf, who expertly sliced it into eight more or less equal pieces.

"I think we got him riled," whispered the Cheshire Cat from the corner of his mouth. "That was a bad move—Beowulf *always* vanquishes Grendel."

But Kaine didn't waste any more time and a moment later there was a living, breathing *Tyrannosaurus rex* tramping the concrete floor, fangs drooling with saliva. It whipped its tail angrily and knocked the engine nacelle onto its side.

"From *The Lost World,*" queried the Cat, "or *Jurassic Park?*"

"Neither," replied Kaine. "*The Boy's Bumper Book of Dinosaurs.*"

"Ooh!" replied the Cat. "The nonfiction gambit, eh?"

Kaine clicked his fingers and the thunder lizard lunged forwards as Beowulf went into the attack, sword flailing. I retreated towards the Cat and asked anxiously, "This Beowulf isn't the original, is it?"

"Good Lord no, *quite* the reverse!"

It was just as well. Beowulf had made mincemeat of Grendel but the *Tyrannosaurus,* in turn, made mincemeat of him. As the giant lizard slurped down the remnants of the warrior, the Cat hissed to me: "I do so love these competitions!"

I wiped my scratched face with my handkerchief. I must say I couldn't really share the Cat's mischievous sense of glee or enjoyment. "What's our next move?" I asked him. "Smaug the dragon?"

"No point. He'd invoke a Baggins to kill it. Perhaps it would be best to make a tactical retreat and introduce an Allan Quatermain with an elephant gun, but I'm late for my son's birthday party, so it's going to be . . . *him!*"

There was another shimmer in the air about us and, with a whiffling and a burbling, a bat-winged creature appeared. It had a long tail, reptilian feet, flaming eyes, huge sort of *catchy* hairy claws . . . and was wearing a lilac-colored tunic with matching socks.

The *Tyrannosaurus* looked up from its feast at the jabberwock who stared back at it while hovering in the air and making dangerous whiffling noises. It was about the same size as the dinosaur and went for it aggressively, jaws biting, claws catching. As the Cat, Kaine and I looked on, the jabberwock and the *Tyrannosaurus* rolled around in mortal combat, tails flailing. At one point it looked as though Kaine's champion had the upper hand until the jabberwock executed a maneuver known in wrestling circles as an "airplane spin and body slam" that shook the ground. The giant lizard lay still, moving feebly. An animal that large does not need to fall from very high to break bones. The jabberwock burbled contentedly to itself, doing a little triumphant two-step dance as he walked back over to us.

"Right!" yelled Kaine. "I've had just about my fill of this!"

He raised his arms in the air and a gale seemed to fill the hangar. There were several crashes of thunder from outside and a large shape started to rise within the empty framework of the half-built airship. It grew and grew until it was wearing the airship skeleton like a corset, then broke free of it and with one tentacle clasped the jabberwock and raised it high in the air. Kaine had cheated. It was the kraken. Wet, strangely shapeless and smelling of overcooked oysters, it was the largest and most powerful creature that I knew of in fiction.

"Now, now!" said the Cat, waving a claw at Kaine. "Remember the rules!"

"To hell with your rules!" shouted Kaine. "Puny Jurisfiction agents, prepare to meet thy doom!"

"Now that," said the Cat, addressing me, "was a *very* corny line."

"He's Farquitt! What did you expect? What are we going to do?"

The kraken wrapped a slippery tentacle several times around the jabberwock's body and then squeezed until his eyes bulged ominously.

"Cat!" I said more urgently. *"What's the next move?"*

"I'm thinking," replied the Cat, lashing his tail angrily. "Trying to come up with something to defeat the kraken is not that easy. Wait. Wait. I think I've got it!"

There was a bright flash and there, facing the kraken, was—a small fairy no higher than my knee. It had delicate wings like those of a dragonfly, a silver tiara and a wand, which she waved in Kaine's direction. In an instant the kraken had melted away and the jabberwock fell to the ground, gasping for breath.

"What the hell—?" shouted Kaine in anger and surprise, waving his hands uselessly to try and bring the kraken back.

"I'm afraid you've lost," replied the Cat. "But you cheated and I had to cheat a bit, too, and even though I've won I can't insist on my prize. It's all in Thursday's hands now."

"What do you mean?" shouted Kaine angrily. "Who was that and why can't I summon up beasts from fiction any longer?"

"Well," said the Cat as he began to purr, "that was the Blue Fairy, from *Pinocchio*."

"You mean—?" asked Kaine, mouth agape.

"Right," replied the Cat. "She made you into a real person, just like she made Pinocchio into a real boy."

He touched his hands on his chest, then his face, trying to figure it out.

"But . . . that means you have no authority over me—!"

"Alas not," replied the Cat. "Jurisfiction has no jurisdiction over real people in the real world. As I said, it's all up to Thursday now."

The Cat stopped and repeated two words as if to see which sounded better. "Jurisfiction—*jurisdiction*—Jurisfiction—*jurisdiction*."

Kaine and I stared at one another. If he was real it definitely meant Jurisfiction had no mandate to control him and it also meant we couldn't destroy him through his book. But then he couldn't escape from the real world either—and would bleed and die and age like a real man. Kaine started to laugh.

"Well, this is a turnaround! Thank you very much, Mr. Cat!" The Cheshire Cat gave a contemptuous snort and turned to face the other direction. "You have done me a great service," continued Kaine. "I am now free to lead this country to new heights without the meddling of you and your fictional band of idiots. I'll be free to put behind me the last vestiges of kindness that I was forced to carry because of my written character. Mr. Cat, I thank you, and the people of the unified Britain thank you." He laughed again and turned to me. "And you, Miss Next, won't be able to even get close!"

"There's still the Seventh Revealment," I said a bit weakly.

"Win the SuperHoop? With that ragtag bunch of no-hopers? I think you grossly overrate your chances, my lady—and with Goliath and the Ovinator to help me, I can't begin to overestimate mine!"

And he laughed again, looked at his watch and walked briskly from the hangar. We heard his car start up and drive away.

"Sorry," said the Cat, still looking the other way. "I had to think of something quickly. At least this way he didn't win—tonight."

I sighed. "You did well, Chesh—I would *never* have thought of invoking the Blue Fairy."

"It *was* quite good, wasn't it?" agreed the Cat. "Can you smell hot buttered crumpets?"

"No."

"Me neither. Who are you going to put on midfield?"

"Biffo, probably," I said slowly, picking up my automatic from where it had fallen and replacing the clip, "and Stig as roquet taker."

"Ah. Well, good luck and see you soon," said the Cat, and vanished.

I sighed and looked around at the quiet and empty hangar. The fictional gore and corpses of Medusa, the *Tyrannosaurus* and Beowulf had vanished and apart from the wrecked airship, there was no evidence of the battle that had been fought here. We had scored a victory against Kaine but not the total victory I had hoped for. I was just walking back towards the exit when I noticed the Cheshire Cat had reappeared, balanced on the handle of a pallet trolley.

"Did you say Stig, or fig?" asked the Cat.

"I said Stig," I replied, "and I wish you wouldn't keep appearing and vanishing so suddenly—you make one quite giddy."

"All right," said the Cat and this time it vanished quite slowly, beginning with the end of the tail, and ending with the grin, which remained some time after the rest of it had gone.

37.

Before the Match

Zvlkx Followers Hold Nighttime Peace March.
All seventy-six members of the Idolatry Friends of St. Zvlkx spent the night silently marching between the places of interest of their worshipful leader, who was hit by a Number 23 bus on Friday. The march began at Tesco's car park and visited places in Swindon that St. Zvlkx held most dear—seven pubs, six betting shops and Swindon's leading brothel—before undertaking a silent prayer at his place of death. The march went off peacefully, except for numerous interruptions by a woman who gave her name as Shirley and insisted that Zvlkx owed her money.

Article in the Swindon Daily Eyestrain, July 22, 1988

I arrived at the croquet stadium at eight. The fans were already waiting at the turnstiles, hoping to get the best seats in the stands. I was waved past and parked my Speedster in the manager's parking spot, then made my way into the changing rooms. Aubrey was waiting there for me, pacing up and down.

"Well?" he said. "Where's our team?"

"They'll be here at one o'clock."

"Can't we get them here earlier?" he asked. "We need to discuss tactics."

"No," I said firmly. "They'll be here on time. It's senseless to try to impose human time constraints on them. They're playing on our side—that's the main thing."

"Okay," agreed Aubrey reluctantly. "Have you met Penelope Hrah?"

Penelope was a large and powerful woman who looked as though she could crack walnuts with her eyelids. She had moved to croquet because hockey wasn't violent enough, and although at thirty-two she was at the end of her career, she might prove an asset—as a terror weapon, if nothing else. She scared me—and I was on the same team.

"Hello Penelope," I said nervously. "I really appreciate you joining us."

"Urg."

"Everything okay? Can I get you something?"

She grunted again, and I rubbed my hands together anxiously.

"Right, well, leave you to it, then."

I left her to talk strategy with Alf and Aubrey. I spent the next couple of hours doing interviews and ensuring that the team's lawyers were up to speed on the game's complex legal procedures. At midday Landen and Friday arrived with Mycroft, Polly and my mother. I took them down to the seating reserved for the VIPs just behind the players' benches and sat them down next to Joffy and Miles, who had arrived earlier.

"Is Swindon going to win?" asked Polly.

"I hope so," I said, not brimming with confidence.

"The problem with you, Thursday," put in Joffy, "is that you have no faith. We in the Idolatry Friends of St. Zvlkx have complete faith in the revealments. Lose and Goliath moves to new heights of human exploitation and unfathomable avarice, hidden amongst the trappings of religious formality and perverted ecclesiastical dogma."

"That was a very good speech."

"Yes, I thought so, too. I was practicing on the march last night. Don't feel you're under any pressure now."

"Thanks for nothing. Where's Hamlet?"

"He said he'd join us later."

I left them to do a live broadcast with Lydia Startright, who was really more interested in knowing where I had been for the past two and a half years than asking me about Swindon's chances. After this I hurried down to the players' entrance to welcome Stig— who was playing—and the four other neanderthals. They were completely unfazed by the media attention and ignored the phalanx of pressmen completely. I thanked them for joining our team, and Stig pointed out that they were there only because that was part of the deal, and nothing more.

I walked them towards the changing rooms, where the human team members greeted them with a good measure of curiosity. They talked haltingly with one another, the neanderthals confining their speech to the technical aspects of croquet play. It was of no matter or consequence to them if they won or lost—they would simply do the best they could. They refused body armor, as they preferred instead to play barefoot in shorts and brightly colored Hawaiian shirts. This caused a slight problem with the Toast Marketing Board, which had insisted that its name be on the team strip, but I smoothed it over with them eventually and all was well. There was less than ten minutes before we were due out, so Aubrey made a stirring speech to the team, which the neanderthals didn't really comprehend. Stig, whose understanding of humans was perhaps a little better than most, just told them to "hoop as much as we can," which they understood.

"Miss Next?"

I turned to face a thin, cadaverous man staring at me. I recognized him instantly. It was Ernst Stricknene, Kaine's adviser—and he was carrying a red briefcase. I had seen a similar case at Goliathopolis and during *Evade the Question Time*. It doubtless concealed an Ovinator.

"What do you want?"

"Chancellor Kaine would like to meet the Swindon team for a pep talk."

"Why?"

Stricknene looked at me coldly. "It is not for you to question the will of the Chancellor, young lady."

It was then that Kaine marched in, surrounded by his goons and entourage. The team stood up respectfully—except the neanderthals, who, completely ambivalent to the vagaries of perceived hierarchy, carried on talking to one another in soft grunts. Kaine looked at me triumphantly, but I noticed, too, that he had changed slightly. His eyes looked tired and his mouth had a barely discernible sag to it. He'd started to show signs of being human. He was beginning to age.

"Ah!" he said. "The ubiquitous Miss Next. LiteraTec, team manager, savior of *Jane Eyre*. Is there anything you can't do?"

"I'm not that good at knitting."

There was a ripple of laughter amongst the team, and also from Kaine's followers, who abruptly silenced themselves as Kaine glanced around the room, scowling. But he controlled himself and gave a disingenuous smile after nodding to Stricknene.

"I just came down here to talk to the team and tell all of you that it would be a far better thing for this country if I stayed in power, and even though I don't know how Zvlkx's revealment will work, I can't leave the secure future of this nation to the vagaries of a thirteenth-century seer with poor personal hygiene. Do you understand what I am saying?"

I knew what he was up to. The Ovinator. It would, as likely as not, have us all eating out of his hand in under a minute. But I wasn't figuring on Hamlet, who appeared suddenly from behind Stricknene, rapier drawn.

It was now or nothing, and I yelled, "The briefcase! Destroy the Ovinator!"

Hamlet needed no second bidding, and he leapt into action, expertly piercing the case, which gave off a brief flash of green light and a short, high-pitched wail that started the police dogs outside barking. Hamlet was swiftly overpowered by two SO-6 agents, who handcuffed him.

"Who is this man?" demanded Kaine.

"He's my cousin Eddie."

"NO!" yelled Hamlet, standing up straight even though he had two men holding him. "My name is Hamlet, Prince of Denmark. Danish, and proud of it!"

Kaine gave a smug laugh. "Captain, arrest Miss Next for harboring a known Danish person—and arrest the entire team for aiding and abetting."

It was a bad moment. With no players, the game had to be forfeited. But Hamlet, actioneer that he had become, was not out of ideas.

"I shouldn't do that if I were you."

"And why not?" sneered Kaine, not without a certain quaver in his voice; he was now acting solely on his wits. He had neither his fictional roots nor the Ovinator to help him.

"Because," announced Hamlet, "I am a very special friend of Ms. Daphne Farquitt."

"And . . . ?" inquired Kaine with a slight smile.

"She is outside awaiting my return. If I fail to reappear or you try any sort of anti-Mallets skulduggery, she will mobilize her troops."

Kaine laughed, and Stricknene, sycophant that he was, laughed with him.

"Troops? What troops are these?" Kaine asked, amused.

But Hamlet was deadly serious. He glowered at them for a moment before answering. "Her fan club. They're highly organized, armed to the teeth, profoundly angry at having had their books burned and ready to move at her command. There are thirty thousand stationed near the stadium and a further ninety thousand in reserve. One word from Daphne and you're finished."

"I have reversed the law banning Farquitt," replied Kaine hastily. "They will disperse when they learn this."

"They will believe nothing from your lying tongue," replied Hamlet softly, "only that which Ms. Farquitt tells them. Your power is waning, my friend, and destiny's inelegant toe creaks the boards to your door."

There was a tense silence as Kaine stared at Hamlet and Hamlet stared back at Kaine. I'd witnessed quite a few standoffs but none with so much at stake.

"You haven't a hope in hell anyway," announced Kaine after considering his options carefully. "I'm going to enjoy watching the Whackers trash you. Release him."

The SO-6 agents uncuffed Hamlet and escorted Kaine out the door.

"Well," said Hamlet, "looks like we're back in the game. I'm going to watch with your mother. Win this one for the Farquitt fans, Thursday!"

And he was gone.

None of us had any time to ponder on the matter further, as we heard a Klaxon go off and an excited roar from the crowd echoed down the tunnel.

"Good luck, everyone," said Aubrey with a good measure of bravado. "It's showtime!"

The crowd erupted into screams of jubilation as we trotted down the tunnel onto the green. The stadium could seat thirty thousand, and it was packed. Large monitors had been set up outside for the benefit of those who could not get a seat, and the TV networks were beaming the match live to an estimated 2 billion people in seventy-three countries worldwide. It was going to be quite a show.

I stayed on the touchline as the Swindon Mallets lined up face-to-face with the Reading Whackers. They all glared at one another as the Swindon & District Wheel-Tappers' Brass Band marched on, headed by Lola Vavoom. There was then a pause while President Formby took his seat in the VIP box and, again led by Ms. Vavoom, the audience stood to sing the unofficial English national anthem, "When I'm Cleaning Windows." After the song had finished, Yorrick Kaine appeared at the VIP box, but his reception was derisory at best. There was a smattering of applause and a few "Hail!"s, but nothing like the reception he was expecting. His anti-Danish stance had lost a lot of popular support when he'd made the mistake of accusing the Danish Women's Handball Team of being spies and arrested them. I saw him sit down and scowl at the President, who smiled back warmly.

I was standing at the touchline with Alf Widdershaine, watching the proceedings.

"Is there anything more we could have done?" I whispered.

"No," said Alf after a pause. "I just hope those neanderthals can cut the mustard."

I turned and walked back towards Landen. On his lap was Friday, gurgling and clapping his hands. I had taken him once to the chariot race in the novel of *Ben-Hur,* and he'd loved it.

"What are our chances, darling?" asked Landen.

"Reasonable to middling with the neanderthals playing. I'll speak to you later."

I gave them a kiss each, and Landen wished me good luck.

"Dolor in reprehenderit—Mummy," said Friday. I thanked him for his kind words and heard my name being called. It was Aubrey who was talking to the umpire, who, as custom dictated, was dressed as a country parson.

"What do you mean?" I heard Aubrey say in an outraged tone as I moved closer. It seemed there was some sort of altercation, and we hadn't even begun play yet. "Show me where it says that in the rules!"

"What's the problem?" I asked.

"It's the neanderthals," he said between gritted teeth. "According to the rules, it seems that nonhumans are barred from taking part!"

I glanced back to where Stig and the four other neanderthals were sitting in a circle, meditating.

"Rule 78b-45(ii)," quoted the umpire as O'Fathens, the Reading Whackers' captain, looked on with a gleeful expression, " 'No player or team may use an equine or any other nonhuman creature to gain an advantage over the opposing team.' "

"But that doesn't mean *players,*" I said. "That rule clearly only refers to horse, antelope and so forth—it was brought in when the

Dorchester Slammers attempted to gain the advantage by playing on horseback in 1962."

"The rules seem clear to me," growled O'Fathens, taking a step forwards. "Are neanderthals human?" Aubrey also took a step forwards. Their noses were almost touching.

"Well . . . sort of," I answered hesitantly.

There was nothing for it but to seek a judgment. Since the rules regarding on-field litigation had been relaxed ten years ago, it was not uncommon for the first half hour of a match to be taken up with legal wranglings by the teams' lawyers, of which each side was permitted two, with one substitute. It added a new form of drama to the proceedings but was not without its own problems: after a particularly litigious SuperHoop six years ago, when a legal argument was overturned in the high court two years after the match was played, it became mandatory that three high-court judges be at readiness to give an instant, unquestionable ruling on any legal point.

We approached the Port-a-Court, and our respective lawyers made their representations. The three judges retired to their chambers and returned a few minutes later to announce:

"It is the finding of this Croquet Appellant Court in the action *Mallets* v. *Whackers* (neanderthal player legality) that the Whackers' complaint is upheld. In the eyes of English law, neanderthals are *not* human, and cannot play."

The Reading side of the crowd erupted into joyous yells as the judges' ruling was run up on the screen.

Aubrey opened his mouth, but I pulled him aside.

"Don't waste your breath, Aubrey."

"We can prepare an appeal in seven minutes," said Mr. Runcorn, one of our lawyers. "I think we can find a nonhuman precedent in the Worcester Sauces v. Taunton Ciders SuperHoop semifinals of 1963."

Aubrey scratched his head and looked at me. "Thursday?"

"A failed appeal could result in a two-hoop forfeit," I pointed out. "I say we get the lawyers working on it. If they think it's worth a try, we'll lodge an appeal at the end of the first third."

"But we're five players down, and we haven't even picked up our mallets!"

"The game's not lost until it's lost, Aubrey. We've got a few tricks up our sleeve, too."

I wasn't kidding. I had visited the lawyers' pavilion earlier, where they were performing background checks on every player on the opposing side. The Whackers' striker, George "Rhino" McNasty, had fourteen unpaid parking violations, and our legal team successfully pleaded that this should be heard here and now; he was sentenced to an hour's community service, which effectively had him picking up litter in the car park until the end of the second third. Jambe turned back to Mr. Runcorn.

"Okay, prepare an appeal for the end of the first third. We'll start with what we've got."

Even with our substitute brought on, we still had only six players to their full complement of ten. But it got worse. To play on a local side, you had to have been born in the town or lived there for at least six months before playing. Our substitute, Johnno Swift, had lived here for only five months and twenty-six days when he began his career at the Mallets three years before. The Reading lawyers argued that he was playing illegally in his first match, a transgression that should have won him a life ban. Once again the judges upheld the complaint, and, to another excited yell from the crowd, Swift walked dejectedly back to the dressing rooms.

"Well," said O'Fathens, putting out his hand to Jambe, "we'll just accept you've conceded the match, okay?"

"We're playing, O'Fathens. Even if Swindon were to lose a thousand hoops, people will still say, 'This was their finest—' "

"I don't think so," interrupted the Whackers' team lawyer with a triumphant grin. "You're now down to only five players. Under Rule 681g, Subsection (f/6), 'Any team that fails to start the game with the minimum of six players forfeits the match.' "

He pointed out the entry in Volume 7 of the World Croquet League rule book. It was there, all right, just under the rules governing the minimum raisin requirement in the buns served at the concession stands. Beaten! Beaten even before we'd picked up a mallet! Swindon could weather it, but the world could not—the revealment would be broken, and Kaine and Goliath would carry on their perverse plans unmolested.

"I'll announce it," said the umpire.

"No," said Alf, clicking his fingers, "we *do* have a player we can field!"

"Who?"

He pointed at me. "Thursday!"

I was gobsmacked. I hadn't played for over eight years.

"Objection!" blurted out the Whackers' lawyer. "Miss Next is *not* a native of Swindon!"

My inclusion would be of questionable value—but at least it meant we could play.

"I was born at St. Septyk's," I said slowly. "I'm Swindon enough for this team."

"Perhaps *Swindon* enough," said the lawyer, consulting a rule book hurriedly, "but not *experienced* enough. According to Rule 23f, Subsection (g/9), you are ineligible to play international-standard croquet since you have not played the minimum of ten matches to county standard."

I thought for a moment. "Actually, I have."

It was true. I used to play for the SpecOps Middlesex team when I was based in London. I was quite good, too—but nothing like these guys.

"It is the decision of the Croquet Appellant Court," intoned the three judges, who wanted to see a good game the same as anyone, "that Miss Next be allowed to represent her city in this match."

O'Fathens's face fell. "This is preposterous! What kind of stupid decision is that?"

The judges looked at him sternly. "It is the decision of this court—and we find you in contempt. The Whackers will forfeit one hoop."

O'Fathens boiled with inner rage, held it within him, turned on his heel and, followed by his lawyers, strode to where his team was waiting.

"Good one!" laughed Aubrey. "The whistle hasn't even gone, and we're winning!"

He tried to sound full of enthusiasm, but it was difficult. We were fielding a six-strong team—five and a quarter if you count me—and still had an entire game to play.

"We've got ten minutes to the off. Thursday, get changed into Snake's spare set—he's about your size."

I dashed off to the changing rooms and dressed myself up in Snake's leg guards and shoulder pads. Widdershaine helped me adjust the straps around my chest, and I grabbed a spare mallet before running back onto the field, fiddling with my helmet strap just as Aubrey was beginning his strategy talk.

"In past matches," he said in a hushed tone, "the Whackers have been known to test a weak side with a standard 'Bomperini' opening tactic. A deflective feint towards midhoop left, but actually aiming for an undefended back-hoop right."

The team whistled low.

"But we'll be ready for them. I want them to know we're playing an aggressive game. Instead of backfooting it, we'll go straight into a surprise roquet maneuver. Smudger, you're to lead with a sideways deflection to Biffo, who'll pass to Thursday—"

"Wait," put in Biffo. "Thursday is here making up the numbers. She hasn't hit a ball in years!"

This was true. But Jambe had bigger plans.

"Exactly. I want them to think Thursday is a dark horse—that we *planned* this late addition. With a bit of luck, they'll waste a good player marking her. Thursday, drive it towards their red ball, and Spike will intercept. It doesn't matter if you miss—I want them to be *confused* by our tactics. And, Penelope—just frighten the other team."

"Urg," grunted the wingwoman.

"Okay, keep it tight, no more violence than is necessary, and keep an eye out for the Duchess. She's not averse to a bit of ankle swiping."

We all tapped our fists together and made a *harump* noise. I walked slowly to my place on the green, my heart beating with the pump of adrenaline.

"You okay?" It was Aubrey.

"Sure."

"Good. Let's play some croquet."

38.

WCL SuperHoop-88

2:00 P.M., Saturday, July 22, 1988, Swindon Stadium, Wessex

Reading Whackers:	Swindon Mallets:
Tim O'Fathens, Captain	Aubrey Jambe, Captain
Molly "The Mark" Stern, Midfield	Alan "Biffo" Mandible, Midfield
Tim "The Mouse" McCall, Forward Striker	"Snake" Spillikin, Forward Striker
Gretchen "Barker" Koss, Striker	~~Grunk (neanderthal), Defense~~
Wallace "Back to Front" Acadia, Defense	~~Warg (neanderthal), Striker~~
~~George "Rhino" McNasty, Striker~~	~~Dorf (neanderthal), Peg Defense~~
Alessandra Lusardi, Roquet Taker	~~Stiggins (neanderthal), Roquet Taker~~
"Bonecrusher" McSneed, Forward Hoop	"Smudger" Blarney, Forward Hoop
Freddie "Dribbler" Loehnis, Peg Defense	~~Zim (neanderthal), Striker~~
Duchess of Sheffield, Wingman	Penelope Hrah, Midhoop Wingman
	Thursday Next, Manager/Midfield

Legal Team: Wapcaplitt & Sfortz	**Legal Team:** Runcorn & Twizzit
Linesman: Bruce Giffords	**Sub:** ~~John "Johnno" Swift~~
Coach: Geoffrey Snurge	**Coach:** Alf Widdershaine

I took up my station at the twenty-yard line and looked around the green. The rhododendron bushes in the center occluded my vision of the back-hoop right; I glanced up at the scoreboard and clock. Two minutes to go. There were three other natural hazards that we were to play around on the green—the Tea Party, which even now was being stocked by volunteers, the garden roller, and the Italian Sunken Garden. Once the Tea Party volunteers were safe and the parson umpire was happy his curate linesmen were all in position, the Klaxon went off with a loud blare.

Many things happened at once. There were two almost simultaneous *clack*s as both teams whacked off, and I ran forward instinctively to intercept the pass from Biffo. Since the Whackers didn't think I was of any use, I had been left unmarked, and Biffo's pass came sailing towards me. I was flushed by the excitement and caught it in midair, smashing it towards the opponent's ball for what looked like an aerial roquet. It didn't work. I missed by about a foot. The opponent's ball carried on to the forty-yard line where McCall blasted it through the back-hoop right—the classic Bomperini opener. I didn't have time to think about it, as there was a shout of "Thursday!" from Aubrey, and I turned to make a swipe at the opposition's ball. The Klaxon went, and everyone stopped playing. I had touched the opponent's ball when south of the forty-yard line after it had been passed from the last person to have hit a red ball in the opposite direction—one of the more obvious offside transgressions.

"Sorry, guys," I said as the Whackers lined up to take their penalty. O'Fathens took the shot and catapulted our ball into the rhododendrons. As George tried to find it, and with our other ball out of play in the Italian Sunken Garden, the Whackers went on the offensive and hooped three times before we'd even realized it. Even when we found the ball, we were too dispersed, and after another twenty-eight minutes of hard defensive footwork, managed to end the first third with only four hoops to Reading's eight.

"There are too many of them," panted Snake. "Eight–four is the worst opening score for a SuperHoop final ever."

"We're not beat yet," replied Jambe, taking a drink. "Thursday, you played well."

"Well?" I returned, taking off my helmet and wiping the sweat from my brow. "I sank the ball with my first whack and dropped us a hoop on the offside penalty!"

"But we still *scored* a hoop—and we would have already lost if you hadn't joined us. You just need to relax more. You're playing as though the world depended on it."

The team didn't know it, but I was.

"Just calm down a bit, take a second before you whack, and you'll be fine. Biffo—good work, and nice hoop, Penelope, but if you chase their wingman again, you might be booked."

"Urg," replied Penelope.

"Mr. Jambe?" said Mr. Runcorn, who had been working on a rearguard legal challenge to the antineanderthal ruling.

"Yes? Do we have a case?"

"I'm afraid not. I can't seem to find any grounds for one. The nonhuman precedent was overruled on appeal. I'm very sorry, sir. I think I'm playing very badly—might I resign and bring on the legal substitute?"

"It's not your fault," said Jambe kindly. "Have the substitute lawyer continue the search."

Runcorn bowed and went to sit on the lawyers' bench, where a young man in a badly fitting suit had been sitting silently throughout the first third.

"That Duchess is murder," muttered Biffo, breathlessly. "She almost had me twice."

"Isn't striking an opponent a red-card three-hoop penalty offense?" I asked.

"Of course! But if she can take out our best player, then it might be worth it. Keep an eye on her, everyone."

"Mr. Jambe?"

It was the referee, who told us further litigation had been brought against our team. We dutifully approached the Port-a-Court, where the judges were just signing an amendment to the World Croquet League book of law.

"What is it?"

"As a result of the Danish Economic (Scapegoat) Act coming into law, people of Danish descent are not permitted to vote or take key jobs."

"When did this law come into effect?"

"Five minutes ago."

I looked up at Kaine in the VIP box, where he smiled and waved at me.

"So?" asked Jambe. "Kaine's dopey ideas have no reflection on croquet—this is sport, not politics."

The Whackers' lawyer, Mr. Wapcaplitt, coughed politely.

"In that you would be mistaken. The definition of 'key job' includes being a highly paid sports personality. We have conducted some background checks and discovered that Ms. Penelope Hrah was born in Copenhagen—she's Danish."

Jambe was silent.

"I might have been born there, but I'm not Danish," said Hrah, taking a menacing step towards Wapcaplitt. "My parents were on holiday at the time."

"We are well aware of the facts," intoned Wapcaplitt, "and have already gained judgment on this matter. You *were* born in Denmark, you *are* technically Danish, you *are* in a 'key job,' and you are thus disqualified from playing on this team."

"Balls!" yelled Aubrey. "If she was born in a kennel, would that make her a dog?"

"Hmm," replied the attorney thoughtfully, "it's an interesting legal question."

Penelope couldn't contain herself any longer and went for him. It took four of us to hold her back, and she had to be forcibly restrained and frog-marched from the green.

"Down to five players," muttered Jambe. "Below the minimum player requirement."

"Yes," said Mr. Wapcaplitt glibly, "it appears the Whackers are the winners—"

"I think not," interrupted our substitute lawyer, whose name we learned was Twizzit. "As my most esteemed colleague so rightly pointed out, the rule states thus: 'Any team that fails to *start* the game with the minimum of six players forfeits the match.' The way I see it, the match has already begun, and we can carry on playing with five. Your Honors?"

The judges put their heads together for a moment and then pronounced, "This court finds for the Swindon Mallets in this matter. They may continue to play into the second third with five players."

We walked slowly back to the touchline. Four of the neanderthal players were still sitting on the bench, staring off into space.

"Where's Stig?" I asked them.

I didn't get an answer. The Klaxon for the second third went off, and I grabbed my mallet and helmet and hurried onto the green.

"New strategy, everyone," said Jambe to myself, Smudger, Snake and Biffo—all that remained of the Swindon Mallets—"we play defensively to make sure they don't score any more hoops. Anything goes—and watch out for the Duchess."

The second third was probably the most interesting third ever seen in World League Croquet. To begin with, Biffo and Aubrey whacked both of our own balls into the rhododendrons. This was a novel tactic and had two consequences: firstly, that we weren't going to score any hoops in the middle third by natural hooping, and second, that we denied the opposition any roquets off our balls. No advantage to win, clearly, but we weren't trying to win—we were fighting for survival. The Whackers had only to score thirty hoops and hit the center peg to win outright—and the way it was going, we wouldn't make the last third. Staving off the inevitable, perhaps, but World League Croquet is like that. Frustrating, violent and full of the unexpected.

"No prisoners!" yelled Biffo, waving his mallet above his head in a display of bravado that would sum up our second-third strategy. It worked. Freed from the constraint of ball defense, we all went into the attack and together caused some considerable problems to the Whackers, who were thrown by the unorthodox playing tactics. At one point I yelled "Offside!" and made up something so outrageously complex that it sounded as if it *could* be true—it took ten minutes of precious time to prove that it wasn't.

By the time the second third ended, we were almost completely exhausted. The Whackers now led by twenty-one hoops to twelve, and we won another eight only because "Bonecrusher" McSneed had been sent off for trying to hit Jambe with his mallet and Biffo had been concussed by the Duchess.

"How many fingers am I holding up?" asked Alf.

"Fish," said Biffo, eyes wandering.

"You okay?" asked Landen when I had returned to the stands to see him.

"I'm okay," I puffed. "I'm out of shape, though."

Friday gave me a hug.

"Thursday?" hissed Landen in a hushed voice. "I've been thinking. Where did that piano actually come from?"

"What piano?"

"The one that fell on Cindy."

"Well, I suppose, it . . . just, well . . . *fell*—didn't it? What are you saying?"

"That it was a murder attempt."

"Someone tried to assassinate the assassin with a *piano?*"

"No. It hit her accidentally. I think it was intended for you!"

"Who'd want to kill me with a piano?"

"I don't know. Have there been any other unorthodox attempts on your life recently?"

"No."

"I think you're still in danger, sweetheart. Please be careful."

I kissed him again and stroked his face with a muddy hand.

"Sorry!" I muttered, trying to rub it off and making it worse. "But I've got too much to think about at the moment."

I ran off and joined Jambe for a last-third pep talk.

"Right," he said, handing out the Chelsea buns, "we're going to lose this match, but we're going to go out in glory. I don't want it to be said that the Mallets didn't fight until the last man standing. Right, Biffo?"

"Trilby."

We all knocked our fists together and made the *harump* noise again, the team reinvigorated—except for me. It was true that no one could say we didn't try, but for all Jambe's well-meaning rhetoric, in three weeks' time the earth would be a smoldering radioactive cinder, and no amount of tarnished glory would save Swindon or anyone else. But I helped myself to a Chelsea bun and a cup of tea anyway.

"I say," said Twizzit, who had suddenly appeared in the company of Stig.

"Have a bun!" said Aubrey. "We're going out in style!"

But Twizzit wasn't smiling. "We've been looking at Mr. Stig's genome—"

"His what?"

"His *genome*. The complete genetic plan of him and the other neanderthals."

"And?"

Twizzit rummaged through some papers. "They were all built between 1939 and 1948 in the Goliath BioEngineering labs. The thing is, the prototype neanderthal could not speak in words that we could understand—so they were built using a human voice box." Twizzit gave a curious half smile, as though he had produced a spare ace from his sleeve, and announced with great drama, "The neanderthals are 1.03 percent human."

"But that doesn't make them human," I observed. "How does this help us?"

"I agree they're not human," conceded Twizzit with the ghost of

343

a smile, "but the rules specifically exclude anyone 'nonhuman.' Since they have *some* human in them, they technically can't fall into this category."

There was another long pause. I looked at Stig, who stared back and raised his eyebrows.

"I think we should lodge an appeal," muttered Jambe, leaving his Chelsea bun half eaten in his haste. "Stig, have your men limber up!"

The judges agreed with us. The 1.03 percent was enough to prove they *weren't* nonhuman and thus could not be excluded from play. While Wapcaplitt ran off to search the croquet statutes for a reason to appeal, the neanderthals—Grunk, Warg, Dorf, Zim and Stig—limbered up as the Whackers looked on nervously. Neanderthals had often been approached to play, as they could run all day without tiring, but no one until now had ever managed to get any.

"Okay, listen up," said Jambe, gathering us around. "We're back in the game at full strength. Thursday, I want you to stay on the benches to regain your breath. We're going to fool them with a Puchonski switch. Biffo is going to take the red ball from the forty-yard line over the rhododendron bushes, past the Italian Sunken Garden and into a close position to hoop five. Snake, you'll take it from there and croquet their yellow—Stig will defend you. Mr. Warg, I want you to mark their number five. He's dangerous, so you're going to have to use any tricks you can. Smudger, you're going to foul the Duchess—when the Vicar gives you the red card, I'm calling in Thursday. Yes?"

I didn't reply; for some reason I was having a sudden heavy bout of déjà vu.

"Thursday?" repeated Aubrey. "Are you okay? You look like you're in a dreamworld!"

"I'm fine," I said slowly. "I'll wait for your command."

"Good."

We all did the *harump* thing, and they went to their places whilst I sat on the bench and looked once again at the scoreboard. We were losing twenty-one hoops to twelve.

Aubrey nodded at Smudger, who took out the Duchess in grand style:
they both careered into the Tea Party and knocked over the table.

The Klaxon went off, and the game started with renewed aggression. Biffo whacked the yellow ball in the direction of the up-end hoop and hit the Whackers' ball. Warg took the roquet. With an expert swing, the opponents' ball tumbled into the Italian Sunken Garden, and ours sailed as straight as a die over the rhododendrons; a distant *clack* was mirrored by a roar from the crowd, and I knew the ball had been intercepted by Grunk and taken through the hoop. Aubrey nodded at Smudger, who took out the Duchess in grand style: they both careered into the Tea Party and knocked over the table. The Klaxon sounded for a time-out while the Duchess was pulled clear of the tea things. She was conscious but had a broken ankle. Smudger was given the red card but no hoop penalty, as the Duchess had been shown the yellow card earlier for concussing Biffo. I joined the fray as play started up again, but the Whackers' early confidence was soon evaporating under a withering attack from the neanderthals, who could anticipate their every move simply by reading their body language. Warg passed to Grunk, who gave the ball such an almighty whack that it passed clear *through* the rhododendrons with a tearing of foliage and was converted by Zim on the other side towards an undefended hoop.

By the time there were three minutes to play, we had almost caught up: twenty-five hoops to the Whackers' twenty-nine. Firmly rattled, the Whackers missed a roquet and, with only a minute to run, scored their thirtieth hoop with us only two behind. All they had to do to win was "peg out" by hitting the center post. Whilst they were trying to do this and we tried our best to stop them, Grunk, with eight seconds to go and two hoops to make, whacked a clear double-hooper that went through one up-end hoop, all the forty yards down the green and through the mid. I'd never heard a crowd yell more.

We had leveled the score and desperately tried to get our ball to the peg in the scrum of players trying to stop the Whackers from doing the same. Warg grunted to Grunk, who ran towards the scrum and tore into them, taking six players down as Warg whacked the ball towards the now unprotected peg. It hit the peg fair and square—but a second *after* the Klaxon had sounded. Play had ended—in a draw.

39.

Sudden Death

Neanderthals Turn Down Croquet Offer
A group of neanderthals unwisely turned down an exciting and unrepeatable offer from the Gloucester Meteors yesterday, following their astonishing performance at the 1988 Whackers v. Mallets SuperHoop on Saturday. The generous offer of ten brightly colored glass beads was rejected by a neanderthal spokesman, who declared that conflict, howsoever staged, was inherently insulting. The offer was raised to a set of solid-bottomed cookware, and this was also roundly rejected. A spokesman for the Meteors later stated that the neanderthal tactics displayed on Saturday were actually the result of some clever tricks taught them by the Mallets' team coach.
Article in *The Toad*, July 24, 1988

Good work," said Alf as we sat on the ground, panting hard. I had lost my helmet in the scrum somewhere but hadn't until now noticed. My armor was dirty and torn, my mallet handle had split, and there was a cut on my chin. The whole team was muddy, bruised and worn out—but we were still in with a good chance.

"What order?" asked the umpire, referring to the sudden-death penalty shoot-out. It worked quite simply. We took it in turns to hit the peg, each time moving back ten yards. There were six lines all the way back to the boundary. If we got them all, we started again until someone missed. Alf looked at the players who were still able to hold a mallet and put me seventh, so if we went around again, I was on the easiest ten-yard line.

"Biffo first, then Aubrey, Stig, Dorf, Warg, Grunk and Thursday."

The umpire jotted down our names and moved away. I went to see my family and Landen again.

"What about the steamroller?" he asked.

"What about the steamroller?"

"Didn't it nearly run you over?"

"An *accident*, Land. Gotta go. Bye."

The ten-yard line was simple; both players hit the peg with ease. The twenty-yard line was still no problem. The crowd roared as Reading hit the peg first, but our side roared equally when we hit ours. Thirty yards was no problem either—both teams hit the peg, and we all moved back to the forty-yard line. From this distance the peg was tiny, and I didn't see how anyone could hit it, but they did—first Stern for Reading, then Dorf for us. The crowd roared its support, but then there was a slight rumble of thunder and it began to rain, the full significance of which was yet to dawn.

"Where are they going?" asked Aubrey as Stig, Grunk, Dorf and Warg ran off to find shelter.

"It's a neanderthal thing," I explained as the rain increased dramatically to a downpour, the water streaming down our armor and onto the turf. "Neanderthals never work, play or even stand in the rain if they can help it. Don't worry, they'll be back as soon as it stops."

But it didn't stop.

"Fifty-yard penalty," announced the umpire. "O'Fathens for the Whackers and Mr. Warg for the Mallets."

I looked at Warg, who was sitting on the bench under the stands, staring at the rain with a mixed expression of respect and wonder.

"He's going to lose us the game!" muttered Jambe in my ear. "Can't you do something?"

I ran across the soggy green to Warg, who stared at me blankly when I implored him to come and take the penalty.

"It's raining," replied Warg, "and it's only a game. It doesn't *really* matter who wins, does it?"

"Stig?" I implored.

"We'd work in the rain for you, Thursday, but we've taken our turn already. Rain is precious; it gives life—you should respect it more, too."

I returned to the fifty-yard line as slowly as I could to try to give the rain time to finish. It didn't.

"Well?" demanded Jambe.

I shook my head sadly. "I'm afraid not. Winning has never been of any interest to the neanderthals. They played only as a favor to me."

Aubrey sighed.

"We'd like to delay the next penalty until it stops raining," announced Twizzit, who had appeared holding a newspaper over his head. He was on legal marshland with this request, and he knew it. The umpire asked the Whackers if they wanted to delay, but O'Fathens stared at me and said that he didn't. So the next person on the list took her turn at the fifty-yard line—me.

I wiped the rain from my eyes and tried to even *see* the peg. The rain was coming down so heavily that the cascading droplets created a watery haze a few inches above the turf. Still, I had the second shot—O'Fathens might miss, too.

The Whackers' captain concentrated for a moment, swung and connected well. The ball went sailing high towards the peg and seemed set to hit it fairly and squarely. But with a loud *plop* it landed short. There was an expectant rumble from the crowd.

The word was relayed up the field—O'Fathens had landed four feet from the peg. I had to get closer than that to win the Super-Hoop.

"Good luck," said Aubrey, giving my arm a squeeze.

I walked up to the fifty-yard line, the now muddy ground oozing around my boots. I removed my shoulder pads and cast them aside, made a few practice swings, wiped my eyes and stared at the multicolored peg that somehow seemed to have retreated another twenty yards. I squared up in front of the ball and shifted my weight to maintain the right poise. The crowd went silent. They didn't know how much was riding on this, but I did. I didn't dare miss. I looked at the ball, stared towards the peg, looked at the ball again, clasped the handle of my mallet and raised it high in the air, then swung hard into the ball, yelling out as the wood connected and the ball went sailing off in a gentle arc. I thought about Kaine and Goliath, of Landen and Friday and the consequences if I missed. The fate of all life on this beautiful planet decided on the swing of a croquet mallet. I watched as my ball plopped into the soggy ground and the groundsman dashed ahead to compare distances. I turned away and walked back through the rain towards Landen. I had done my best, and the game was over. I didn't hear the announcement, only a roar from the crowd. But whose crowd? A flashbulb went off, and I felt dizzy as the sounds became muted and everything appeared to slow down. Not in the way that my father could engineer, but a postadrenaline moment when everything seems odd, and *other.* I searched the seating for Landen and Friday, but my attention was distracted by a large figure dressed in a duster coat and hat who had vaulted over the barrier and was running towards me. He drew something from his pocket as he ran, his feet throwing up great splashes of muddy water on his trousers. I stared at him as he came closer and noticed that his eyes were yellow and beneath his hat were what appeared to be—*horns.* I didn't see any more; there was a bright white flash, a deafening roar, and all the rest was silence.

40.

Second First Person

Yacht Choice of Famed Literary Detective a Mystery
The shooting of Thursday Next last Saturday leaves the question of her favorite yacht unanswered, our Swindon correspondent writes. "From the
look of her, I would expect a thirty-two-foot ketch, spinnaker-rigged and
with a Floon automatic pilot." Other yachting commentators disagree and
think she would have gone for something larger, such as a sloop or yawl,
although it is possible she might only have wanted a boat for coastal day
work or a long weekend, in which case she might have gone for a compact
twenty-footer. We asked her husband to comment on her taste in sailing,
but he declined to give an answer.

Article in Yachting Monthly, July 1988

I was watching her, right up to the moment she was shot. She
looked confused and tired as she walked back from the penalty,
and the crowd roared when I shouted to get her attention, so she
didn't hear me. It was then that I saw a man vault across the barrier
and run up to her. I thought it was a nutty fan or something, and
the shot sounded more like a firecracker. There was a puff of
blue smoke, and she looked incredulous for a moment, and then
she just crumpled up and collapsed on the turf. As simple as
that. Before I knew what I was doing, I had handed Friday to Joffy
and jumped over the barrier, moving as fast as I could. I was the
first one to reach Thursday, who was lying perfectly still on the
muddy ground, her eyes open, a neat red hole two inches above her
right eye.

Someone yelled, "Medic!" It was me.

I switched to automatic. For the moment the idea that someone had shot my wife was expunged from my mind; I was simply dealing with a casualty—and heaven knows I'd done that often enough. I pulled out my handkerchief and pressed it on the wound.

I said, "Thursday, can you hear me?"

She didn't answer. Her eyes were unblinking as the rain struck her, and I placed my hand above her head to shield her. A medic appeared at my side, sloshing down into the muddy ground in his haste to help.

He said, "What's happened?"

I said, "He shot her."

I reached gingerly around the back of her head and breathed a small sigh of relief when I couldn't find an exit wound.

A second medic—a woman this time—joined the first and told me to step aside. But I moved only far enough for her to work. I took hold of Thursday's hand.

The first medic said, "We've got a pulse," as he unwrapped an airway, then added, "Where's the blasted ambulance?"

I stayed with her all the way to the hospital and let go of her hand only when they took her into the operating theater.

A friendly casualty nurse at St. Septyk's said, "Here you go," as she gave me a blanket. I sat on a hard chair and stared at the wall clock and the public-information posters. I thought about Thursday, trying to figure out how much time we had spent together. Not long for two and a half years, really.

A boy next to me with his head stuck in a saucepan said, "Wot you in here for, mister?"

I leaned closer and spoke into the hollow handle so he could hear me and said, "I'm okay, but someone shot my wife."

The little boy with his head stuck in a saucepan said, "Bummer," and I replied, "Yes, bummer."

I sat and looked at the posters again for a long time until someone said, "Landen?"

I looked up. It was Mrs. Next. She had been crying. I think I had, too.

She said, "How is she?"

And I said, "I don't know."

She sat down next to me. "I brought you some Battenberg."

I said, "I'm not really that hungry."

"I know. But I just don't know what else to do."

We both stared at the clock and the posters in silence for some minutes. After a while I said, "Where's Friday?"

Mrs. Next patted my arm. "With Joffy and Miles."

"Ah," I said, "good."

Thursday came out of surgery three hours later. The doctor, who had a haggard look but stared me in the eye, which I liked, told me that things weren't terrific but she was stable and a fighter and I wasn't to give up hope. I went to have a look at her with Mrs. Next. There was a large bandage around her head, and the monitors did that beep thing they do in movies. Mrs. Next sniffed and said, "I've lost one son already. I don't want to lose another. Well, a daughter I mean, but you know what I mean, a child."

I said, "I know what you mean."

I didn't, having never lost a son, but it seemed the right thing to say.

We sat with her for two hours while the light failed outside and the fluorescents flickered on.

When we had been there another two hours, Mrs. Next said, "I'm going to go now, but I'll be back in the morning. You should try and get some sleep."

I said, "I know. I'm just going to stay here for another five minutes."

I stayed there for another hour. A kindly nurse brought me a cup of tea, and I ate some Battenberg. I got home at eleven. Joffy was waiting for me. He told me that he had put Friday to bed and asked me how his sister was.

I said, "It's not looking very good, Joff."

354

He patted me on the shoulder, gave me a hug and told me that everyone at the GSD had joined the Idolatry Friends of St. Zvlkx and the Sisters of Eternal Punctuality to pray for her, which was good of him, and them.

I sat on the sofa for a long time, until there was a gentle knock at the kitchen door. I opened it to find a small group of people. A man who introduced himself as Thursday's cousin Eddie but whispered that actually his name was Hamlet said to me, "Is this a bad time? We heard about Thursday and wanted to tell you how sorry we were."

I tried to be cheery. I really wanted him to sod off, but instead I said, "Thank you. I don't mind at all. Friends of Thursday are friends of mine. Tea and Battenberg?"

"If it's not too much trouble."

He had three others with him. The first was a short man who looked *exactly* like a Victorian big-game hunter. He wore a pith helmet and safari suit and had a large bushy white mustache.

He gave me his hand to shake and said, "Commander Bradshaw, dontchaknow. Damn fine lady, your wife. Appreciate a girl who knows how to carry herself in a scrap. Did she tell you about the time she and I hunted Morlock in Trollope?"

"No."

"Shame. I'll tell you all about it one day. This is the memsahib, Mrs. Bradshaw."

Melanie was large and hairy and looked like a gorilla. In fact, she *was* a gorilla, but she had impeccable manners and curtsied as I shook her large coal black hand, which had the thumb in an odd place, so was difficult to shake properly. Her deep-set eyes were wet with tears, and she said, "Oh, Landen! Can I call you Landen? Thursday used to talk about you all the time when you were eradicated. We all loved her a great deal—I mean, we still do. How is she? How is Friday? You must feel awful!"

I said, "She's not really very well," which was the truth.

The third member of the party was a tall man dressed in black robes. He had a very large bald head and high arched eyebrows. He put out a finely manicured hand and said, "My name's Zhark, but you can call me Horace. I used to work with Thursday. You have my condolences. If it will help, I would happily slaughter a few thousand Thraals as a tribute to the gods."

I didn't know what a Thraal was but told him it really wasn't necessary. He said, "It's really no trouble. I've just conquered their planet, and I'm not sure what I should do with them."

I told him that this really, *really* wasn't necessary and added that I didn't think Thursday would have liked it, then cursed myself for using the past tense. I put on the kettle and said, "Battenberg?"

Hamlet and Zhark answered together. They were obviously quite keen on my mother-in-law's speciality. I smiled for the first time in eight hours and twenty-three minutes and said, "There's plenty for everyone. Mrs. Next keeps on sending it over, and the dodos won't touch it. You can take away a cake each."

I made the tea, Mrs. Bradshaw poured it, and there was an uncomfortable silence. Zhark asked if I knew where Handley Paige lived, but the big-game hunter gave him a stern look and he was quiet.

They all talked to me about Thursday and what she had done in the fictional BookWorld. The stories were all highly unbelievable, but I didn't think to question any of them—I was glad for the company and happy to hear about what she had been doing over the past two years. Mrs. Bradshaw gave me a rundown of what Friday had been up to as well and even offered to come and look after him whenever I wanted. Zhark was more interested in talking about Handley but still had time to tell me a wholly unbelievable story about how he and Thursday dealt with a Martian who had escaped from *The War of the Worlds* and turned up in *The Wind in the Willows*.

"It's a W thing," he explained, "in the titles, I mean. Wind-War, Worlds-Willows, they are so similar that—"

Bradshaw nudged him to be quiet.

They left two hours later, slightly full of drink and very full of Battenberg. I noticed the tall one in the black cloak had riffled though my address book before he left, and when he looked, he had left it open on Handley's address. I returned to the living room and sat on the sofa until sleep overcame me.

I was wakened by Pickwick wanting to be let out, and Alan wanting to be let in. The smaller dodo had some paint spilled on him, smelt of perfume, had a blue ribbon tied around his left foot and was holding a mackerel in his beak. I have no idea to this day what he'd been getting up to. I went upstairs, checked that Friday was sleeping in his cot, then had a long shower and a shave.

41.

Death Becomes Her

SuperHoop Assailant "Vanishes"

The mysterious assassin who shot the Mallets' team manager has not yet been found, despite a vigorous SpecOps search. "It's still early days in the investigation," said a police spokesman, "but from clothes left at the crime scene we are interested in interviewing a Mr. Norman Johnson, whom we understand had been staying at the Finis Hotel for the past week." Asked to comment further on the rumored link between the attack on Miss Next and a grand piano incident last Friday, the same police spokesman confirmed that the attacks were connected, but wouldn't be pressed on details. Miss Next is still in St. Septyk's Hospital where her condition is reported as "critical."

Article in the Swindon Daily Eyestrain, July 24, 1988

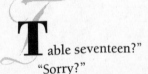able seventeen?"

"Sorry?"

"Table seventeen. You are table seventeen, I take it?"

I looked up at the waitress in a confused manner. A second ago I had been taking a penalty during a SuperHoop—and now I was in a cafeteria somewhere. She was a kindly woman with a friendly manner. I looked at the table marker. I *was* table seventeen.

"Yes?"

"You're to go . . . *Northside.*"

I must have looked confused, because she repeated it and then gave me directions: along the concourse, past the *Coriolanus* Will-Speak machine, up the stairs and across the pedestrian walkway.

I thanked her and got up. I was still dressed in my croquet gear, but without mallet or helmet, and I touched my head gently where I could feel a small hole. I stopped for a moment and looked around. I had been here before, and recently. I was in a motorway services. The same one that I had visited with Spike. But where was Spike? And why couldn't I remember how I got here?

"Well, looky what we have here!" came a voice from behind me. It was Chesney, this time wearing some sort of neck brace, but with a bruise on the side of his head where I had kicked him. Next to him was one of his henchmen, who was minus an arm.

"Chesney," I muttered, looking around for a weapon, "still in the soul-reclamation business?"

"And how!"

"Touch me and I'll knock your block off."

"Ooooh!" said Chesney. "Don't flatter yourself, girlie—you've just been called to go Northside, haven't you?"

"So?"

"Well, there's only one reason you go over *there*," replied Chesney's sidekick with an unkindly laugh.

"You mean . . . ?"

"Right," said Chesney with a grin. "You're dead."

"Dead?"

"*Dead*. Join the club, sweetheart."

"How can I be dead?"

"Remember the assassin at the SuperHoop?"

I touched the hole in my head again. "I was shot."

"In the head. Get out of that one, Miss Next!"

"Landen must be devastated," I murmured, "and I have to take Friday for a health checkup on Tuesday."

"Ain't none of your concern no longer!" sneered Chesney's sidekick, and they walked off, laughing loudly.

I turned to the steps of the pedestrian footbridge that led towards the Northside and looked around. Oddly, I didn't feel any great fear about being dead—I just wished I'd had the chance to say good-bye to the boys. I took the first step on the staircase when

I heard a screeching of tires and a loud crash. A car had just pulled outside the services, jumped the curb and collided with a rubbish bin. A large man had leapt out and was running through the doors, looking up and down in desperation until he saw me. It was Spike.

"Thursday!" he gasped. "Thank heavens I got to you before you went across!"

"You're alive?"

"Of course. It took me two days of driving up and down the M4 to get here. Looks like I was just in time."

"In time? In time for what?"

"I'm taking you home."

He gave me his car keys.

"That's the ignition, but the engine starter is a pushbutton in the middle of the dash."

"Middle of the dash, okay. What about you?"

"I've got some unfinished business with Chesney, so I'll see you on the other side."

He gave me a hug and trotted off towards the newsagents'.

I walked outside and got into Spike's car, grateful that I had a friend like him who knew how to deal with things like this. I'd be seeing Friday and Landen again, and everything would be just hunky-dory. I pressed the starter, reversed off the rubbish bin and drove towards the exit. I wondered if we'd won the SuperHoop. I should have asked Spike. *SPIKE!!!*

I stomped on the brakes and reversed rapidly back to the services, jumped out of the car and ran across the footbridge leading to the Northside of the Dauntsey services.

Only it wasn't the Northside, of course. It was a large cavern of incalculable age lit by dozens of burning torches. The stalactites and stalagmites had joined, giving the impression of organic Doric columns supporting the high roof, and snaking amongst the columns and the boulder-strewn floor was an orderly queue of departed souls who had lined up ready to cross the river that guarded the entrance to the underworld. The lone ferryman was doing a brisk trade; for an extra shilling, you could be taken on a guided tour on the way. Another entrepreneur was selling guides to the underworld: how best to ensure that the departed soul went to a land of milk of honey and, for the more dubious characters, a few helpful hints on how to square yourself with the Big Guy on Judgment Day.

I ran up the queue and found Spike ten souls from the front.

"*Absolutely* no way, Spike!"

"Shhh!" said someone ahead of us.

"Nuts to you, Thursday. Just look after Betty, would you?"

"You are *not* taking my place, Spike."

"Let me do this, Thursday. You deserve a long life. You have many wonderful things in front of you."

"So do you."

"It's debatable. Battling the undead was never a bowl of cherries. And without Cindy?"

"She's not dead, Spike."

"If she pulls through they'll never let her out of jail. She was the Windowmaker. No, after the shit I've been through, this actually seems like a good option. I'm staying."

"You are not."

"Try and stop me."

"Shhh!" said the man in front again.

"I won't let you do it, Spike. Think of Betty. Besides, I'm the one that's dead, not you. SECURITY!"

A moldy skeleton holding a lance and dressed in rusty armor clanked up. "What's going on here?"

I stabbed a finger at Spike. "This man's not dead."

"Not dead?" replied the guard in a shocked tone. The queue of people all turned around to stare as the guard drew a rusty sword and pointed it at Spike, who reluctantly raised his hands and, head shaking sadly, walked back towards the footbridge.

"Tell Landen and Friday I love them!" I yelled at his departing form, suddenly realizing that I should have asked him who'd won the SuperHoop. I turned to the queue behind me that snaked amongst the boulder-strewn cavern and said, "Does anyone know the results of SuperHoop-88?"

"Shhh!" said the man in front again.

"Why don't you poke your 'shhh' up your— Oh. Hello, Mr. President."

As soon as he recognized me, Formby gave me a broad toothy grin. "Eeee, Miss Next! Is this that theme park again?"

"Sort of."

I was glad that the trip across the river led up as well as down. One thing was for sure: unless there had been some sort of dreadful administrative mix-up, Formby was certainly *not* bound for eternal torment within the all-consuming flames of hell.

"So . . . how are you?" I asked, momentarily lost for words when confronted with the biggest—and last—celebrity I would be likely to meet.

"Pretty good, lass. One moment I was giving a concert, next thing I was in the cafeteria ordering pie and chips for one."

Spike had said he'd driven for two days to get to me, so it must be the twenty-fourth—and, as Dad had predicted, Formby had died as he had been meant to, performing for the Lancaster Regiment Veterans. My heart fell as I realized that the days following Formby's death would mark the beginning of World War III. Still, it was out of my hands now.

The boat arrived for the ex-President, and he stepped in. The ferryman pushed the small craft into the limpid waters of the river and dropped his pole into the dark waters.

"Mr. Formby, isn't it?" said the ferryman. "I'm a big fan of yours. I had that Mr. Garrick in the back of my boat once. Do you do requests?"

"Ooh, aye," replied the entertainer, "but I don't have me uke with me."

"Borrow mine," said the ferryman. "I do a bit of entertaining myself, you know."

Formby picked up the ukulele and strummed the strings. "What would you like?"

The ferryman told him, and the dour cavern was soon filled with a chirpy rendition of "We've Been a Long Time Gone." It seemed a fitting way to go for the old man who had given so much to so many—not only as an entertainer but as freedom fighter and elder statesman. The boat, Formby and the ferryman disappeared into the mist that drifted across the river, obscuring the far bank and muting the sound. It was my turn next. What had Gran said? The worst bit about dying is not knowing how it all turns out? Still, at least I'd got Landen back, so Friday was in good hands.

"Miss Next?"

I looked up. The ferryman had returned. He was dressed in a sort of dirty muslin cloth; I couldn't see his face.

"You have the fare?"

I dug out a coin and was about to hand it over when—

"WAIT!!!"

I turned around as a petite young woman trotted up, out of breath. She brushed the blond hair from her face and smiled shyly at me. It was Cindy.

"I'm taking her place," she told the ferryman, handing over a coin.

"How can you?" I said in some surprise. "You're almost dead yourself!"

"No," she corrected me, "I'm not. And what's more, I pull through. I shouldn't, but I do. Sometimes the devil looks after his own."

"But you'll leave Spike and Betty—"

"Listen to me for a moment, Thursday. I've killed sixty-eight people in my career."

"So you *did* do Samuel Pring."

"It was a fluke. But listen: sixty-eight innocent souls sent across this river before their time, all down to me. And I did it all for cash. You can play the self-righteous card for all I care, but the fact remains that I'll never see the light of day when I recover, and I'll never get to hold Betty again, or hug Spike. I don't want that. You're a better person than me, Thursday, and the world is far better off with you in it."

"But that's not the point, surely?" I asked. "When it's time to go—"

"Look," she interrupted angrily, "let me do *one good thing* to make up for even one-quarter of one percent of the misery I've caused."

I stared at her as the skeleton in rusty armor clanked up again. "More trouble, Miss Next?"

"Give us a minute, will you?"

"Please," implored Cindy. "You'd be doing me a favor."

I looked at the skeleton, who probably would have rolled his eyes if he had any.

"It's your decision, Miss Next," said the guard, "but *someone* has to take that boat or I'm out of a job—and I've got a bony wife and two small skeletons to put through college."

I turned back to Cindy, put out my hand and she shook it, then pulled me forward and hugged me tightly while whispering in my ear, "Thank you, Thursday. Keep an eye on Spike for me."

She hopped quickly into the boat before I had a chance to change my mind. She gave a wan smile and sat in the bows as the ferryman leaned on his pole, sending the small boat noiselessly across the river. Against the burden of her sins, saving me was only small recompense, but she felt better for it, and so did I. As the boat containing Cindy faded into the mists of the river, I turned and walked back towards the pedestrian footbridge, the Southside of the Dauntsey services—and life.

42.

Explanations

State Funeral Attracts World's Leaders

Millions of heartbroken citizens of England and the most important world leaders arrived in Wigan yesterday to pay tribute to President George Formby, who died two weeks ago. The funeral cortege was driven on a circuitous route of the Midlands, the streets lined with mourners, eager to bid a final good-bye to England's President of the past thirty-nine years. At the memorial service in Wigan Cathedral, the new Chancellor, Mr. Redmond van de Poste, spoke warmly of the great man's contribution to world peace. After the Lancashire Male Voice Choir sang "With My Little Stick of Blackpool Rock," accompanied by two hundred ukuleles, the Chancellor invited the Queen of Denmark to sing with him a duet of "Your Way Is My Way," something that "might well serve to patch the rift between our respective nations."

Article in *The Toad*, August 4, 1988

It was touch and go for a moment," said Landen, who was sitting by my hospital bed holding my hand. "There was a moment when we really didn't think you'd make it."

I gave a wan smile. I had regained consciousness only the day before, and every movement felt like daggers in my head. I looked around. Joffy and Miles and Hamlet were there, too. "Hi, guys."

They smiled and welcomed me back.

"How long?" I asked in a whisper.

"Two weeks," said Landen. "We really thought . . . thought—"

I gently squeezed his hand and looked around.

Land divined my thoughts perfectly. "He's with his grand-mother."

I raised a hand to touch the side of my head but could feel only a heavy bandage. Landen took my hand and returned it to the sheet.

"What . . . ?"

"You were astonishingly lucky," he said in a soothing tone. "The doctors say you'll make a full recovery. The caliber was quite small, and it entered your skull obliquely; by the time it had gone through, most of the energy was gone." He tapped the side of his head. "It lodged between your brain and the inside of the skull. Gave us quite a fright, though."

"Cindy died, didn't she?"

Joffy answered. "Looked to be improving, but then septicemia set in."

"They really loved one another, you know, despite their differences."

"She was a hit woman, Thursday, a trained assassin. I don't think she regarded death as anything more than an occupational hazard."

I nodded. He was right.

Landen leaned forwards and kissed my nose.

"Who shot me, Land?"

"Does the name 'Norman Johnson' mean anything to you?"

"Yes," I said. "The Minotaur. You were right. He'd been trying to slapstick me to death all week—steamroller, banana skin, piano—I was a fool not to see it. Mind you, a gun's hardly slapstick, is it?"

Landen smiled.

"It had a large BANG sign that came out of the barrel, as well as the bullet. The police are still trying to make sense of it."

I sighed. The Minotaur was long gone but I'd still have to be careful. I turned to Landen. There was still something I needed to know.

"Did we win?"

"Of course. You pegged a foot closer than O'Fathens. Your shot has been voted Sporting Moment of the Century—in Swindon, at any rate."

"So we aren't at war with Wales?"

Landen shook his head and smiled. "Kaine's finished, my darling—and Goliath has abandoned all attempts to become a religion. St. Zvlkx does indeed work in mysterious ways."

"Are you going to tell me?" I said with a wan smile. "Or do I have to beat it out of you with a stick?"

Joffy unfolded the picture of St. Zvlkx and Cindy's fatal pianoing on Commercial Road, the one from the *Swindon Evening Globe* that Gran had given me.

"We found this in your back pocket," said Miles,

"And it got us to thinking," continued Joffy, "exactly *where* Zvlkx was heading that morning and why he had the ticket for the Gravitube in his bedroom. He was cutting his losses and running. I don't think even Zvlkx—or whoever he was—believed that Swindon could possibly win the SuperHoop. Dad had always said that time wasn't immutable."

"I don't get it."

Miles leaned forward and showed me the picture again. "He died trying to get to Tudor Turf Accounting."

"So? Oldest betting shop in Swindon."

"No—in the *world*. We made a few calls. It had been trading continually since 1264."

I looked at Joffy quizzically. "What are you saying?"

"That the Book of Revealments was nothing of the kind—*it's a thirteenth-century betting slip!*"

"A what?"

He pulled Zvlkx's Revealments from his pocket and opened it to the front page. There was a countersigned receipt for a farthing that we had thought was a bookbinder's tax or something. The small arithmetical sum next to each revealment was actually the odds against that particular event's coming true, each one counter-signed by the same signature as on the front page. Joffy flicked through the slim volume.

"The Spanish Armada revealment had been given the odds of 600–1, Wellington's victory at Waterloo 420–1." He flicked to the final page. "The outcome of the croquet match was set at 124,000–1. The odds were generous because Zvlkx was betting on things centuries before they happened—indeed, centuries before croquet was even *thought* of. No wonder the person who had underwritten the bet felt confident to offer such odds."

"Well," I said, "don't hold your breath. A hundred twenty-four thousand farthings only adds up to . . . up to . . ."

"One hundred and thirty quid," put in Miles.

"Right. One hundred and thirty quid. Nelson's victory would net Zvlkx only—what? Nine bob?"

I still didn't quite get it.

"Thursday—it's a *totalizer*. Each bet or event that comes true is multiplied by the winnings of the previous event—and any prophecy that didn't come true would have negated the whole deal."

"So . . . how much are the revealments worth?"

Joffy looked at Miles, who looked at Landen, who grinned and looked at Joffy.

"One hundred and twenty-eight *billion* pounds."

"But Tudor Turf wouldn't have that sort of cash!"

"Of course not," replied Miles, "but the parent company that underwrites Tudor Turf would be legally bound to meet all bets drawn up. And Tudor Turf is owned by Wessex Cashcow, which is itself owned by Tails You Lose, the wholly owned gaming division of Consolidated Glee, which is owned by—"

"The Goliath Corporation," I breathed.

"Right."

There was a stunned silence. I wanted to jump out of bed and laugh and scream and run around, but that, I knew, would have to be postponed until I was in better health. For now I just smiled.

"So how much of Goliath does the Idolatry Friends of St. Zvlkx actually own?"

"Well," continued Joffy, "it doesn't *actually* own any of it. If you recall, we sold all his wisdom to the Toast Marketing Board. *They* now own fifty-eight percent of Goliath. We told them what we wanted, and they wholeheartedly agreed. Goliath has dropped its plans to become a religion and decided to support another political party other than the Whigs. There was something in the deal about a new cathedral to be built, too. We won, Thursday—*we won!*"

Kaine's fall, I discovered, had been rapid and humiliating. Once he was without Goliath's backing and minus his Ovinator, parliament suddenly started wondering why they had been following him so blindly, and those who had supported him turned against him with the same enthusiasm. In less than a week he realized just what it was to be human. All the vanity and plotting and conniving that worked so well for him when fictional didn't seem to have the same power at all when spoken with a real tongue, and he was removed from office within three days of the SuperHoop. Ernst Stricknene, questioned at length over calls made to Cindy Stoker from his office, decided to save as much of his skin as he could and talked at great length about his former boss. Kaine now had to face the biggest array of indictments ever heaped upon a public figure in the history of England. So many, in fact, that it was easier to list the offenses he *wasn't* indicted for—which were: "working as an unlicensed nanny" and "using a car horn in a built-up area during the hours of darkness." If found guilty on all charges, he was facing more than nine hundred years in prison.

"I almost feel sorry for him," said Joffy, who was a lot more forgiving than I. "Poor Yorrick."

"Yes," replied Hamlet sarcastically, "alas."

43.

Recovery

Toast Party Unveils Manifesto

Mr. Redmond van de Poste, whose ruling Toast (formerly Commonsense) Party took control of the nation last week, announced the party's manifesto to raise the country from economic and social collapse. Mr. van de Poste began by announcing mandatory toast-eating requirements for all citizens on a sliding scale based on age, then proposed a drive to place a new toaster in every home within a year. "In the long term," continued Mr. van de Poste, "we will instigate a five-year plan to upgrade all our manufacturing facilities to build a new brand of supertoaster that will sweep aside all competition and make England the toast capital of the world." Critics of the Toast manifesto indicated alarm at Poste's strident calls for a North Atlantic Toast Alliance, and pointed out that by excluding non-toast-eating nations it would create unnecessary international tension. Mr. van de Poste has not yet responded, and has called for a reform of parliament.

Article in The Toad, August 4, 1988

I went home two weeks later to a house that was so full of flowers it looked like Kew Gardens. I still didn't have complete command of the right-hand side of my body but every day it seemed a little bit more like part of me, a little less numb. I sat and looked out the open French windows into the garden. The air was heavy with the scents of summer and the breeze gently played upon the net curtains. Friday was drawing with some crayons on the floor and I could hear the *clacketty-clack* of Landen's old Underwood typewriter next door, and in the kitchen Louis Armstrong was on

the wireless singing "La Vie en Rose." It was the first time I had
been able to relax for almost as long as I could remember. I was going to need an extended convalescence but would go back to work
eventually—perhaps at SpecOps, perhaps at Jurisfiction, perhaps
both.

"I came to say good-bye."

It was Hamlet. I had learned from him earlier that William
Shgakespeafe had managed to extricate *Hamlet* from *The Merry
Wives of Windsor,* and both plays were as they should be. The one
enigmatic, the other a spin-off.

"Are you sure you're—"

He silenced me with a wave of his hand and sat down on the
sofa while Alan gazed at him adoringly.

"I've learned a lot of things while I've been here," he said. "I've
learned that there are many Hamlets, and we love each one of them
for their different interpretation. I liked Gibson's because it has the
least amount of dithering, Orson because he did it with the best
voice, Gielgud for the ease in which he placed himself within the
role and Jacobi for his passion. By the way, have you heard of this
Branagh fellow?"

"No."

"He's just starting to get going. I've got a feeling his Hamlet will
be stupendous."

He thought for a moment.

"For centuries I've been worrying about audiences seeing me as
a mouthy spoiled brat who can't make up his mind about anything,
but, having seen the real world, I can understand the appeal. My
play is popular because my failings are *your* failings, my indecision
the indecision of you all. We all know what has to be done; it's just
that sometimes we don't know how to get there. Acting without
thought doesn't really help in the long run. I might dither for a
while, but at least I make the right decision in the end: I bear my
troubles *and* take arms against them. And thereby lies a message

for all mankind, although I'm not *exactly* sure what it is. Perhaps there's no message. I don't really know. Besides, if I don't dither, there's no play."

"So you're not going to kill your uncle in the first act?"

"No. In fact, I'm going to leave the play exactly as it is. I've decided instead to focus my energies towards being the Jurisfiction agent for all of Shakespeare's works. I'll have a go at Marlowe, too—but I'm not keen on Webster."

"That's excellent news," I told him. "Jurisfiction will be very happy."

He paused. "I'm still a bit annoyed that someone told Ophelia about Emma. It wasn't you, was it?"

"On my honor."

He got up, bowed and kissed my hand. "Come and visit me, won't you?"

"You can count on it," I replied. "Just one question: where on earth did you find Daphne Farquitt? She's the recluse's recluse."

He grinned. "I didn't. By the morning of the SuperHoop, I had managed to gather about nine people. There's a limit to how much anti-Kaine sentiment you can muster going door to door in Swindon at two in the morning."

"So there never was a Farquitt Fan Club?"

"Oh, I'm sure there is somewhere, but Kaine didn't know it, now, did he?"

I laughed. "I've a feeling you're going to be an asset to Jurisfiction, Hamlet. And I want you to take something with you as a gift from me."

"A gift? I don't think I've ever had one of those before."

"No? Well, always a first for everything. I want you to have . . . Alan."

"The dodo?"

"I think he'd be an invaluable addition to Elsinore Castle—just don't let him get into the main story."

Hamlet looked at Alan, who looked back at him longingly.

"Thank you," he said with as much sincerity as he could. "I'm deeply honored."

Alan went a bit floppy as Hamlet picked him up, and a few moments later they both vanished back to Elsinore, Hamlet to further continue his work as a career procrastinator, and Alan to cause trouble in the Danish court.

"Hello, Sweetpea."

"Hi, Dad."

"You did a terrific job over that SuperHoop. How are you feeling?"

"Pretty good."

"Did I tell you that as soon as Zvlkx got hit by that Number 23 bus, the Ultimate Likelihood Index of that Armageddon rose to eighty-three percent?"

"No, you never told me that."

"Just as well really—I wouldn't have wanted you to panic."

"Dad, who *was* St. Zvlkx?"

He leaned closer. "Don't tell a soul, but he was someone named Steve Schultz of the Toast Marketing Board. I think I might have recruited him, or he might have approached me to help—I'm not sure. History has rewritten itself so many times I'm really not sure how it was to begin with—it's a bit like trying to guess the original color of a wall when it's been repainted eight times. All I can say is that everything turned out okay—and that things are far weirder than we *can* know. But the main thing is that Goliath now answers to the Toast Marketing Board and Kaine is out of power. The whole thing has been rubber-stamped into historical fact, and that's the way it's going to stay."

"Dad?"

"Yes?"

"How did you manage to jump Schultz or Zvlkx or whoever he was all the way from the thirteenth century without the Chrono-Guard spotting what you were up to?"

"Where do you hide a pebble, Sweetpea?"

"On a beach."

"And where do you hide a thirteenth-century impostor saint?"

"With . . . lots of other thirteenth-century impostor saints?"

He smiled.

"You sent all twenty-eight of them forward just to hide St. Zvlkx?"

"Twenty-seven, actually—one of them *was* real. But I didn't do it alone. I needed someone to whip up a timephoon in the Dark Ages as cover. Someone with remarkable skills as a time traveler. An expert who can surf the time line with a skill I will never possess."

"Me?"

He chuckled. "No, silly—*Friday.*"

The little boy looked up when he heard his name and chewed a crayon, made a face and spat the bits on Pickwick, who jumped up in fright and ran away to hide.

"Meet the future head of the ChronoGuard, Sweetpea. How did you think he survived Landen's eradication?"

I stared at the little boy, who stared back, and smiled.

Dad looked at his watch. "Well, I've got to go. Nelson's up to his old tricks again. Time waits for no man, as we say."

44.

Final Curtain

I was well enough to be given an award three weeks later at a
mayoral lunch. Lord Volescamper presented the whole SuperHoop
team with a special "Swindon Star" medal, especially struck for the
purpose. The only neanderthal to show up was Stig, who understood what it meant to me, even if he couldn't truly understand the
concept of individual aggrandizement.

There was a party afterwards, and everyone wanted to chat to
me, mostly to ask me if I would play any more professional croquet. I met Handley Paige again, who jumped when he saw me and
downed a drink nervously.

"I've decided not to kill off my Emperor Zhark character," he announced quickly. "I'd just like to make that point right now, in case anyone might think I was going to stop writing Zhark books, which I'm not. Not at all. Not ever." He looked around nervously.

"I'm sorry?" I said. "I'm not sure I understand."

"Oh . . . right," he replied sarcastically, tried to drink from his empty glass and then strode off to the bar.

"What was all that about?" asked Landen.

"Search me."

Spike was at the party, too, and he sidled up to me as I was fetching another drink.

"What did she say to you when she took your place?"

I turned to face him; I wasn't surprised that he knew Cindy had replaced me. The semidead was his field of expertise, after all.

"She said that she wanted to make up for some of the misery she had caused, and she knew she would never hold either you or Betty again."

"You could have refused her, but I'm glad you didn't. I loved her, but she was rotten to the core."

He fell silent for a moment and I touched him on the arm.

"Not entirely rotten, Spike. She loved you both very much."

He looked at me and smiled.

"I know. You did the right thing, Thursday. Thank you."

And he hugged me, and was gone.

I answered lots more questions regarding the SuperHoop match, and when I decided enough was enough, I asked Landen to take me home.

We drove towards home in the Speedster, Landen driving and Friday in a baby seat in the back, right next to Pickwick, who didn't want to be left alone now that Alan had gone.

"Land?"

"Mmm?"

"Did you ever think it odd that I survived?"

"I'm grateful that you did, of course—"

"Stop the car a minute."

"Why?"

"Just do as I say."

He pulled up, and I very carefully climbed out and walked towards where two familiar figures were sitting on the pavement outside a Goliath Coffee Shop. I approached silently and sat down next to the larger of the two before he'd even noticed. He looked around and jumped visibly when he saw me.

"Once," said a sad and familiar voice, "you would never have been able to sneak up on a Gryphon!"

I smiled. He was a creature with the head and wings of an eagle and the body of a lion. He wore spectacles and a scarf under his trench coat, which somewhat dented his otherwise fearsome appearance. He was fictional, to be sure, but he was also head of Jurisfiction's legal team, my lawyer—and a friend.

"Gryphon!" I said with some surprise. "What are you doing in the Outland?"

"Here to see you," he whispered, looking around and lowering his voice. "Have you met Mock Turtle? He's now my number two at the legal desk."

He gestured towards where a turtle with the head of a calf was staring mournfully into space. He was, like the Gryphon, straight out of the pages of *Alice in Wonderland*.

"How do you do?"

"Okay—I suppose," sighed the Mock Turtle, dabbing his eyes with a handkerchief.

"So what's up?" I asked.

"It's quite serious—too serious for the footnoterphone. And I needed an excuse to do some Outlander research on traffic islands. Fascinating things."

I felt hot and prickly all of a sudden. Not about traffic islands, of course, about my *conviction*. The Fiction Infraction. I had changed the ending of *Jane Eyre* and was found guilty by the Court of Hearts. All that was missing was the sentence.

"What did I get?"

"It's not that bad!" exclaimed the Gryphon, snapping his fingers at the Mock Turtle, who passed him a sheet of paper now stained with his own tears.

I took the paper and scanned the semiblurred contents.

"It's a bit unusual," admitted the Gryphon. "I think the bit about the gingham is unnaturally cruel—might be the cause of an appeal on its own."

I stared at the paper. "Twenty years of my life in blue gingham," I murmured.

"And you can't die until you've read the ten most boring books," added the Gryphon.

"My gran had to do the same," I explained, feeling just a little puzzled.

"Not possible," said the Mock Turtle, drying his eyes. "This sentence is unique, as befits the crime. You can take the twenty years of gingham anytime you want—not necessarily now."

"But my gran had this punishment—"

"You're mistaken," replied the Gryphon firmly, retrieving the paper, folding it and placing it in his pocket, "and we had better be off. Will you be at Bradshaw's golden wedding anniversary?"

"Y-es," I said slowly, still confused.

"Good. Page 221, *Bradshaw and the Diamond of M'shala*. It's bring-a-bottle-and-a-banana. Drag your husband along. I know he's real, but no one's perfect—we'd all like to meet him."

"Thank you. What about—"

"Goodness!" said the Gryphon, consulting a large pocketwatch. "Is that the time? We've got a lobster quadrille to perform in ten pages!"

The Mock Turtle cheered up a bit when he heard this, and in a moment they were gone.

I walked slowly back to where Landen and Friday were waiting for me in the car.

"Dah!" said Friday really loudly.

"There!" said Landen. "He most definitely said 'Dad'!" He noticed my furrowed brow. "What's up?"

"Landen, my gran on my mother's side died in 1968."

"And?"

"Well, if she died then, and Dad's mum died in 1979 . . ."

"Yes?"

"Then who is that up at the Goliath Twilight Homes?"

"I've never met her," explained Landen. "I thought 'Gran' was a term of endearment."

I didn't answer. I had thought she was my gran but she wasn't. In fact, I'd known her only about three years. Before that I had never set eyes on her before. Perhaps that's less than accurate. I had seen her whenever I stared into a mirror, but she had been a lot younger. Gran wasn't my gran. *Gran was me.*

Landen drove me up to the Goliath Twilight Homes, and I went in alone, leaving Landen and Friday in the car. I made my way with heavily beating heart to her room and found the ward sister bending over the gently dozing form of the old, old woman that I would eventually become.

"Is she suffering much?"

"The painkillers keep it under control," replied the nurse. "Family?"

"Yes," I replied, "we're very close."

"She's a remarkable woman," murmured the nurse. "It's a wonder she's still with us at all."

"It was a punishment," I said.

"Pardon?"

"Never mind. It won't be long now."

I moved closer to the bed, and she opened her eyes.

"Hello, young Thursday!" said Gran, waving at me weakly. She took off the oxygen mask, was roundly scolded by the nurse and put it back on again.

"You're not my gran, are you?" I said slowly, sitting on the bedside.

She smiled benevolently and placed her small and pink wrinkled hand on mine.

"I *am* Granny Next," she replied, "just not yours. When did you find out?"

"I got my sentencing from the Gryphon just now."

Now that I knew, she seemed more familiar to me than ever before. I even noticed the small scar on her chin, from the Charge of the Armored Brigade way back in '72, and the well-healed scar above her eye.

"Why did I never realize?" I asked her in confusion. "My *real* grandmothers are both dead—and I always knew that."

The tired old woman smiled again. "You don't have Aornis in one's head without learning a *few* tricks, my dear. My time with you has not been wasted. Our husband would not have survived without it, and Aornis could have erased everything when we were living in *Caversham Heights*. Where is he, by the way?"

"He's looking after the boy Friday outside."

"Ah!"

She looked into my eyes for a moment, then said, "Will you tell him I love him?"

"Of course."

"Well, now that you know who I am, I think it's time to go. I *did* find the ten most boring classics—and I've almost finished the last."

"I thought you had to have an 'epiphanic moment' before you departed? A last exciting resolution to your life?"

"This is it, young Thursday. But it's not mine, it's *ours*. Now, pick up that copy of *Faerie Queen*. I am one hundred and ten, and it is well past my out time."

I looked across at the table and picked up the book. I had never read the end—nor even past page 40. It was that dull.

"Don't *you* have to read it?" I asked.

"Me, you, what's the difference?" She giggled, something that turned into a weak cough that wouldn't stop until I had leaned her gently upright.

"Thank you, my dear!" she gasped when the fit had passed. "There is only a paragraph to go. The page is marked."

I opened the book but didn't want to read the text. My eyes filled with tears, and I looked at the old woman, only to be met by a soft smile.

"It is time," she said simply, "but I envy you—you have so many wonderful years ahead of you! Read, please."

I wiped away my tears and had a sudden thought.

"But if I read this now," I began slowly, "then when *I* am one hundred and ten years old, I will *already* have read it, and then I'd be—you know—just before the last sentence before I . . . that is, the younger me . . ." I paused, thinking about the seemingly impossible paradox.

"Dear Thursday!" said the old woman kindly, "always so *linear!* It does work, believe me. Things are just so much weirder than we *can* know. You'll find out in due course, as I did."

She smiled benignly, and I opened the book.

"Is there anything you need to tell me?"

She smiled again.

"No, my dear. Some things are best left unsaid. You and Landen will have a wonderful time together, mark my words. Read on, young Thursday!"

There was a ripple, and my father was standing on the other side of the bed.

"Dad!" said the old woman. "Thank you for coming!"

"I wouldn't miss it, oh, daughter-my-daughter," he said softly, bending down to kiss her on the forehead and hold her hand. "I've brought a few people with me."

And there he was, the young man whom I had seen with Lavoisier at my wedding party. He laid a hand on hers and kissed her.

"Friday!" said the old woman. "How old are your children at the moment?"

"Here, Mum. Ask them yourself!"

And there they were, next to Friday's wife, whom he had yet to meet. She was a one-year-old somewhere, with no idea of her future either. There were two children with her. Two grandchildren of mine, who had yet to be even thought of, let alone born. I continued reading *Faerie Queen*, slowly pacing myself as more people rippled in to see the old woman before she left.

"Tuesday!" said the old woman as another person appeared. It was my daughter. We'd vaguely talked about her, but that was all—and here she was, a sprightly sixty-year-old. She had brought her children, too, and one of them had brought hers.

In all, I think I saw twenty-eight descendants of mine that afternoon, all of them somber and only one of them yet born. When they had said their good-byes and rippled from sight, other visitors appeared to see her. There was Emperor and Empress Zhark, and Mr. and Mrs. Bradshaw, who were never to age at all. The Cheshire Cat came, too, and several Miss Havishams, as well as a delegation of lobsters from the distant future, a large man smoking a cigar and several other people who rippled in and out in a polite manner. I carried on reading, holding her other hand as the fire of life slowly faded from her tired body. By the time I had started on the final verse of *Faerie Queen*, her eyes were closed and her breathing was shallow. The last of the guests had gone, and only my father and I were left.

I finished the verse, and my sentence was complete. Twenty years of gingham and ten boring books. I closed the volume and laid it on the bed next to her. Already her face had drained of color, and her mouth was partly open. I was alerted by a quiet sniffle next to me. I had never seen my father cry before, but even now large tears rolled silently down his cheeks. He thanked me and departed, leaving me alone with the woman in the bed, the nurse discreetly waiting at the door. I felt sad in that I had lost a valued companion, but no great sense of grief. After all, I was still very much alive. I had learned from my own father's death many years ago that the end of one's life and dying are two very different things indeed, and took solace in that.

*   *   *

"Are you okay?" asked Landen when I got back to the car. "You look as though you've seen a ghost!"

"Several," I replied. "I think I just saw my whole life pass in front of my eyes."

"Do I feature?"

"Quite a lot, Land."

"I had my life flash in front of me once," he said. "Trouble is, I blinked and missed all the good bits."

"It will need more than a blink," I told him, nuzzling his ear. "How's the little man?"

"Tired after a lot of pointing."

I looked into the backseat. Friday was spark out and snoring. Landen started the car and pulled out of the parking space.

"Who was the old woman, by the way?" he asked as we turned into the main road. "You never did tell me."

I thought for a moment. "Someone who knew me really well and turned up when it mattered."

"I have someone like that," said Landen, "and if she's feeling up to it, I'd like to take her out for dinner. Where do you fancy?"

I thought of the old woman in the bed, dressed in gingham, hanging on for the last verse, and all the people who had come to see her off. Life, I decided, would be good and, more than that, *unusual*.

"If I'm with you," I told him tenderly, "SmileyBurger is the Ritz."

Credits

My great thanks to Maggy and Stewart Roberts for the illustrations in this book.
My thanks to Mari Roberts for huge quantities of research on everything from the Danes to Hamlet to conflict resolution and the piano gag, and for companionship, and love.
Mr. Shgakespeafe's quotes and Hamlet kindly supplied by Shakespeare (William), Inc.
Lorem Ipsum usage suggested by Swaim & Rogan.
For the purposes of this narrative, it should be noted that Zeffirelli's excellent version of *Hamlet* starring Mel Gibson and Glenn Close was made in 1987, not 1991 as previously thought.

My grateful thanks to John Sutherland and Cedric Watts for their *Puzzles in Literature* series, which continues to amuse and delight, and to Norrie Epstein for her excellent *Friendly Shakespeare,* which is every bit as the title suggests. Also to the Reduced Shakespeare Company for much-needed Bard-related tomfoolery in times of stress. Pulp western research by Gillian Taylor, author of *Darrow's Word* and many others. Visit www.gillian-f-taylor.co.uk.

My grateful thanks to Landen Parke-Laine for being willing to undertake a guest first-person appearance at short notice.
No penguins were killed or pianos destroyed in order to write this book. The penguin meal on page 146 and the piano incident on page 305 were merely fictional narrative devices and have no basis in fact.
My apologies also to Danish people everywhere for the fictional slur undertaken in the pages of this book. I am at pains to point out that this was for satirical purposes only, and I like Denmark a lot, especially rollmops, bacon, Lego, Bang & Olufsen, the Faeroes, Karen Blixen—and, of course, Hamlet, the greatest Dane of all.
Mandatory toast information, as required by current toast legislation: Bread was originated in a Panasonic SD206 breadmaker, sliced with an IKEA bread knife on a homemade breadboard and toasted in a Dualit model 3CBGB. Spread was Utterly Butterly, and Seville marmalade was homemade.
The appearances of Zhark in this book and the use of his name and exploits were monitored and approved by Zhark Enterprises, Inc., and we gratefully acknowledge the Emperor's help and assistance in the making of this novel.
This book was constructed wholly within the Socialist Republic of Wales.
A Fforde/Hodder/Viking Penguin production.

CROQUET!

GOING TO THE SUPERHOOP THIS YEAR? TAKE THE

SWINDON EXPRESS

TRAINS RUN TWICE HOURLY FROM PADDINGTON. SEE YOUR LOCAL TRAVEL AGENT FOR DETAILS.

Battenberg

The cake of Princes!

"After I've spent a hard day musing upon questions of mortality and existence, there is nothing I like better than to relax with a slice of Battenberg cake."

-Hamlet, Prince

Battenberg cake, as sponsored by Hamlet, Prince of Denmark.

Battenberg, Inc., is a wholly owned subsidiary of the Toast Marketing Board.

STRENGTH - JOY - NUTRITION

HAVE YOU EATEN YOUR TOAST TODAY?

TOAST

Issued by the TOAST Marketing Board in the interest of public safety and nutrition. Failure to meet mandatory toast-eating requirements is an offense.

Croeso I Gymru!

Take your holidays in the

Socialist Republic of Wales

Not *ALWAYS* raining.
See your local tourist office for details.

Look for the next
Jasper Fforde adventure in 2005.